Words
of My
ROARING

Also by Ernest J. Finney

Birds Landing
Winterchill
Lady with the Alligator Purse

Words
of My
ROARING

Ernest J. Finney

Crown Publishers, Inc.
New York

Published by Crown Publishers, Inc., 201 East 50th Street, New York, New York 10022.
Member of the Crown Publishing Group.
Random House, Inc. New York, Toronto, London, Sydney, Auckland
Manufactured in the United States of America

Library of Congress Cataloging-in-Publication Data
Finney, Ernest J.
    Words of my roaring - Ernest Finney.
    1. World War, 1939–1943—California—San Bruno—Fiction.
    I. Title.
    PS3556.I499W65   1993
813'.54—dc20   92-34134
                                                                      CIP

ISBN 0-517-59107-3

10 9 8 7 6 5 4 3 2 1

First Edition

For Nan

Thanks to the sailors who told me the stories:

Virgilio Del Zompo
Al Hope
Joe Jodoin
Tommy McDonald
Ed Nash
Clyde Smith

and two whose names I never learned: the retired chief I met at the USS *San Francisco Memorial, who served on that ship in 1942, and the sailor at the Carson* City Historical Museum, who was on the USS *Nevada* at Pearl Harbor in 1941.

Look at any California map and you'll find San Bruno just south of San Francisco. You can still go for a walk around the hearts there, and there *was* an Edgemont School, but Miss Walker didn't teach there. She and all of the other characters in this novel are entirely imaginary, and any resemblance to actual persons, living or dead, is purely coincidental.

My God, my God, why hast thou forsaken me?
Why art thou so far from helping me,
And from the words of my roaring?
Psalm 22

Words
of My
ROARING

1943

Mary Maureen

We waited just on the other side of the hedge where Grammy couldn't see us until he came out. I knew how to be patient from Miss Walker. It was part of being polite, like decorum and the proprieties. He edged out of Aunt May's house quiet, twisting his way through the small crack he'd made when he opened the door, holding the knob turned so there would be no click.

He wore his sailor cap and his jacket with the army patches sewn on the back like the other boys had, and he combed his dark hair in the morning with hair tonic until the cowlicks were laying flat like they did, but he didn't act like them. One reason, I thought, was because he'd lived here all his life, where most everybody else had just come during the war. He looked like he was always worried, as if he could hear the first wail of the air-raid siren and the rest of us couldn't yet. He never looked at you when he spoke, usually down at your shoes, or his own. And for no reason he'd go crossed-eyed and then to make it funny he'd wiggle his ears. For nothing. And then the stuttering all the time, that left spit on his lower lip.

He was brown as a walnut from working in Aunt May's garden all the time. And he was strong; he'd let the other boys punch him in the shoulder and never feel it. He'd just smile. And his clothes were always clean. But he was different.

My Grammy hated him now. Said Aunt May only kept him because he'd be in reform school otherwise, and would end up there anyway. He was the stupidest boy she'd ever seen, she liked to say.

I went first. "Good morning, Avery."

"Good morning, Mary Maureen." He had to answer. And to Ruthie too: "Good morning, Ruthie." She didn't have any manners and was only half awake, but she took his hand and we started. Every morning we waited to walk to school with him, but some mornings he didn't let us. He'd say, "You'll have to excuse me, but I have to go," or "I just remembered something," and he'd be off, or we'd meet Leroy and they'd take off together.

But it was worth the wait, because on the way something always happened that didn't seem likely to happen again. It never snowed here, but it got cold. There was ice on our car's windows and ice on Abner's water bucket. We had crossed San Mateo Avenue and were going down the other side, trying to blow rings with our breath. Nothing got by Avery, whether it was a lost penny or a gum wrapper for his foil ball or a loose marble. He'd spot it. I didn't see what he was picking up at first because they were the same color as the leaves. There were too many, and he put some in his jacket pocket. Dead sparrows, nine of them.

"You're going to catch a disease," I said. "Those birds died of something that made them sick." He never listened. He had two of them between his hands, looking at them through a crack between his fingers. Ruthie was trying to see; she had picked up two too.

All at once they gave off a chirp and he opened his hands and they both flew off, straight into the air. It must have been the cold that made them seem dead, and the warmth of his hands brought them back. Then Ruthie's took off, and Avery was trying to get them out of his pockets before they hurt themselves. I'd never seen anything like it in my life. Avery jumped up and down yelling, "Did you see that, did you see that?" Ruthie was waving her arms as if she was a bird. In the end they all flew off but left their fingers full of bird shit they had to wipe off on the frosted grass.

In class it wasn't the same as walking to school. Avery usually just sat there not saying one word or doing one thing anyone told him to do. He was like those birds, frozen stiff at his desk. But once in a while he would have the class in stitches. "Please take off your hat, Avery," Miss Walker would remind him when he sat down. "You're inside now."

"Yes, ma'am," he'd answer, "but if you don't mind, I was going to do my times tables and I'll need my thinking cap on."

"You'll have to pretend, Avery; it's not acceptable."

"Could we pretend it's not on my head?"

"Avery, do what you're told." Then he'd take the sailor cap off.

We got to the schoolyard gate and Avery was warming up to say something. It's when he was in a hurry that he stammered. He almost danced his feet as if to match his tongue trying to speak. But he never gave up trying until he thought he'd got it all out. "I must be going now, Mary Maureen," and he'd be off.

I took Ruthie over to where the kindergarten and the first grade were supposed to play, and then went to where Miss Walker was standing on yard duty. Most of the other girls stood around her; it was too cold to play jacks. The boys were playing as if they were airplanes having dogfights, arms out, thumbs extended for guns, shooting each other down in flames. The bell rang and we all lined up at our room door to go inside two by two and stand for the salute of the flag, then roll call.

I was ready to start third grade when we came to San Bruno, California. It was the end of summer. California: the name wasn't the same as the place. In Tennessee I thought a duck lived in a house out here and the two mice drove a car, because of the funny papers. I really expected I'd see them, or at least some animals, if not talk, then stand upright and wear clothes. I never told anyone that except Avery. He took his time before he said anything, not just because he stuttered; it was always like he wasn't sure where the words were going to come from. He'd feel under his shirt, roll his eyes and pant like he was taking in extra breath to speak. He told me back that he used to think there were little people who lived in the back of radios and they did the talking.

California was the end of the rainbow for us, for our family. My father said that to us. We were sitting at the dinner table. "I second the motion," my mother said. Grammy, who never agreed with my mother, said, "I miss Tennessee." Ruthie was feeding her fat face and didn't even hear. Michael wasn't there, was out with Sammy next door. It was 1941, before Pearl Harbor. But my father saw the war coming and we came west and he got a job in the shipyard. Before that he was a partner with his first brother-in-law in a hardware store. They had arguments, and there wasn't enough business for two families.

Once we got used to California, it was like we were always here. Our street was close enough to downtown to walk to the movie theater for the Saturday matinee or to go shopping with our mother. Michael would drive us sometimes; he was my father's son from his first marriage. He was too serious, everyone said, but my mother could get him to talk and laugh sometimes. Usually he was busy fussing with his radios or shortwave set. Doing his homework or going to his job at the appliance store or running around with Sammy next door.

My father talked; he was always talking. He had more opinions than your average politician, my mother would say, and sometimes she would creep up on him where he couldn't see her and put her hands over his mouth while he was telling us something. We'd all laugh. "Save some for tomorrow," she'd say, holding both hands flat around his mouth until he gave up.

But my father knew what he was talking about. He had a year of business college and had been a sergeant in the First World War and had been in four different countries. England, France, Germany, and Belgium. "Those Huns like to march and fight; we didn't defeat them; they just ran out of ammunition and supplies. They'll try us again," he said before the war started. But he admitted later he didn't think the Japs would try a sneak attack.

My father not only liked to talk, he liked to help people. Before, whenever he had time, he'd go over and get someone's car started or fix their plumbing.

Aunt May next door would always yell over the fence, "Dennis, do you know anything about gas furnaces?" and he'd stop whatever he was doing in the garage and go around the back gate. Everyone said she was a character, Aunt May. She was Sammy's mother. Dressed up like she was going to a dance, my Grammy said. But she was a cripple; she could barely get around on two canes. She had the same disease as the President, and he wrote her a letter when she was in an iron lung. She never left the house except to work in her garden or when it got dark. Sammy was a second-year apprentice meatcutter at Swift's. We could hear them arguing about money through the walls sometimes. The houses were a lot closer together here than in Tennessee.

"Cripples always spoil their kids," Grammy said.

"Why?" I asked.

"To make up for being a cripple," she said. I still didn't understand. "Because they're not normal." She was almost yelling at me. I still didn't get it, but I gave up.

Grammy could be gruff, but she took me and Ruthie with her to the drugstore on Main Street for a Coke when she got her check from my grandfather's Post Office pension. He'd been postmaster in Martin, Tennessee, for forty-one years. Ruthie was too small; she had to sit on her legs to reach the counter and bend her straw to drink, but she spoke up and ordered her favorite of everything in the whole fountain. I always tried something different: rainbow, where they give you a short squirt of everything, or lemon phosphate, or chocolate. Ruthie always asked for the same thing: cherry Coke, please. Always the same, even after I thought I had her talked into something else. Grammy always had iced tea. Sometimes Mrs. Hughes walked up with us, who was friends with my grandmother. She knew everything about the neighborhood, had been born and raised in the same house she lived in. Never had any kids, and was married to a streetcar conductor who had died. Rented out the other side of her house, and had worked for the telephone company when she was younger. She always said, "If I can't say something good about someone, I won't say it," except when it came to Aunt May. Everyone called her that, even Sammy, her son; it was because she got married late or some such thing. She introduced herself like that the day we moved in, came to the fence separating our house and hers and said, "Welcome to the state of California." She'd seen our Tennessee license plates.

My father introduced us all back. Then I took Ruthie for a walk while Michael and my father untied the canvas on our trailer. My father had come out before to get the job and find this place. "Don't go any further than the end of the block," Grammy said. My mother had already started scrubbing the shelves in the kitchen.

Ruthie didn't like to walk, and I had to pull her to get her started. The street was like the street we'd just left, except for the cool wind. Same houses, some nice and some not. Trees, fences, lawns, and hedges. Sidewalks. But there were sweet peas still, in August. I had to look twice to be sure. When we got to the corner we went across our street and walked back on the other side. Just before we could see our house, there was a two-lot street that ran off our street, with only one house. Mrs. Hughes was standing out watering the biggest hydrangea bush I'd ever seen. She said hello and I said hello back. "My, what a pretty accent you have," she said. I thought she meant I smelled nice, even if it wasn't true about Ruthie, who wet the bed. I told her I was going to be in the third grade and my sister was going to be in kindergarten and my mother had once sung over the radio in the church choir and was my father's second wife because the first one died of complications. "Be sure you go for a walk around the hearts," she said. "If you go down to the end of this street and cross over, you'll be right on the fat end of the heart. The blocks down there are laid out in the shape of two big hearts that point at each other. What do you think of that?"

Ruthie just nodded, but I knew what people wanted to hear. "I like things like that," I said. And I liked crazy people too, but I didn't say that. This street was going to be better than Tennessee. Mrs. Hughes went into her house and came back with two penny Tootsie Rolls. Even Ruthie thanked her. When we got back they had let Abner out of his box, which was a mistake, because the first car that passed us he took off after it, and we had to chase him.

When school started it was the same as back in Tennessee too. Same kind of teacher, same kids. But we were ahead back there, and without even trying I got the best grades in the class. They said I was going to skip the fourth grade if I kept it up.

On Sunday we took drives. Up to the city for the zoo, to Playland to ride the roller coaster. And we had Chinese food in Chinatown. Took ferry rides across the bay. Saw the aquarium and the museum of natural history in Golden Gate Park. We took a picnic over to the coast and saw the Pacific Ocean for the first time. We couldn't swim because of the undertow, but we jumped in the waves. It didn't bother my father or Michael, who floated around on their backs past the breakers like they were in a bathtub.

One Saturday we went to the Tanforan Race Track. It was so close we could have walked. It was too crowded in the grandstand so we stood by the rail. When the man came out in the red uniform and blew his bugle for the next race I saw him, but I never got to see the horses because I was too short, and Ruthie was on my father's shoulders. My mother won eighteen dollars.

We went to see Michael on the San Mateo High School swim team. He did the butterfly and the Australian crawl and we cheered for him. We went to the movies and had big dishes of ice cream at the creamery after. Sometimes we'd go on a surprise: just get in the car and drive. We ended up at the ice-skating rink at Sutro's Baths one time. Drove to where they were setting off fireworks, once. My mother always asked Mrs. Hughes, who sometimes came. Sammy always did. Aunt May, never. Some kids down the street, who moved away when the war started.

I was lying down on the front room floor reading the funnies out of the paper to Ruthie, "Prince Valiant," when the news came over the radio. It wasn't until I saw my mother cry that I understood something had happened. Sammy came running over, then Aunt May. It was the only time that I ever saw Mrs. Hughes and Aunt May in the same room talking to each other. Then there was another news flash and we'd all stop and listen.

A couple from down the street knocked and my father let them in and gave the woman his chair. My mother kept crying, like she was cutting up onions. She was standing over me and I could feel the tears on my knees when they dripped down her cheeks. By the time the President came on the radio she was saying, "Why, why did this have to happen? Why can't everyone leave each other alone? Why can't we just be happy here?"

"You can't expect the good times to last forever," Aunt May said.

The day we met Avery, my father had been working on the Packard, changing the oil, hurrying; we were supposed to go to a Labor Day picnic for the shipyard workers, down in a park in San Mateo. We were all in and backing out the drive when we heard someone yelling. It was a boy, but we couldn't understand what he was saying. He chased after the car, one hand trying to hold on to the silver swan on the hood, the other waving as the car backed over the sidewalk and onto the street. It sounded like *nol, nol, nol.*

My father turned off the ignition, and then as we were all getting out the boy slid under our car. My father saw what had happened and followed the trail of oil and came back running with the plug he'd forgotten to cinch up on the oil pan. It'd come out when we backed over the bump in the driveway. He got down in his blue suit to screw the plug in while the boy had the palm of his right hand over the drain so all the rest of the oil wouldn't come out.

I watched on all fours. When they both backed out from underneath the car, my father was still thanking him. "It would have frozen up for sure," he said. "I'd have had to replace the whole engine."

The boy was smiling at all of us. There was black rot on his bottom teeth that looked like he'd been chewing licorice. He was half a head taller than I was. It was hard to tell about California people because there were no Negroes out here. In Tennessee you have the white and the colored so you have a way of telling what the in-betweens are. The sun had cast him the same color as Gladys, but he wasn't Japanese. It turned out he was half Italian, like Sammy next door.

Both he and my father put their knees on the curb and started wiping their hands on the strip of grass there. "Dennis, let's forget about the picnic," my mother said. "It's already eleven-thirty." I knew better than to whine when my mother said anything, but Ruthie didn't. "I want to go, I want to go," she started up. "Quit it," my mother told her. Grammy kept her lips pressed together, waiting for my father to say something. The boy had got his hands clean and went over to Aunt May's and, like he did it every day of the week, reached over the picket fence and drew up a shovel, went over to where a gopher had left a big mound of soft dirt, and started sprinkling it over the stream of shiny oil down our driveway.

"And what do you think you're doing?" Grammy said to him. The boy kept smiling away, moving the dirt over the edge of the shovel.

"He's putting dirt down so it'll absorb the oil, so it won't get all over our floors, Mother Mitchum," my mother said.

"Let's all have some orangeade," my father said. "We can go next year." He went over and picked up Ruthie, who was still sniveling. My mother was unlocking the front door when she asked, "Will you join us?" to the boy. He was still smiling like that was all he could do. He nodded. Then Grammy asked, "Who might you be?"

"I am Avery," he said.

He didn't say much else, never stuttered that time, drank his orangeade and ate only one sugar cookie, little bites he broke off with his front teeth and chewed and chewed. My father came out of the bedroom wearing his work clothes. Drank his glass standing up by the table. "I better go put some oil back in that Packard," he said. No one said anything when Avery just got up and followed him out.

I could see my father pouring from the five-gallon oil can into the quart can with the long spout that Avery held with both hands just the right level from the ground. Then they moved off so I couldn't see them through the screen door, to put the oil in the car. Then they came back again and did it over, not saying one word, like he'd been helping my father for years.

Just before she went up to bed my grandmother always wrote on her Rexall calendar that hung next to the ironing-board door. In small writing she put over the number, but only in that box for the day, what happened.

September 7, 1942.

Never got to the picnic. Both the leghorn and the Plymouth are setting. Next door Aunt May took in a boy named Avery Fontana. Same weather holding for the last five months, cool and windy. But the sun shines every day.

• • •

My father worked from six to six every day of the week. Some of the swing shift and some of the graveyard, he liked to say. When we got home from school he'd get up. After a while he'd go get his shaving things out. He had a round mirror as big as a saucer on a stand, and he'd gone back to using his father's ivory-handled straight razor because you couldn't get razor blades anymore. And his shaving mug and brush were all in a wooden box with dovetailed corners. He had told me that word. There had been something inside the box before, but we couldn't read the blue printing anymore on the outside. It was about the size of the bottom half of a lunch bucket, and when he set it down on the table Grammy would lay out a clean towel and the white basin with the red line on the rim full of steaming hot water.

By that time Ruthie would be in her chair, elbows on the table. Avery would never knock or ring the bell, when he could sneak away from the victory garden, but you could hear him on the porch because it was old and creaked when anyone walked across it. One of us would run for the door and open it and Avery would be standing there, and me or Ruthie would invite him in. My mother said he was just shy, but sometimes after I'd opened the screen door wide he wouldn't step over the threshold, he'd just look down at his feet. "You're invited in the house," I'd repeat. He'd act like he didn't want to come in, but then why was he standing there on the porch? I'd yell, "Are you coming in or not?" Sometimes he'd run and sometimes he'd step across. If Ruthie went to the door, she'd just grab his arm and take him in.

When he came in, he'd sit in the spare chair next to Ruthie. My father would say, "Look who's here." He'd already stropped the razor and he'd show us how sharp by holding up a newspaper page and cutting a big circle out of the middle. Grammy would start getting his meal ready. After glaring at Avery once or twice when he came into the kitchen, she'd pretend he wasn't there.

Then my father started soaping his face with the shaving brush. Working up a lather first in the mug, going around and around, then coating where his beard was with the soap. "Now you kids don't get too close, here; I know you don't like soap." We'd all lean in then. When we got too close, he'd get us with the brush on our noses. He took his time soaping, going over and over his chin and his neck, dipping the brush back into the hot-water basin, then into the mug. "It softens the skin," he explained once when I asked him why he kept soaping his face.

He'd answer all our questions until he got to a subject he liked. Then he was off, until Grammy would say, "Finish, Dennis, or you won't have time to eat." He could go on about President Roosevelt or his wife, Eleanor Roosevelt, the whole time. Or the state of California. The shipyard, where there was a woman who could rivet faster than any man. And the First World War, where he was gassed twice. Avery always had questions about something my father had said before, a day before or a week, it didn't matter. "Why did the German artillery always hit what they were aiming at?" The Saturday before, he had told us how the German gunners would play with the American soldiers hiding in their trenches, letting them think they were perfectly safe after a barrage, then dropping a 75 right on their dugout.

That Saturday he'd got down on the floor on his stomach. Showed how he had stayed low in no-man's-land, wriggling along on his elbows and knees to escape the shells. We all got on the linoleum, our cheeks pressed against the green-and-yellow pattern. "We tried to be quiet," he said, "or as quiet as possible, not to alert their attention. But if they thought we were there, all hell would break loose. Shells would start coming, a sound worse than ten, even a hundred of these locomotives passing. Smoke. Dirt flying, shrapnel zinging around us." He started moving across the floor to escape, and under the table, and we all followed right behind him.

If Avery's questions were always like the opening part of a serial on the radio, my father's answers were as if he were just thinking them over for the first time. "They had observation balloons. And at night they had flares and patrols out." He was still moving his shaving brush against his chin, slow, as if the bristles could stick there like a beard. "They had good forward observers; they'd get up close to our lines and see what we were up to. Then get the information back to their field artillery."

"How?" I asked.

"There might be a runner. They could use pigeons. Radio, maybe. The Germans were smart. And they had since 1913 to figure out ways to use their artillery. They had a lot of practice on the English, French, and Italians."

"The Italians weren't the Axis that time, Dad?" I asked, just for Avery's sake. My father had explained a couple of times about the Italians, who were with us in the first war and against us in this one.

"They were our friends in the last war," he said.

My mother came home from work after my father left for the shipyard. She would walk if she wasn't too tired, or take the streetcar. My father drove the Packard to the city and picked up five other men on the way.

The electronics plant was across the tracks and over by the street that went to the airport, but on this side of El Camino Real. It always surprised me when she came into the house wearing her scarf like a turban around her hair to keep it out of the machinery at the plant, and her wool slacks and sweater, because in her section it was drafty, the building as big as five barns put together. In those clothes she didn't look like her. My mother did soldering, along with seventy-two other women in her section; they soldered wires that went into radios the army used. Her eyes were always tired because the wires were so tiny, and they had to finish their assignments on each shift or they didn't get a pin for their lapel after a year. She already had one pin. Grammy had one for giving two gallons of blood. I had one for giving twenty cents to the Red Cross. Ruthie had one from the bond drive because she had a twenty-five-dollar bond. My father had his shipyard badge with his picture, besides four or five other pins he could wear if he wanted to.

She would sit down, take off her glasses at the kitchen table, and I'd go get her slippers; her feet hurt from standing all day. She got up before we did and was gone by five-thirty and came home at five-thirty at night. But she got Sunday off. When she was tired she forgot to keep her mouth shut, and you could see her buck teeth. I heard Sammy say to Aunt May how my mother could eat corn through a picket fence. But I never understood why he said that until later, when I asked Avery. She sometimes soaked her feet in hot water while Grammy got our dinner on the table. And Grammy would be talking away. That's how I think my father learned how to talk so much, from her. She'd talk to herself if there was no one around to listen.

My mother was a hired girl back in Tennessee and lived with a family whose father was a dentist with a wife and two kids and a Negress cook, Maureen, who I was named after, with the Mary for my grammy. If it wasn't for the cook, my mother told us, she would have hanged herself. The dentist's wife used to slap her, pull her hair, and sometimes hit her with a piece of kindling when she did something wrong. Then put her down in the cellar and yell through the door, "You'll thank me for this when you get older. You'll be worth something." She was twelve when she went there and twenty when she married my father.

She only talked about the dentist's house when she talked about Maureen, who was older than Grammy and tried to protect her when she was a girl and treated her like a daughter. My mother wrote Maureen and sent her presents on her birthday and at Christmas. Perfume and embroidered linen handkerchiefs. "You never forget a good friend," my mother said when she sat down at the kitchen table to write back to Maureen. She would tell us Maureen stories. How Maureen could cook anything. Her kitchen was always spotless. She had named the chickens and they would come when they were called. Taught her how to embroider and crochet.

Ruthie and I would dry my mother's feet and get her slippers when Grammy called us to supper. "This certainly is tasty," my mother would say with the first mouthful. Grammy would say, "Why, thank you, Dora," like my mother was a guest in the house she'd just met. Then she'd go into how they were rationing sugar now.

My mother would stay up, no matter how tired she was, to make sure we did our homework. Ruthie didn't have any in first grade, but my mother made her go over her letters and read to her. She'd tell me, "I might only have an eighth-grade education, but I know better than that," when I tried to get out of doing something for school, like book reports. I hated them worse than any-thing. I didn't mind reading the book, but then having to write the same thing again as proof got me. So I'd just read some of the front and some of the back and then write the half-page. It seemed fair to me. But not to my mother. She would catch me and make me read the whole book before I could listen to the radio or go out and play.

At eight o'clock she'd run the water for a bath in the tub, putting some pink bubble bath in, and then when the mirror over the sink was clouded up, we'd come in and she'd let us wash her back. Her skin was soft and there was a birthmark on her shoulder in the shape of a half moon. She'd just lay there like she was asleep with the steam rising.

We liked to hear her stories, but she wasn't like Grammy. She could lie in that tub for an hour and not say one word, or go a whole day without speaking except at the dinner table. I'd ask her questions to get her going, but she'd ignore me if she wasn't in the mood. If she wasn't talking. "How come you only went to the eighth grade?" I'd try.

"Because that's how many grades there was at the school. Then I had to go to work. It's not like out here. I knew girls two or three years older than you that got married. I got a job."

"What about your folks? Didn't they want you to go to school?"

"My mother and father never saw the inside of a school. They thought it was a waste of time. My father signed his name with a cross in a circle at the mill, but my mother could read and write. I had six sisters and five brothers. Everyone had to help out. I had a cousin who was working in a laundry in Martin, and she took me back with her on the bus to look for work. And it was my bad luck that Dr. Burns needed a hired girl. But I had no choice in the matter."

"What happened to your cousin?"

"She was scalded at the laundry and had to go back home."

"Was Maureen already at Dr. Burns's?"

"She was the family cook for his mother. Mrs. Burns didn't dare mistreat Maureen; her husband, Carl, was an electrician who worked for the govern-ment; they had two cars and owned a house. Mrs. Burns had a stone where a person's heart ought to be. She didn't treat her own kids well either."

"They got locked down in the cellar too, with the spiders and the rats?"

"Too many times to count. I used to start shaking when Maureen would say good-bye after dinner to go home."

"Didn't they have the police then?"

"It wouldn't do any good. It was because of the money. The Burnses were rich. Out here it's different. I work right beside a Filipino lady at the plant, I never knew one before, and there's Negro ladies and Spanish and Italians.

Sometimes I look around and I think I must be dreaming. We all get eighty cents an hour. Same lunchroom, same toilets, same water fountains, and we get paid the same. We all can buy a car or a new house, if they were building any during the war. It's your money, not your color or how educated or how you look, that people respect. If I was making the money I'm making out here in California back in Tennessee, I would have been sitting pretty. I could have worked where I wanted, not for five dollars a month and room and board. But I wasn't. So Mrs. Burns could kick me black and blue and there wasn't nothing anyone could do about it. Except put compresses on the bruises."

At nine my mother put me and Ruthie to bed. Made sure we brushed our teeth. Tucked us in. She never hugged us like Grammy did, or stayed longer like Dad did when we wouldn't let him go, held on to him with our arms to keep him there. When she got up, she got up, and turned off the light.

It was only during the air raids, when the siren started up, that she let us sleep with her. Ruthie never wet there because she was too scared to shut her eyes. Grammy never even woke up at the siren; she slept through every time. Abner howled along with it, higher pitched, almost louder than the siren sometimes. Then he would stop, just before the siren quit.

Whenever we heard the airplanes taking off at the airport, I would make my body as small as it would go, in case a bomb came through the roof. The whole world was gone outside, dark as the inside of the bedroom. Ruthie lay stiff; I could feel her beside me like a hard cushion.

"Mom, should we pray now?"

"You go ahead, then."

"Will you pray with me?" Ruthie was too scared for me to ask her. I knew my mother didn't believe in God. Grammy believed. Maureen had believed. My mother's mother had read from a Bible. But my mother said you were better off reading a seed catalog; at least you could get something for your time and money. She and Grammy had almost stopped arguing about it, by the time I could remember. I heard Grammy tell Mrs. Hughes that her daughter-in-law was an atheist. That was after my mother told us at dinner we ought to ask someone closer than God to help us, or do something for ourselves, when Grammy wanted to thank God for food with a blessing. Mrs. Burns's uncle, who came to dinner every Sunday, was a Methodist minister. The Burnses made her go to church with them. The old windbag yelled at her too, and tried to trap her in the pantry. Grammy used to take us to church when we first came, Congregationalist. But not anymore, after the reverend's daughter was caught with a sailor and her husband divorced her.

"I can't pray, Mary Maureen. I just can't. Try and think of your dad. Hope he's safe at the shipyards. That's where they'll bomb."

"And Michael too," Ruthie said.

"And Michael," my mother said.

I knew my dad would be safe because he knew what to do from the first war, so I thought of the street over on Cupid Row, one of the best places to go when it got hot, where we'd look for the soft places and pull up long stretches of tar and chew and chew, until I went to sleep.

When Michael left for the Navy with Aunt May's Sammy, we didn't know what was going to happen to Abner. He was Michael's dog and slept at the foot of his bed and always waited for him to come home from school on the porch. He was a peculiar dog, not because he bit people or chased cars and fought with other dogs, but because he was a one-master dog; he only minded Michael. He never did what I said, or even my father. Just Michael. He bit Ruthie on the rear end a bunch of times because she teased him when he was eating. Avery was afraid of him and wouldn't come in the yard when he was loose. So was Aunt May, who Grammy thought had tried to poison him, because Abner was sick once, after he dug up all her onion sets in her victory garden. And she told Grammy his nuts ought to be cut off. He didn't bother Grammy because she fed him. And he was older than she was, sixty-three years in human age and nine in dog years. He weighed forty-one pounds when we weighed him on the scale in front of the Rexall drugstore, and was supposed to be a golden retriever with a little terrier and beagle mixed in.

But Abner didn't pine like I thought he would after Michael left, or bite any more than he used to. He still chased cars, but that was because he saw himself in the hubcap and thought it was another dog. We kept him chained all the time now because people complained, especially the mailman. He just lay in front of the wash shed during the day, getting the sun. He still got loose occasionally, but he didn't run off like he used to. He stayed in the yard or on our street. When he chased Miss Walker that morning before school, it was Ruthie's fault. She unhooked him because he was tangled in the chain and he made a run for it. My face was red. I apologized at least ten times. Abner was leaping against her screen door, trying to bite her. I got the rope around his neck and tried to drag him away, but it wasn't easy. Every time I apologized, Miss Walker would say, "Nice dog," or "That's all right, Mary Maureen, it can't be helped." Mrs. Hughes was yelling, "Get that dog off the porch." I wished I were a tiger; then I'd bite Abner's head off. Miss Walker was my fifth-grade teacher. They had skipped me over fourth grade, so I was in the same room as Avery.

Miss Walker came over to our house twice when we invited her, the first week she moved in. But mostly she stayed over in her apartment at Mrs. Hughes's, when she wasn't at school. Sometimes the light would be on late in her window that we could see from our upstairs. Grammy would say, "Miss Walker must be grading papers late," because her light was on at one-thirty in the night when she got up to go to the bathroom.

When I walked with Avery we couldn't take the shortcut off Cupid Row because we might meet Miss Walker. I knew she left at seven o'clock, an hour before school started, but it didn't do any good to tell him that. "She must be conscientious," Grammy would say; "it's only a fifteen-minute walk." My mother said she might be lonely away from home for the first time and all, and we should be nice to her.

Everyone was nice to our teacher the first week of school. Miss Walker wore suits, and her dishwater blond hair came down to her shoulder blades with a natural curl. She had never taught before she came to our grammar school and was from the capital of Nevada. She was pretty and had the most beautiful manners possible. She wrote a thank-you card to my mother for inviting her over to listen to Jack Benny on Sunday night. She wore white gloves and high-heeled shoes and a hat when she went to the Episcopal church on Sunday morning. If we learned anything, she told us the first day, during our year in the fifth grade, she hoped it would be good manners. They were important and would be with you your entire life.

Until Miss Walker became our teacher, I thought doing cartwheels and walking on my hands were the most important things to learn. When we went to the circus at the Cow Palace we saw acrobats dressed in purple sequined bathing suits doing that. I could do eleven cartwheels in a row, walk on my hands four squares on the sidewalk, and ride with no hands for a block on my bike, when it had tires. Ruthie was a butterball, but she could do cartwheels.

One time my mother came home from work when I was holding Ruthie's legs up and she was trying to walk on her hands. My mother put her sweater down and kicked herself up on her hands. Started right down the driveway toward the garage, me shouting, "You can do it, you can do it," Ruthie jumping up and down yelling, "Mama, Mama!"

Her face was red as a beet but she made it to the wash shed and rested her heels against the door. Then she flipped herself over onto her feet.

"All your blood is in your head, Mom," I said.

"I haven't done that in so long, I don't remember when," she said, picking up her sweater and lunchbox.

I still practiced after Miss Walker was our teacher, but I didn't want to join the circus anymore; I wanted to be like her. And I was the teacher's pet, and I didn't care who knew it.

From the first day it was like I had just moved in, not Avery. He showed us how to follow the ice truck, the water dripping from the back onto the street, before it made a stop where there was a sign put up in the window, ICE. The driver would open the canvas back and with his icepick work a twenty-five-pound block off, then grab it with his tongs and carry it on his shoulder up into someone's house, to put in their icebox. We'd wait until he came back, standing behind Avery. "It's going to be hot today," he'd start out as if he'd never stuttered in his life. "You're probably going to sell a lot of ice today." Without us asking, the ice man would chip us off some slivers of ice. We'd hold them in our hands and put them in our mouths as long as we could, running back and forth yelling, "I'm freezing, I'm freezing to death."

It wasn't always like that; some of the things we did, I never understood why. I'd ask Avery, "What are we doing this for?" but it was only after I got tired. From down by the railroad tracks we collected eleven wagonloads of eucalyptus-tree acorns that smelled like the worst medicine in the world. He'd never give us an answer. When Aunt May found them in her shed and started yelling, "Get them out of here," we had to haul them back. I didn't mind when we filled the wagon with scissors. They were parts of weeds with purple flowers and needlelike points; you could make a hole in one and put the other through, and they acted just like scissors. They grew in vacant lots. We put them together for hours. But it was always down by the tracks that we had to go for the eucalyptus acorns. I didn't like trains. They made too much noise, and gave me a headache. It was ammunition, he told me finally, when I was ready to quit. "We'll be able to throw them." I didn't ask him at who.

We collected old tires too, for the war effort. Hauled them out of ditches and vacant lots and from beside the road. They were worth money, he told me, and I believed him. We took them and stacked them behind the streetcar station until we had fifty-three, and then someone stole them.

He found about a thousand old flashlight batteries behind a factory, and we hauled them down to the tracks and hid them. They would hurt you if they hit. We practiced for hours. The acorns turned out to be too light.

Avery was always going down the alleys and looking around at things. He found the tickets behind the El Camino Theater that way. They must have been cleaning out ten years' worth, because there were boxes and boxes. Most of the tickets were torn in two, but if you kept looking you'd find some whole. We looked at every single ticket and must have found a hundred good ones. Then we buried the ones that weren't any good so everyone would think the garbage man had taken them. It was the only time we got something for our efforts, and the only time I got in trouble. He gave some to Leroy and I had some and so did Ruthie, because we all helped. Grammy was washing my dress; I thought I had taken the tickets out and put them back in my hiding place underneath the corner of the linoleum in our room. We'd only gone to three matinees with the tickets, spent the money we got for the movie on jujubes, red vines, and popcorn. We'd stay twice, see the double feature and cartoon over, come out in the sunshine blinded. But there they were, in my pocket.

"Where did you get these?" she yelled at me. She had me by the braids. "Do you hear me?" Then she gave me a slap. Then another. My mother woke up and came running. I was screaming back at Grammy and trying to kick her. Ruthie was just screaming.

I told my mother, "I found them; I didn't steal them."

"I'm going to tell your father," she said. He never said anything to me. Grammy tore them all up. Ruthie and Avery shared their tickets with me.

At recess I made Ruthie wash her hands in the water fountain so she wouldn't catch anything from those birds. I told Avery he better too, but he pretended he didn't hear me. Because of the sparrows coming back to life, I knew today was going to be different, and it was. This wasn't only going to be library day, where we walked downtown, and George Washington's birthday, when we made our hats, but there was going to be a surprise too. Because of the paper shortage we used newspaper for our hats, and I pasted my cut-out feather I had colored red, white, and blue on the side. Then I started drawing.

Across the room where the boys sat, Avery was coloring his sunrise on the newspaper, orange and yellow waves that went out like strips of yarn. Miss Walker was going up and down the aisles. "That's a very elaborate cockade, Mary Maureen," she said when she got to me.

"Thank you, Miss Walker." It was good because I had done this before, as long as I could remember, even back in Tennessee. We had the same framed picture of George Washington with white hair up in the front of the class over the alphabet and next to the flag. My brother Michael's birthday was February 23, the same month as my father's.

"Interesting color scheme, Arnold." Arnold did what he always did, laughed out loud, made Miss Walker jump, sprayed Leroy's back with his drool; then his head, big as a full-grown pumpkin, rolled as if it would come off.

Sharon, the only girl who sat over on that side, behind Avery, was writing on his hat for him. She was the best cursive writer in the whole class, probably the school, too. "Sharon, why have you cut off Martha Washington's head?" If Arnold didn't have any decorum, Sharon didn't have any manners in general. She only answered the teacher when she felt like it. Everyone was afraid what would happen if they yelled at her. She got away with murder. Without even looking up, she started printing under the bottom of the headless body. We were all drawing scenes of George Washington's life, like chopping down the cherry tree, with famous quotations. "I can not tell a lie," is what I wrote. The dead woman wasn't George's wife. I could see Sharon had printed BETSY ROSS underneath for Miss Walker to see.

When Avery didn't like someone, you knew it. Avery raised his hand. Miss Walker nodded. "Pardon me, Miss Walker, but that hat is mine, not Sharon's. She was just spelling for me." He almost got it all out except for spell, spell, spell. It seemed the more he stuttered the more he tried to say. "I asked her to."

"Do your own work, Avery," Miss Walker said, interrupting herself to yell, "Leroy, don't use so much paste!"

We marched. The sun had come out and warmed up the sidewalks. But instead of going across at El Camino, we turned right, away from the library, just as we could see the dome. There was the second, third, and fourth grade behind us, each carrying their classroom flag, and the sixth in front, carrying their flag high so you could see it over everyone's head. I had worn my coat. It was windy, and I had to keep one hand on my hat and the other with the person I was walking with. Avery wouldn't hold my hand, just my sleeve, to make it look like he was. If she saw, we'd both be in trouble. I didn't know where we were anymore; I had never been on this street. Avery did. He could go any-where. "Where are we going?" I asked.

"It's supposed to be a surprise."

"Tell me."

"It wouldn't be a surprise then," he said. That's the way he was.

We stopped in the middle of the block, where a house had burned down to the foundation. Even the ground was burned, up to the vacant lot on either side. Then I recalled the news. This was the place where the P-38 came down, day before yesterday. The family wasn't home and the pilot got out safely, but before he could open his parachute he was cut in two by the tail. Half of him had come down farther out, in the mud flats, and another part in the bay.

No one giggled or laughed or pushed or shoved now. Everyone had perfect deportment. The sixth-grade teacher made all the flag carriers stand up on the front steps facing us. Miss Walker took out her pitch pipe and gave us a G and we sang "God Bless America."

On the way back to the library my hat blew off and was run over by a Navy bus going back to the base. The sailors hung out the windows and cheered as they passed. They started whistling when they saw Miss Walker, who turned red and looked straight ahead until she had to yell at Leroy for dipping the flag on the sidewalk, trying to hit someone with the brass eagle on top.

Avery didn't say yes or no, but I helped anyway. There was no telling how he found things, but he knew where the railroad ties were lying. I knew I mostly wanted my scooter to use, but I met him and Leroy down by the tracks after school, with the scooter and Ruthie. I had to take her because my mother was still at work, and it was Monday, washday, and Grammy was doing the clothes in the wringer and didn't allow anyone in the wash shed or the garage.

Avery didn't say anything but Leroy did. "You bring that pisspot?" Everybody knew when Ruthie wet. For shame, Grammy hung the sheet on the clothesline so everyone in the street would know. It didn't make any difference. Avery had his wagon and he had his rope across his chest. He put Ruthie in and started down the middle between the rails, bumping along. We had rules at home like Miss Walker had manners at school. Our street was one over from the railroad tracks, and we were never to go over there. Never. We'd get whipped and not sit down for a month of Sundays. I remember when we moved in, we were all sitting down to supper and a train went by. Michael was still home then, and the whole room started to shake. I was watching the salt shaker move across the bouquet of flowers on the oilcloth. "It's a tornado, Dad," Michael said, jumping up fast enough to knock his chair over. My father laughed until the tears came and he had to blow his nose. "It's a train, it's only a train," he said. Later, when the next one came, my father said, "Well, at least we're on the right side of the tracks." My mother said, "We're right *on* the tracks."

Now there were more trains, and longer. Avery told me once he counted one that had 191 boxcars. If I wasn't supposed to be here, neither was Avery. If Aunt May found out, he would have to leave. Aunt May was always talking about sending Avery back where he came from. Leroy would get in trouble too.

There were four ties, big, square-ended, that smelled terrible and lay like pick-up sticks dropped off a flatcar. The first one was easy because it was close to the track. We hefted one end on the wagon and the part that hung over we rested on my scooter. Went right down the ties again until we got to the trestle and tipped it off. It landed in the canal with a splash.

Everybody knew what to do next. Avery and Leroy went down the bank, and Avery fastened the rope around the tie with one of his knots, then gave one rope end to Leroy, kept the other end for himself, and they moved the tie down the middle of the water, one on each side of the canal, till they got it around a turn beside some willows, where no one could see it.

The next ones were harder. They were farther down the bank and had to be dragged up with the rope. Ruthie got the tar all over her and in her eye too, and started to bawl. Leroy fell in the water up to his knees and blamed Avery and left, calling Avery a shit-ass. And trains kept coming and we'd have to stop and hide.

I would have given up too; it was late now, past when our programs were on. My mother would be home and my father already at work. But I knew what would happen if I didn't keep at it. He kept saying if they were all gone, no one would know. If we left one, they would. They have to disappear, they have to disappear, he kept saying.

I stayed to the end. And we had to run back all the way to our street. And all the time I knew Avery would never take me when he built his boat out of the ties and sailed out in the ocean, because I heard him tell Leroy.

"You're excused," Miss Walker said every day at three o'clock. We filed out of the old building, still quiet, like shadows moving to get outside in the daylight to escape. Once past the double doors the boys would whoop and holler and start running, dragging their jackets, papers flying, hitting on each other, jumping over fire hydrants, pushing and shoving. Kids spread out for blocks, like the pattern on our quilt.

As we got farther and farther from school, more peeled off, like planes in formation, until it was just Ruthie and me. I could sometimes see Avery and Leroy ahead, stopping to pick something up, climb a tree, or circle a parked car. I'd get close to them and they'd speed up.

"Come on, Ruthie." I had to keep after her; she'd dawdle to watch a caterpillar cross the sidewalk. One time she picked a black-and-orange one up by the hair to put in her mouth. I was already carrying her coat and lunch bucket and had tied her shoelaces and wiped her nose. It seemed longer, walking home.

When we rounded the corner onto Main Street, two men had Avery and Leroy by the collars of their shirts. The men had their shipyard badges on and were still blinking from coming out of the bar into the sunlight. "What's your name?" one kept asking. The other said right in front of me, "Where are you little Japs going?" I didn't know why they were talking that way to Avery and Leroy, but I knew the sound whiskey made in someone's voice from Tennessee. When my uncle, my mother's brother, talked, it was like whiskey had frozen his lips and the words didn't come out round.

I could tell Leroy was ready to cry. Avery was up on his toes, was almost smirking, like he always did when he got in trouble. "We're not Japs," Leroy said. I looked closer at the two of them. I noticed for the first time their eyes were squinty. And Avery had dark eyes, and his hair was black when it was wet. They were the same color as both Gladys and Wilma, who they took out of our third-grade class and locked up first at the racetrack and then at some prison because they were all spies for Tojo and Emperor Hirohito.

I spoke up then. "They aren't Japanese. My father said Leroy's got Mexican blood, and he's half Italian." I pointed at Avery. They acted like they didn't hear me. "And his cousin Sammy is in the United States Navy," I said louder. Someone yelled from inside the bar, "Leave them alone, you 4F-ers. That's Chet Gorman's boy. If you know what's good for you, you'll take your hands off him. He's got plenty of uncles left."

The men let go and both Leroy and Avery were across the street like they were released from the end of a rubber band. I grabbed Ruthie and caught up.

Leroy was embarrassed. He didn't say anything, but he was. His father had shown up drunk at school once and sat on the curb handing out pennies to the kids as they came out to go home. Leroy tried to get him to leave, but he wouldn't, pulling on his coat and saying, "Come on, Dad, come on," until his father punched his face. Someone called the principal then.

"Neither of you has to thank me," I said. Leroy stopped. He took another street and didn't live near us. He went to our school because he got in trouble like Avery did and they didn't want him anymore at the other one.

"You didn't do anything," Leroy said.

"They were just having fun. Kidding," Avery said.

"No, they weren't; you do look like Japanese. My Grammy said so too."

After Leroy turned off, the three of us took the shortcut across the vacant lots. Avery must have been thinking, because he didn't run off. "You're invited," I said. "To listen to the programs on Sunday night." Since Aunt May didn't have a radio anymore because the FBI came and took it away, I could invite him. But Avery almost never answered when you asked him anything. Not only because he stuttered; because he was that way.

When we got to Aunt May's, he surprised me. "You want to see how big my tinfoil ball is?" Before I could answer he went around behind the house and came running back. I hadn't seen it since it was the size of a walnut, but now it was the size of a California orange. He let me hold it. "You're going to win the city school contest," I told him. I had started one, but I never kept at it for long.

"It's going to be bigger," he said. "A lot bigger." There was a prize. Avery's was ahead of everyone's that I had seen at school.

"Avery, where did you go?" Aunt May yelled. "You have something to do." He had to go work in Aunt May's victory garden. He held the ball down so Ruthie could touch it. "You can come with me tonight if you want," he said.

I couldn't believe my ears. "What time?"

"At the back lot, after the seven-thirty streetcar passes. I'll meet you there."

"Avery," Aunt May called out, and he ran.

It wasn't hard to get out of the house. All I had to do was learn to wait. Do my chores, the ironing, now that my mother was too tired, and help Grammy with the mending, darning the holes in socks while she used the Singer. We had piles of sewing: my father kept getting burn holes in his clothes from the hot slag from welding, and Ruthie could tear anything. We still had Michael's old socks that had holes in them too. "The Navy gives him clothes now; he doesn't need these," I said. "We'll have them ready when he comes back," she said back, working the treadle. I put the wooden darning egg in the next sock. I thought I remembered working on it last month with that rotten thread that didn't hold. I pulled the old out with my fingernails and started in. You couldn't get thread or needles anymore.

After supper I did the dishes and made my mother's lunch. She'd gone to bed after we ate, not even bothering to listen to the radio. When I really started noticing the time, Grammy was snoozing in her chair and I had put Ruthie to bed. Which was a chore. "Go pee," I told her.

"I don't have to." She was half asleep.

"It doesn't matter, go anyway." She just lay there and I had to lug her out to the bathroom and lift up the big baby. "Go on now." She just sat there. "Pee." She was obstinate. "I'll tell you a story." Then she peed. It didn't make any difference; she still wet the bed most nights and got me all wet. I got my coat and put my pin on the lapel that showed I gave to the American Red Cross. I was a little early but I couldn't wait anymore and went outside.

You could hear the streetcar coming for a mile, not just the squeaks and creaks or the ding-dongs of the bell but the yelling and singing of the sailors coming in from the base. They were hanging all over it as it swayed down the track. Out the windows, in front over the cowcatcher, out both doors; the car was packed with sailors and with their white caps against their dark uniforms it looked like the blue field on the flag hanging in the corner of the classroom.

There was a noise over by the garage, and I thought it was Avery. I was going to call out "Over here," but then the gate opened and he was beside me. He took me by the sleeve and we moved through the rows of vegetables. Aunt May's were already coming up, and the stakes were up for her beans. The winter cabbages looked like big heads rolling along with us and gave me a start.

We went around the back way and came out by the show. The main street was a surprise, all lit up, neon signs, headlights on the cars going up and down. Most of the houses we'd passed had their blackout curtains up and were dark, but not downtown.

I didn't know how many sailors were out at Tanforan now, but there were about a million on that street. There were big gangs going up and down the sidewalk, roaming the downtown. There were so many they couldn't get into the bars at one time, so there were big crowds of sailors standing outside on the sidewalk, getting drinks passed over the others' heads from friends inside. Standing out in the cold, talking to each other like they were having the time of their life. As it got darker the neon signs looked brighter; the letters hummed zzzzzt and went off and on up and down the street. The lights blurred the buildings and they looked like a lined-up deck of playing cards and the bars were all jacks and kings. Every once in while a shore patrol would come by in a jeep, and the sailors would hide the bottles and pretend they were just out for the air and straighten their clothes.

We were hiding behind the gas pumps of the Mobil station, looking out between them so no one could see us. "Stay here," Avery said into my ear. I wanted to go with him, but I never had a chance to speak, much less move. I could see him at first when he went by a light, picking up thrown-away cigarette packs, peeling off the foil, going in and out around the sailors. Then he disappeared and I started worrying. How was I going to get back home in the dark? What if he forgot me here?

I kept looking for him, and I saw it wasn't only the bars and eating places that were open, but two of the grocery stores were full of sailors too. They came out eating from big boxes of ginger snaps and drinking out of bottles of pop and milk, leaning up against the buildings or standing there, passing it all around to the other sailors.

Main Street made a **V** into El Camino Real and had a waiting line of cars two blocks long trying to get off it onto the highway. If a car went by with one sailor in it, the next time it came by it was full. The big drugstore on the corner was crammed with sailors; so was the restaurant by the bus station.

A group of sailors came over by the gas station. Some stood and some sat on the curb and started passing a bottle back and forth. One went over by the Mobil sign and peed. I didn't breathe. I didn't notice Avery was back until he pulled my sleeve, motioning me to come. I started out but lights flashed on us and we got back behind the pumps. "It's the SPs," Avery said.

A sailor stood up in the shore patrol jeep and called down to the sailors on the curb, "If you gentlemen want a ride back to the base, I can accommodate you. If not, put your covers back on and get out of the gutter before some civilian reports you to the mayor."

They griped but stood up and put their caps back on and started off, except one. He stayed where he was. The SP got out of the jeep and strolled over to the sailor. He wore white leggings and a white belt, a white holster and hat that made his sailor suit look black. "If I said 'please,' would it make a difference?" He sounded like my mother cajoling me into something. "Go up to the USO and get yourself a cup of coffee." A lot of other sailors stopped to watch. But the sailor on the curb didn't move.

The SP put his hand out to give the sailor a lift up. The sailor took hold but when he came upright he let loose a roundhouse swing with his other fist. The SP leaned back out of the way, his cap falling off his head.

Some of the friends came running back and grabbed the sailor by the arms. The SP picked up his hat, stepped closer to say something, but the sailor spit a mouthful in his face, then tried to kick him. "He's an Indian," one of the other sailors said, getting ahold of him again; "he's drunk; he doesn't know what he's doing." The SP hadn't got mad or upset, had perfect manners, just wiped the spit off his face with a handkerchief, turning it over to a dry place once.

"An Indian, you say. What kind would that be?"

"Arapaho, Navaho. Something like that," one of his friends said.

"Let the blue-eyed Indian go," the SP said. There were more sailors stopping now to see. A big crowd. His friends let go of the Indian like they were loosening a wild animal. "When I shit," the SP said, "I pass more Indian than you are."

The Indian just swayed, mumbling, his big fists like potato mashers hanging at the ends of his arms. The SP made a motion with his hand to the driver of the jeep. That SP got out and came around behind the Indian. "You can come along the easy way," the SP said, taking out his club, "or you can come along the hard way."

The Indian lunged, swinging and cursing, but the SP stepped aside and then suddenly slipped the long club between the Indian's legs. The other SP grabbed that end and they both heaved up. The Indian's feet came off the ground and they dropped him back down hard and then lifted again. Fast. Again. Again. I put my hands over my ears but I could still hear the sound the Indian was making. Avery was holding my hand so hard it went numb. They did up and down up and down until the Indian fell off to the street, holding himself with both his hands, moaning.

One of the Indian's friends came forward then. "You didn't have to do that," he said. The SP clubbed him right on his ear and it split like a juicy tomato. Then he started hitting out at anyone that was close. The whole bunch of sailors started running away, and he was after him. The other SP tried to hold him, yelling, "Chuck, enough, Chuck, Chuck, enough."

Avery had me by the arm and we were running. I could hear the sailors howling all the way to the corner.

We walked the five blocks home in the middle of the street so nothing would get us in the dark. In passing, Avery told me he knew the sailor personally and was a friend of his, the one who beat up on the others. I didn't say anything, but it was hard to believe. But on the other hand, Avery didn't brag.

Elaine

By nine o'clock Monday—her seventh Monday—she felt like she'd never been off the weekend. She was tired out already. "Now, class, take out your readers; each group start taking turns reading the assignment. Group leaders, please check the readers' errors. I'll come around." The kids moved their desks or got chairs from the back and formed their groups. She stood up behind her desk and watched. They knew she was looking and made a minimum of fuss.

There were eight girls in the first group; why were they always the best readers? It had been that way when she was in school. She stopped to listen to Mary Maureen. She should be in the seventh- or eighth-grade reader and she was younger than the rest too, had skipped fourth grade last year. "Excellent," she said after Mary Maureen sat down. "But don't read so fast out loud. This isn't like reading to yourself." The rest of the group laughed.

The second group were all good readers with slight flaws: they mispronounced, didn't sound out well enough yet, didn't always know what the words meant. Seven girls and seven boys.

The third group mumbled, still used their fingers to keep their place on the page, though they were in a much easier book. They read after a fashion. Most couldn't sit still long enough or pay attention long enough to follow a story of any length. It was a puzzle to her how some of them were promoted. Five girls and nine boys.

The fourth group sat silent, as if waiting for Sharon to have an epileptic seizure. She was supposed to be the leader and go first. "Read, Sharon." The book was a third-grade reader, simple. Leroy couldn't even find the right page. "Twenty-nine," she said, and reached and turned to the page. "Here." Avery had the page and was following with his finger, tapping his right foot against the floor. Why did he irritate her, just looking at him? Sharon read as if she were singing rhythmically, starting out low, then raising her voice to the period. She stumbled. "Separate by syllables, Sharon; you know that word." Arnold was drooling, his big hydrocephalous head balancing on his narrow shoulders. He shouldn't even be in public school. But his parents insisted. Who was she to argue anymore? Just send Arnold out to stand in the hall when he made one of his noises, and his mother would be in the principal's office the next day. Same with Sharon's father, who was a marine engineer at the shipyard. He had wanted to sit in the classroom. Imagine. Mr. Allen had stuck up for her that time. It would be too disruptive.

Avery, sitting there waiting his turn, scared. He was almost shaking. He would stutter or do something when she said, "Avery, you read": fall out of his chair, try to touch his nose with his tongue to make the other kids laugh, anything but what he was supposed to do. These four took more time than the rest of the class put together. And she was going to have them again next year. They were talking about her teaching sixth. "Avery," she said in her loud voice, "you read." It was as if she'd struck him. He dropped his book. Everyone laughed; the other groups all waited for him to do something else. The thing was, he could read well enough to get by. The stutter was distracting for everyone, but he would keep trying, like a car turning over on a cold morning. Whir, whir, whir. Then he crossed his eyes at her, just what the class was waiting for, and they roared. She was yelling before she knew it. "Quiet, quiet down, where are your manners? You just encourage him." She couldn't send him to the office. "Mary Maureen," she said, "come down and help the fourth group."

What next? She collected the milk money. Now she had to listen to them slurp their half-pint and watch them masticate their graham crackers without closing their mouths. Her mother wouldn't have let her get away with that. None of them had any manners. Looking down the rows, she saw that none of the girls had been taught to cross their legs or at least hold their knees together. That was something she could work on.

Avery, hiding behind Arnold, was entertaining again. Taking his milk straw, putting it in his inkwell, and sucking the black line almost to his lips, then letting it drain back down, for the amusement of the students around him. Never drinking his milk, giving it to anyone who asked, and he was getting it free, he and Leroy and four others. Didn't have to pay the nickel, can you imagine. She'd heard the stories about Avery's parents; they had plenty of money for other things.

"Milk monitors, please collect the empty bottles." She hated the clanging when they put the bottles back into the wire crates. She was getting irritable. Already. It wasn't even time for ten-o'clock recess. Did she have yard duty? Was she having her period? She felt something wet. That was all she needed. Should she excuse herself and see? It was too early. "Class, those who have brought money for Victory stamps, please raise your hands." The same ones, every time. "Please come up by your seat number." She was more a bookkeeper than anything else. Collecting money, pennies and nickels for the Red Cross drives, Sister Kenny, tuberculosis: it was one thing after another.

Mary Maureen came up with five nickels and pasted her stamp into her book. The twenty-five-cent stamps were supposed to add up to enough to buy a twenty-five-dollar bond when you filled the book. But no one had ever come close. Sharon had a dollar, four stamps. And Leroy had fifty cents; he couldn't afford to pay for his milk, but he could buy stamps. Five more came up with their sweaty coins.

She was just finished putting the cigar box with the money in her locked drawer when the air-raid siren went off. She could have *goddamned* out loud. Not at recess time, when she could have a smoke. Mary Maureen was up, closing the curtains to protect everyone from flying glass. She had to have her class register in her hands and not hurry. The children were under their desks on their rumps, faces pressed against their knees, hands laced over their heads. This was the only time there was no twittering, their eyes shut tight, waiting, listening. Then she flicked off the lights.

This was all foolhardy, she'd pointed out at a teachers' meeting. It wouldn't take a bomb to knock this old building down; it was going to come down on them by itself. The third and fourth floors were already condemned; kids hadn't been allowed up there for the last couple of years. They should be outside hiding in the row of eucalyptus trees on the other side of the schoolyard. But this was district policy. There was enough light coming from around the curtains to see back to her desk. She got down on all fours to get under it. When she'd first seen the school, she'd wanted to turn around and go right back to Carson City. From a distance it had looked abandoned, old enough to have been built in the last century. Four stories, painted gray shingles, square, as tall as it was wide, with ranks and ranks of schoolroom windows up and down the outside. There was very little playground, and that was hard-packed gravel. Teeter-totters, swings, one short slide, and a big sandbox outside what must be the primary rooms. It had been like coming on one of those schools in the desert, out by itself, desolate, except this one had single houses nearby, on each side. The closer she got, the worse the place looked. Some of the shingles had come off, exposing tarpaper, and there were holes in that, with pigeons flying in and out, and broken windows covered over with boards. She could have taught in a comfortable school in Nevada.

The siren stopped. Then Leo the janitor came down the inside hallway banging a broom handle inside a metal wastepaper can, yelling "Bombs away, bombs away." She knew it was coming, but it always gave her a start. Mr. Enoch, the superintendent's idea, to simulate a real attack. Give the situation authenticity. It was too much for some of the kids in the lower grades: it had never happened in her class, but she'd heard in the lunchroom that several third-graders had wet themselves.

Then it was quiet. She could hear the clock ticking away her break. She did have yard duty, she remembered. This whole week. That meant she'd stand out there and watch the kids, with maybe ten minutes to smoke, go to the bathroom, and eat her sandwich while the kids were eating their lunches.

The siren signaled the all clear. Her knees hurt and she had the beginnings of a headache and one of her legs had gone to sleep. She limped over to the light switch as Mary Maureen pulled the curtains open. The light blinded everyone. The kids were standing, stretching, stiff. "Sharon, come out from under your desk." She hadn't meant to yell. Don't have a fit now, she thought as the girl didn't move. Please. Avery crawled over to her desk. Rubbed through the toe of her shoe until she raised her face, smiling at him. She wasn't the only one relieved. No one would taunt Avery, girlfriend, girlfriend, either. They were all afraid of the sound Sharon made more than any siren. She just had to roll her eyes back and that would be it.

"Please take your spellers out, class, and turn to lesson five."

She lit a cigarette while unwrapping the waxed paper from her tuna fish sandwich. Exhaled, took a bite. Then another; she was hungry. Other teachers came in, old-timers, sitting down at the table, full of advice for a first-year teacher. All women. The only man was the principal, Mr. Allen, who had a club foot and hadn't been called up yet. She'd read that they were drafting men with one eye now, with more than seven dependents, and over forty too.

Eunice, the sixth-grade teacher, came in and put down her purse. She had made the mistake of telling Eunice some of the problems she was having the first few weeks: kids making noise, not listening to instructions, getting out of their seats all the time, laughing for no reason. She was yelling at them too much. Eunice had to know; her room was right across the hall. You never heard a peep from that class. "I'll drop by," she'd said.

Eunice was as short as some of the kids, round, wore wraparound skirts and cardigan sweaters over starched blouses, and was her mother's age, at least forty. She got a beauty parlor wave every week. She wore thick glasses, but there was nothing wrong with her. The kindergarten teacher was seventy-one and almost deaf. One second-grade teacher had a withered arm. The other second-grade teacher had one leg shorter than the other, and the sole of her left shoe was five inches thick. The fourth-grade teacher had a cataract in one eye and wore dark glasses that made her look completely blind. And the principal: it was like a home for cripples. None were married. One of the third-grade teachers, who might have been insane, had been sent home. She had stripped to her underwear, locked herself in the teachers' lounge, and wouldn't come out. Threw her clothes through the transom, yelling, "I just want to jitterbug, dance my way down the street."

No one else had been to a university. Eunice had a degree from a normal school; the other teachers, two years at most. Mr. Allen had a degree from a Catholic college. She'd just found out the girl who had replaced the third-grade teacher was only a high school graduate. What had she got herself into, she wondered the first week, after she'd met her colleagues. By Armistice Day she'd stopped wondering, was always tired, and just wanted school to be over each day.

"You have yard duty," Eunice said.

"I know," she said, taking the last bite of her sandwich, putting out her second cigarette. Eunice was the senior teacher, kept track of whose turn it was to do what. She had been here for seventeen years. She had been offered the principal's job but refused. "I like the classroom too much," she'd said. Mr. Allen had been a last-minute replacement after the former principal was drafted. Teaching wasn't a deferment.

Eunice had promised to visit her classroom; she came in at eight-thirty one morning. The kids still hadn't settled down after the roll call and flag salute. Leroy was in the corner facing the blackboard where she had put him, still giggling, for getting a mouthful of water from the faucet and spitting it out the window. Mary Maureen was passing out lined paper for penmanship. Eunice came in like she owned the place, put the stopper down on the door with her foot, and left it open. She asked Leroy, who was still grinning, "What did you do?" He didn't get a chance to answer; she grabbed him by the collar and slammed his head into the blackboard. Arnold gave one of his wild shrieklike laughs, and she walked over to his desk and picked up his ruler and cracked him over the head. The ruler snapped in half and he started sobbing. Mary Maureen, who was standing in the aisle, said, "Leroy spit water."

"Did anyone ask you, miss?" Mary Maureen stepped backward, almost falling over someone's legs, and dropped the paper. Eunice saw Avery then, took two quick steps, and lifted him up out of the seat by his hair. "Who's forgotten to take off his sailor cap?" Tears started coming down his cheeks, but he wouldn't answer, and Eunice said, as if she were just asking a big favor, "What did you forget?" He wouldn't say anything. "What?" she yelled, shaking him back and forth with a tight grip on his cap and his hair. "You'll answer if you know what's good for you. What did you forget?"

"NNNNNNothing," he got out. She had him out of the desk, yanked him into the aisle, still holding him by the hair, and threw him down against the floor. "Don't sass me." Then Sharon made her noise.

It caught even Eunice by surprise, because she let go of Avery. Startled, she went over to where Sharon lay on her back in the aisle, frothing at the mouth and making a sound that was terrible to hear, loud, unbearable, as if she were burning up inside, being consumed by pain, as if by listening you would catch fire too. Eunice took Sharon by the heels and dragged her down the aisle and into the cloakroom and shut the door. It was so quiet in the classroom now that she felt, heard, her own heartbeat, not in her chest, but the reverberation in her left wrist. Then, behind her forehead, the start of a migraine. She had the crazy idea that she should be polite and introduce Eunice, say something like, "Class, this is Miss Cameron, who has come to visit."

Eunice went up and down the aisles now, daring them. Avery was back at his desk, looking straight ahead. Sharon had stopped kicking her heels. It was perfectly quiet now. "I like this class," Eunice said. "I'm looking forward to having them become sixth-graders. They're going to be a real challenge for me."

She never complained to Eunice again. Never. Neither of her parents had ever even spanked her. She remembered her father shaking her by the arm once for something. But not like that, like Eunice. She'd thought she was going to be sick. For a week after that, all she had to say was, "I think I'll call Miss Cameron from across the hall," and there was dead silence.

There was only one other time that Eunice came in. She knew Eunice was trying to help, but the woman scared her too. Everyone was to write right-handed, that was the rule. It was essential for cursive. No lefties. She had four in her class. None remembered; they'd always go back to their left hands, again and again. She'd been talking it over with Mr. Allen when Eunice walked in. "I know how to handle that," she said. After recess, Eunice followed her back into her room. When the kids came through the door and saw who was there, it was instant quiet. Instant.

Eunice took over. "Students," she said, "take out some scrap paper and write the alphabet in cursive. Do the best you can; this is just a practice, but we always try our best, don't we?"

She went over to Mary Maureen first. Kindly she asked, "Do you know your right hand from your left?" Mary Maureen looked surprised. She nodded, raising her right hand. "That's the hand you're supposed to be writing with; try it. See, it's easy. Everyone is supposed to write right-handed. It's not a difficult task."

Avery had switched his yellow pencil from his left hand and was writing away with his right. "Here," Eunice said, taking Mary Maureen's hand. Opening the inkwell, she dipped in turn each of Mary Maureen's fingers into the blue-black liquid, then dropped her limp hand onto her paper to dry. "You'll remember now," she said. "The hand with the ink on the fingers is your right hand, your writing hand." Surprised, Mary repeated, "My right hand is my writing hand."

Eunice didn't ask Avery any questions, didn't say a word to the other two boys either. Took his limp right hand and dipped the fingers in the inkwell. Dropped the hand back on the desk as if it were dead. They both stared at each other.

"What are you looking at?" she said. Avery kept his eyes on her face.

From where she was standing by the door, she could see him slide his unstained hand along the wrought-iron scrollwork inside his desk until he found the sharp-pointed metal pencil compass he used for drawing circles. She stopped breathing, couldn't even yell out. Neither Avery nor Eunice blinked, just stared at each other until Eunice said, "I can wait. There's plenty of time. That's if you even make it to the sixth grade," and she went out.

She almost enjoyed yard duty. The kids were playing nicely; usually there was some scuffling among the boys, but not today. A few had been bringing their baseball gloves to school and they were playing one-a-cat. The girls were jumping rope and playing jacks. Some kids were playing war with the scaled-down plastic airplane models that were used to instruct the civilian airspotters. Last month she'd had to teach enemy aircraft identification, holding the planes up in front of the class. It was Leroy who knew every one, who could tell a German Heinkel from a Japanese Mitsubishi Zero, no matter what angle she held them at. Mary Maureen and the rest of the first reading group, who'd always shot their arms first for nearly everything, spent a lot of time looking the planes up in the book. Avery wasn't interested. He might know, if she called on him, but he didn't volunteer. Even Arnold knew and put his hand up with a shriek.

Mr. Allen came limping up with his whistle at the corner of his mouth, smiling. He had taught in private schools before the war, was always even-tempered. He never mentioned the noise coming out of her classroom, and those first weeks when she used to send too many kids up to his office, he'd told her in a kind voice, "You have to try to deal with them in the classroom, Elaine." She never did that anymore. "Baseball?" he said. "You'd think it was spring instead of November."

They looked over at a group of boys making airplane noises and landing their planes on the field they'd smoothed out in the soft dirt at the bottom of the bank. She tensed herself, looking around, as Mr. Allen blew his whistle and yelled at some kids. "No pushing at the drinking fountain. Take turns."

"Six more months." She said what she'd been thinking. He had commented to her several times that there were only a hundred and eighty-three teaching days in a year.

"The first year is always the hardest," he said. "It gets easier."

She noticed Avery lying on his back in the right field of the baseball diamond. Sharon was there, and several other kids from her class, all looking at the sunny sky. "It's an unusual time," Mr. Allen was saying. "But the war can't last forever. And then everyone can get back to normal. In some ways, the war has meant opportunities; I would never have got this job as principal if the war hadn't come along." They both looked down at his club foot, and he stamped it lightly on the cement. "My wife is afraid they'll draft me." He laughed. "It's good for something anyway," he said. "What are those kids all lying down over there for?" You could see everything from this spot. Eunice had showed her where to stand.

"I'm not sure," she said. When he blew his whistle, most of the kids looked. He waved his arm for the kids lying down to come over. They all came running. If she'd blown her whistle and motioned, no one would have moved. She always worried when anyone else dealt with the pupils in her class, though she told herself not to. It was no reflection on her.

"What are you troublemakers doing over there?" he asked.

Arnold answered with his shrieking voice, "We're waiting for the Jap balloons." "What balloons?"

"The ones that start fires. Avery told us," Sharon said.

Before he could ask, Avery stepped forward, standing straight, his arms stiff at his sides. "I read about it in the paper, Mr. Allen. They caught the woods on fire." Avery wasn't stammering at all, she noticed. "They started sending them over. I thought we ought to keep a lookout. Mr. Mitchum said they can do more damage than a five-hundred-pound bomb."

"I'll find out about this. Go play some, don't just lie there and get your eyes tired looking at the sun. Get some exercise; you won't grow if you don't run. Go on now." They all ran off.

"He's a good boy," he said. She tried not to look surprised. Shocked. Avery? "I was looking at his file. I think we should promote him, Elaine, I really do. But it's up to you."

After lunch was the best time in the classroom. The kids were docile, subdued. Sleepy. Sandwiches eaten, the food in their stomach; did that make their eyelids slide halfway down?

Mrs. Beason, the district music teacher, came in after lunch, so she got to sit in the back listening, relaxed. All the kids were grouped by their instruments: flutophones, triangles, wooden blocks, tambourines, and sticks. They played and they sang. Mrs. Beason was good about letting them choose songs from the book. They did all the military songs first, the kids competing to raise their hands first for their favorites. "Anchors Aweigh," "The Marine Hymn," "The Caissons Go Rolling Along." But their real favorites came next: "The Song of the Volga Boatmen"—yo heave ho, and then everyone gave out a loud grunt—and "Row, Row, Row Your Boat" as a round, and "Rachel, Rachel, I've Been Thinking." When Mrs. Beason raised her pitch pipe and sounded a key and all the kids burst into song, keeping time with their instruments, she had the feeling sometimes it was almost worth it to be a teacher.

She had never been allowed to sing at this age. The music teacher had said she was a monotone, and she could help best by passing out and collecting all the music books. That always bothered her, especially because her sister Mona had such a beautiful voice, and her mother too. She could have been allowed at least to hum. She was humming now, and no one noticed.

Art. Drawing time. The kids seemed to like art, because everyone kept busy. She gave them all the Crayolas and paper they needed, as long as they used both sides. Most of the boys did battle scenes, airplanes shooting each other down, battleships sinking. The girls drew themselves, jumping rope or in elaborate long gowns, or standing outside their houses with their dogs on the front steps. She went down the rows, trying to encourage everyone. There was no time to teach them to draw. You couldn't do it in a half hour with forty kids.

She'd learned by chance. Her grandfather took up painting after he retired, and he'd taught her. The other kids in grammar school never improved because no one knew enough to show them anything. In high school there had been a good teacher, Mrs. Long, the wife of the vice-principal, who came in just for the art classes. She could do anything: charcoal, pen and ink, oils, watercolor, pastels. She'd been to an art school in Chicago. She'd been to Europe and studied one summer in London. "First you have to learn the technical part. Then, slowly, carefully, you develop your style. But you're young: don't be impatient," she'd say.

Her mother and father encouraged her, took the whole family to San Francisco to the de Young and the Palace of the Legion of Honor to look at paintings. Her mother entered her in everything from the county fair to the National Women's League Youth Art Contest. She'd won, too, not every time, but enough to half-expect the blue ribbon to be on her canvas, or the telegram notifying her that she'd placed somewhere. In her last year in high school she'd started doing portraits. That was the most interesting, to see how close you could come to copying the person, then go beyond that to what the person might become, or what they had been. It was like a game of double-dare.

Mrs. Long commissioned two, one of her husband and the other of her son. Insisted on paying her for them. She did one of an old Linotype operator in his best suit; he worked for her father. A state senator and his wife. A dozen at least. She learned something each time she tried one. Portraits. She couldn't stop. Looking hard, trying to make your hand move true to your eyes, you caught them out in a way that made you guess things about yourself.

The spring that she graduated, her mother wrote to several art schools in the East, sent portfolios, all without her permission, of course. All three schools accepted her with full scholarships. Large stipends, enough for tuition, supplies, housing, living expenses.

Even then she had wanted to get out of Carson City, and this was her first opportunity. As far away as possible. But then she hesitated; she didn't know if she wanted to become an artist. She didn't understand at first why she was resisting. Why she wanted to stop.

After a while she understood. It was a question of not knowing what was going to happen anymore when she started a portrait. She was going too far beyond what she was seeing. It was like having a regular dream that slid into something else that woke you, terrified, though you couldn't remember what it was. "That's not me," George, the old Linotype operator, had said. He used to buy Mona and her Popsicles in the summer when they went down to the print shop. Her portrait of him was supposed to be a surprise gift. "I don't want it, if it's all the same to you. What good is it to me? I thought it was going to be my picture, or I wouldn't have sat there all that time." She'd gone too far and didn't know how to get back.

She was in her studio, that's what her mother called it, her grandfather's old room. After he died and she started getting serious about painting, her mother fixed it up for her. For weeks she'd been sticking her brushes in a jar of turpentine, just cleaning one when she needed it. She decided to clean them all. Out of the three art schools she had decided on one, and her mother had phoned the other two. But she felt uneasy—about the art part, not about going to New York. Did she want to do this the rest of her life? Could you get out, once you got in? Would she end up like Mrs. Long?

Her studio had nine windows; the three outside walls were nearly all glass. "What light for a painter," her mother said almost every time she came into the room. But she didn't need light; she just needed the right person to paint, and the uninterrupted time, for everyone to leave her alone. As she finished the brushes, she lined them up on the top of the table. There were a lot, different sizes, different kinds of bristles, different colors of wooden handles. She tried out the thought: I'm never going to use these again. She was astonished at how relieved she felt.

The hardest part was telling Mrs. Long. But Mrs. Long had warned her. "I've been painting for the past twenty years with no particular success or recognition. The art world attracts more charlatans than serious people and is guided by fads, bad teachers, and bad critics. The best get out as soon as they see how degrading it is to have to turn out mediocrity to be accepted. Oh, I'm in an awful mood, Elaine. Don't pay any attention to me." She knew Mrs. Long had just been fired from the WPA project in Reno; she'd been painting a section of mural in the post office. She didn't want to ask why. They were having tea at Mrs. Long's house, sitting in the kitchen. "I don't know why I don't just say the hell with it. I've thought of it enough times. I just don't know how to stop. It's become a such a bad habit, I can't stop." That had been during her junior year.

She phoned instead of going over, though the Longs lived only three blocks away. But Mrs. Long was cheerful. "It's your decision," she said. "But I wouldn't rule it out completely. It might surprise you and not let you quit."

She would have liked to explain more to Mrs. Long, but she wasn't sure she could.

She told her father. He was calm. "It's up to you," he said. "You have to decide." Her mother yelled, "Are you crazy?" Even Mona was surprised. "Why did you spend all that time, if you weren't going to try?" She didn't have an answer.

She went to Reno and registered at the university. She applied to the education department; she was going to be a schoolteacher. She didn't want to work in the print shop and she didn't want to be a nurse and she couldn't think of anything else. And three of her friends from high school were going to be teachers.

"That's wonderful, Arnold." He had an unusual color sense. He'd used the side of a white crayon first, then a blue and a green to shape the waves. His ocean looked real. So did the conning tower of a submarine. The more you looked, the more you saw. The magnetic mine. Sharks. Birds flying overhead.

Sharon, using just ink and a wooden pen, could line-draw anything. Trees, a dog scratching itself. Then she'd color them in with four or five quick strokes and ruin everything. Sharon started a big fat cat while she watched. She couldn't help herself; she leaned down, taking the black Crayola, and shaded just the flank of the animal. Sharon looked up at her and grinned.

Leroy was doing a tank, shooting, running over soldiers, their entrails coming out of their mouths. "Very realistic," she said as she passed. Avery was doing another in his series of circles, the point of his compass digging a hole in the wooden surface of his desk. She didn't say anything. The circles, not more than a quarter of an inch apart, got bigger and bigger until they ran off the page. Then he'd start again on the other side.

The bell rang. Everyone jumped. The noise started, all the kids rushing to put things away. It was time to go home. She tried not to hurry up to her desk so she could stand behind her chair and say, "You're dismissed, class."

Crossing from the heart to Cupid Row, she tried to think of a new greeting for Mrs. Hughes, who always was waiting on the porch for a little chat when she came home from school. "Lovely weather for November"? "Another day, another dollar"? It was the funniest thing; there was a certain resemblance between her mother and Mrs. Hughes. If she were to draw their faces, she would use the same loose curve, same stroke for the chin. They had similar bone structure. The skin was another matter; her mother was forty-three and Mrs. Hughes had to be in her sixties, with pure white hair. Both wore their hair pulled back into a bun. Her landlady didn't wear any rouge or lipstick either. They both stood erect. Good posture. She had her mother to thank for hers; she'd never slumped, though she was almost five nine. How were they different? Mrs.

Hughes wore glasses and had blue veins like vines going up her unstockinged legs. "The San Bruno wind didn't blow me away, Mrs. Hughes," she called out, starting up the porch steps.

I will not be lonely, she told herself, kicking off her shoes in the kitchen. Now that she'd thought it, would the feeling disappear? Did ideas have a certain shape and color or odor that lingered after they'd evaporated?

She was going to become the best teacher in the district and then in the whole state of California. That's what she'd thought in September. Now she came home each night so tired that she felt like she'd been running the whole day. She'd sit down on the couch, numb, unable to move. She had gone to bed at seven-thirty one Friday night. Her mother had phoned—she usually phoned on Sunday—and Mrs. Hughes had kept knocking until she woke up: "Telephone, Elaine, you've got a call." Because she was half asleep, her mother had thought something was wrong. "Do you want to come home, Elaine?" Mrs. Hughes was sitting in her chair pretending to read the paper she held like a curtain between them. "Elaine, can you hear me? Do we have a poor connection again?"

"Everything is fine, Mother," she'd said. What else could she say? That she was having a terrible time and she'd be on the next bus? That she was a lousy teacher; she couldn't be sure the kids were learning anything? That you had to yell at them all the time, threaten them? They didn't want to be in the classroom. They hated her and she hated them. "Everything's fine." She went back to her apartment and had a bowl of shredded wheat. She had forgotten to eat dinner. From then on, she made herself stay up until at least nine o'clock, even if it was only to make up her lesson plan at the kitchen table.

She wrote long letters to her brothers Damon and Daryl in New York, at West Point. Her mother and father, of course. And to Mona, who never wrote back, but that didn't stop her from sending letter after letter to Carson City. They had always got along, as different as night and day, her mother always said, but she missed Mona most of all.

For the first time in her whole life, she had time to really think. More time than she needed. On Saturday nights she allowed herself to stretch out on the couch in her robe and listen to the radio in the dark, dipping crackers into a quart jar of sandwich spread for her dinner. Her mother would be horrified. At home they never ate without linen napkins rolled up in their own silver rings, without a fresh tablecloth at dinnertime. Her father at the head of the table. Her brothers, Mona. No one started until her mother sat down.

She had three jars of sandwich spread left. She'd brought a lot of things from home. Forty cans of tuna fish, her favorite for sandwiches with dill pickle, red onion, and mayonnaise, if you could get it anymore. For the rest, the coffee, sugar, and butter, you had to have ration stamps. Everybody hoarded; you weren't supposed to, but when things came in the store you bought as much as you could carry off or did without later because everyone else had bought it all up. Three cases of home-canned fruit and vegetables and jam. And four of the biggest boxes of Kotex, a year's supply at least, wrapped in gray paper. Why the company bothered to try to conceal what was inside was beyond her. Everyone knew. Mona was almost two years older than she was, but she had gotten her period first. Mona didn't get hers until she was almost sixteen. She started hers in junior high. It had something to do with how much you weighed, her mother explained. She had been fat; Pudge, they called her in junior high. Their mother bought them sanitary napkins until she was in high school: then she told them they should buy their own. They were getting paid for working at the shop. And they did when they remembered. The agreement was the person who used the last one was to go down to the drugstore and buy the new box, but she usually forgot. One time Mona needed a napkin and there weren't any and she started yelling, bullying her to go down to the drugstore: she threw a hairbrush at her to make her go. She got the wrapped box and stood in line with nothing else to hide it, she hadn't brought enough money, so everyone would know, think it was her period. She was so embarrassed. "It's for my sister," she told the woman clerk, turning bright red. Why did she have to explain?

Why had it taken so long for her to work things out? She had become a teacher because her mother had wanted her to become an artist. Is it reaction from one choice that always makes you choose its opposite? Her mother was always telling her don't be so sensible all the time. So she was sensible. Sensible clothes, sensible looks, and sensible thoughts. What was that an indication of? That she never had a good time? That wasn't true.

She was in California for the same reason; her father wanted her to teach in Carson City. He could have arranged a job in that school district. Not because the Japs were going to invade, but because he knew what was best for her. Was she ever going to initiate her own choices?

Her mother called her strong-willed. That was funny, because it was Mona who did any damned thing she wanted. She remembered coming home from the university one Friday night when she was a junior. "You'll do what you're told," her mother was saying in that controlled voice.

"You're jealous," Mona yelled back. Her mother started laughing. Mona ran from the kitchen. Her mother turned then and saw her. "Home for the weekend, Elaine?" They had all sat at the dinner table together like nothing had happened. Her mother and Mona passing bowls and platters, making small talk.

She thought what she always thought when she'd been away for a while and looked at her family, how much she and her brothers looked like their father. It was all right for her brothers, as boys or men, to have sharp noses, high foreheads, thick thighs, hands almost bigger than their feet. She'd asked her mother—she must have been Mary Maureen's age, old enough to know what she looked like—"When am I going to be pretty like Mona?"

"There are different kinds of pretty. It's not all the same. You'll grow up and be attractive. I guarantee it." Had she believed her mother? She didn't remember. She had started drawing by that time, and could make everyone beautiful. But Mona wasn't only beautiful; it was as if she were sending out some secret code, not only to men but to women and kids too. They had to turn and look at Mona. She could be wearing an overcoat and stocking cap in the winter and still turn heads. She didn't need to flirt. She had to repel. Men her father's age, acting foolish, offering her cigarettes, fawning when she answered them. In high school there were always boys hanging around their front porch. "How long is this going to go on?" her father would ask her mother before they sat down at dinner, and her mother would go to the front door and say, "Go home, you boys. We're eating now."

Later that evening she went into Mona's room. Mona was lying diagonally on her bed, reading a book on the new offset Linotype machine they'd ordered for the plant. She knew as much as the foreman about the printing business. They had both worked there as kids, but it was Mona who had paid attention. Both her mother and father had been happy when she came back from school to work in the business.

She sat down on the bed and leaned back against the headboard. "How are you?"

Mona looked up and grinned at her. "You busybody," she said. They both laughed. They had always confided in each other. "You still a virgin, El?"

She didn't know what to answer. She had always been honest with Mona but she didn't want to admit she was. Mona went on, "Because if you are, the best is yet to come."

That made her start to giggle. "Better than tapioca pudding?" she got out, doubling up.

Mona started laughing too. It was their favorite thing. "With mandarin orange slices," she said.

When they'd both stopped, Mona went on. "I was just trying to work out where we should put this. We're going to double production with this press. And at the same time I was thinking about—am I going to embarrass you, El?" She shook her head. "Sex becomes . . . once you try it, you think about it a lot. It's irresistible. You don't have to really love the person; this is hard to explain. You just want to feel his weight on you, breathe in the smell of his skin, wrap your arms around his back, and then you just sort of merge and take off with the movement and all you're noticing is how good it feels." Mona paused to look at a diagram in the manual.

She knew her face was red. She thought of mentioning a film she'd seen in Health, where a woman with an advanced case of syphilis wasn't able to answer a simple question. Was Mona a nymphomaniac?" "Do you hear from Ben?" she asked. She didn't want her to go on. Mona and Ben had been high school sweethearts.

"Not since he got drafted. El, I don't love anybody. I don't want to marry him or anything like that. He's already married. That's why Mother's giving me a bad time."

"You told her?"

"She found out. His wife phoned. What a mess. I'm not going to see him anymore."

Though she'd tried to put it out of her mind, it had bothered her, what Mona'd said, all that evening. It wasn't that she didn't know. In girls' PE, she had seen the little two-by-three books that you thumbed, making Blondie and Dagwood do things to each other. Then Mona showed her one with Olive Oyl and Popeye. She took her time letting the pages flip back, making the cartoon characters move in slow motion. She was considered a nice girl. She French-kissed, took and gave long embraces, clinches, they called them. Passionate kisses. But that was all. She had never wanted to go on, or had anyone panting for more. Did she hear music or see flying cupids, hearts? Nothing like that.

She had two brothers; she knew how they were made. She'd looked over the anatomy books; the male models in the life classes Mrs. Long talked her father into letting her take at the university were of only mild interest; it was like drawing someone's nose, though she never included that in the drawings she turned in.

It was all perfectly normal, except for the professor in her dreams. She didn't know why he was even there, because in the restaurant he'd been at their table less than five minutes. It was on a museum trip to San Francisco with Mrs. Long and two other art students, and Mrs. Long had taken them to a famous restaurant. Bohemian. A man came up to their table, his cigarette in a long holder. He actually wore a monocle. There was paint splattered on his shoes, a few sprinkles on his white shirt. He was shorter than her five-nine and had a fat belly that sagged both above and below where his belt cut into the fat, as if it were two sausages. His face wasn't interesting, the way it was twisted from trying to hold the glass to his eye. He was going bald in front and had combed his hair forward into bangs. Mrs. Long stood up to shake hands with him. He stayed at the table and they were all introduced. She had been drawing faces of the people sitting around them; she knew it was an affectation, she carried the sketchpad around like a badge, *I am a painter*, but she did it anyway. She had Mrs. Long down, as plain-looking as a housewife or someone who worked in a five-and-dime store, sensible hair, comfortable dress, glasses. A nice face. A kind one. The professor—Mrs. Long had introduced him as Professor someone—picked up her pad and looked through the drawings, flipping the pages back. It irritated her; he hadn't asked. She didn't usually show anyone her sketches.

"Facile," the professor said. "You haven't really grasped your subjects. No feeling."

She got mad. "I usually don't go into any depth when I sketch. They're just to remind me what I have seen, what I've liked." Why was she explaining to him? "I'd like to see some of *your* work. I'd like to give you my opinion."

He grabbed up her pad, picked up several strands of dripping spaghetti from someone's plate, and smeared them across a fresh page. They all watched him as he handed the pad back with a bow. The sauce had soaked through three pages. Without thinking, she tore them out and crumpled them up, and as he started to march away she bounced the ball of paper off his neck. "No talent," she yelled after him.

She never made scenes. Everyone was looking at them. Mrs. Long was roaring with laughter. The two other girls looked scared. She was feeling sick to her stomach.

In the cab going back, Mrs. Long explained that the professor did collages, wrote art criticism, and taught at the university across the bay. "It's one thing to be a mediocre artist, but why do they all have to teach?" Mrs. Long sounded indignant. "Then play critic, when they're safe in a classroom with their salaries."

That night she had the first dream. She couldn't believe it when the professor appeared naked, just walked into her studio while she was painting and watched her for a while without any clothes on. She remembered the dream the next day. What was going on? Disgusting, she kept thinking every time she remembered. But it got worse when she was in college.

He was always naked. Then something changed; he was painted in watercolors. An orange ear. An eyelid black. His toes were green. Then he put his hand up her sweater. The sneak. The strangest part was she didn't struggle. Didn't yell out or hit him with her wooden palette. She kept painting while he massaged her right breast. Not like he kneaded her buttock, but gently. She was annoyed to feel her nipple get bigger and bigger. She was amazed; it had never happened before. But the sensation wasn't all bad.

Then the bastard blew in her ear. He was disgusting; it made her jump. Started nibbling on her ear; then he stuck his tongue in. She woke up with a start, looking around the dormitory room, trying to see him. Her roommate was in the next bed. She couldn't go back to sleep.

It got worse. She went to the library and started reading the books on abnormal psychology. Case studies on perverts. Something was wrong with her.

What was a foot fetish? Some man would sit around across from a row of women in a train station and watch their feet through a hole in his newspaper and ejaculate. She read the psychoanalysts too; they dealt with dreams, but not hers. It was a bunch of hooey. She didn't want a penis; she wanted to be left alone. She'd have liked to talk to a doctor, but her family doctor had white tufts of hair coming out his ears, and besides, her mother always came in with her. She'd never undressed below the waist for anyone.

She had to talk to someone. She went to see Mrs. Long. She couldn't even mention what was going on to Mona, much less her mother. She had taken a course in psychology, an elective, the last semester, but they never came close to discussing anything like her dreams. She still read, but couldn't make any of the books apply to her problems. She brought the conversation around to the professor, in hopes—she didn't know what she was hoping for anymore. "You know that time," she started out. She could talk to Mrs. Long. They were in Mrs. Long's studio, a small house in the back where she painted; several fresh canvases were against the wall.

"I'm coming back from a journey," Mrs. Long interrupted, "back to representational. That's what it feels like. I never should have left."

"They look a little like Rouault." She had stopped painting but allowed herself to take one course in art history a semester. "Those colors, that stained-glass effect."

"It's an improvement, let's say," Mrs. Long said.

"What I wanted to ask you about was . . ." She felt something on the bottom of her foot, a sensation. As if someone were just running a finger over her instep, on her right foot. It made her jump. It was happening while she was conscious. He was rubbing her foot in broad daylight. "I have to go now," she said, "I just remembered something."

She had hinted to her mother about coming home for Thanksgiving, if someone would come and get her. She'd been away three months now. Christmas was when they'd agreed on. Her mother didn't take her up on it. It was the gas rationing, she decided. She couldn't take the bus either, because there wasn't enough time. She was stuck.

Mrs. Hughes invited her then. She had no choice; it was either next door or eat alone. She made a pumpkin pie for their dessert and went over at two-thirty. She tried to appreciate the effort Evelyn made—Mrs. Hughes wanted her to call her that—but it was too hard. "Dinner is served," Mrs. Hughes said, and put down a baked chicken in the middle of the table. Her family had always had turkey. The chicken was tough, too. There were no creamed carrots or giblet stuffing. "Wonderful," she said, pulling a piece of meat from a leg with her front teeth. She was being ungrateful.

She made an effort to finish everything on her plate, and had two pieces of pie. Listened to all Mrs. Hughes's complaints. Physical: varicose veins, palpitations, toothache, arthritis, and dandruff. House: the roof leaked and the planes flying over had cracked the cement foundation. Listening, nodding in agreement, suddenly it seemed to her that this was going to be her life forever. Living like this. Time was going to pass her by. She wasn't going to get out of this rut she was in. Ever. She'd always done what she was told. She had been going to school her whole life because everyone said get an education, and where did it get her? Here, drying the dishes while Mrs. Hughes washed. There had to be more.

"You can't get anything without rationing," Mrs. Hughes said. "Sugar, coffee, butter, meat, and now tea." She would sit here tonight and listen to Mrs. Hughes and the radio until nine o'clock, excuse herself, then go next door to her apartment and go to bed.

"I have to leave early, Evelyn," she said. "They're having a Thanksgiving service at church. I promised I'd attend." Liar, liar, pants on fire. She'd find one open if she had to climb through a window.

She was never going to get used to this California weather. You had to wear a sweater at night, but not in the afternoon, and it was almost winter. But the fog made up for the mild weather. She got her hat, gloves, and purse, went down the stairs, knowing Mrs. Hughes was watching her, and started down the block.

Where? The Episcopal church didn't have a service. She could go downtown; there was still enough daylight. It was when it got dark that the servicemen came to town. She'd heard the stories, mostly from Mother Mitchum and Mrs. Hughes. No woman was safe after dark. "It's not just the servicemen," Aunt May had told her. "The shipyard workers leave a lot to be desired when it comes to decency." It couldn't all be true.

The town was too spread out; where was she going, for heaven's sake? She was walking uphill, almost to the park. She could see the stands of eucalyptus trees; they were in the most unexpected places. Not native to the state. It was getting dark; she'd have to get back. The sun was almost down; there were just white-yellow gleams left in the sky. She crossed the street and went back the way she'd come. She hadn't ever been in this neighborhood before. These were better homes, newer; working people didn't live here; must be the businessmen that took the train to the city.

She had to look twice to be sure, but it really was a poinsettia, that big shrub in the front yard ahead, in full bloom. Only in California. At home they bought them at Christmastime in pots. Here they grew as big as trees in people's front yards. She'd better hurry; it was getting really dark, and Mrs. Hughes would be watching for her, waiting for her to reach the porch before opening her door and inviting her in for tea. She was never going back. Never. If Mrs. Hughes was lonely, what was she?

She didn't know where she was, her feet hurt, and she could count the first stars. She'd lost her way but she was aimed in the right direction; she could see El Camino. A front door opened up ahead, a cone of light, and three girls came down the front walk, talking, laughing, putting on their scarves, adjusting their coats over their cashmere sweaters. They wore pleated wool skirts and saddle shoes. She'd never worn those kind of clothes, what everyone else wore in high school or college. Her mother had bought her clothes. That was the awful truth of the matter. The clothes she was wearing now they'd bought last July. She just couldn't decide. "You're too old for me to do this," her mother had said; they were in Penney's in Reno, going through the size-eight rack. "Mother, I can't make up my mind," she'd said.

The last girl, the one walking behind the other two, she almost bumped into when they stopped at the corner. "Are you going too?" the girl asked.

"I'm just trying to find my way home," she said. They all laughed at that like she was trying to be funny. But she wasn't.

"This is going to be fun," one of them said. "Come on." They included her. She tried several times to introduce herself, but they were chattering and she never got a good opening. They were college students home for the holiday. They were in nursing training somewhere down near Los Angeles.

She went along. It was in the right direction for home. When they turned the corner and the three girls started across the yard, she knew where she was. It was Edgemont, that square, four-story silhouette, she couldn't mistake it, even in the pitch dark. She followed them through the main entrance and up the three flights of wooden stairs—she had never been up to the condemned floors—and into the auditorium.

"Who's a first-timer?" a woman a little older than herself, wearing a blue uniform with a USO patch on the shoulder, asked as they were all taking off their coats. Without thinking, she raised her hand, and so did one of the girls she'd come in with.

"There are rules posted up behind the counter; please read them and re-member the one that says you're not to leave with the servicemen. We've been having trouble with parents complaining. Read the rules. What can you do?" she asked. What did she mean? The other girl said, "I can dance."

"Everyone can do that. I meant, can you be master of ceremonies? Sing? Tell jokes? Something to make our boys forget they're far away from home?"

"I can draw," she said. The woman waited for her to go on. "I could sketch portraits, something they could send home to their mothers."

"How long would it take?"

"Three or four minutes."

"Here," she said, and handed her a small five-by-seven pad out of her purse. She made the woman prettier than she was, made her mouth smile and didn't put in the acne scars on her cheeks. It was her first effort in four and a half years. She was relaxed; she didn't feel that tension that made her think she was going to vomit when she started an oil.

"You're good," the woman said. "There's a supply room off the stage; get what you need. The rest of you are going to help me set out the trays of doughnuts and make the coffee."

The supply room was full of games, box after box. She found chalk and some good drawing paper. There was more paper up here than the whole school had down on her floor. She was sitting in a chair across from another empty chair by the entrance when a soldier wandered in. He watched her a minute, then looked around the big auditorium at the stage and the open beams strung with red, white, and blue streamers. "Sit down," she said, "and I'll draw your picture."

Then the sailors came in. She did seventy-four the first night, with a long line of men who had to be turned away. She made them all look handsome and all happy.

Veronica, the USO officer, made her take a break, let her dance. Got her into a game of Ping-Pong. "You're supposed to have fun too," she told her, taking away her drawing paper. She didn't have to worry about her colleagues coming here. It didn't matter if they did know. Veronica gave her a ride home; it was twelve-forty-five when she unlocked her front door; and the whole house was dark.

Chuck

*0*422. It was too early to get up. He found his father's railroad pocket watch under his pillow. The same. He watched the eight minutes until the ship's clock he'd found in an empty office and requisitioned dinged one bell: 0430. The time. The hour. The minute. They were all satisfactory.

He wouldn't sleep again now, but that didn't make any difference. Not with this duty. He was the engineer on the gravy train. No more saltwater sailor. He was safe for now. For however long the war took. No more sea duty, as long as he kept his nose clean.

Stateside was unbelievable. Before the war he blew his pay on the first liberty and then sat the time out until the ship went to sea again, back to Pearl or Subic Bay or Yokohama or somewhere. It was easier to have a good time in a foreign port. Why was that? For a dollar you could fuck, drink, and get a shoeshine. But it wasn't only that. They treated you better. It wasn't like stateside, where you were a piece of shit no matter how much money you had.

But that had all changed now. He still couldn't get over how it had been, coming back last month to San Francisco. The war had been on a year. He didn't know what to expect. He didn't expect anything, certainly not what he saw. The scuttlebutt was the Japs were getting ready to invade the West Coast. He'd take his chances: anything was better than waiting in some steel coffin to sink into the blue salt. He'd got off the hospital ship in Hawaii and flown into California on a PBY. Over all that water, he couldn't look out. It wasn't his mind, it was his body that wouldn't move. It kept stiffening, became rigid when he tried to turn his head to see out a window. Eleven days on the raft, up to his neck in the ocean. He was as much water as any wave. He was liquid inside, with his skin like a bulkhead keeping him together. They couldn't make him go back to the Pacific because he was full of salt water, and he wouldn't float if he got blown over the side this time, he'd dissolve.

Stateside was a madhouse, sailors everywhere, he'd never seen so many. He hadn't been back since '39. Market Street San Francisco was like a Navy Day parade: no civilians as far as he could see out the back window of the ambulance, not one.

When they had him on the street on a gurney, taking him to sick bay, some woman in a party dress kissed him on the lips. He was so surprised he said thank you ma'am. The next day some young college girl came in and read to him. He'd put his hand on her knee the first thing to see what he could get. He couldn't imagine a woman coming around if she didn't have some fun in mind. She picked his hand up and put it back on the bed. "If you don't mind," she said.

It was the same with the other women that came to the hospital. They came to write letters for him or shave him or read. There was a certain interest in him because he had been on the USS *San Francisco*, which had made it to drydock at Mare Island. Most of the crew had gone home on leave, the live ones anyhow.

He was a novelty of sorts, the only one on the raft to survive. Picked up by submarine after all hope was gone, with four others that died later. They didn't know he survived because he'd given up and died too, before the others. So he didn't particularly care what happened to his body. As long as he knew the time. Both of his watches kept ticking. He listened at night. When the sharks came he fought them off, using his sheath knife lashed to a wooded paddle, kicking them in the snout when he could see them nosing around in the phosphorescent water as they circled. "It's 2100 hours," he'd call out. By the fourth night everyone had stopped talking except him. During the day the sun cooked them red, especially the ones that had lost their clothes, and during the night the sharks came to feed. "2300," he'd call out.

"Something's got me, something's got me," someone would scream. "Help." Everyone else but him would try and pile into the raft to escape. He'd swim around to where the shark was trying to drag away the sailor and stab at the fish until he let go or until the sailor lost his grip on the raft. "2400 hours." But he did care enough to drink the rainwater they caught on a piece of canvas.

He noticed it didn't matter whether you wanted to live or not; the sharks didn't care. It didn't keep you from going crazy and swimming away, insisting you could see the ship's forward gun turret where you'd left three cheese sandwiches. Or just letting go of the raft. I have to get back to my family, a third-class told him. I can't die. That night he started drinking saltwater and was dead the next day. Everyone was so polite, helping each other. Here, pal, let me use my belt to put a tourniquet around that leg, with the sharks snapping their jaws, waiting. Out of sixty men, he was the only one to get out of the water and live.

An all-female orchestra came to play in the dayroom. They pushed everyone that couldn't walk in wheelchairs. He was down forty pounds from his usual one-eighty and felt weak. When the musicians started playing and he heard the first notes he started sobbing, loud, and he couldn't stop. The melody caught him unawares. He was so embarrassed he put his face inside his robe but couldn't stop making that awful noise, trying to get his breath while he was crying. Some sailor leaned over to him. "Hey buddy, knock it off; we can't hear." He stopped, finally.

When they let him go out the first time, just for the morning, he took the streetcar all over the city. It was like a beehive. People were on the move night and day. He talked to a shipfitter from Washington State who told him he shared a room with eleven other men. Six on each twelve-hour shift: when they left for work at the shipyard, the other six were coming home. Flags everywhere. Women in dungarees with lunch buckets, going to work as riveters and welders. It made you wonder what it was going to be like if the war ever ended.

He found some willing women among the hospital volunteers: Lynn, Gloria, and Wendy. They worked at a place where they ground lenses for gunsights on antiaircraft guns. They wore him out. The three of them were from Wisconsin, came west to work. All single, robust and rosy, healthy. Wendy had been married before. They worked different hours, or they would have had to bury him. It was the best kind of banging. Just like calisthenics. Jumping jacks. Good for your body. No crying or falling in love or this or that forever. Only feeling good about it after, squeezing each other tight and giggling while their sweat ran down their backs.

But the worst happened. They were always asking about the sailor's life. So he'd accommodate them, tell them sea stories. About the comradeship in the Navy, which was bullshit; good times, which were few; chance to learn something, which was nil. They knew he'd been on the USS *San Francisco* and knew how it had come back from the South Pacific. That's how they'd met; the three women came to visit the wounded at the Navy hospital on their one day off. People couldn't do enough. He told them that he was a chaplain's assistant and his only duty was to pray with most of the officers in a special compartment with special bulkheads and decks that bombs and torpedoes couldn't penetrate. Unsinkable, too. They were skeptical. "It's true; the paradise room is what we called it; we all just prayed for victory." Gloria was a Catholic too. He crossed himself for her. "Swear to God," he said.

"Then how did the admiral get killed?" she asked.

"He wouldn't listen to me and went back topside for his Bible."

"Oh come on," Lynn said. They could laugh. He made them laugh.

All three joined up. He couldn't believe it when they told him, only a couple of weeks after he'd met them. "The Navy? You enlisted?" He tried to talk them out of it, but it was no use. They were going to do their part. He went to the train station to see them off. After they got seats, they kept getting off the train to hug him again as the train waited for the last passengers to get on. He was too surprised to feel sad, though he stood there waving and waving until the train was gone.

He'd thought it was some kind of a joke, when they cut his orders after five weeks in the hospital. A Navy base at a horse-racing track? And before that they kept the Nips there?

He took the bus down, feeling better the farther he got away from the sea. There were mountains now between him and the ocean, and there was just a faint salt smell from the bay side. They were passing acres of headstones, cemeteries on either side of the road. It made him think of all the sailors that were going to die before the war was over. Would they win, the Allies? You couldn't prove it by him. More shipyards. Somebody said they were building a Liberty ship a day. It must be faster than the rate they were being sunk. Big steel mills now, thousands of men getting off shift.

Besides the Navy, he'd never had a job. Never got a paycheck for working. What did that make him, a loafer? Could he find a job now if he had to? He'd missed the whole Depression, joining the Navy in '33. He never even saw the hard times that hit later. It was hard times in Montana all the time. The Depression just made it worse.

He saw his stop and picked up his seabag. Went down the aisle with the white canvas bag up on his shoulder. Feeling the weight of his gear there always made him think that things were going to change. Not just that the new place would be different, but himself. It had never happened before. Changing in rank or rate from baker to yeoman to master at arms or from the *Arizona* to the *San Francisco* or from St. John's to the U.S. Navy, he always stayed the same.

An hour later he was standing at attention in front of the desk of the base executive officer, who was wearing a European theater ribbon from this war and a Yangtze River Campaign ribbon from the twenties. He'd been around. He was leafing through his personnel file. LT. COMMANDER VAN BEEK was engraved on the brass nameplate. "It's always a fair-weather day when we get a man with your experience," the XO said.

"Yes, sir," he answered, looking just above the officer's bald head. Never into their snake eyes.

"Discipline has gone to hell in this wartime Navy."

"Yes, sir," he said.

"We're in a touchy situation here. These boots are supposed to be trained and ready to serve in the fleet. But they get into trouble in town, or go AWOL, or injure themselves. As I said, we can use you. I can use your experience as a master-at-arms." As he talked he kept looking through the file. "You don't have to worry; I'll send you back to your ship. This is only temporary for me too. They sent me here from the Mediterranean. And I didn't want to come, but I've convinced myself the Pacific is where we're going to see some major sea battles. In my estimation, anyway. And I've been on five convoys to Murmansk plus the North African Campaign. You'll get to smell the black powder again, I can guarantee you that."

He knew he shouldn't say anything, but it came out anyway. "I don't want sea duty, sir."

The XO just laughed. "I don't wear them, but I rate six good-conducts. I was an enlisted man eighteen years, the last eleven as CPO. There's nothing you've experienced or even dreamed of that I haven't done. Twice, at least twice. And I know you'll want sea duty again. You'll request mast, standing right where you're standing now. You don't believe that, but you will. And I'll tell you why. You've been too long away from our so-called civilization. You can't come back here and expect to be comfortable. Survive, even. You had a better chance on the *Arizona* or the *San Francisco*. Not only you don't fit in; they don't want you either. Don't believe me. I'll stop boring you and myself too. But don't be fooled by this war now. It might look like everyone is glad to see you, but that's because they're afraid. For now. Wait till they're not."

"I have some questions." He started looking down at the file again and picked up a pencil. "How old were you when you enlisted?"

"Sixteen, sir."

"You have here nineteen. All Depression sailors lied. Who is this Cord?"

"He was a staff officer on the *Arizona* and the *San Francisco*."

"I've never seen or even heard of such a personnel evaluation. Recommendations for citations. Did you ever receive your Navy Cross?"

"No, sir."

"It takes time; that goes all the way back to the admiralty for approval in Washington, D.C. I don't like to make personal judgments about sailors under my command, but I have to know certain things. It's better to know now than be surprised later. You weren't his bunboy, were you?"

It took a second to understand what he was talking about. "You can go take a fuck in a rolling doughnut, sir."

Laugh, the XO laughed and laughed. "Nothing personal meant by that, and I won't take your answer personal either. What else? You finished tenth grade at St. John's Indian school. Does that make you an Indian?"

"My mother was." He wasn't going to answer, but this bastard would wait him out.

"What kind?"

"Blackfoot."

"You're a reservation Indian?"

"No. My mother was Indian; I'm not." The XO just looked at him. "I never lived on a reservation. I wasn't raised an Indian. I don't speak Blackfoot. And I don't know any Indians and I don't want to know any."

"If you don't want to be an Indian, that's fine with me. I was just asking." He wrote something down, then went back to turning the papers over. Took off his regulation glasses. "You'll be acting CPO here, in charge of security. You report to me. We don't have enough officers. For some reason, even after talking to you, I have a lot of confidence that you'll do the job. If you don't, I'll shitcan you to the fleet. I won't wait for you to come in here for a transfer. On the other hand, I'll push for your chief's rate, and I'll do my best to make sure you get the decoration you earned. It's the least I can do for another non-Indian. I never admitted having any blood in me either. But I'm less than you are. Dismissed, First Class Petty Officer Sweet."

He had seen worse. All officers could do or say anything they liked. People who had power over other people were all the same; they all insisted they were doing what was best for you. He didn't care what they did to him as long as he didn't have to go to sea.

He couldn't just lie there in his rack anymore, checking the time, listening for the bells on the half hour from the ship's clock. There were no other sounds in the Quonset hut. This room had been a lucky find. He didn't want to live in a barracks anymore. Just the thought of having people around him and he'd never close his eyes again. It was bad enough now, waking up all the time. He used to be able to sleep anywhere. He once dozed off during a night attack by five Japanese cruisers. That was after three days at battle stations.

The room was supposed to be the company armory, but as soon as he could, he went over to supply and got a rack, mattress, fart sack, pillows, blankets, and enough sheets to last a year. He'd put the weapons in the other Quonset hut assigned to the section.

After checking in with the XO, he spent the rest of the day walking around the new base. They were building faster than seemed possible; a regular city of two-story barracks was going up on the other side of the highway from Tanforan. The racetrack grounds were used mainly for training, the big concrete bleachers for lectures, the infield and track for a parade ground. You could still smell horseshit from the stables when the breeze was right.

He got up and took a shower and dressed. Went out in the dark and wandered some. Found the twenty-four-hour galley and had breakfast. He was back in his room by five o'clock and heard reveille. The place wasn't full yet, but he could hear enough voices counting out cadences for calisthenics and marching to chow to know there were a lot of sailors around. He shined his shoes, then got his iron out. Put two footlocker boxes on top of each other, then a blanket, and smoothed out his blues. It was the uniform of the day for permanent staff.

By six-ten he'd dusted and swabbed out his room. Took his time and made up his rack.

The water was still clean, so he went out into the office and started there. He was almost finished when a seaman came in and stood watching him from the doorway. At four minutes to seven. "What are you looking at, sailor? I want to see just your asshole and elbows while you empty out these wastebaskets first. Then get a rag and start wiping these desks off. And if there's any covers for these typewriters, they better be put on, fast."

More staff came and started helping the first sailor after he whispered to them. He wrung out the swab and dumped the dirty water in the sink. He always found it relaxing to swab, or roll out dough when he was a baker, or type. Chipping paint, even; he liked that too.

He thought he should say something at seven, when everybody was supposed to be there, but he couldn't. He had heard so many introductions from superiors that he couldn't bring himself to say one too. Tough ones, trying to scare the sailors into doing what they were supposed to. Funny ones. Everyone was pretending to work. He set a three-by-five blackboard up on his desk and wrote, First-Class Chuck Sweet, 1468735 USN. Then he went around and stood behind each man, asking questions. "Where did you learn to type?"

"Right here, sir, at this desk."

"How long have you been here?"

"Ten days now, sir."

"First, I'm an enlisted man; you don't sir me. Second, you better start practicing. You can learn to type. I'll see if I can get you a manual."

There were worse. Boots. All strikers, never been to school, assigned for no reason. Only one had any experience. Rated Third Class Randolph Smith. Drafted in '40, at nineteen, for one year; went through Great Lakes; sent to eight weeks of yeoman school. War started, and he got extended for the duration. And they promoted him. He considered himself old Navy. Never been on a ship. Never. And proud of it.

"Where do you draw for your shore patrol, rooster?"

"Permanent staff." Randolph had got up and half sat on the edge of his desk as he came up to him. Lit a cigarette.

"They have any training?"

"We call the police, the city police, if we can't handle the situation."

"What do they do?"

"They lock them up."

He didn't know what to answer. Just looking at Smith made him mad. He wanted to punch that smirk off his clodhopper face.

"They have a temporary brig on base, over by the stables. The Marines are in charge," Smith said.

"Don't send anyone there unless I say so. I don't care what he's done."

"The city police are worse."

"You ever been in Marine brig, Salty?" He didn't bother to listen to his answer, and interrupted. "Then don't tell me." All the typing stopped in the room. He felt the strain on his arms because his fists were clenched and he was ready to swing. Smith wasn't smirking now. He took a step backward, looking around the room. The typing started up again. The front door opened and two sailors came in for liberty passes, and Smith went over to the counter.

He had to be careful. This wasn't shipboard, where if someone gave you some guff you settled it right there. Never let any argument fester on a ship. Even a battleship was too small. He had learned that on board. Just like shore patrol. There was a second-class on the *Arizona* who would teach anyone interested how to use a baton, disarm and frisk a drunk sailor, and never even consider using your sidearm. He'd pulled shore patrol first when he was a seaman, but always with an experienced man.

He tried to figure out what to do until he could get enough men in the section. He went back to the only desk with a cubicle and sat down. He looked over the patrol rosters. They were on four and off eight, for twenty-four hours. Why did they need a shore patrol when the sailors were only on liberty from 1600 to 0400? It would save two patrols. If the Marines were on the front gate and in the brig, he didn't have to worry about the base. It was the towns he'd have to be concerned with.

He was feeling his way, never sure if he was going in the right direction. The base was going to build up to sixteen thousand recruits. It was too many sailors in one place. That's all he could think about. And he was supposed to stop them from killing each other.

Some mornings he didn't know where to start. He had the crazy idea he'd lock the door and give speed typing tests to the yeomen. Make them type faster and faster. Tear the phones out too. Until the XO found out; then he'd be shitcanned to the fleet. He had to try.

He got a call from a Lieutenant jg Sikes, the recreation officer for the base, who was setting up a temporary outdoor movie theater as fast as he could, for use until the indoor one was finished. "Entertainment is fine," Sikes said, "but we've got to let the men know what this war is about. What we're fighting for. I've got hold of some films on what the Japanese army did to whole cities of people in China in '35 and '36."

The phrase stuck in his head. What were we fighting for? So it could be like it was before the war back in the states. The Depression? So he could go back to fucking the whores in Hong Kong? He asked Third-Class Smith: Salty thought he knew everything. "To kill Japs," he said.

After talking to him on the phone two or three times, he finally met Lieutenant Sikes. "Mr. Sikes," he addressed him; you didn't have to sir a lieutenant. Sikes caught on right off. "Call me Sikes or Russ, I don't care." They were walking across the parade ground; he had automatically fallen a pace behind and made sure Sikes was on his right. Sikes didn't know anything about respect for officers and he didn't want to know. He had four months in the Navy. He'd been drafted from his job as assistant manager of a bank.

Sikes was the worst slob of an officer he'd ever seen. He looked like he slept in his uniform, and had a belly on him big enough to stretch the place between his shirt buttons so you could see his skin. But he acted himself with Sikes; he was relaxed. Not so relaxed that he was ever familiar in front of another officer or any of the men. He wished there was some way to suggest to Sikes that he square himself away.

He asked Sikes, "What are we fighting for?"

Sikes gave what for him was a short answer. "When it comes to the Nazis and the Italians and the rest, we have to stop fascism. We can't allow Hitler to dominate the world. With the Japs, they attacked us and we have to respond in kind. And we're fighting for our way of life here, as unjust and capricious as it is at times. What do you think we're fighting for?"

"It's my job. I'm regular Navy."

"You didn't have to be on board the San Francisco." Van Beek had mentioned that at a meeting when he'd introduced him as the new base master-at-arms: "This man has had three lives so far. He was on board . . ." and the rest of it.

He thought about saying, "For my country." But if he had his way he'd live somewhere other than stateside, Singapore, maybe. "For the money," he said. "I'm up to a hundred twenty-eight dollars a month now as an acting chief." They both laughed. He couldn't think of anything better.

Sikes was always talking about transferring back to the East Coast where he was from, and had applied for submarine school to get back. "You're crazy," he told Russ. "It's bad enough on top of the water. Underneath has to be worse."

"I tried to get them to send me to a university program they have for officers, but they wouldn't take me."

He thought Van Beek included him in the permanent staff meetings, which were mostly made up of officers, to embarrass him. He sat in the back, hoping not to be noticed, as morale and the number of courts-martial and AWOLs were discussed. Sikes had a lot to say about everything, from the chow to how the obstacle course should be set up. He'd stand up with his potbelly hanging over his civilian belt, not wearing his collar bar, one or both of his scuffed shoes untied. But everyone listened. Some of the officers took notes.

He met Sikes's wife when she came on base to pick him up. She dressed the same way Sikes did. There were coffee spots on her blouse. An inch of her slip was hanging half-mast below her skirt. She might have been a little older than her husband, thirty-one or -two. She had an opinion on everything too. When he asked her, "What are we fighting for?" she said, "Oil, rubber, and the right not to get bombed." She wasn't fat, but she was like Sikes in that she didn't notice things. Sikes would stand looking at cloud formations right where every recruit in the base would pass, and they'd all have to salute him. Whole companies would be given eyes-right as they marched by. She wanted to see the galley, which made the cooks think they were being inspected, and the new barracks, Sikes leading the way, with the sailors in their skivvies yelling attention when they saw an officer. Then Mrs. Sikes walked in.

Myra, Mrs. Sikes, invited him to dinner. He went, nervous, trying to act like he sat down and ate roast beef with an officer every day of the week. But after a while he relaxed, listening to the two of them argue. About anything. Sikes had been to college a couple of years, but Myra only had a high school education. She had worked her way up to manager of a home heating oil company with thirty-one employees. They'd met when she'd gone to get a loan from his bank. "And Russ wasn't going to give me the money."

"We weren't loaning money then; it was 1938."

The house was brand-new, just-built officers' housing. They had already filled in all the built-in bookshelves. Neither liked California. "There's no seasons here. It's not natural for it to be summer all the time," Myra said. "What do you think, Chuck, you're not from here."

"San Diego used to be a good liberty town."

They both laughed; he knew it was because he always thought about everything from the sailor's point of view. He made sure he was consistent, too, and always got a rise out of Myra. "Forget liberty. Do you miss Montana weather?"

"Sometimes," he said. "Especially the way your ears freeze at forty below." He liked being with them, making them laugh.

The town chief of police and the county sheriff had each been trying to get him on the phone for days. They left messages with the clerks. They wanted to see him. He hadn't even gone on liberty since coming here, much less gone into town on patrol, just on the off-chance he might run into them. They refused to come to the base. He kept telling the clerk to say he was out. Finally he talked Sikes into going into town with him. "You'll be a help, as an officer."

"What do they want?"

"I don't know, but I'd appreciate your coming with me."

The chief's office was too small for all four of them, and he and Sikes had to share a short bench where suspects sat. The sheriff had a kind of gentleman's cowboy hat on, a tie and a suit, and a permanent grin, like he was hearing funny stories all the time. The chief was a sourpuss, wore his blue uniform with more brass on the collar than a rear admiral's. They were Van Beek's age, old, in their forties; both had gray hair. The sheriff had a gut, but not half as big as Sikes's. The sheriff talked while the chief just tried to stare them down. "You boys know that the racetrack used to be one of the major sources of income around here."

Sikes jumped right in. "Well, I'm sure sixteen thousand sailors are just compensation. And their families, let's not forget them now. There isn't a place to rent in a twenty-mile radius. And the bars, eateries, and stores in general benefit. The whole county benefits."

"You're misunderstanding me," the sheriff interrupted, still grinning, patient. "Tanforan Race Track was the source of our income."

Even Sikes was puzzled during the silence that followed. "I don't think I understand."

"There used to be a lot of illegal betting, off-track wagering, we called it."

"Bookies," the chief yelled, as if they were deaf.

"They use to compensate us for our assistance, and we put their gratuities into a slush fund. A benefit fund. The annual policemen's ball, benevolent society for the widows and orphans, and such."

"I don't know what to tell you," Sikes said, "but I don't think, gentlemen, that the U.S. Navy has the authorization to disburse compensation to you for former bribes."

"Are you trying to be funny?" the sheriff said, and he wasn't grinning now.

He should never have brought Sikes. He had to say something. "We can't bring the horses back; you're going to have to wait just like we are for the war to be over to get things back to normal. What if I get you PX privileges and a card to eat in the CPO dining room? No rationing there, all the butter and steaks you can eat. And cigarettes are only four bits a carton at the PX." The sheriff was grinning again. "All you want," he added.

"That would help," the sheriff said.

"Yeah," Sikes pitched in, "the war won't last forever."

As they were going back to the base, Sikes kept exclaiming. "They were trying to shake down the U.S. Navy; can you imagine that? I've heard everything now." Going through the front gate, as the Marine guard was saluting, Sikes started laughing. He finally got out, "Chuck, why didn't you ask them what we're fighting for?"

He once knocked Sikes to Van Beek. "If he ever gets in the submarine service, how's he going to get through the hatches with his gut?"

"What do you mean?" Van Beek asked in just the right tone to let him know that he'd gone too far.

"Nothing, sir."

"Lieutenant Sikes will be missed." He knew why Van Beek liked Sikes. He got things done. He knew something about everything, and would find out if he didn't. And he was able to make his ideas stick. Why was he such a brown-noser, backbiting Sikes, someone he respected? Everyone did it; say the bad before they said it about you. Not Sikes. Sikes never bad-mouthed Van Beek or anyone else.

He usually went over to Sikes's office in the morning at 1000 hours for coffee. He stopped at the bakery for a dozen cinnamon rolls. With his mouth full, Sikes said, "Did I mention they accepted me for submarine school in Connecticut? I leave Wednesday after next."

In peacetime he was used to seeing a friend sent to another duty station or to a school. Go up another rate, transfer ships. But with the war it happened faster; everyone was moving around a lot more. He did what he'd seen others do, went around to the enlisted men in both Sikes's section and his own and asked if they wanted to contribute to a gift for Sikes. With the money he bought a Navy officer's sword.

"Just what I need in a sub," Sikes said when Van Beek presented the gift. He thanked everybody. Went around shaking the enlisted men's hands, then the officers who had insisted they contribute when they found out about the sword.

He took Sikes and Myra to the club for a drink. Mrs. Sikes didn't shave her legs like most women did, now that both silk and rayon stockings were impossible to get. The hair was dark and curly and there was more than on his own legs. "Chuck, you can do better than the Navy," she told him.

"There's nothing wrong with the Navy," Sikes defended him.

"There's nothing wrong if you like never having to think for yourself."

"Thinking is not a prerequisite to anything."

"There's no freedom in the service; you can't make mistakes."

"The hell you can't," he put in. "I spent thirty days in the brig." He just played the dumb sailor; he knew what she meant.

"Not that kind, the kind where you learn something."

She kissed and hugged him when it was time for them to board the bus the next day. Sikes shook his hand and didn't let go. "Chuck, take care of yourself." It was as if he were the one that was going to be shipped out to the war zone. He didn't know what to say, he felt so awkward. They like me, he kept thinking. I'm their friend.

He tried to walk into town, but every civilian that went by offered him a lift. He didn't even have his thumb out. He finally took a ride with a woman, but he hadn't seen the three kids asleep on the backseat. He tried anyway. "You like to go dancing with me?" he asked.

She looked over at him to see if he was serious. She was a little overweight but had a pretty smile. "My husband is in the Coast Guard and he wouldn't be too happy at your offer. Or my mother-in-law either, who I'm living with."

"Just asking," he said. "You remind me of my sister."

"Go on," she said.

At the first bar he promised himself only a couple of beers but was bought more by a factory worker who sewed canvas tents for the Army. Everyone who stood near him had to explain why they weren't in uniform. He'd heard it all, he thought: I'm 4F because of my eyes or flat feet or too thin, or I'm deferred because I have five kids, or I was in the first one. I'm just waiting until they call me. I'm going to work three more months, then I'm going to join up. I can't leave now; I'm making almost a dollar an hour. I never made that a day, back in Wyoming. I'm too old or too young.

But the one that had just edged up to the bar said, "I'm a pacifist." He had to think a minute before he knew what he was talking about. He'd read somewhere about them. Conscientious objectors. COs, they were called. He was interested, surprised. "Not if they were hurting your family?" he asked.

"I might fight then," he said matter-of-factly. "But not wholesale."

"Is there a difference?"

"I don't want to have to kill another human being. I don't think it's right." This was interesting. He remembered, now, hearing the arguments of men that didn't want to kill on board ship. But as far as he knew, they always did what they were told to do, whether it was stacking ammo or cleaning the gun or shooting it. "What did your draft board say when you told them that?"

"They said I was going to have to go to prison."

"What did your family say?"

"They think I'm a coward. Both of my brothers are in the Army. I have another hearing."

"I've never been in prison," he said, "but I've been in a couple of brigs and they're not pleasant. Let me buy you a drink."

"No, no, I've had enough; I'm going to finish this. I got a room on the street behind the bar, over a garage. I just stopped here for one before I hit the sack." He raised the brown bottle of Blatz he was drinking out of for the last swallow, then set the bottle back on the bartop. "Can I ask you a question?"

"Ask me anything, sure, go ahead."

"What do you think it feels like to kill another man?"

He had to think about it a minute. "In the Navy," he said, still thinking it over, "you don't actually get to shoot another person, individually. What I mean to say is, you're usually shooting at other ships or airplanes. I never took it personally that I was killing other sailors or they were trying to kill me."

"You've been in the war zone, then?"

"I was on the *Arizona* at Pearl." It was the first time he'd voluntarily told anyone that since he got back. The conscientious objector looked like a young Santa Claus, chubby, red-cheeked, with glasses and a big grin. It was already seven o'clock. He'd been in the bar an hour and a half. He checked his wristwatch; the bar clock was nine minutes slow. Looked at the railroad watch in the pocket of his jumper. Nine minutes to.

The CO was peeling the label off the bottle with his thumbnail. "Didn't it bother you, seeing all those men die?"

He had never thought about it; there were too many things happening after. To gain time he said, "I'll comment if you allow me to buy a round." He was ready when the bartender took their order.

"I had some friends that went down with the ship. Don't get me wrong now, but there were a lot of shipmates I didn't know and a few I didn't particularly like. But no one should have to wake up and die like that." Was that what he thought? "But again, I never took it personally. And I know it could have been me that's still down there."

He stopped, trying to make the words that were coming out line up with his thought. He wondered if they ever did. Do you ever say the exact right thing? The CO was looking at him, waiting. What made the telling perfect? It had to be the retelling and the retelling again until you had all the possibilities right, like taking a lead on a plane coming at the ship with the forty-millimeter, the tracers going out, lining up, until you get right on the target and the plane explodes. Disintegrates.

He noticed the CO was signaling the bartender for more beer. When the bottles were set in front of them, he took his money out and paid. "I'll get it," the CO said.

"My turn, my turn."

"I never tell anyone I'm a conscientious objector," he said. "No one ever understands. A couple of fellows at work tried to beat the piss out of me."

"I never tell anyone I was on the *Arizona* for eight years either." They both laughed. "It isn't just because it was hard on a person; I saw a lot worse later, in the South Pacific. Things that wouldn't happen to you if you were sent to hell for eternity. Hell is in the ocean, in the sea, and is made of blue water and salt." He didn't care if the CO understood or not.

Before the words started coming out, he knew he was going to tell. And the CO was waiting, wanting to hear if it was right not to go.

"I got up for early chow to go to mass. I was a yeoman then, a pencil-pusher, but I played the clarinet in the ship's band for church services. As a kid I'd played the bassoon; it's got the same fingering as the clarinet, but harder if you don't know. Mass was at 0800 but we were all standing around tooting, warming up. Until then I always thought, playing music, nothing bad could ever happen to you. Like a kind of grace.

"I had the advantage over a lot of the other sailors; I knew the ship. And I was topside. A lot were asleep in their hammocks and a lot had just come on board the last few months." He paused, trying to remember. It was being on the *San Francisco* afterward that kept confusing him.

"What I was worried about most was the clarinet. It was the best instrument I ever played; it was silver-plated, and you can bet I kept it polished. I couldn't stop thinking if it was damaged the Navy would hold me responsible." The CO laughed. It surprised him: was that funny? He went on.

"It happened before I could be afraid. It was like I was reading pulp magazines and I had to find out more. Cowboys riding into town shooting and yelling, drunk after a long trail drive. You have to supply the pictures in your head; it's not there on the page. You have to see the horses lathered up and the dust from Main Street rising up higher than the storefronts. The empty shell casings and the noise, powder exploding, smoke. Especially the smoke and the booms. The booms. You have to supply all that later, because there's not time then to register the details.

"I ended up in a compartment, after the ship went down. The ship hadn't settled yet, part of the compartment was underwater and part wasn't. There were about twenty of us; it was dark but there was plenty of fresh air.

"The steel plates of the ship were still buckling, breaking up from the pressure as it settled. You could hear the echo through the bulkhead of the compartment. The water was rising, not very fast, lapping at the sides like the tide was coming in.

"There were bodies floating facedown. A chief was at the top of a ladder where there was a hatch, trying to break off a padlock with the blade of his deck knife. I still had my clarinet; through it all I kept hold of it. I had it stuck under my jumper so it wouldn't get scratched. I could taste blood in my mouth, but I didn't feel hurt. I thought I'd bitten my tongue in all the excitement. I wasn't feeling scared or anything. It just didn't come to mind. It was better without all the noise now and the smoke from the burning oil. It was almost like we were at sea. For some reason I was feeling like I'd just got up from chow and I was going topside to smoke a cigarette. Talk to my shipmates. See who was going to be in the movie.

"There were two men on the step above me, officers by their uniforms, who had their arms around each other's shoulders and were sniffling. I could hear someone saying their prayers, one after another. Hail Marys, Our Fathers, louder and louder, as if that sound would fill up the compartment instead of the water. A gunner's mate next to me was saying, 'I thought the general quarters was a chaplain's trick; they just wanted to get us up to go to church.' Somebody else was shouting above that, 'I had a forty-eight-hour pass; I shouldn't be here.'

"The chief kept yelling goddamn sons of bitches over and over, after he broke the blade of his knife, and he started kicking the hatch. Everyone was perched on the fifteen feet of ladder that was out of the water. When I tried to edge up they kept me down. No one wanted to lose their place. I was up to my knees in water when something bumped against my legs. It was a sailor face up, just in his skivvies, wearing a cork lifejacket. I had to take my clarinet out from under my jumper before I could haul him up partway out of the water, enough to put my knee on his stomach. He smelled awful. Stunk. Some kind of crap had got all over him. He spit water when I pressed down and started coughing. He started breathing and I held on to him.

"While I was doing all that, one of the officers grabbed the clarinet. 'Try this,' he said to the chief.

" 'That's mine. It's too light to do any good,' I said.

" 'As you were,' the officer said. I could hear the chief battering the clarinet to pieces. It gave off a sound, a wheeze, like the reed was split.

"The half-drowned sailor started rambling about something. It sounded like he was giving the range. I tried to calm him. 'We're going topside in a little while.' 'Four hundred yards, four hundred yards,' he kept saying. I took the cork life preserver off so I could haul him a little farther up the ladder, whether anyone moved or not. He started yelling, 'I want this man's name.' Kept saying it over and over. To humor him I kept saying back, 'Chuck Sweet 1468735 third class.' He did smell. The officers wanted me to put him back in the water."

He stopped. He'd forgotten he was talking to someone. "I'm almost through," he told the CO.

"I'm listening. You're better than the radio. Believe it or not." They both took big swigs from their beer bottles.

"The worst was not knowing the time; my wristwatch had stopped. And of course the ship's bell wasn't sounding. I kept thinking if I knew the time I'd be all right. If I knew how long I was down there, trapped, it would be enough to get me out. I kept asking the time, but no one had a watch that worked.

"My father liked to know the time; he was a brakeman on the Northern Burlington. This is my father's watch and chain. I had a good Waltham pocket watch from St. John's, where I went to school, but it was in my locker on the *Arizona*. Most watches just have twelve-hour dials: this one I got off an aviator has a twenty-four-hour dial so you know exactly where you are. No P.M. or A.M." He held out his wrist.

"This one's your regular watch, twelve-hour dial." He cocked his leg, pulled up his bell-bottom trousers, and pushed down his sock. "I keep this one for emergencies, Bulova, twenty jewels. Waterproof. And a good timepiece. Where was I?" He noticed the bar was jammed with men. Most wore sailor suits; the civilians had gone home.

"I saw a hose floating like a big sea snake. The longer you were in there, the more you could see. I swam out; it was a four-inch hose and had a brass nozzle on it like a club. I couldn't get it loose and swam back to the ladder. I banged it on the rail then to wake it up and had the smelly sailor hold the hose while I unscrewed it. We got it loose. He was vomiting up now. The sound made everyone nervous, it echoed so much, like he was dying. 'Pipe down. Stow it.' Everyone was yelling at him.

"'Move over,' I yelled. 'I can bust that lock.' I hauled the sailor up with me. Everyone was yelling back there was no room, leave him, but I wasn't going to. Just to piss them off, you see. I was going to take him with me. 'If you want to get out of here, let us up,' I kept yelling.

"I got him up with me. Three blows with that nozzle was all it took. I could have battered the entire hatch down, given the time. It opened into a partly flooded companionway, and because of the angle we all started crawling. I kept my place first; everyone was shoving and wanting to get out. But I was in front, pushing the sailor ahead of me. I saw a vent grating when I looked up. The companionway was on its side; we were crawling on the bulkhead. I could see the Hawaiian sun through the grating. I had to pull the sailor into the vent; it was about three feet by two. He did smell bad and he couldn't crawl. When we got to the end of the vent, I could see past the sailor that we were hanging about twenty feet above the water. Small boats were circling the part of the ship that was out of the water.

"I always had a funnybone. And I yelled down, 'Ahoy, permission to leave ship.' The chief behind me yelled, 'You asshole, double time, move it.'"

He smiled, pleased with himself for getting it mostly right, promising himself he'd never, never tell about it again. The CO was shaking his head. He had to explain a little further.

"It all happened so fast, it's only when it's over that you have to suffer the time. It must be like coming back from the dead."

"Then they sent you back here?"

"No," he said. He felt tired; the beer was making him sleepy. "They put me in the hospital. I got this." He ran a finger down the scar on his face. "I was regular Navy, I had a duty." He lifted up his sleeve with his two hash marks to show. "It was my vocation." He noticed there were several more full beer bottles in front of him. He looked around; a civilian in a gray suit lifted his glass, and he nodded back. He put one bottle in front of the CO. "Where was I?"

"You were regular Navy."

"I was. It's hard to explain. I was raised in Montana. No ocean. When I joined up I didn't know what sea duty was like. How being out on a ship . . . I didn't know what to compare it to. I was raised Catholic. And I used to think it was like heaven. Living on the sea was like being on a watery cloud in the blue sky. It was so peaceful. Lookout at night. In the fog, quiet. Even when we were in rough seas. Storms, hurricanes. I always felt secure. I'm getting off the subject." He took a mouthful of beer.

"I was in the hospital. I was all right; they'd taken the stitches out. I never even had a headache. Guess who comes into the ward?"

The CO started laughing. "Someone who wants you to pay for the clarinet?" He laughed too.

"The smelly sailor in skivvies, but he's a full commander with his clothes on. He's going to do this and that for me. He was grateful for all I'd done and so forth and so forth. I was satisfied to lay on my bed the rest of the war and just look out at the palm trees through the window. I was a little disillusioned with the ocean.

"But he started talking about getting back at the Japs. Carrying the flag into the Pacific. I was his luck. In a few minutes I was out-patrioting him. 'I'd like to get those slant-eyes in my sights.' But that had been the farthest thing from my mind a couple of minutes before that. I know myself, and I know it's always afterwards that I realize what I've done.

"Anyway, he'd been assigned to the USS *San Francisco* and he suggested I sign on. I threw the covers back and put my bare feet on the deck, ready to go right then. I was crazy. His word was good; he made me a first class with my name up for chief. He tried like hell to make me CPO, but my rate was frozen. That's how I became master-at-arms; there was a better chance for me than as a yeoman. The *San Francisco* was a flagship and there was an admiral aboard. Commander Cord was his attaché. He'd been to Annapolis. He was a good officer."

He stopped talking for a second. A thought occurred to him. "How come you're working in the shipyard? That's war work; you're helping to kill."

"They made me, until my hearing. I volunteered to work on the ships that were sunk and raised, or damaged so badly that we cut them up for scrap. I was at Mare Island when they brought in the *San Francisco* last December. We used a cutting torch to open some of those compartments."

He started laughing. He couldn't help it. And he couldn't stop. He didn't know if the CO was laughing or not. He tried to stop. "See, what's so funny, what's so funny is, you've met Clarence. Yes you did. He fried crisp as a piece of bacon on that ship in the forward gun turret. You met my old shipmate Commander Cord." He started laughing again.

They were on the street. "You sure you're all right?"

"I'm fine. I just needed some sea air. Feel good now. I'm going to play some checkers. Come on."

"No, I can't. You take care of yourself, Chuck."

"I will, I will." He had been thinking about it the whole time they were in the bar. "You're not a coward," he said to the CO, who was starting to walk away. "There are no cowards. Just like there's no devils. It's all bullshit. We're all even. Even," he yelled. It's the same, he thought, and cupped his hands around his mouth to yell, "We're all the same."

He wasn't sure the CO heard. He started walking full stride, shoulders back, one hundred twenty steps a minute.

Avery

I got up when Aunt May yelled to wake me, and I washed and dressed, ate my puffed wheat. She never came out of her bedroom in the morning. Never opened the door, just yelled through it, "You're going to be late. Be sure and lock the front door. It's Wednesday; put the bottles out for the milkman. You were supposed to rinse them out." I never answered, just did what she yelled. Then hurried, though I had plenty of time before the first bell at school, to meet up with Leroy, to be gone before Mary Maureen was there waiting for me.

Last night had been the big USO party for the week. There was no telling what we'd find. A lot of tinfoil: sailors got all the cigarettes, gum, and Life Savers they wanted. Leroy once found a brass USN with a rope-and-anchor insignia. We'd both found pennies and nickels. Once a watch, which we turned in to the janitor. Also five wallets—they fell out easy because a sailor suit has no pockets but the small one on the jumper—and a lot of dog tags, religious medals, and glasses. When sailors fight, they just beat on each other, tearing their clothes half off. I saw that a lot of times at the bars.

We were the first in the yard, and went around and around. We must have picked up a hundred sticks of gum wrappers and so many empty packs of cigarettes I had to take out my orange from my brown paper lunch bag because my pockets were filled. There was no time to separate the foil from the paper wrappers, hopping around yelling here's another, another seven by the sandbox, twenty by the swings. They were everywhere.

"My foil ball is going to be as big as a cabbage," I said.

"Mine is going to be as big as a basketball," Leroy called back from over by the teeter-totters.

We never went inside before it was time, but this morning the door was open, so we went up the stairs, picking up more wrappers. The janitor hadn't swept yet. It was a true miracle and like playing a game at the same time: red rover red rover come over, and we did, up the stairs. I had my lunch bag filled and my shirt front too.

We kept going right up to the fourth floor, which was absolutely forbidden. I had never been up here before. At the top there were big open double doors that led into the auditorium. There were long school tables with wooden folding chairs, and red, white, and blue streamers across the ceiling like a net. We didn't go farther; Leroy kept saying, "Let's get out of here." When we heard the noise he ran for it, down the stairs three at a time.

I went to follow, and my lunch bag split. All my tinfoil flew out. I got so excited I started putting things in my shirt pocket when there was no more room. The noise got louder behind the closet door, like something banging in the nighttime.

Once I had all my wrappings picked up, I went over just to see, maybe open the door and then run. I was calmer now, not shaking, like I did when the cat got my tongue and I had the stutters. With a long arm I turned the handle and let the door swing open, stepping back fast. There was a naked sailor lying with his head behind some pushbrooms. Looking closer, I saw he had his cap on, pulled down over his face, and a rag tied through his mouth. His hands were tied behind him, and his ankles were tied too, with the rope from the curtains in the classroom.

He had a tattoo on each foot, a pig on one and a rooster on the other, and a wristwatch on an ankle and another on his arm by his elbow. He made the noise again, banging his head against the wooden wall. Besides his hat and dog tags he was wearing a red crêpe-paper streamer in a big bow around his radiator hose.

I got the hat off and worked the rag over his chin where it was loose. "Good morning, sir," I said.

"Time check," he yelled back. The first bell sounded and made me jump. "Time check, goddamn sonofabitching bastards. Time check."

I had to think. "0800 hours," I yelled back. "0800."

He stopped banging his head. "That's good, because when I get loose, I'm going to have to kill somebody by 0930."

I wasn't going to shake. I tried to think; if you're going to be a sailor, you have to know knots. I knew thirty-one, not counting the easy ones: over-and-under, granny, and clove hitch. Sammy knew a hundred and two. I kept some clothesline rope handy and did them while I was walking, and at night when we were listening to the radio. There was enough slack in the cord to snap back the square knot until it parted, and I worked the end through. The sailor lay still, stopped saying what he was going to do. I got his feet free and then the last bell sounded and I started to feel sick to my stomach.

After I got his hands free he couldn't use them very well. I picked up his cap for him. His name was stenciled inside like Sammy's but his had a ship's name too: SWEET, USS ARIZONA. He tore the crêpe-paper bow off when he noticed, and then tried to stand up at the same time. He fell over and hit the top of his head on a shelf. "Where are my shoes, who has my shoes?" he said, and just lay there on his back, watching. I looked in the back of the long closet. His blouse was in knots, tied up with his trousers. I started taking them apart too. Hearing the school building was quiet and all the kids were in the classroom made me nervous and I started to shake. He yelled at me, "What's wrong with you?" I tried to answer, but it took seventeen *n*'s before "Nothing" would come out.

He didn't wear the bars of ribbons like some had. There were two red hash marks for eight years in on the one sleeve, and he had the crow with the three red chevrons of a first-class. The nap was gone from the blue wool from ironing, but the jumper had been tailored and the military creases were still sharp.

He was older, and had more regulation hair than Sammy had in his last photo he sent, too. There was a scar that went down out of his hair over his forehead, left a white knob as it passed through his eyebrow, and ran halfway down his cheek to the corner of his mouth. He was a battle-wagon sailor if his ship had been the USS *Arizona*, the best and the toughest. If Sammy looked like the sailors on the recruiting posters, Join the Navy, the first-class looked like the sailors that you were supposed to be giving blood for.

"What are you looking at, boot?" he yelled at me.

I got the trousers loose and he put them on. There weren't any skivvies or socks. The blouse took more time. I found his shoes.

"Somebody is going to pay," he said, doing the buttons on his sleeves. I handed him over his hat, folded right. He took his time tilting it before he set it on his head as good as if he were looking in a mirror.

Then he started down the steps to the landing. He was squared away. Stopped there. "What's your name?" I told him. "I appreciate your help," he said.

"You're welcome," I said. Then added, "I'm going to join the Navy too."

"You wouldn't make a pimple on a sailor's ass," he said, laughing, going down the rest of the stairs.

I was used to the place now, but for a long time it made me nervous to go up Aunt May's front walk. It seemed as long as the letter *m* I got stuck on once for two hundred times. There were just flowers in the front yard. No lawn. Violets, the geraniums, of course, and the iris leaves were coming up like swords. When I first came, it was five colors of hollyhocks, fading California poppies, white daisies, and nasturtiums. She told me the names, of course. When my sister stopped the car, I saw the curtain pulled back. I didn't want to be dragged by the arm up the walk, so I followed her and listened to the chimes when she pressed. It was early, just when the sun was warming up and the flowers were getting calls from the hummingbirds and bugs that were flying around.

The front room was full of furniture. There was something wrong with the woman. We all sat down and my sister talked. The woman asked me, "Do you like working in a garden, Avery?"

"If I can do it with my shoes off," I said. She laughed. You can say anything, when they can't get you. I didn't look at my sister.

"Why don't you go take a walk and look around and see what there is to see?" the woman said. I didn't want to go because my sister would tell her about the fires I started, or when I ran away, and why they wouldn't let me go back to the school where I used to live.

I listened outside the door. "My husband is going to kill him next time. I had to take him to the hospital. He can't stay with us."

I went down the street one way and then back again to the next corner. It was the same as where I used to live, and it was different. I came back to her house and went down the drive, looked in the space where the garage door didn't close. There was no car, but there was a pit for getting under them in the cement floor so you could work on them. Small backyard, most was out front, but there was a vegetable garden spread over two big lots, the one behind her house and the one next door. There was a lot of weeds, and the climbing beans needed water. I knew about gardens; we picked strawberries when school was out this last summer. Peas too. My brothers and sisters. Since the war started, there was a lot of work for everyone. It's where I learned patience, filling those crates up one strawberry at a time.

I went along the path through the rows of vegetables. It was the biggest victory garden I'd ever seen. On the far side was sidewalk, then a street and the tracks. Two sets of streetcar tracks first, then a gully, and then train tracks. Past that was the mud flats, and I could see Bayshore Highway. Then the airport. I watched an airplane, a Navy PBY, come in, making a big arc over the bay.

When I heard the sound, I didn't want to believe for sure what it was until the train blew its whistle. And I crossed the street and stood on the crossties of the streetcar tracks. I couldn't see yet, but I could hear; the old sound was all around me now. Then I saw the engine coming down the track. I had never allowed myself to be this close. Never. I'd never been on a train. I wanted to run more than anything, just run down the street away from the noise and the hot steam that was pouring out from beneath the engine, away too from the sounding of the horn as it approached the crossing. But this time the confusion drew me across the streetcar tracks toward where the train would pass. I couldn't stop myself like before. The engine was passing over the trestle, bigger and blacker, coming down the track, faster and faster. I went down the gully and up where the mound of railroad rocks was spread out even like mattress ticking to cushion the rails.

As the engine passed I saw the sparks of steel that shot out from where the wheels heated the rails up. The noise made me forget who I was and I stepped closer, feeling the rocks making the soles of my shoes slip me forward, and I took another step. If I wanted, I could reach out and touch the train; the wind was blowing my shirt and pants like flags. I took a half-step; the rocks were firmer here, but it was like standing on the mouths of beer bottles. I could feel the pull of the train trying to suck me under; it made me feel free. I breathed in, my eyes shut, feeling the racket of the boxcars as the gusts came around the lettered sides until they hit the space where the couplings were and there was a bigger crash that made me swallow my lips until the train was past. Then I ran.

I went back inside her house and interrupted. "I like it here," I said. "Your yard is better than anyone else's on the street," I added. "I can weed all day if need be." She smiled at me and I sat down.

I was as good as my word. I could weed like a demon for hours. The flowers in front were to look at; the garden in back was to eat, and that's where the work was. I pretended I was a rabbit that ate weeds, sometimes, going up and down the rows of beans on my hands and knees, around the tomatoes and through the carrots.

Aunt May on her canes, sun hat, cotton gloves, moving the hose, then harvesting the zucchini for our supper. Reminding me, "Don't forget the beets. See if you can find the tomato worm; that plant looks like a cactus, he's eaten so much."

"Yes, ma'am," I always answered, till she went in to fix lunch. Saturday we worked the whole morning in the back lots. I had a bucket for the weeds and I emptied them in our pile. I had to hurry because Aunt May could see me from the kitchen window when I stood up and she'd yell at me to get down where the work was.

Mary Maureen got on top of her fence to watch me. The boards were so old that the weather had made the knots and grain stand out like cobwebs. The fence was going to fall down; it sagged inward where a post must be broken off in the ground, and where it was supposed to be nailed to the wash shed it hung loose, but the six-foot boards were high enough to keep the chickens out of the the garden.

"We got something, Avery," Mary Maureen called to me. If I stuttered the alphabet, she talked funny too. Aunt May called them hillbillies. You could barely understand their grandmother. She knew I had to work. "Come over and see."

Ruthie came out into the garden through their gate. She wasn't supposed to be here. "Go back, Ruthie," I told her, but she just grinned at me and picked a green tomato and threw it toward Aunt May's house. She didn't have the strength or the arm. I crawled over. "Ruthie, quit that." She'd already picked two more. I grabbed her, and on my knees I dragged her over to their gate and into her yard, squirming and giggling.

Mary Maureen jumped down and then did one cartwheel after another to the garage. "Look," she said. She had a gold can of malted-milk pills from the rafts. Mr. Mitchum worked on the Navy ships that came back from the Pacific. He brought home forty-millimeter and twenty-millimeter shell casings, two of each, in his lunch box, that he put on top of the radio. And he brought home old rations from the life rafts, the gold cans of pemmican, peanut butter, and malted-milk pills.

She poured me out a handful of them and I put them in my mouth and started chewing. I'd had them before and knew what to expect. We all chewed and chewed up those pills. They tasted good, but you couldn't swallow it down your throat. That's one reason I never ate the white paste at school. I was always worried it would harden and I'd suffocate. Mary Maureen went over to the faucet by the wash shed and took a drink to be able to swallow, and I followed her. You had to be careful here because of Abner, who could bite right through your shoe, but he was gone from where he usually slept. I took a drink and the pills tasted like candy.

Mary Maureen gave us some more and I filled up my mouth. We were just standing by the open door of the shed when Mother Mitchum yelled. "What do you think you're doing?" She had the old yellow broom handle she used to fish out clothes to put through the wringer, and as I watched she hit me over the head. Broke the handle in two and I bit my tongue and saw green and blue spots. "What, what, what?" she yelled, "Look what you've done, you've broken my stick."

It's only the first hit that hurts the worst and you have to consider that and just wait and not think about the next one. I started backing up, trying to get my legs to run.

"Grammy, he wasn't doing anything, Grammy."

"Don't you tell me," she said to Mary Maureen, and swatted her on the back. She ran and so did I, her grandmother yelling, "And don't you come back in the yard."

Sammy showed up the second night I came to Aunt May's, just out of boot camp. He gave me one of his white hats to wear, and we had long talks. He showed me the knots and left me his copy of *The Blue Jacket Manual* so I could look things up.

Sammy had enlisted with Michael from next door, Mary Maureen's brother, who I had never met, but he was stationed somewhere else. They got separated in the confusion at the Federal Building. "The first thing they had us do after they swore us in was to sweep Market Street, sixty or seventy of us, all sweeping with new kitchen brooms. The whole block," Sammy told us. "Then, when we were all done, damned if a street sweeper didn't come along, right after us." I could listen all night, the three of us sitting around the kitchen table. His first Navy meal in San Diego was SOS, white gravy on toast for breakfast: shit on a shingle. His hair hadn't grown back; he kept rubbing it and looking in the mirror over the sink saying his ears stuck out like flaps.

He was going to radio school and he'd practice with his spoon on the table-top in Morse code. I decided I was going to join the Navy too. And before Sammy left, he said I'd have to learn to obey the rules and be able to follow orders. That was the hardest part.

I wanted to obey the rules, like at school, and in the classroom, where we had to have manners, but it never worked out that way. I would have to, if I wanted to be a sailor. When I wanted to be a transmission man, my Uncle Johnny used to say rules were meant to be broken. I always thought he meant the church's rules; they had, when I thought about it, more than even the Navy. Unk told me I'd outgrow religion when he caught me with my eyes closed and asked me what I was doing and I said I was praying. "Do you believe in the Easter bunny too? Or Santa Claus?"

Unk was clever. He once fixed a priest's transmission that came into his shop. I was with him at the time, and so was Leroy's mother, Helen. Leroy was living with his father. I made myself useful around the place, swept, washed parts, cleaned tools, and she kept the books and cooked. The priest wasn't from this parish, but up in the city. He wouldn't pay, when Unk got after him. He said he was never going to pay: he would consider it a contribution to the church, and if Unk didn't like it he could lump it. "I'm going to change my name from Gorman," Unk said. "These priests are giving the Irish a bad name. I never learn."

We went up there on a Saturday night. The priest had locked his black Chrysler in the garage, but it didn't take us long to get in there and take out that transmission. I'd seen him do it before: five minutes, you wouldn't know it wasn't there until you reached for the knob. We took it back and sold it the next morning before the cops came.

Unk always took things in trade to get someone back on the road. Spare tires, guns, clothes, and tools. He once took a stamp collection for rebuilding a transmission. He told the cop he didn't know anything about it; why would he do such a thing? The priest had paid. Helen showed him the receipt, PAID IN FULL, stamped across the top. Then Unk showed them what the priest had paid with. A suitcase full of women's red and black underwear that had words printed on them that you could read in the dark. The cops knew my uncle. And the bishop who made the complaint got introduced too. "If that's the way they feel about it," he said to the sergeant, "they can have their goods back." The cops had the suitcase delivered to the bishop's cathedral by a process server. Unk used to tell that story a lot.

I thought of the Army too, because of Mr. Mitchum. The Army made a man out of you, he said. I don't know how many times he said that. But Sammy said the soldiers had to sleep in the mud. And when it rained you got wet. And the chow was cold. In the Navy you had a dry bed and hot food. And they sold candy bars on shipboard.

We went slow after Sammy left. Sometimes, listening to the radio, we pretended we weren't in the same room. I was more used to that than Aunt May was, and could sit quiet for a long time. She had to speak. "You don't have to stay if you don't want to," she told me once. "But on the other hand, I don't want you to say you're going all the time either." I nodded. I had no ideas about leaving. I hadn't done anything yet.

I knew more about her than she knew about me. She only knew about me from what my sister told her. And I knew about her not only from what all the neighbors said, but what she said. She was always talking about Newton, her husband, who was dead. And Sammy too, of course. About her legs that were shrunk and had braces so she needed canes. Her husband was older than she was and worked for a scavenger company for fifty-three years. "The cleanest person I ever met," she said, when I learned from the neighbors that meant he was a garbage man.

"And we're not related," she'd point out to me, even before I got the first report card. She refused to sign any paper where it said parent or guardian. When she did, she put "no relation." Because we had the same name now, Fontana, she always explained that Newton was a great-uncle to my mother by marriage, and it didn't count.

When she was mad at me, I wasn't to call her Aunt May. And I said "yes ma'am" like for the manners and etiquette at school. She was moody. Because her legs hurt. Because I did things wrong. Because Sammy was gone. I didn't always know. But I decided I was glad to be here. I was to help and be her company until Sammy came home again. I had my own bed. And she let me stay up late to hear the programs on Sunday. And I would get used to her ways. And I didn't miss anyone where I used to live.

When she started working herself up, I'd get the rag out and dust the furniture, or fluff the pillows on the couch and chairs. Empty the ashtrays. She liked me to do things like that without being told. I was starting to be different from before. It was an effort not to yell back or run the way I used to do. But I also knew things never turned out the way you expected them to, so you had to be ready.

When she made us dinner she wore her braces and boots and she could shake the entire house when she moved across the blue linoleum floor. But sometimes she was too tired and didn't put them on and she'd groan then because her cane had to hold up all her weight. Ahhhhggh. Ahggh. I listened to Red Ryder laying on the floor. There was enough light from the kitchen that I could pay attention to both of them, especially Little Beaver, who I'd like to be like if I wasn't going to be a sailor. I knew Aunt May didn't like to cook. "Come and get it," she'd say, "before I throw it to the hogs."

After dinner we might take a walk, and we'd be very polite to each other. "Would you like me to take your arm, Aunt May?" I could call her that; she insisted. Encouraged me. But later she might take it back again and correct me, "Don't you Aunty me, you little snotnose." The walks would start out just to go to the end of the street to see. Short walks, because she got tired. Had to use her canes, plant one at a time in the sidewalk like she was going uphill, then swing out one leg in its brace after the other, like the pendulum in the library clock. Her arms tired first. Then she'd hand me the canes and hold on to my shoulder and she'd shuffle her feet. It was slow but we stopped all the time anyway to admire other people's gardens. "Too much direct sun on those petunias, they'll burn up. And look at those roses over by the faucet; they have enough aphids on them to supply the rest of the town. These carnations are too leggy. And look at the mums, will you."

We never stopped at the end of the block but went on and on. She would kid me, well, it's time to turn around, as she worked herself down off another curb with me holding her up. When she got far enough from our street, she'd start taking people's plants. She'd yank up a whole pink geranium bush and put it in her shopping bag. "I haven't seen that color for years," she'd say, moving along in the dark with only the streetlights coming on. She carried scissors, for slips, and wore her cotton gloves.

She only did it when no one was home and it was getting dark enough where no one could see her. "They wouldn't mind," she said to me. "I'd ask if they were home." We didn't walk every night, maybe once or twice a week, but always in a different direction.

I had been with her seventeen days and nothing bad had happened. We were someplace I'd never been before, in front of a big house and lawn, bigger than any three on our street. "Look at that red," she said. It was a carnation the color of blood. A row of them like drip spots along the white stucco wall. Too far away for her to take.

I tried to get her to walk along, but she wouldn't budge. It was getting darker. "Go up there on the porch, Avery, and ring the doorbell. Ask them for a slip." I could just look at her. It was as if someone socked me, put me in a sack, and was going to take me back where I used to live. We never rang doorbells and we never answered ours. "Go on, Avery, they'll give it to you." There were two Chryslers in the driveway, and the yard looked like a magazine photo. "Go on, Avery."

I knew why she didn't want to go up there her own self. Because of her legs. They would look down and see while she asked. She never minded on our block. She noticed Mary Maureen staring too long once and she told her, "The President of the United States of America has polio too. And I happen to have a letter from him." Some older boys made fun of her once when we tried to get across the street, called her a gimp and a freak. She yelled back, "My son Sammy is in the U.S. Navy and he's going to come back and kick the shit out of you." She was angry for days after that and wouldn't go out for a walk or leave her chair and kept a blanket on her lap so neither of us could see her legs.

I couldn't go up those rich people's walk. I told myself to go. Go. But I still couldn't. "Go on," she said. And she raised her cane and gave me a push with the rubber tip in the stomach. I ran.

I didn't stop until I got back to the house. I started putting my clothes in Purity bags. She came in the front door when I was done. I heard her put up her canes on the knob of the closet door, using the backs of the couch and the big chair to get to the hallway. I didn't breathe. I didn't look when she stood watching me from the doorway.

"If it makes any difference to you, I had no right to do what I did back there. I wouldn't like for anyone to do that to me and I'm sorry." We were both looking at each other now. "Are you going to accept my apology?"

"I accept," I said. Nothing surprised me, I told myself.

All the next week she would bring up what happened. "You better not try that again." Or, "There's nothing wrong with being shy, but you have to make your views known." She went over and over that time. I always tried to forget things that I didn't want to remember. Never, never say them aloud, because they'd stay. They were always creeping around anyway, waiting for you to let them in. Remind your memory, remember, remember, look, look.

But I understood. It wasn't only because I was shy or only because they had money or I was different or what happened before. I couldn't think why, but I understood. It was a while before we went back walking. I wasn't paying attention, because when I saw the deer on the lawn, it surprised me and I stopped dead. The carnation flowers were as big as coffee cups now. Darker red now, more like dried blood.

"Come on, Avery, let's go back; if we get caught out in another air raid they'll think we're spies." There was a light on in the front room and a man reading the newspaper. I let go of Aunt May's arm and went up and rang the bell. My body started making trouble. I had started to melt. My clothes were getting too big for me by the minute.

A woman opened the door. "Good evening, ma'am. We were wondering if it might be possible if you'd give us a slip off your red carnations." I could see back, see Aunt May had put her canes behind her and was smiling.

"Wait a minute," she said and went away. I could see the polished wood floor inside and rugs as thick as a hairbrush. Cut flowers on the piano I didn't know the name of. The woman came back with a section of newspaper. She broke off some slips from different plants along the row. Then wrapped them in the paper after wetting it under the faucet. Handed the bundle to me. "Thank you," I said. "Thank you a hundred times," I said as I backed away.

"My azaleas are always good," she said. "Come back in the fall. I'll be glad to give you some."

"We will, we will," I kept saying.

Aunt May didn't have to say it; I tried to keep away from the train tracks at first. I kept away farther by not going to the streetcar stop either, except on occasion. And then I didn't cross over the tracks but went underneath the trestle.

At night from my bed I could see the boxcars slide past good enough to count. Across the back lots, between our shed and over the Mitchums' fence. I reached 306 one night. It was better counting from the toolshed roof during the daytime, when I could see the names of where they came from. Some trains were all flatcars loaded with olive-drab tanks, or jeeps or trucks or cannons, going up to the port to be sent out to the Pacific.

I sat up there for hours, watching, waiting, seeing the planes land and take off like dragonflies at the airport. Sitting hidden, in the middle of three rubber tires like an antiaircraft turret, watching farther out over the bay the specks of planes like dust come out of the sunlight, diving down on the target behind the tow planes.

I kept my eyes peeled too for the balloons in the sky. At school we all took turns watching the sky at recess to try and spot them no matter what anyone said. The Japanese army was sending them over by the hundreds to start fires when they came down and kill anyone who touched them.

It always put me to sleep, watching the sky. But I would come awake with a start when a locomotive sounded. You could hear a train coming in my schoolroom blocks away. In Aunt May's house the noise could make waves in your milk glass and open a cupboard door. But I got used to the sound, could sit still and let it pass. Aunt May would stop talking, like she was resting, then continue what she was saying when the caboose passed.

I was in my gun turret when I heard the car doors open and shut out on the street in front of the house. Three men in gray suits and hats stood on the sidewalk. I didn't go see, didn't move. It wasn't that I thought they might be coming for me, but it's better not to have anyone know where you are. That way nothing can happen to you.

I could hear one of them talking to Aunt May at the front door. "But I can't understand Italian," she said. "I don't even like the Pope. I'm not Catholic. My son Sammy is in the U.S. Navy. I'm a widow. It was my husband who was Italian."

I could hear them going over the house. Closet doors opening. Cupboards. Drawers. Two of the men came out carrying the console radio. The other had the binoculars Sammy had brought home from the Navy, and the box camera. His homemade radio.

Aunt May had stopped talking by then. One came back behind the house and looked around the yard. Came over to the shed and looked into the doorway. I didn't breathe, heard him kick the tire on the wheelbarrow and some of the buckets to see what was inside. Then he went back and all three got back into the car and drove away.

I climbed down the ladder and went around front to make sure they were gone. Then I went inside. Aunt May sat in her chair with her legs up, staring at the place where the radio had been. They had put Sammy's picture on the dining room table. His hat wasn't on regulation, but on the back of his head so his wave would show. Smiling. Enough of his shoulder showing to see his new third-class patch.

You had to say the right things in a time like this. It was part of good etiquette and probably decorum too. The binoculars never focused right. You couldn't get film for the camera anyway. The radio, there was nothing to say about that; she was going to miss the radio. Nothing I could say would fix that. I didn't speak out.

I started fluffing the silk pillows on the couch. The ones Sammy sent with the USN and anchor, from San Diego. And the one from Long Beach. And the last from Hawaii. Everywhere they put Sammy, he sent a pillow cover to Aunt May. They were lumpy, filled with old socks and rags.

There was no telling what she was thinking or what she planned to do. "I can go ask Mr. Mitchum if we can listen to the war news with them," I said.

"Keep your big mouth shut," she told me.

On Saturday morning I did the shopping with my wagon and the list and the ration books. Sugar, if there was any, and coffee the same way. Butter there never was. For six ration stamps and the money she'd counted out, I bought the pound can of tobacco, whatever they had, Tops or Raleigh, and never forgot the papers. There was no getting cigarettes, Pall Malls, Aunt May's favorite.

We had our own vegetables and we traded with the Mitchums for eggs. I bought bread, of course, sardines, Spam, a box of soft cheese. And mustard, we always had plenty of mustard. Macaroni. I never waited in line to buy meat, if they had any. Only sometimes a pound of hamburger. I followed the list. And I hauled Sammy's old wagon, taking my time, not going off curbs, so nothing would break. I was always the first one at Purity when it opened and they let me put the wagon inside by the door. Aunt May didn't like to be in the kitchen. So she didn't bake. But she liked Jell-O, orange, and for Saturday night she put a can of fruit cocktail in.

When I came back I unloaded the wagon at the back door. Aunt May was sitting in her chair smoking, looking at the old *Life* magazines I got her at the paper drives. She could tell everything I was doing in the kitchen. "Did you put the bread in the bread box?"

"Yes, Aunt May."

"Did you put the receipt on the table with the change? The ration books in the drawer?" I had to eat the mustard sandwich and drink the V8 juice she had out for me, or she'd know. It was what she'd made for Sammy, so she made them for me when I came home from school or shopping and after church on Sunday. I never had this much mustard before in my life, but I ate the sandwich every day. "You're not getting crumbs on the table?" she asked.

"I'm being careful," I said.

"We'll get ants, ants around the sink already; I killed one while you were away."

"I'll put the ant powder down on the list."

"Do that."

I finished fast, put the plate in the sink, ran the water to rinse out the glass, and stuck my tongue under to clean off the burning. Mustard should be rationed.

Aunt May always dressed up, even if she didn't go outside, in her purple silk dress that went around her like she was a bottle of vinegar; in her jewels, pearls that were as long as a one-person jump rope that she had to loop over her head four times. Her hair was the color of magazine ashes, mostly gray, with the black at the ends. When she put on her red lipstick and patted her face with the powder puff she looked really nice.

I told her that once. And she told me to mind my own business. She wasn't interested in my manners as long as I didn't bring ants with my crumbs and ate with my mouth shut.

Saturday afternoon we wrote letters. I cleaned off the oilcloth good on the table and we set to. We read Sammy's last letter to get everything straight. He never got caught by the censors; he was too sharp for that. We had to look for the secrets. When he wrote, "I hope you find all your pearls and will leave them in the drawer," we knew he was leaving Hawaii. Or, "Did Southern Pacific Railroad ever put up that gate at the crossing so people will stop getting hit by the trains?" meant South Pacific. I looked in the atlas, followed the map to the war zones. Aunt May finished reading. "I hope the canal doesn't overflow its banks this winter," she read. She read it again. I looked around the islands. There were too many. "Look in the back at the names," she said. I looked, but there was nothing right. I had to think. Remember the war news. What Mr. Mitchum said when we listened. When I thought it over, it came to me. It had to be Guadalcanal. There was a battle there. I put my finger on the island and showed her. She looked with her magnifying glass for a long time.

Then we wrote back. Mine was on lined paper I took from school, in block letters. I didn't like writing cursive.

DEAR SAMMY, THIS IS YOUR COUSIN AVERY. (I could spell. When I couldn't she told me . . . M-U-S-T-A-R-D.) I BET YOU MISS YOUR FAVORITE SANDWICH, MUSTARD. I HAVE ONE EVERY DAY NO MATTER WHAT. MUSTARD IS NOW MY FAVORITE TOO. EVERYTHING IS FINE. THE WAGON IS FINE. THE VICTORY GARDEN IS FINE. I CAN DO FORTY-THREE KNOTS NOW. DON'T WORRY ABOUT THE CANAL, WE'LL KEEP AN EYE OUT AND HOPE THAT NOTHING HAPPENS.

"You're a clever boy," Aunt May said when she read my letter.

P.S. I WISH I WERE THERE TO HELP YOU. KILL A FEW JAPS FOR ME.

YOUR FRIEND, AVERY

She always folded my paper in hers and put it in an envelope to give to the mailman when he came later.

After dinner we played cards, double solitaire, usually, rummy, of course, and spit-in-the-ocean. She won them all. There was no beating her. I came close in solitaire a couple of times, but something always happened. She'd have a spell or there'd be an air raid. Or she'd point out a mistake, where the cards stuck together, and she'd declare a misdeal. And we'd start over.

After the radio was taken, things changed a lot. There was no friendly sound, and she didn't want to go over to the Mitchums' very often. She got grumpy then, not wanting to talk, and sometimes went in her bedroom and slammed the door. I went into my room then and sat in the dark, ready to count boxcars.

There was nothing to say. She had told me all her life stories and I knew them by heart. She went to school in the city like everyone else, then went to work for the Western Union company. Went dancing. Swimming at Sutro's Baths. She could dive from the highest platform. She had a picture of herself and some friends when they were wearing their bathing suits. Her parents had owned a grocery store. She got polio when she was nineteen and was sick a long time. "How would you like to lie in a tank the size of a bathtub for five years?" she yelled, when I asked how was it to be in an iron lung. But she got better and was able to get around with crutches and her boots, and met Newton at the place where she made brooms. And had Sammy, who the doctor said was impossible to have. Newton died when Sammy was eleven years old.

"And Newton didn't believe in your priests either," she said. "They owned everything and took all the money when he was a boy in Italy. All fat as pigs. Mussolini should have been made pope, and then the Italians wouldn't have joined the Axis."

Every Sunday she gave me a nickel and sent me to mass. She'd done the same thing for Sammy, she said. I never tried to explain we only went to church when we had to see the monsignor. Of course, she wasn't Catholic herself, but Newton had been, and Sammy too. But I went now because she sent me. Sat in the back. I'd had my first communion and knew what they were doing up there at the altar.

The place was always filled with people, even at the earliest mass. People waiting to get a seat. "Because of the war," I heard two women saying. This wasn't where we had to come before. So I didn't mind if the priest saw me, but I never went to communion or confession. I didn't see anyone from before, which was a big relief, because I didn't have to pretend I didn't notice them.

I waited through the whole time, but I didn't put my nickel in the plate when it came around. I just sat there pretending I was deep in prayer. I could pray when it came to it, but I'd learned only to ask for things you didn't want to happen. Kick me out, Aunt May, I don't give a rat's ass. I'd pray hard for her to get rid of me. If I prayed to stay, I'd be gone the next day. That's the way things worked in the church. God only heard what he wanted to hear. Your only hope was to confuse him.

I used to think too that your true prayers had to pass through all the people, pew by pew, the altar boys, then the priests, that's where the real changes started, then the statues, Virgin Mary, Saint Francis, and the rest of them, go right up the steeple to the bell, up the cross and up and up to heaven, but by then the prayer was worn out and no one paid attention. But you had to keep trying. That was the trick, again and again until it was loud enough.

It was like stuttering; I always started out with the best of intentions, not even remembering I ever stuttered in my life, but before I knew it I was saying *AAAA* sixty-one times. I had pretty much given up on regular prayer. And I liked to stutter now.

One Sunday the monsignor appeared to give a special sermon. I opened my eyes when I heard his voice asking for money to finish a chapel at the new

Navy base. He was the same one, and I slumped down in the pew so there would be no chance of him seeing me. He'd seen me enough before.

We always went between eight and ten o'clock mass, when he allowed people into the parish house that needed something. He sat at the breakfast table eating slow, picking up a strip of bacon, taking a bite and putting it back down, chewing. The housekeeper that let us in kept coming back to fill his coffee cup. Bringing more hot toast. We stood in the big room at one end of the long table in a row. I could feel my heart get louder and louder, making my whole body want to jerk. My older sister who drove the car did the talking. My mother stood behind us, trying to hide.

We had all been here before. My sister, like Uncle Johnny, could talk to anyone about anything, charm monkeys out of trees. "It was a tragic accident, Monsignor. They were brothers. Just kidding around. No one knew the gun had a bullet. There's no one to work at home."

Monsignor interrupted her, chewing his eggs, wearing his black skirt. "Who can say a Hail Mary?" We all raised our hands, and recited when he made a motion with his arm like a music teacher for us to start.

"What's wrong with that one?" And he pointed at me. I was starting to shake. "Nothing, Father," my sister said, and my mother pulled me back behind her so the monsignor couldn't see me.

The monsignor played golf with the judge that was going to sentence my father. He never said yes or no. He just stood up in the middle of what my sister was saying and said, "I have to get back to work." It was time for the next mass. We all watched him walk out. Then waited a minute, went after him, and sat in the front of the church where he could see us. I prayed hard then to have my father free as a bird, not put in Alcatraz for a thousand years where he belonged.

I thought for a minute about giving my nickel for the sailors like the monsignor said, but it was too risky. On the way back from church I stopped at the drugstore and spent the nickel for a chocolate Coke. I sat on the stool taking deep breaths, pushing my stomach in with my hands, storing up air, letting it out, my lungs getting bigger and bigger, the straw floating, bobbing up and down by itself, ready. When I got enough air I drank the Coke down to the bottom in one inhale. I always liked to drink it like that. It was like looking at the sun for a long time; I got dizzy and one time fell off the stool.

I was dreamy and Miss Walker caught me unawares. We'd had three air raids that day; all the windows were opened against concussion now, and that made the curtains blow out like clouds. I wore my hat in the dark under my desk and made believe I was in a sled dashing through the snow like in a picture of Christmastime. I could think of things easier when I couldn't see. I used to hope for a big bomb to drop. Those people in London were lucky to hide all day in a cellar. I considered what I was going to do once I was at Aunt May's, and how big my tinfoil ball was getting.

I must not have heard the last bell because no one could get out of that room faster than me after the bell and the *you're excused*. I could be out on the sidewalk before some of the kids had got out of their seats.

"Avery," Miss Walker said. It was twenty-three days counting this Friday since school started. I had big hopes that this year would be different. "I was wondering if you would accompany me tomorrow at ten A.M. to pick up a chair I ordered, with your wagon, of course." Etiquette. She turned to pick up a paper. The back of her skirt had chalk dust from the floor from when she'd sat under the desk.

"I would be happy to," I said.

"Mrs. Hughes recommended you. And I'll pay you," she said.

"That won't be necessary," I said. That was decorum. She was smiling at me; her two front teeth were a little chipped at the corners. I'd never noticed before.

"Ten o'clock sharp, then, Avery."

"Yes, ma'am," I said, and did a good about-face per uniform military code of conduct and went out.

I didn't sleep that night very well. I had checked the wagon over. It was Sammy's wagon, of course, when he was my age. He got it out for me from under the house and we hosed off the cobwebs and dirt. He said he was giving it to me; I would need it to help Aunt May.

I had done all my chores Friday night to be free in the morning. Washed my sailor cap in the tub when I took my bath. Got up early like I always did on Saturday and got the shopping done.

"Avery, I'm glad to see you're on time. Promptness is as important as good table manners." It confused me sometimes: manners, etiquette, now promptness and the rest. It was like the chicken and the egg. Which was most important? Which was first? How many chickens were there going to be?

We went up Mastick instead of taking the shortcut through the alley behind Purity. Four blocks instead of three. I didn't correct her, just pulled my wagon, counting the rubber wheel bounces over the cracks in the sidewalk. It was the same kind of sound train wheels made when they went over where the rails joined. Miss Walker didn't pay attention until we passed St. John's. "Do you go to church, Avery?" she asked then.

"Sometimes," I said, pulling the wagon with my arms behind me now like I was an ox in yoke.

"I'm an agnostic," she said. "I still go to the Episcopal church but I'm an agnostic. Do you know what that means?" She didn't wait for an answer and went on to explain. If people knew more than you, they always went in that direction. It never failed.

The furniture store was in an old building below the Odd Fellows hall. They gave calendars, but they were all on one page. You never got to tear a month off. I stopped going there a long time ago.

The owner loaded the chair, knew what he was doing, too; put two boards crossways so the chair would ride even. He let me tie; I did a square knot, a bowline, two half hitches, and finished off with three clove hitches. Seven different knots in all. They watched, standing behind me.

"Last chair like that we have in stock," the owner said. "They stopped making them for the duration, the company wrote me. They're making seats for military vehicles now. I'm going to end up not having anything to sell. I can't even make deliveries anymore with the gas rationing."

"That's enough, Avery," Miss Walker said. I tucked the loose ends behind and stepped back.

"You have a handy helper," the owner said, and he reached behind the counter and came out with a yardstick. "I have a present for him. I'll put it here under the cushion of the chair," he said when I didn't reach for it. I felt sick, even though it didn't have brass tips, and I tried to stop my cheeks from jerking like that and closed down one eye and most of the other. I got shooting pains in my hands and I didn't want to look at them. I tried to maneuver the wagon around to get away, but forgot both sides of the door weren't open and ran full into the glass with the top of my head. I saw flashes like staring at the sun until your eyes melt out, but I stayed on my feet.

"You all right, Avery?" I had to open my eyes to clear the door and get to the sidewalk. I started pulling for home. Having that yardstick on the chair was like I was being chased. "Slow down, Avery, what's wrong?" I stopped, and the front part of the wagon hit me in the ankles and hurt. I hated that worse than anything. I always wanted to kick the wagon back.

"Nothing," I said. "I just like to keep working once I start."

"Well, don't go so fast; we have another stop. We don't want the chair to fall off." And she laughed. I liked to watch her mouth when she did. It was like an instrument in a band. I never heard her laugh at school.

Sammy, when he came home, said Miss Walker had fat legs. But I couldn't say so; they looked like anyone else's. Except Aunt May's. And a nice big ass. I never understood that part, how a woman's behind was so important in the general run of things. Shit was shit, no matter who it came from. But she smelled like violets and her hair was always combed. Her lipstick was the color of the pink gladiolus flowers we had. And sometimes she said things that were wonderful. "I feel like we're the last people on earth, Avery. No school. The streets empty of people. My new chair. I could sing and dance." I never heard anyone like her in my life. Not on the radio. Maybe in the movies. Before she could do that, we stopped in front of the creamery. It had the best fountain. "What about a milk shake, Avery? Could you drink a whole one?"

"It would be a pleasure to join you," I said. I'd had five milk shakes in my life. Three Sammy bought me when he came home. I didn't like going in places regularly by myself. People stopped what they were doing and looked at you. It made me uncomfortable. But with Miss Walker, they all looked at her. The four sailors in the first booth using all the straws up by blowing the covers at each other; the cook who was yelling through the opening to the kitchen, "You boys stop that"; another sailor talking to the waitress at the end of the counter: they all looked.

I ordered strawberry too, sat straight, my hands folded in my lap. And tried to pay attention to the polite conversation. She liked to talk, too, and didn't leave any spaces for me to answer, about her father who was a businessman somewhere and was a member of the draft board and had been asked for advice by a congressman in Washington, D.C.

The milk shakes were put down on the counter and I did everything by the numbers. Pick up the cold metal container with both hands, one. Pour in the glass, not all the way to the top, two. Set it back down, peel the straw out of the wrapper, deposit it in the ashtray, three. Carefully, without slurping, draw the milk shake up, FOUR. Everything was sweet and cold and perfect astonishment. Ice cream in general, milk shakes in particular, root-beer floats—I'd had one with Sammy—hot fudge sundaes, never banana split, never. Cokes, Pepsi, 7-Up, Dr. Pepper. All cold. Cold peaches. Jell-O. Fruit salad in Jell-O.

Cold lima beans. You could die if you ate them. I sat for hours trying. I couldn't. "Wasting food helps Hitler." I still couldn't. A beating was better than forking one lima bean into my mouth. We never had lima beans at Aunt May's; she didn't like them either.

"How's it going, buddy? You and your sister enjoying yourselves?"

"I'm Avery's teacher," Miss Walker spoke up. I kept drawing up my milk shake with decorum, not spilling or making any disgusting sounds. I recognized the sailor, first-class; he had been the one I'd untied in the broom closet at school. He had his knee on the seat next to mine and leaned his elbow on the counter toward Miss Walker. It made it hard to keep an eye on the chair in the wagon outside.

"Avery, huh, and what's *your* name, good-lookin'?" She didn't answer. I kept drawing up milk shake as if I'd tapped into a whole barrel under the counter. I watched all three of us in the mirror behind the stacked glasses.

"My name is Chuck Sweet; we can be civil, can't we?" he added when no one said anything.

"My name is Elaine Walker," she said.

"I'm pleased to meet both you, Elaine, and Avery here."

The waitress came over with the check, put her initial on the bottom, and placed the paper in front of Miss Walker. The first-class tried to reach for it, but she grabbed it. I'll pay for ours, thank you," she said. I was finished and ready to go.

The first-class whispered to me as Miss Walker was at the cash register, "I meant to remind you last time, boy; you don't wear your cover indoors unless you're under arms." I took off my hat.

When we were back on the sidewalk, all of us stood there for a while. "That's a pretty big load for one person, Avery," he said.

"He can manage," she said, to be polite.

I said, "I've pulled more," and gave the wagon a nudge.

"Well, until we meet again," Chuck said, taking a step backward, waving so long.

"It was a pleasure," Miss Walker said as I started pulling. Just before we turned the corner she looked back, and he had waited and waved at us again. "What do you think of that, Avery?" I couldn't think of anything to say. "Brash," she said, "bordering on rude." I kept pulling.

When we got to Mrs. Hughes's I untied the rope and we got the chair into her front room. I helped her pull the staples out of the cardboard wrapping and we were careful and didn't make a mess on the floor. She gave me the cardboard for the paper drive, and I was tying it on the wagon when she asked, "How much do I owe you?" I didn't understand and watched her more carefully. "I want to pay you."

"It's not necessary," I said. I was more happy just using that word again without stammering than finding a dollar in the street.

"Thank you," she said.

"Thank you for the milk shake," I said, happy I remembered.

She went in, but before I got to the sidewalk she came running back out with the yardstick. I kept my face turned away. "Your yardstick, Avery."

"I'd appreciate it if you'd keep it."

"He gave it to you."

"Please," I said. "Please."

"If you like," she said, "I'll do that," and she hurried back inside. I got away then as fast as I could go, jumping the curb and going across the street without looking.

I did my best. The first report card was on Columbus Day and I passed my grades and Aunt May signed. Without looking. The next one, after Thanksgiving, Miss Walker knew me better then, and must have forgotten I helped her with the chair. I got five unsatisfactories in deportment and three D's, but Aunt

May signed without reading the report card.

I don't know how these things happen. The harder I tried, the worse it got. It was like stuttering; I could go for days and never make a fool of myself. Then other times, it was all I could do to speak. All Miss Walker would have to do was say "Avery," and it was as if I was hit or woke up at night and heard the footsteps on the stairs. I knew you had to do good in school if you wanted to go in the Navy. They didn't allow stupid people. But I couldn't understand what Miss Walker wanted me to do. I always did the wrong thing. She was yelling at me now.

"Do you want to get promoted to the sixth grade? Do you? Answer me when you're asked a question." I couldn't speak. My eyes tried to change places. I couldn't say yes ma'am. It wasn't the stuttering then. I could speak but I didn't.

"Go stand in the hall."

I stood straight, not leaning on the wall, like a sentry at parade rest, feet apart and my hands behind my back. It was quiet out in the hall. I didn't look right or left, not wanting to see if anyone was coming out of the principal's office.

I was going to be in the Navy because I could stand that way for hours, days if need be. They had sentries out at the horse track when they rounded up the Japs, before it was a navy base. My Uncle Johnny and his friends used to drive by and throw their empties at the Japs over the barbed-wire fence; you could hear them crashing against the stable roofs. The sentry wouldn't move, would stand there even if they stopped and yelled at the Japs, who would go inside the old horse stables, getting away from the fence, fast. Sometimes Leroy was there with his mother. I yelled once, at night, walked right up close to where I could see the sentry with the white helmet holding the rifle and yelled, "You dirty shit-assed Japs, die. Die." The lights started going off in all the stables.

When the recess bell sounded, the other kids went out to play and I stood my ground. Miss Walker went right by me to the teachers' room. I never moved my eyes. I stood perfectly still. I could stand here forever, if need be.

Chuck

*H*e couldn't say why at first, but he started going to early mass, not on the base but in town, sitting in one of the side sections in the back among the shipyard workers with their lunch pails, going off or on shift. He came because it was peaceful in the old church. It looked like it might fall down, long water-stained cracks in the pink plaster, but it was big and quiet. The small chapel on the base was crowded, shared by all the denominations, one after another. It was like selecting pogey bait from a candy machine. He didn't take communion or go to confession. It was too easy to pray, so he didn't allow himself the pleasure. It was a joke, the whole business; everyone was Christian in a foxhole. Fear would make you pray to your big toe if you thought that would make it all stop. *God* was another word for *help*.

At mass he thought he saw the kid, he wasn't sure, that knew the teacher, that he'd seen at the fountain. The kid who'd untied him that time. He couldn't remember their names and he wasn't good at faces either. Going out, he caught up with him on the steps. The kid was wearing a Navy cover. "Ahoy, sailor," he said. The kid smiled, shy, and stopped. "You need a lift? I forgot your name."

"Avery," he said.

"Come on, my jeep is right down the street."

"I usually walk."

"This is Sunday, you're supposed to rest up. I'll give you a ride. There's no top or sides on the jeep, but it's warm enough. Where to?"

They went down the main street. He couldn't think of anything to talk about. When they came to the El Camino Theater the kid piped up, "You can let me off here."

"Do you live near here?"

"No, but if you drive me to Aunt May's she'll worry, think something happened to Sammy, or they're coming to take her radio again."

"Where does your teacher live?"

"Down the street, over by the heart."

"What heart?"

"It's the way the streets are shaped."

"Show me," he said. "We don't have to go by your house. And don't sweat things so much; you make me nervous too."

He wouldn't have believed it. He drove slow, following the curve-shaped blocks. The hearts met at their points, then went around again to the **V** at the top. Each side was one or two blocks long. He stopped at the second one's **V**. Avery hopped out of the jeep.

"Where does your teacher live?"

"Over there," he pointed, "on Cupid Row."

He looked over at the street sign. It did say that. In Montana this wouldn't be possible, he thought. "Okay, sailor, you take care of yourself. I'll take you out to the base one of these days and run you through the obstacle course. You like that?" The boy nodded. He saluted and drove off while the kid stood at attention.

When Salty Randolph came around with two letters and laid them down on his desk, he was more than surprised. They were from Myra. He had stopped going to mail call years ago. The last letter he got was in '38 or '39, from his father. One time Myra had asked him about his folks. "What about them?" he'd said.

"Are they alive? Do they live in Montana? What kind of work did they do?"

"Don't be so nosy," Sikes told her.

"They're both dead now. My father worked on the railroad. He was away a lot."

"And your mother?"

"She left us when I was in the second grade. We were put in St. John's."

"You have brothers and sisters?"

"A sister, lives in Montana still. Married. Molly."

He was thinking more about Montana, but he had no intention of going back for a visit. Molly had invited him. She had been notified when he'd been reported missing from the *San Francisco*. He had her name on his GI insurance. When he was rescued she sent their father's railroad watch to him in the hospital in Hawaii. It was the first time she had written since he'd left to join the Navy. He hadn't exactly departed with Molly waving good-bye and wishing him luck. And he'd never written her, although he had written his father three or four times a year, and once sent him a coconut still in its hull, carved and painted like a monkey's face. His father always had another brakeman, Toby, write for him. The last one he knew by heart.

"Dear Chuck, It's me Toby writing for your Dad, we're working out of Glasgow yard just down the line from Havre now. He asked me to write again because he doesn't like to. He's feeling good and says he got a letter from your sister Molly and she's fine. We're still not working more than fifteen hours a week. Things can't go on like this forever. We have to get back outside, we're all in the switchman's shack where it's warm. Toby."

Below the signature, in another hand, was "Your father Charles." It didn't matter, but his father could read and write. Had once been a telegrapher before he worked for the railroad. He had kept his father's and Toby's letters for years. Took them out at odd times and reread them. He put both of Myra's in his wallet like he used to his father's.

Was he going to think about 1943 in 1953 or '63 like he thought about 1923 now? When his father didn't have any seniority on the railroad and was always getting bumped and was out of work? When he was seven he didn't care if they were going to be put in a home because there was no rent money, as long as Molly was there.

St. John's wasn't the Indian Music School when they were first taken there; it was an orphanage. But only a few of the kids didn't have a mother and father. Most were there because their parents couldn't feed them anymore. His sister explained that all to him, after their father left them there, after their mother went off. Molly was the most patient person he'd ever known, not because she was his sister and took care of him, but because she always knew what she wanted and was waiting for it. "We'll have a house someday," she'd say. "I'll have a job and wear high heels." She could go on like that for hours when she was twelve and he was seven and they'd first arrived at the school.

He'd liked the place from the beginning. There was plenty to eat, and the classes the brothers taught were easier than public school. He never cried at night like some of the new kids, keeping everyone awake. And he didn't mind doing the outside chores, which were mostly feeding the flock of sheep and the turkeys, the only animals left from when the order had tried to be self-sustaining.

There was mass every morning at nine, between classes. He was an altar boy because he didn't want to go outside at recess in the Montana cold, and recess was when they practiced assisting. Mass was in the dining room, and you sat in your same chairs as in the orchestra and listened to the sounds in the kitchen of the cook making lunch. All morning he'd sit at his desk, watching the big hand go round and round the clock. Lunchtime. More classes. Then three o'clock, orchestra practice in the dining room. No one had to be reminded after recess where to go, or asked to help move the heavy dinner tables to make space for the chairs placed in a half-circle.

Then Brother Ralph would appear, his back straight, as if it were the first time he'd seen them in months, instead of just an hour and a half ago outside as umpire at the baseball game. They all sat up, their instruments at the ready. Then Brother Ralph would tap his stick on the rim of his music stand. Tap. Tap. On the third tap they all started to play.

Between pieces, Brother Ralph would make brief suggestions, especially when they sounded bad. "You're only as good as how much you practice," he'd say, while they all blew through their instruments to clear the spit out, or wiped off their mouthpieces. It was easy to believe Brother Ralph that practice makes perfect. He could play any instrument, from the old piano to the bass tuba. "Try it this way," he'd say, picking up your instrument. His family had owned a circus, and he had grown up playing in the band.

No one wanted to leave when practice was over, because Brother Ralph would usually sit down at the piano and play, or take out his flute, or sing with some of the other brothers. They all knew music. At one time or another they had tried to raise money as a group called the Melody Brothers, and they'd had a choir called the Heaven Tones, when there were more members in the order. There were framed playbills in the office.

Brother Ralph would finally stand up and make his last announcement: "When I was your age I thought I knew everything about music. And compared to a lot of fifteen-year-olds, I did. And through pride I decided I was perfect. Was I perfect? Think about that until tomorrow. Let's put the tables back; it's almost dinnertime."

No matter how little you were, you sat in with the orchestra. You sat in your chair and listened, if nothing else. When he started, there were forty-one members in the orchestra, all the kids in the school. The first chair in each section was responsible for the others. Molly was always reminding them, "These are not toys." She had been made first chair after three months, but she'd had four years of playing in public school before St. John's. He was put last, sixth chair. His clarinet had a wooden shaft, it was so old. All the instruments had been used up, donated from the public schools.

The most exciting part would be when they'd go somewhere. Brother Ralph would make the announcement: "We have been invited to entertain Moose Lodge 435 at their annual dinner." The orchestra would go anywhere if they were provided a bus and lunch. Then he'd tap his baton on the top of his music stand, "Let's try that last part again," quieting the whispers: "Oh boy, we're going, we're going."

Brother Ralph was always experimenting. Usually they wore long-sleeved white shirts and blue ties, but they had red ties for Christmas and cloth rabbit ears for Easter. This time the whole orchestra dressed as Indians to play at a veterans' home outside Missoula. Mrs. Hanley, the cook, and the older girls made the costumes. They used cut-up gunnysacks for vests and turkey feathers for headdresses, with black shoe polish and lipstick for the face decorations. Some of the kids made bows and arrows. He had found a tree root that looked like a club. Everyone was looking forward to it: all they could eat and the audience clapping, asking for encores. They practiced hard, going over and over their music until they had it right.

Brother Ralph surprised them by dressing like an Indian too, at least with the headdress and two dashes of color, white poster paint, across his forehead. But nothing could hide the scars. He had been burned in a circus fire that killed most of his family and all the animals. He had been cared for by the Sisters of Clare. Later he had joined the Order of Delphinius. The skin on his face looked like it had melted like wax from a candle, then hardened into small laps and overlaps of paraffin. He always wore a freshly laundered white cassock. He got on the bus last, after the other six brothers, Mrs. Hanley, and the teacher, Miss Clay.

In the Navy they used to sit back at the fantail and tell why each of them had enlisted. The Depression. Hard times. One he'd heard more than once was the family passing through some country seat. "My Pappy stopped the Model T in front of the Navy recruiting office. 'Well, son, this is where you become a man'"; the boy's mother in the front seat chewing her lip as he says, "I can get a job, Pa." "There are no jobs in this United States of America anymore." Younger brothers and sisters beginning to wail. Another popular one was "So the judge said one hundred years in the penitentiary or six years in the Navy. I should have taken the hundred years," the storyteller would always add. He had had it so good at St. John's that he never even tried to make up a hard-luck story. It was even good the first two years, before the big changes came because of their concert at the veterans' home.

Brother Ralph sat next to Miss Clay on the bus, whispering something, the other brothers sitting behind and across, leaning out to listen. Mrs. Hanley sat with Molly, both finishing the last vests. She was a widow who was always yelling at the boys, "Wash behind your ears," when they went in to take showers.

From where he sat he could see Molly, her head down as she basted big stitches through the burlap. She was fat at fourteen and looked more Indian than Welsh, dark, with brown eyes and the stiff black horsetail hair. He had the same hair, but his eyes were hazel and his skin was the dull shade of the bacon fat they used to fry meat in. No one made fun of them here as Indians or half-breeds. There were two other kids darker-skinned than his sister, brothers who had come north from Mexico with their family to harvest sugar beets and were put in the orphanage when they were abandoned.

Miss Clay got up and came down the aisle speaking to each of the kids. She had been hired by the bishop from a business college in Chicago to teach in the orphanage, and Brother Ralph was to pay her out of the funds the state gave for each orphan. "As if there was anything left," Brother Ralph said when he heard. The bishop was always trying to tell the order what to do because it was in his diocese, but the brothers contended that he had no authority over it.

Miss Clay fit in, earned money by doing typing for the county courthouse, when the order couldn't pay her. All the kids tried to get her goat, but she never fell for it. The most she'd say was, "Don't give me any of that backtalk." But she never yelled or hit them. In five months she'd made typing almost as important as the orchestra. It was her typing demonstrations that fascinated everyone. She'd sit up front of the typing class, with good posture, so you never got tired, and start out slow, like she was playing a prelude on a piano. "Always warm up," she'd say, "make sure your fingers are limber; it'll mean more words," exaggerating the movement of her hands. As she talked she'd be going faster, beginning to look down more and more at what she was typing, going faster and faster but still talking. "Typing is all eye-hand coordination; anyone can learn." All this time she was slamming the carriage back, the bells dinging, her hands flying. Once she went for fifteen minutes, then asked all the students to come and check for mistakes. There weren't any. Molly had been keeping time. It worked out to 104 words a minute. She always looked the same, dressed in her brown suit and white blouse, always composed. When the timer buzzed she'd stop typing and raise both hands over her head, all the kids standing up and cheering and clapping, the brothers whistling. She'd bow her curly gray head toward them, flexing her fingers, her glasses slipping down her nose a little from the effort.

Molly wasn't her favorite; Miss Clay let all the older girls use her makeup and showed them different ways to do their hair. She slept in a rooming house in town, but was always at the school. She didn't just teach the commercial courses but took turns sitting with kids in the dining room. Each orchestra section sat together at a table. She talked to them about learning a vocation: "If you can play a musical instrument or, of course, type, repair shoes, if you can just do something, you can always fall back on that and get a job." Molly wanted to go into town and get a job. She was ready, she told Brother Ralph. She could do housework. He said she was too young. So did their father, who was now working only one shift a week for the railroad. The rest of the time he waited around in hotel lobbies with the other men out of work, playing pinochle. He came to visit every five or six months, bringing presents, winter mittens, handkerchiefs, always telling them, "I'll have you out of here by spring. Or fall. Things are going to pick up with Hoover in the White House." He never mentioned their mother; it was like they never had one. Neither did Molly, who remembered her better than he did. He asked once when they first came to St.

John's, "Did you see Mom?" His father looked away like he never heard. "Shut up, Chuckie," Molly told him.

The veterans' home was a big building made out of stones the size of a loaf of bread and the color of a copper penny. Some of the veterans were already sitting in the rows of benches. The oldest, Miss Clay said, were from the Civil War; they had badges on their lapels, and some had long gray beards.

They set up their music stands on the stage and took out their instruments. The turkey feathers kept falling out of the piece of cloth he had tied around his head. Molly kept ordering the clarinets around. "Put your chair here. You, there." She was too bossy.

More veterans filed into the hall. There were a few already from the First World War; you could tell by their American Legion hats. Miss Clay said they'd been gassed. Some were from the Spanish-American War. One wore a hat like a Boy Scout's.

They had all done this before a number of times. No one was expecting anything different. Nothing had happened at the Florence Crittenden Home for Unwed Mothers, though the bishop had worried that it might cause a scandal for the orphanage. But when the first veterans from the Indian wars came in and saw the orchestra dressed as Indians, they started yelling out war whoops, *Wha-wha-woo*, moving the flats of their hands against their open mouths, chanting. Some of the other veterans started in, too. Brother Ralph came out and bowed to the audience, waving his baton in a sweeping motion. There was applause, like always, and then there were more Indian yells. He didn't understand why they had started and why they were keeping it up.

Tap. Tap. Tap. They started playing the regular Sousa marches. Then they tried something they'd practiced for a year, the Pastorale in Beethoven's Sixth Symphony. It was a hit, because the veterans started clapping and wouldn't stop until they played it again and then again. They did nine encores that afternoon.

Later they had lunch in the cafeteria, chicken and gravy and mashed potatoes. After that a veteran went to his footlocker and got out a beautiful set of moccasins to show them what they looked like. There were thousands of blue and white beads sewn into the leather. The veteran explained how the squaw chewed the deer hide to soften it. He had an Indian scalp on a leather thong, too.

A photographer came later from a newspaper because a veteran from the Mexican War was celebrating his one-hundredth birthday. There was a big flat cake with pink and white frosting. Another veteran had picked up one of the Mexican kids to sit on his lap. Molly was standing in front with him, wearing the moccasins, and he was twirling the scalp by the leather thong in a circle when the photographer's flash went off, blinding them all.

That was all, until a week later, when Brother Ralph showed them the headline in the feature section of the Denver newspaper someone had sent in with a contribution: INDIAN ORCHESTRA MAKES MUSIC FOR VETERANS OF INDIAN WARS. The article went on to say how the orphaned Indian musicians practiced for hours each day on old cast-off instruments, taped or wired together, that had been discarded as junk.

Within a month they were getting donations, contributions from every state in the Union plus the territories of Alaska and Hawaii. From Canada, Central America. From places no one had ever heard of before. Tasmania, Liechtenstein, San Marino. Molly had a collection and saved all the stamps.

Miss Clay had to stop teaching, except for one advanced typing class, to keep up with all the mail, just to open the letters and count the checks, cash, and money orders that people were sending the school. For each contribution they sent back a blessing and a photograph signed by the whole orchestra.

Brother Ralph started building an auditorium. There were new Underwood typewriters for Miss Clay's students. A new bus. Along with everyone else, he got his first wristwatch. And he was second chair now, next to Molly. The Bishop invited the school for dinner at his palace in Helena. After the orchestra performed, each musician went up to kiss his ring. They took a train ride to Chicago to play on the radio, and stayed overnight in a hotel.

He'd always been able to practice for hours, both the clarinet and typing, but now he did even more. Sometimes he daydreamed when he was playing with the orchestra, his mother water-combing his thick hair, trying to get the cowlicks to stay down in front and the part straight, both their faces in the mirror, the beads of water running down his neck and forehead, making him wiggle, both laughing as she tried to wipe them with a towel. He'd wake up with a start when he'd get elbowed in the side because everyone else had stopped playing.

They were given pocket money, Brother Ralph called it, plus a dime for whatever chair they had in the orchestra. Molly got a dollar and he got ninety cents a month. He was better than Molly now, but that didn't stop her from ordering all five of the clarinets around, telling them what to do. She was bossier than ever.

When they went into town it was a different story now. The shopkeepers couldn't do enough for them. They bought funny books and white paper sacks of hard candy, and spent hours at the pictures watching the cowboy movies and eating popcorn.

When the name of the orphanage was changed to St. John's Indian Music School, Brother Ralph undertook a ten-day fast and vow of silence in thanksgiving for their good fortune. He continued to lead the orchestra, but only with gestures now. When he had to, he wrote on a pink tablet and tore out the page with a rip that made the members jump. Everyone whispered during practice. "He's a saint," Miss Clay told them in the dining room, while everyone in the room pretended not to watch Brother Ralph sitting at his place, staring into space.

He wondered how old you had to be before Brother Ralph talked to you about joining the order. There had been only a few boys old enough to think about entering at seventeen, and one left to join the Army and the four others got on with a harvesting crew. He started thinking about becoming a brother, but he didn't tell anyone. Not even Molly. He started making promises to God. If I can type forty words per minute I won't eat the peach cobbler we're having tonight for dessert. If I can play this music perfect I'll put a piece of gravel in each shoe and keep it there for the whole day. For fifty words per minute he didn't eat for three days, just sipped water and sucked on lemons. He wasn't the only one that tried God. The girl who played the harp was fasting too, to make her solo perfect. Molly found out and yelled at him when he got dizzy and fell forward and banged his head on the music stand.

Brother Ralph changed him from the clarinet to the bassoon. "Why?" he kept asking. "Why?"

"Because you're our best, and we need a bassoonist now. You can do it; I know you can."

"But if I'm the best, why can't someone else play it, and I'll just get better?"

"Try the bassoon. Please."

He didn't like it at first. It was too big. The fingering was like the clarinet, but the instrument was too long, almost to the floor. He didn't like it, although as the only bassoonist he got the double dessert for sitting in the first chair, and the same amount of money as Molly. Then, in spite of himself, he started to like the resonant sound the instrument made. The lower register. The vibration he could feel with his fingertips as the tone went lower and lower. Brother Ralph would point his baton at him as he stood to solo.

There were special hours for visitors now. Most of the kids wore their Indian costumes then, better ones than the first. Brother Ralph ordered them from a catalog. Visitors came from all over to hear the orchestra, which was getting better and better. The string section had grown the most: nine violins, two violas, and two basses. But they still played the Sousa marches and took requests from their audiences. There were twenty-three new students and two new brothers, the first in twelve years, who'd joined the order from New York State.

Molly wouldn't stay when she turned eighteen. Miss Clay tried to hire her for the office, but she wouldn't apply. Brother Ralph wanted to send her to the Normal School in Dillon, but she refused. "I want to live in a house," she told him. "I never liked the clarinet." She got herself a job as a bookkeeper for a big spread north of town owned by a Catholic family, the Cutlers, who came to mass on Sunday at the school's new church.

He tried to talk Molly out of going. "You're up to seventy words per minute. You could get seventy-five and win the gold pen for this year." She just shook her head, packing her trunk. She wouldn't stay.

He was in his typing class when the note came for him to come to reception. He was almost one of the older boys now, but he had an advantage over the rest of them, as an Indian, as the first and only bassoonist, and maybe as a future brother. "If you get the call you'll know," Brother Ralph said. He had gone in to talk it over when he was thirteen.

"How will I know?"

"You just will. But it's important not to make a mistake. To make a false claim. To be prideful in your ambitions."

When he got to the office the secretary said, "There's someone outside to see you. I asked them if they'd like to wait in the reception room, but they didn't want to. And tell them to stop honking their horn out there."

He went outside. The wind was blowing, blasting right through his Indian vest. He had to hold on to his headdress. He looked around. There was only one car and he didn't see anyone inside it. He was half turned around to go back when he heard the sound of the car door opening and then cans falling, rolling on the concrete driveway. Someone started calling his name, the one Molly used. "Chuckie, Chuckie." He walked back toward the car. A pair of legs came down against the cement. Then a woman's head appeared, her black hair resting on her arm on the open window.

He knew who it was before he got close. He could see someone else in the front too, but it wasn't his father; he didn't know why he expected it to be. She was resting her chin on her wrist now. Her head moved back and forth as if she were saying *no no*.

"You grew up, Chuckie, I knew you must be big. But you're grown up. You were always such a little squirt. And look at you, all dressed up like an Indian."

"Ma?"

"You remember your mother, then."

"You look like Molly." He didn't know why that came out. There was a resemblance, the same round face, the coloring. The hair.

"I came to see you, Chuckie. It's been a long time. I've been working over in Seattle, steam press in a laundry, cannery, you name it. So I thought I'd drive over here; I forgot how cold that wind was. Your father finally told me where you were. He didn't want to but he did." As she talked there were spaces, like on a typewriter, where she stopped, but for no reason, then started up again.

"I stopped and saw Molly first, but she didn't want to see me. Sent someone to tell me she didn't want to and I was to clear out. I can't blame her, me taking off like that and all."

The man in the front seat sat up, then looked around like he wasn't sure where he was. He couldn't tell if the man was an Indian or not. He wore a hat and dark glasses. "We got to go," he said.

"We got to go now, Chuckie," his mother said. The engine started. The car moved a little and more beer cans fell out and his mother pulled up her legs as the door swung shut. She waved as the car went past down the driveway. Yelled back, "You look nice."

He stood exactly where he was for a while, feeling the wind get stronger. The nine empty green-and-silver cans had rolled into a half circle and were shuddering from each gust. Like a snake ready to coil itself.

Molly phoned that night. "Did she come there? The drunken Indian. What a nerve. But I have good news. Lawrence asked me to marry him. And I said yes. We're going to build a house up above the woodlot. You can come and live with us. He said you could. You don't have to live in that place anymore." She had tried to get him to join the haying crew each of the two summers she'd worked for the Cutlers, but he'd always got out of it: the orchestra had engagements; Brother Ralph couldn't let him go. "We'll have a home, Chuckie."

"I want to play the bassoon."

"You can get an instrument."

"I want to type eighty words per minute before I leave."

"We have a typewriter."

"I think I might have a calling, Molly." She couldn't make him, so he stayed where he was.

When the Archbishop sent his own accountant, Brother Ralph refused to show him the books. He came into practice late and instead of starting he gave a long talk about pride and responsibility, covetousness and avarice. They fiddled with their sheet music, impatient to start playing, but they didn't rehearse that day or the next. That was when the trouble started.

It was Molly, who knew more about what was happening at the school than he did, who told him at Sunday dinner. "Brother Ralph bought another Lincoln."

"A big Lincoln," Lawrence said. Molly was a good cook, but not as good as the one they had at St. John's now. He knew he should eat all that was on his plate. He was sorry he'd come. Usually he got out of it by saying he had to practice. He had nothing against Lawrence; he was just a dumb cowboy with a red face from being out in the sun too much.

"It's bigger than the Bishop's DeSoto and he's not going to like that," Lawrence said. He didn't say it but he thought it; Brother Ralph was right; envy was an awful thing. Lawrence had a beat-up '25 Plymouth.

"Do you know how much money the school took in last year?" Molly said.

"More than our father ever made in his whole life." He didn't know how to answer back.

But Brother Ralph knew what people were saying. When the whole school stuffed envelopes after dinner with the photo and a small feather dyed blue, "Don't pay attention to gossip," he'd say. "St. John's is well thought of in the state of Montana."

He'd hear little snips of things at the school from the brothers. The bishop had got a court order allowing him to audit the books of the school. No one seemed concerned, least of all Brother Ralph.

On his fifteenth birthday they had his party. When they turned off the light he watched the candles burn, taking in a deep breath, thinking, I'm never going to leave this place. Never. Brother Ralph presented him with a gold pocket watch engraved with his name. The fob was in the shape of a bassoon.

Kids came back after they left. There was one who had joined the Navy, Sonny, who'd played the slide trombone. He came back wearing his white uniform. Had tattoos on his feet of a rooster and a pig. "You'll never drown with these," he told the boys. Brother Ralph always welcomed the former students back, invited them to stay if they didn't have anyplace to go. Sonny was an orphan and spent his whole twenty-day leave at the school. He was a bandsman on the battleship USS *Pennsylvania*. During practices he took his old chair in the orchestra. "I'm rusty," he told Brother Ralph. "We play the same things all the time, either 'Anchors Aweigh' or some piece by Sousa."

It was only the good musicians that came back, he decided. Sonny was first chair. Generally the kids that left were poor players anyway and never showed up again. He was going to be a brother. At night they sat around the study table and listened to Sonny tell about the Navy. And they asked questions. About the whores, and how you join up. That wasn't him, he had no intention of ever leaving. "I went to Seattle and found the Navy recruiter. Three hours later I had a meal voucher and was on the train for San Diego. I was a happy fellow too, let me tell you. I couldn't find work. Sawmills, the logging camps. There's thousands of men looking for jobs. There was nothing. I'm glad I joined up."

Brother Ralph never made anyone leave the school, but when a student reached eighteen he started writing letters to people he knew at Fort Peck, where they were building a dam, or the railroad or ranchers or the U.S. government for applications for the new WPA or CCC. "There are jobs if you have a trade," he always said, but he had to change that to "if you have the *right* trade." It was hard times in '33.

Money wasn't the only thing that Molly and Lawrence talked about when they went on about the school. "They caught a brother in the girls' dormitory again last night." Or, "One of the matrons is pregnant; the town doctor said so." Or, "All the girls have head lice." He never listened, checking his new watch, holding it out so they could see him look to see if it was time to go back. The school was his home.

The orchestra had just returned from playing at the governor's ball in Helena, where they were put up at a big hotel at the state's expense. He had used room service for the first time. Everyone was tired from the bus ride and wanted to go to bed. Two former students who'd left the school five years ago had come back the night before. He didn't even remember them. They were going to stay and help with the livestock. That night they beat and kicked Brother Ralph to death in his office, then drove away in the Lincoln with the money from the safe. He was on the *Arizona* when they hanged the two men in Helena; one of the brothers sent him the clipping.

The Bishop closed the school, and he went to live with Molly and Lawrence. He had no choice. Things happened so fast he didn't know if he was coming or going. The next thing he knew he was living in the bunkhouse with a twenty-five-man haying crew that borrowed his towels and never gave them back and spit tobacco juice into old coffee cans they kept by their bunks.

He lasted almost four weeks bucking hay up on a wagon in 109-degree July heat, getting eaten up by mosquitoes. He'd worked on the school grounds before, but not twelve hours a day, not tearing his hands to pieces.

He kept an eye on what was happening at St. John's, hoping he could go back. But the Bishop wanted the school moved to Helena. Some of the brothers quit the order. Miss Clay went back to Chicago. All the school equipment was hauled to the capital, along with the kids that didn't leave. The orchestra was disbanded there. So were the commercial courses. The bishop set up more vocational shops and started football and basketball teams to play for the school. The old buildings were sold, taken down for the lumber. He avoided going by the place. Couldn't even get himself to go into town.

The first time he got paid he hitched a ride. He was big for his age, almost six feet. He could tell them, like Sonny said, that he was nineteen. "Don't stop at seventeen," he'd said. Molly wouldn't care, he thought. Now they were always arguing: him and her, him and Lawrence, Lawrence and Molly. "You're not at St. John's now, Chuck; put your back into it."

"We all have to work," Molly would say.

When he got to Seattle it was just like Sonny said. There was the ocean. Ships. And the Navy recruiter.

Because of St. John's and Brother Ralph dying, he missed learning about girls like he should have. American women. He learned about the women in the Caribbean, Central America, and every port in the Pacific, once he was in the Navy, but it didn't do him any good, he decided. It wasn't anything he could use.

There were whores in the States, to be sure, but it wasn't the same thing. Once you got saltwater between you and the States, everything changed. Especially with women. Not just for sailors either. He'd seen those Englishmen in Hong Kong and Singapore, the Portuguese in Macao and the French in Saigon. They weren't going back to their countries if they could help it. And it wasn't that they'd gone native. It was that you could do anything you liked. Especially with women. He had heard the stories and was ready for anything.

The first port of call was in American Samoa: he was a seaman apprentice standing guard on a loading dock with a third-class steward, three hash marks, from Hawaii. The *Arizona* was offshore. Their division hadn't got liberty. They had guard duty: rifles and leggings, walking up and down the docks. The liberty boat went back and forth from the ship. As soon as they were posted, the Hawaiian sat down on the stores they were protecting and started whittling on a stick, whistling, telling him, "Keep moving; they'll see you from the bridge." They had been at sea for three months.

He was so happy. He was in the Navy, on an island. This was what they had heard about from the salts for months now. Ass. He would get liberty the next day. He hadn't missed St. John's. There hadn't even been time to think about the place. Boot camp. Bakers' school. Then sea duty. He hadn't written Molly or his father yet to let them know where he was. On the forms when he'd enlisted he'd marked the musical instruments he played, and they came looking for him with a clarinet. He was going to play tomorrow night on shore at a lawn party the American consul was having for the officers of the ship. Everything was new, for the first time: the ship, making bread, and the ocean.

He heard voices and went back to where he'd left the third-class. He'd never realized how big the natives could get: he was over six feet now and they were taller than he was, three women, one with a nursing baby, on the other side of the barbed-wire fence. "Hey kid, come here," the third-class said. He went over. The women had flat faces and dyed hair, orange. Two of them were fat, and their tits stretched down like brown skin bags. He didn't know where to look. There were sores on their legs, festering. It was his first close look at the native women. It wasn't what he'd expected.

"Keep a lookout for me," the Hawaiian said as he unbuttoned the front flap of his trousers. The woman got down on her knees and at first he wasn't sure what she was doing until she started making the sounds. The other two women were watching. He started backing away. He almost broke into a run for the end of the pier.

Smoking, the Kanaka joined him. "You should have stuck around. Two bits. It relaxes you, cleans out your pipes. A man needs that. You get stopped up." He was still holding the stick he'd been whittling. "But you have to be careful in these places with these women. Did you ever think what if one of them got too excited or had a fit or something and bit off your cock? Then what you got? So I always put something in the corner of their mouth, between their teeth. A rope end, if I can't find anything else." He tossed the stick into the water.

He didn't go on liberty there when it was his turn, but in Subic Bay he did. Waited in his crisp whites in line with other sailors to fuck at the whorehouse. Not just because it was going to feel good or because his shipmates expected him to; he had to find out for himself. Experience. He sometimes thought, look what I'm doing now. Just look. Sin. Squalor. He forgot all that after the first year or so. He didn't go to mass anymore.

He got his first four-year hash mark, and when his hitch was up he reenlisted and was a rated yeoman third class. He wasn't getting up at 0300 hours to roll dough anymore. He lay in his hammock and slept until reveille. Yeoman typed in a clean office every day, wore fresh uniforms every day, and were feared because they made the duty rosters and the liberty rosters and worked directly with the officers.

When they got to port now, liberty was different, because the senior yeomen knew where the officers' whorehouses were. The women wore dresses, evening gowns. He didn't believe it when the ship got to Hong Kong. They washed his pecker in a basin of warm water before and after, and wore something that looked like a wedding dress. On a soft double bed in a room by themselves, not next door to a bunch of other sailors arguing with the whores if they'd already come or not, trying for seconds for the price of a short time.

He played in the ship's band at the officers' club when they got to a port with a Navy base. Navy wives, daughters, and sisters danced with the officers. This was the life, he thought. The bandsmen took breaks and ate in sitting rooms off the dance floor and went back to the ship loaded down with booze. They'd get special liberty for playing, so they had their turn to raise some hell. He always tried to get away from the port or Navy base; the women were not only cheaper but a lot cleaner. Every whore within miles headed for the port when the fleet was in.

He had never seen a naked woman until he joined up. There were the girls at St. John's, but no one he knew had ever bothered to try anything. With town girls it was different; he'd heard stories of cheap feels in the movies and fingerfucking in someone's barn. In the Navy he heard the bullshit stories. There were married men with children who told about what their wives did, what they liked. He never knew whether to believe them or not, though he often wondered what it must be like to live with a woman day in and day out, fuck anytime you want, never have to go looking. But he couldn't resist listening. An electrician's mate explained how he kept his finger on his wife's trigger. You could never ask what they were talking about. Everybody agreed: yeah, yeah.

She goes off like a string of firecrackers. Again and again. I got to hold on to her handles or get bounced off.

But the whores didn't like any experimenting or exploring. He was always too embarrassed to even try and suck on their tits. He didn't know if he'd do it right. He'd heard the comments of other whores through the paper-thin walls. "What do you think you're doing? Keep your hands to yourself. That's off limits, sailor. Two dollars for fucking and three for sucking."

It was a mystery, but he was sure there was a way to pleasure a woman, get her to say more, more. It wasn't until just before the war, when he picked up a woman in a bar at Pearl who took him back to her apartment, that he found out. He had stopped drinking so much when it looked like there was any chance of getting a woman down on her back. It turned out she was the ex-wife of a torpedoman first class. She had had a lot to drink before he met her and she had a lot more after, which he paid for.

When they got to her place they both started taking off their clothes and he stopped to help her tug her dress up over her stretched-out arms. She was funny; she made them both laugh. "You say you're a friend of the working girls. Next you'll be telling me you're saving yourself for your sweetheart back home."

She had hardly any tits, and a potbelly, and she wanted to screw with the lights on. "Nothing you can see can get you then," she said. He took his time; if he had learned anything, it was endurance. He could go the old up-and-down as long as he wanted. Timing. He always thought, I can just keep going forever if that's what they want. When the whores started pretending, moaning and such, he shot his wad. It was that simple.

But Jeanette kept getting louder and louder and started bucking like she was going to throw herself off the bed. She was arching her back and calling him sweet names. Then she reached down between them with one of her hands, and he could feel her knuckles moving on his stomach. And he kept going faster now, trying to keep pace, but it was impossible and he started holding his breath, then gasping for air, and he had to hold on because she popped like a cork from a bottle, but he kept moving as she slowed, then stopped.

He rolled off, mystified. What had happened? What had she done? "You're okay, Chuck," she said, gasping. He hadn't come. His cock was changing directions like a weather sock in a high wind. She noticed. "Get up here," she said, patting her chest.

Later he asked. "What did you do?" He didn't care if she laughed. She put his hands over the hair between her legs. "Feel that. That's my pecker." She laughed again. "Only it's the size of a pea, not a pickle. And just like you, I use it to piss through too. You touch that at the right time, it makes a woman very, very, very happy. Easy. Not hard. That's it. That's it."

It was the only time he ever thought of missing the ship, going AWOL.

Not just because of the sex. But Jeanette. She was wonderful. She took him to a zoo; they tossed popcorn at the monkeys. They went to the movies. She worked in a drugstore in Honolulu. She told stories about the men who came in to buy rubbers. "Some whisper so low that I can hardly understand what they want. 'Peacocks, you say?' I ask them real loud. Others want to open the box and blow one up to see how strong they are." She'd been married twice before. Was from Indiana. She wasn't even pretty. She was almost fat and she was at least ten years older than he was.

He made a fool of himself. Told her he loved her. After two nights. "Quit it," she said; "you're just trying to make me feel good."

"No, no, I'm serious. I'm serious." She wouldn't have it. Took him back to the ship in a taxi. "I'm coming back," he kept saying to her. He didn't care if the driver was hearing, grinning. "I love you."

"I'll be waiting," she said. But she wasn't when he got back in '41. The landlord said she'd gone back to the mainland. It wasn't as bad as when a sailor fell in love with a whore and wanted to marry her and they shipped him out somewhere. But he still thought about Jeanette, how they ate cornflakes and bananas together in her little kitchen, laughing their heads off, and wondered how he could get in touch with her.

He got a ride in on a shore patrol jeep. Went right by the bars on San Mateo Avenue and got out at El Camino Real. He didn't want anyone to see him get out of the jeep. He walked up through the residential area toward the USO, giving out good evening ma'ams and sirs right and left to people working in their yards. A sober sailor: he must be the first one some of them had ever seen at 1800 hours.

Some kids on the other side of the street were playing hopscotch, using their roller-skate keys to lag with. It was peaceful here, away from downtown. Someday he was going to be out of the Navy, retired; you couldn't stay in your whole life. Thirty years. But he'd seen some stay longer. They wouldn't just kick you out. There were a lot of retirees called back in for the duration.

A banner over the doorway read USO. He was early; there were only a few sailors around the entrance. A notice said CHECKER TOURNAMENT UPSTAIRS. He'd almost made it to the third floor when he realized he'd been here before. This was where that kid had untied him. He'd been so hung over that time he didn't think he was going to live until noon.

There were women behind the coffee-and-doughnut counter by the auditorium door. He didn't drink coffee because his mother had told them it would turn your skin brown. Even after he found out it wasn't true, he didn't like it. And doughnuts: everywhere you turned around, people were handing you doughnuts. He didn't care for sweets in general after his hitch as a baker.

Over where the tables and folding chairs were set up, he could see broken stacks of black and red wooden checkers in piles on one of the tables. He went over there. "I'd like to play," he said to the woman at the table. Her name was printed on a piece of paper and stuck with a straight pin on the lapel of her jacket. Elaine. He'd seen her someplace before; she looked familiar. He called her ma'am. She was too young for that, but it made it easier, and he was used to calling all civilian women that now.

"Sign here," she said. "We'll start at seven o'clock. 1900 hours," she corrected herself. He grinned at her. She was trying to be pleasant, not accommodating, which meant she wasn't going to throw herself down on the tabletop so he could hump her. He signed his name.

"Would you like to play a warmup game?" she asked. She was almost pretty when she smiled, but too much of her pink gums showed, and her nose was too big. Just by the careless way she set out her pieces, he knew she thought checkers was a kid's game. Probably didn't have any idea how complicated it was. More so than chess. Everyone had played chess at St. John's, but checkers were more interesting. You had to know human nature in checkers; with chess, you just had to remember the old moves. The game was too rigid. In checkers anything could happen. A king in checkers was the best piece ever invented.

He let her go first. "You have to jump," he said. "If you don't see the jump, you lose your piece." She was amused, didn't pay attention, he felt. He'd taken his cover off and rolled his cuffs up once.

She tried to distract him. "May I call you Chuck?"

"Sure," he said. She moved without even looking at what she was doing. He always liked the confusion of the game opening, positioning his pieces that were going to run the board for a king.

"You've been to the Pacific already?" she asked, touching his two hash marks.

"They don't mean that; they represent four years each in the Navy. And besides, you've been to the Pacific if you've been over to Half Moon Bay." He was going to beat her in eight moves.

"That's right," she said. "But it was just a question: have you been to the South Pacific?" He looked up. She was serious; she wanted to know.

"I was in the Pacific from 1933 until three months ago. Does that answer your question? I'm not trying to be rude, ma'am, but I like to concentrate on my game."

"Call me Elaine," she said, and looked down at the board. She started playing then. She gave him a good game. He had four kings to her two, and it took some doing to pin her. There were people around watching at the end when he won. There was clapping, and some sailor raised his arm like he was champion.

"You were lucky," she told him.

"Lucky?" He couldn't believe it. "Lucky, you don't know what you're talking about." She was laughing at him. And he remembered the fountain, sitting at the counter, where he'd met her before.

The tournament, which he'd read about in the base paper, started out slow; winners played winners in the first elimination, and everyone in the auditorium wanted to play. It was 2100 hours before they got down to the last ten players. He'd had a couple of close calls. But it was always that way in checkers; anyone could win. No matter how good you thought you were, there was always someone better or luckier. It had happened on the *Arizona*; some signalman walked up after he'd beaten everyone else and finished him off in five moves. When he did ninety-four words per minute as a yeoman, some boot did one-eleven.

When it got down to four, himself and two sailors and a sergeant in the Army Air Corps, he knew he was going to win. The sailors were taking turns going out in the schoolyard to swig headcrusher. The Air Corps sergeant he was playing kept his attention on the woman who was running the tournament. Elaine, he remembered.

The place was full now, mostly sailors. This was the first time he'd come into town on liberty that he wasn't drinking. A band was tuning up on the stage, getting ready to play for the dance. Everyone was waiting for the game to end so they could turn the lights down and dance. But he was having trouble with the sergeant, who was good when he paid attention. It went back and forth, back and forth. The two sailors never returned. The woman interrupted them to ask if they wanted coffee. He ignored her, but the sergeant asked for a cup and lost his concentration, watched Elaine walk away before he moved his piece. He took a king for not jumping, and beat him in three more moves.

"It looks like we have a tournament champion," she said, taking his hand. If he'd known what she was going to do, he would never have followed her. She went right up the stairs onto the stage. When he tried to go back, she grabbed him by the arm. "Ladies and gentlemen," she said into the microphone like a boxing announcer, "and all the ships at sea, may I have your attention." There was some cheering. "We have a winner here." His face must have been red because the skin on his cheeks was burning up. "Chuck Sweet," she read off the clipboard, "of the United States Navy has won the USO Checkers Tournament. And the prize is . . ." She paused. "A gallon of SOS and ten pieces of toast." The crowd roared. "No, no. I'm sorry, I'm sorry, that's already been sent to the officers' club. What Mr. Sweet has really won is this silver-plated checker piece for his key ring or dog tags, with his name engraved free of charge from the donor, San Bruno Jewelry. Thank you all for your participation."

In the confusion he never got the prize. The lights went out and he could barely see his way back off the stage. He sat by the wall, just listening to the music, enjoying himself. The musicians were good.

"There you are," she said. "I didn't give you the prize." He stood up when she handed him the small white box. Thank you was all he could think to say.

"Congratulations," she said. He stood there feeling awkward. "Are you going to ask me to dance or not?" she said. He went around the floor holding her away from him, feeling the smooth cloth of her jacket at her waist, her moist hand.

"You're a good dancer," she said. "For some reason I didn't think you would be."

"I've had a lot of practice," he said. "But I'm a better checker player." They both laughed. "Do you remember where I met you before?" When she didn't answer, he went on, "At that fountain on San Mateo Avenue. You were drinking a strawberry milk shake with one of your students. And he was pulling a wagon. That was you?"

"It was me. I've seen a lot of sailors lately, but I remember now."

When the music stopped she went behind the counter and started making a fresh batch of coffee. And he stood around for a while, then went back to the base.

Elaine

She couldn't get him out of her mind. She kept going over the things he'd said, the expression on his face. His arms. His legs. Another hour and he'd pick her up.

He was Catholic. How had she found that out? He'd mentioned going to mass one morning at St. Bruno's. You had to be something. She was Episcopalian. Her family weren't churchgoers. When she thought about it, she was the only one who went. When she was home at Christmas she had talked Mona into going with her. "I'll go the day that Jew Roosevelt dies," her father had said when she asked him.

She hadn't been her father's favorite. Mona was. Her mother didn't have favorites, she always said. Did it make a difference now?

Was this serious between Chuck and her? All of Mona's boyfriends had asked her to marry them. How old had Mona been when she'd told her that? She had gone out too, had gone to the proms, doubled with Mona. But it wasn't the same for her. It wasn't that she didn't enjoy herself. She always said thank you for the good time. When she thought about it, though, had she had a good time? No, she hadn't. There was always something missing, as if having a good time on a date should mean more, leave some mark on you. Like Mona's laugh: it sounded reckless, wild, almost, as if she were having the time of her life. It drew men. It was as if the sound attached itself to everyone in the room and demanded their attention.

She had practiced a laugh when she was sure no one was home, watching in the bathroom mirror. Ha ha ha. A gay, modest laugh to start with. Haa haa haaa. A hilarious laugh. The bathroom floor and the walls halfway up were tiled: that laugh echoed as if she were in a canyon. A laugh that meant she was having a good time. But not only that, a sound past that, a laugh that was a foundation for a million more laughs. Then she worked on a little laugh.

Dancing at someone's party, front room of the house with the lights off, she tried a moderately loud one. It was her throaty laugh. It sounded fine. The boy didn't seem to notice at first. He slowed down at the second one, only swaying back and forth, and held her tighter. She didn't have the nerve to try another.

She kept practicing in the bathroom till she could laugh half a minute by the second hand of her wristwatch. She developed one she thought of as a trill laugh, high and exciting. A nasal laugh, which was dangerous because it made her nose run. And a dirty laugh. She couldn't sing, but she could laugh. Her laugh was her music.

She'd never got to use the dirty, lowdown laugh she'd perfected before she graduated from high school. At college in Reno it was all so different. Most of her high school friends had gone away to other colleges or to work. There were so many new people. And she had to work harder to get through the education courses, because they were so boring. There were a lot of times she could have used her laugh in college, but mostly she either forgot or didn't concentrate enough to catch the moment. Then there was that basketball game. Their team had won, and the long line of cars returned to Reno honking their horns, people yelling out the windows. The car she was in stopped at one of the places coming into town. There was a jukebox, a bunch of cowboys still wearing their leather chaps, drinking and playing cards. Other cars stopped and the place filled up with students. The saloon must have been there forever, one of those old bars with dark engraved wood and a big mirror in back. High wainscoting, embossed tin ceiling, a dozen tables, a dance floor. Small restaurant in the back. Students kept coming in, and the cowboys started asking the girls to dance. She had been one of the first.

She knew she had nice legs. These were authentic cowboys from some cattle ranch. The first one she danced with had the tag from a Bull Durham tobacco sack hanging out of his shirt pocket. When the second cowboy asked her to dance she gave her best laugh, a long, long trill. The cowboy stopped dead in his tracks. She had managed to laugh just when the records were changing in the jukebox and it was quiet except for her best high laugh. A cowboy walking by asked her partner, "What are you dancing with, Adolph, a horse?"

"Beats me," he answered. How many others heard? Everyone was looking. She let go of his hand and went into the rest room and never came out until one of her friends came in and got her because the car was leaving. Why did she dwell on things that turned her red to the toes? Even now, just thinking about it, she could feel the heat from her cheeks, could hear the sound of the laugh. Was the professor in the same category, embarrassments of the past that haunt you forever? He hadn't made an appearance for a while. Did she miss him?

Chuck opened the door for her, and she got in and waited for him to start the car. Then she took the air-mail envelope out of her purse. "Listen to this. It's from my mother.

"'It will be perfectly all right to bring your friend home for Easter,'" she read. "'As you know, we have plenty of room. By the way, both Daryl and Damon might be able to come home over the holiday too. If you take the train, we'll come and get you in Reno, or if you decide to drive up, there's no need for a chaperone as far as I can see for an eight-hour drive. Ha ha, I know you were kidding. I hope the weather stays nice.' Then she says something about the times for mass. I told her you were Catholic. Then she says, 'Chuck is more than welcome.' Well?"

He looked surprised.

"Will you come?"

"I'll have to request permission from the Commander-in-Chief of the Armed Forces, Mrs. Roosevelt." She laughed. "I don't know if I can take a week leave or not. I'll have to see the XO. But I appreciate your invitation."

"Find out." She hugged his arm. "You'll like my family, you will."

"I'll let you know tonight at the USO," he said as she got out of the car in front of Mrs. Hughes's house.

When the phone rang she had been dozing on the couch. She hurried when she realized Mrs. Hughes wasn't home, thinking it must be her mother, though it wasn't Sunday. She was still half groggy when she picked up the phone and heard, "Hello, ma'am, has Kilroy been there?"

"Who?" she asked.

"Kilroy."

"Chuck," she said, recognizing his voice.

He started laughing. "Don't you know who Kilroy is? That little man with a big nose looking down over a fence? There's drawings of him all over the place, on walls in the heads. I've even seen civilians wearing little Kilroy pins. He's famous; I saw in a newsreel in the base theater where some GIs captured a town and as they walked into the main square somebody had already drawn Kilroy on a wall, 'Kilroy was here.' That Kilroy."

"Oh, the one the kids draw."

"What I phoned about is, I'm going to be late to the dance tonight. Something's come up, and I have to stick around. But I'll be there, I promise."

She went back to her apartment and took off her jacket. She had forgotten to ask if he'd found out about going to Carson City. She was still only half awake; she just dropped on the couch and fell asleep when she got home now. She couldn't help it. She should write some letters, she was at least two behind with her mother, or she'd start thinking about Chuck.

The other night at the USO he'd had to wait through four or five dances she'd promised before he could have a turn. When they finally got into the mass of couples moving around the floor, he didn't speak to her at first. "My feet are past hurting," she'd said.

"Then why do you dance so much?" She was going to answer, because that's why I come here, to dance with servicemen, but he went on, "I'd like to be able to see you sometimes without waiting in line. I do enough of that in the goddamn Navy."

She was surprised. She understood why he was angry but was amazed that he cared that much. It was so hard to know what other people felt. She either overworked her own feelings or overlooked the fact that she had any.

"It's my turn to work behind the counter," she said. "Go play checkers, and when I finish I'll come and get you." He looked skeptical, as if it were some trick. They kept dancing, and she stopped glancing over at the refreshment counter to see if anyone was filling in.

A sailor tried to cut in, tapping Chuck on the shoulder. He stopped dancing. "Beat it," he said. The sailor stepped back. They started again. They must have gone around a dozen different times. She was dizzy when they finally stopped. He started kissing her on the neck.

After that she worked behind the counter, passing out the doughnuts that the local bakeries donated. Veronica had stopped asking her to do the drawings: there were just too many sailors now, and not enough women to dance, and that's why they came to the USO.

He was later than he said, but he made it twenty minutes before the USO closed at eleven. The sailors had to be back at the base by twelve. When they danced she couldn't let go of him, held him closer than she'd ever held anyone else. She could smell his shaving lotion, cigarette tobacco. "I'm sorry I'm late," he kept saying.

"That's all right."

"There's a war on," he said to be funny, but neither laughed. They were holding each other so tight they could barely move.

At home, after he'd dropped her off, taking off her clothes to go to bed, she was so worked up she couldn't unfasten her bra until she sat down on the chair to stop herself from—not shaking, but from a kind of vibration, like she was just a skeleton and her bare bones were tingling. Delicious. A whole bowl of tapioca pudding. And he was going with her to Carson City for Easter. Leaving on Wednesday, coming back late Sunday. She didn't have any doubts. He didn't have any relatives here, just a sister back in Montana. He'd be happy to have a home-cooked meal. Meet her folks. They knew he was a Catholic, but not a strict one, she didn't think; she had to warn them about that. But not that he was in the service. She was bringing home a sailor. She couldn't wait until she saw her mother's face.

She drove first; he'd just got off duty and was tired. She had been worried that the Navy car they'd use might be painted battleship gray or olive drab, but it was a black Ford. No one would know it was a government car except for the license plates, and it was brand new, a hundred and three miles on it, the same 1941 model they turned out every year now for the military.

He was asleep before they got out of the neighborhood, just dropped off in the middle of explaining where he'd been all night. A battleship had come back and the sailors had all got liberty on the same day that two troopships of soldiers got their orders to embark at midnight. There were pitched battles up and down Market Street in the city, but he'd fallen asleep before she had a chance to ask why. When the soldiers were going out to fight in the Pacific and the sailors had just come back, why did they have to fight each other?

There wasn't much traffic for a weekday morning. Just as she thought that, she got behind a convoy of military trucks, each pulling a cannon, that must have been three miles long. She tried not to be impatient, and went all the way to Vallejo, where the convoy turned off, at twenty miles an hour. She tried to make up time by going faster once they turned off, but then it started to rain just before the foothills.

Chuck woke up at a stop sign and asked, "You tired?" She just shook her head. The only time she stopped was when he came awake and noticed the gas gauge. "You're going to run out if you don't pull over." He got out and filled the tank from one of the five gallon cans in the trunk. Even if you had ration coupons, you couldn't be sure you could find a station that had gas.

The road began winding but she didn't slow down, just braked to get around the curves. "What's your hurry?" he asked. "We'll get there before dark."

She snapped back at him, "Because I want to get home, that's why." Then she tried to soften what she said. "You know the reputation sailors have in San Bruno after sundown." She had teased him in the past: Why are you so worried about the proprieties? Shall I leave the door open to Mrs. Hughes's apartment and notify her that you won't even sit down? He didn't laugh. He was trying to stay awake, so she slowed down going through the last of the small towns.

It started sleeting; then the sleet turned into snow and started sticking to the road but not the windshield. She kept going at the same speed. Chuck started snoring, his head resting on the door window. He looked so handsome, even sleeping: never a hair out of place, taking short breaths through his nose, his hands clasped on his lap.

She didn't reach her hand out and pull the knob to start the wipers when the snow began to dot the glass. It was like being inside a cocoon, looking out through all that white. How much difference did the yellow make from the headlights? She pushed in the knob: everyone else would have their lights on and she'd be able to tell if anyone was coming. It was better, no glare. There was just enough light to see the single snowflakes sailing, sailing toward her face. The moth wasn't in the cocoon; it was outside. Thousands, millions of snow moths. She wished she could open her mouth and catch a snowflake on her tongue like she used to do when she was little. She missed the snow. She and Mona outside in their snowsuits, no hands, trying to get under the biggest snowflake.

"Jesus," Chuck yelled, "turn on the wipers." He almost made her slam on the brakes, she was so startled.

"I don't like the noise they make," she said, but pulled out the light knob too before he would say something. "I thought you were from Montana, where it really snows." The wipers cleared away the snow in two back-and-forths.

"When it snowed like this we used to pull over in the school bus and pray until it stopped."

She laughed but couldn't look over to see if he was kidding. Catholics, they might do that. "This stretch of road is always like this in a storm. It's supposed to be the coldest place along the whole border of the two states." She thought of colder than a witch's tit. Colder than a well digger's ass; she'd heard that in grammar school. Her family didn't talk like that. Her father said, "There'll be frost on the pumpkins tonight," when it got cold.

"Go back to sleep," she said. "You make me nervous."

He laughed when he said, "I don't know if I can." But he closed his eyes again and his head started rocking back and forth.

She was going home.

He woke up looking groggy. "I'll drive," he said, stretching his legs out, then his arms.

"We're there. This is Carson City, capital of the state of Nevada."

He opened the window and reached out and got a handful of snow off the door, wet his handkerchief, and then wiped his face. He was like a cat, the way he kept himself so neat. It wouldn't have surprised her if he'd taken out a razor and started shaving. Then he looked at his watches, first the pocket watch, then the wristwatch on his right arm. To see if they were the same, she guessed. She knew he had another watch around one of his ankles; she'd seen it when a soldier asked him for a cigarette at the USO. A lot of sailors kept their packs in their socks, so they wouldn't have a bulge in their jumper pockets, someone told her, but she'd never seen anyone else with a watch there before. "That's the Capitol," she said, "and that's the city's finest bordello."

"Looks like it's closed for Easter."

"As a sailor with a girl in every port, did you ever go to one of those places?"

"As a former altar boy and second-place winner for the bassoon in the whole state of Montana, I had a certain reputation to maintain."

"You did go, didn't you?"

He sounded irritated when he said, "What difference does it make?" What difference did it make if he didn't want to admit it to her? Who cared?

"Home sweet home," she said, stopping the car at the curb. The minute she reached the sidewalk she started running, yelling out, "I'm home, I'm home," when she got to the porch. Daryl opened the front door and she hugged him. He hadn't been home for Christmas. Then she was inside, hugging her father and mother and the rest, everyone talking at the same time just as she'd pictured it in her mind a thousand times at school.

Then she remembered Chuck. He was standing at the threshold, holding her luggage. She raced back and took him in by the upper arm, keeping hold of him as he shook hands with her father first, her brothers, and then Ben, Mona's old boyfriend. She made the introductions: her mother, Mona, and Loretta, Damon's fiancée.

Then she took Chuck upstairs, still holding on to his arm, to wash up. Past the spare bedroom—"Here's where you sleep; you'll have to share with Ben." She was glad to see both twin beds were made up. Mona must have done it; her mother hated doing housework. "And this is the upstairs bathroom." He had that look on his face, so she grabbed him and kissed him as hard as she could on the mouth. Then pulled away. He still looked the same. She heard someone coming or she would have tried another one.

When Chuck came back down, she and Mona were helping their mother in the kitchen. Everyone else was in the front room. Her father got up and insisted Chuck take his chair. She kept an eye on him through the doorway. He sat stiff, a hand on each knee, shoulders back, his shiny black Navy shoes catching the flame from the fire as if they were made of glass.

What was he seeing? The big opening to the dining room, the walls paneled up to the twelve-foot-high ceiling, the built-in bookcases on either side of the fireplace, with her mother's collection of glass paperweights scattered down the shelves. The curving banister going to the bedrooms upstairs. Why hadn't she ever tried to slide down that thing? Mona had, and her brothers, when her parents were gone. Her mother told stories about when she was a girl, getting caught and getting a swat from her grandfather. She heard Daryl speaking, and tried to listen while she sliced the bread.

"They're accelerating our program; I'll be out a year from this June. With any luck the war won't be over by then."

"They say by 1949," her father said. "What do you think, Ben?"

"The Germans are going to win," he said, "or the Germans aren't going to win. It's as simple as that."

Her father went on to another subject, as though he hadn't heard. "I don't know about the rest of the country, but the state of Nevada is doing its fair share. Both the sheep and cattle industries are pulling out the stops. I don't know what the production records look like, but I've never seen so many cattle cars passing through. And the training camps in this state: airfields, bombing ranges, millions of acres for the tank corps and the field artillery. They closed down all the mining so the men could go into the service or the defense industries. Just in the last year we doubled our employees, up to forty-one, with two shifts, seven days a week. And we're lucky to have them. It's hard to find anyone that needs a job. The Depression is over as far as I'm concerned. We've got a government contract now, and I'm not sure how I'm going to fill it unless I can get another building and more equipment. And the government won't take no for an answer. The work is all classified, or I'd tell you about it."

"It's all about how to maintain truck engines," her mother butted in, going out into the front room. "Booklets for the soldiers to read. If anyone would like to wash up, hurry; dinner is served."

Her mother had outdone herself: a roast, mashed potatoes, and two kinds of vegetables. She couldn't help asking, "How many ration stamps?" as she passed the platter of roast. Her mother winked. "We have friends," she said.

"What's next, Ben?" her father asked.

"Well, if I have any luck, I'll stay stateside awhile. Then they'll send me back. I did nine missions as a waist gunner, and when I got hurt I had time to look around some. And I got my name on a list to go to navigators' school. And they took me. I still can't believe it. It was such a fluke; they made me take some tests, math, mostly, and I passed. Yeah, I passed, Elaine." He poked her in the ribs when she laughed. They had gone through this before. "After all, I took four years . . ."

"But it was four years of Algebra 1. You were in the same class you started out in when I got to high school." Everyone laughed at that.

"It doesn't matter; I was so happy when I saw my name on the list, I would have swum home." He sniffed like he had a runny nose. "The only problem is they're going to send me back to England when I graduate."

"I wish I had your problems," Damon said. "I'd go in a minute if they'd let me."

"You wouldn't say that if you'd been there. It's not like playing baseball in high school. No one wins or loses, no one's keeping score. You just die or get crippled up. And no one cares. All the Army needs is more bodies, more kids growing up that they can train to shoot a fifty-caliber."

"The Army wants to win the war, like the rest of us. I personally don't want the world dominated by the Germans or the Japanese. And I'm willing to do what's necessary to win," Damon said.

Now Daryl, she thought. He would say something. A year and a half older than Damon but not as bright. He'd be in her C reading group. Ben and her two brothers had stopped eating, but Chuck kept shoveling the food in as if he couldn't hear the argument starting up.

"There've been plenty of other men that have made the supreme sacrifice for this country, and I'll bet none regretted it, either. Or their families," Daryl said.

"Well, wait until it's your turn and see what you're willing to offer. Being an officer doesn't make you an authority on patriotism," Ben said.

"And you're not an authority on the war, either, just because you flew nine missions," Damon said. "You never even graduated from high school."

Ben jumped up. "Wait until you hotshots have someone shooting at you. Then we'll see what kind of heroes you are. I need some fresh air," he said, walking out.

"May I be excused?" Mona asked.

"Certainly," her father said. She went out the front door too, letting in another wave of cold air.

"Well, I like scintillating table conversation at dinner," her father said.

Her mother laughed. "You three USO veterans will have to remain humble until you get at the Axis."

"He never even made the varsity baseball team," Damon said.

"Dad, Chuck was on the *Arizona* at Pearl Harbor." She had to say it; then she added, so they'd be sure to understand, "on December seventh."

Everyone stopped eating to look at him. He looked around at them as if the lights had gone out and he couldn't see. He held his wristwatch up to his ear as if to make sure it was ticking. She wished she hadn't said anything. She had found out from Avery. If he didn't tell her, she guessed it was because it wasn't important to him to say it. Probably that was the same reason he didn't wear his ribbons.

"Imagine that," her mother said.

"I had got up early that Sunday," her father said, "planning on going down to the shop and fill some orders. Business cards, I think it was. Mother had got up with me to fix breakfast. Elaine was here from Reno. Sleepy-bones Mona was still in bed. Daryl was already at the Point. And Damon was—"

"I had gone down to Sacramento to a basketball game."

"I opened the paper and was reading. The radio was on. I took a sip of tomato juice, and the war started. 'We interrupt this program to announce Pearl Harbor has been bombed by the Japanese,' blah, blah, blah. We had to look it up to see where the place was. All the Pacific Fleet sunk. What a day that was."

After lunch Thursday they took a walk, her arm through his, around her old neighborhood. "This isn't walking the heart from Cupid Row, but I'm glad to be here," she said. "When I was growing up, we used to go down to San

Francisco to shop. It used to scare me, so many people in one place. Also, no blackouts here, have you noticed?"

"Speaking for Montana, this is a big city. Some of the railroad towns I lived in weren't any bigger than this street."

She was hit by a sudden surge of feeling; she wanted to hug the very breath out of him. She squeezed his arm and stopped him in front of someone's garage, the '36 Plymouth up on blocks, tires and rims gone. "Kiss me," she said. To her surprise he did, right there on the sidewalk. He held her, finding her lips. She opened her mouth and stuck her tongue between his teeth. Startled, he jumped back. She couldn't help giggling and tried to pull him to her again.

"Somebody's coming," he whispered. She looked around; it was only a mailman across the street. No one could see them, but he started walking, taking her with him by the arm.

When they got back to the house, everyone was there in the front room. Mona and Benny moved over so they could sit on the couch. "Did you go to church?" her father asked, and everyone laughed, but Chuck took the question seriously.

"No, Good Friday is tomorrow; I'll go then."

"Where did you say you were from, Chuck?" Damon asked.

"Montana."

"Never been there," her father said. "Your folks still up there?"

"No sir, my father died two years ago, and my mother when I was a kid."

"You're an orphan," she blurted out. Then she added, "He has a sister in Montana."

"That's not many for a good Catholic family," her father said. "Only two."

"You didn't do so badly yourself with four," Mona said. "And you're an Episcopalian." Everyone laughed again.

When her mother got up and went into the kitchen to start dinner, she got up too. She wanted to ask Chuck to come with her, but that wouldn't do. She set the table and let Mona and Loretta help in the kitchen. She couldn't get enough of him. It felt as if she were leaving part of herself on the couch, getting up like that.

At dinner she made sure she sat next to Chuck, the chairs so close together that the full length of their legs were touching. She pretended to feel the pulse from his heart at her hipbone. She wanted to tell him something. Whisper. She had no idea what. What would he say if she asked to draw him without any clothes on?

Everyone was too full for dessert, but her mother insisted they have the canned peaches over sponge cake with whipped cream now, before the cream separated. There were no shortages here. They'd had pork chops for dinner. Country sausage for breakfast, roast last night. That was more meat than she'd had in the last month.

They all groaned, they were so stuffed, when they got up and went into the living room. Her mother kept saying, "Go on, go, I'll clear up." So she did. Mona stayed to help, but Loretta came too. Her father turned on the radio, but the news was already over, so he turned it back off. Her mother came out to announce, "Just for you, Chuck, we're going to have salmon loaf tomorrow night, since it's Friday." She could feel him twitch beside her.

"Thank you, ma'am," he said. No one said anything after that until her father asked Loretta, "How's your brother George doing?"

"Fine, they promoted him to captain. He's still in Louisiana with the field artillery." She stopped listening, wondering how you could define love. A romantic attraction between two people. Reciprocal admiration. Mutual respect. Wanton sex. Lust. A legal union. Marriage. Cupid Row. Living with someone for fifty years. She wanted to brush the hair on his wrist with her fingertips. When she went back to the conversation, Ben and her brothers were into it again.

"Wait until you're an officer and we'll see what your attitude is then."

"My attitude will be exactly the same. The Army generals are a bunch of nincompoops who won't be able to find work after this war."

"You could be court-martialed for that kind of talk," Damon said.

"Report me, that would be fine with me."

"They'll never make you an officer, Ben." Loretta's voice was too loud. "You're just not the right material."

"If your father hadn't owned half the county, your brother wouldn't have made buck private if the war lasted twenty years."

"God forbid," her father said. Before Loretta could go on, he added, "I have to go down to the plant early tomorrow, so I'm going to say good night now."

Her mother came out of the kitchen wiping her hands on her apron, with Mona behind her. "I'm going to turn in too; you young people can stay up as long as you like." Everyone listened as her mother shut the hallway door behind her with a click.

"Where's the booze?" Ben whispered.

"It's rationed," Mona said. "I don't think there's any left."

"Let's take a walk," he said to Mona, and they put their coats on. "Anyone want to come?" Ben asked before they went out.

"No, thank you," Loretta said.

"He should be put in the stockade, not officers' school," Daryl said.

"He always had a big mouth," Damon said.

She got up and started getting the games out from the drawer under the china cabinet. "We have a USO world champion checker player here tonight," she said, opening the board on the coffee table in front of Chuck. "Who wants to play him?"

"I will," Loretta said, "I hate pick-up sticks." And she started setting the red pieces out on the board.

Damn it, she had planned to play Chuck herself. She was just being polite. She played pick-up sticks with Damon and Daryl. "Did you ever play this?" she asked Chuck.

"No, I don't believe I have."

"You go like this, it's easy." She held the sticks in her fist. Had she put the black one on the side where it'd fall on top? She let go and the sticks fell in a jumble. She started rolling away the ones that had fallen clear. She extracted a red one stuck to the others with the end of her finger, then lifted one end of a green with her thumb like a seesaw and swung it clear. Chuck stopped watching and Damon started yelling. "You moved the yellow one." She lost her turn. Loretta was flirting with Chuck, grabbing his hand and trying to pry it open to get a piece out, squealing, "King me, king me."

She had never been in a Catholic church before. She watched Chuck dip his fingers in the font and make the sign of the cross. There were a few people, like lumps of clothing, sitting down by the altar, heads covered with bandannas. It was quiet. The light from the candles cast dark shadows on the wall and made the statues move as though they were alive. She could smell something thick and sweet over the smoke from the candles. Chuck genuflected at a pew and let her go first, and then he knelt down and began to pray.

She didn't have a scarf, but she put her handkerchief on her head. She'd read that somewhere. Now she saw there was a crowd of people over to one side, a big group standing in front of a picture, a priest in front of them, altar boys. The Episcopal church had some of this, the altar, the crucifix, no statues, but the same kind of stained-glass windows. The priest looked the same, wore the same vestments. But there was a big difference.

The priest, of course, because he didn't marry. And all the sins, and then confessing them. Who would want to live under such strict rules? The Catholic girls in high school did the same things that she and Mona did. Smoked. Drank beer. Swore. And got felt up in the back rows of the movie theater. She was being facile. She had never been felt up. The Catholic kids couldn't read *Les Miserables* in English class. She still didn't know why. The real difference was this church was an everyday proposition. They had to be Catholics all the time. Like the Masons, with the secret handshake, even though her father only went on Wednesdays and hardly ever wore his funny hat and sword. No, it was more like the Boy Scouts. She had helped Daryl and Damon become Scouts, memorize the Scout's Oath, and learn the Scout's Code. You were supposed to abide by these rules all the time. Why hadn't she become a Girl Scout? Because she hadn't liked Brownies. She'd got sick at a meeting and thrown up all over herself and had to be taken home by Mona. She had never wanted to go back. But there was no Jesus in the Scouts, and you went to heaven instead of becoming an Eagle. She was being silly.

He sat back on the pew. "Who did you pray for?" she whispered.

"My mother, I always pray for her first. My father. My sister. For you."

"What did you pray for me?"

"That you'd have good health. That you'd be happy."

"I'm happy you're here," she said.

They were going to have Easter dinner on Saturday afternoon because she and Chuck were going to leave early Sunday to get back to San Bruno. She'd never been so surprised in her life, coming down that morning to see Chuck in an apron rolling out dough with a rolling pin. She was ready to laugh, but he asked, "What's your favorite pie?"

"Apple," she said. Then her mother came in from the pantry with a five-pound sack of flour.

"He was up when I came in, and volunteered to make the pies for dinner. He's already got dough rising for cinnamon buns for breakfast and bread for dinner."

"Imagine that," she said. As everyone came into the kitchen he asked, "What's your favorite pie?" She started peeling the apples. When Mona came in she wanted a pecan pie, but they didn't have any pecans. She pulled his apron strings loose and he threw a pinch of dough at her.

"Isn't he full of surprises," her mother said at least twice. "He'll make someone a good wife." She kept peeling until her father came in and said he wanted a lemon pie. Then she started grating lemon peel. They had blackberries canned from summer for Ben. Custard pie for her brothers. When Loretta came over, apple was her favorite, too.

All of them were in the kitchen, their mouths full of cinnamon bun, drinking coffee, all talking at once, watching Chuck. She had never seen him like this, laughing, teasing back, so relaxed that he took a few dance steps with her mother when someone turned on the radio to music. She felt uncomfortable, not because her father or brothers would never think of making a pie, even if they could. She couldn't explain it. She felt uneasy.

She wanted to help more, but he didn't need any help. He could do everything by himself. She'd never seen anyone work so fast. The lattice on the blackberry pie was like the design on needlepoint. And he talked the whole time, and was funny. "Before I was best policeman in the Navy, and the fastest typist, I was the—"

"The most extraordinary cinnamon bun maker," Mona put in.

"That and the most prolific baker in the U.S. Navy." Everyone clapped.

They had both turkey and ham for dinner. Her father stood up at the head of the table, asking each person what he or she wanted. When he got to her, she asked for her favorite, a wing. When he asked Chuck, he started laughing and could barely get out, "Give me the Pope's nose, please." Everyone roared, and her father cut off the tail and put it on his plate with a bow.

She kept watching Chuck, thinking, Am I happy? Am I happy? Everyone else looked as though they were ecstatic.

The pies were even better than they looked. There was just the right amount of cinnamon in the apple. The custard pie wasn't runny, the bottom crusts weren't soggy. Everyone was oohing and aahing. "Yum, yum," Loretta kept saying. Chuck had cut himself a wedge out of the apple, but asked for a bowl instead of a plate. He sliced some cheese over the top and then poured milk over that. Perfectly at home, she thought, with everyone watching.

"I've never seen anyone eat pie like that," Mona said.

"My father used to fix his pie like this."

"What did he do?" she asked.

"He was a brakeman on the Northern Burlington line."

"When I worked on my dad's ranch, there was a hand one summer who drank a half-inch of kerosene every night before he went to bed," her father said. Everyone started hooting and jeering.

"What did he think he was, a lamp?" her mother said.

"It's the truth," her father kept insisting.

Daryl, Ben, and Damon did the dishes. She and Mona went upstairs to change clothes. Her father sat in his chair reading the paper, Chuck on the couch, leafing through magazines. He had offered to help with the dishes, but her mother had said, "No you don't. You made those pies; let them do something for a change." Loretta had gone home to get her coat.

She was the first one downstairs, and Chuck stood up when she came into the living room. "He has beautiful manners," her mother had told her the night before. He was handsome, too. Even with the scar. When he smiled you forgot the pink welt that ran down his temple through the very tail of his eyebrow and on down to his jawbone. She would paint it in, if she did his portrait. It was part of his face, like the gap between his teeth and the way his forehead creased when he smiled.

Everyone was waiting on Ben to go out dancing. She had halfheartedly invited her mother and father, but they had refused to go, which was a relief to her. It was just easier this way. Everyone looked so . . . She couldn't think of a good word. Adult. Young. And military, because the men were wearing their uniforms. She and Mona and Loretta were wearing their best dresses for the occasion.

Loretta, Damon, and Daryl went in her father's Lincoln, and she and Chuck got in the back of Ben's '39 Ford. She was so excited her hands shook when she tried to take a cigarette from Chuck's pack of Lucky Strikes. They were going dancing, a night out on the town.

The spring sky still had that kind of mysterious light, as if either a sun or a moon might appear. Ben kept honking his horn at people he recognized, yelling out the window. Damon, driving behind them, was doing the same. It was like coming back from winning a high school football game.

Once they got out of town, Damon drew alongside Ben's Ford on the dark two-lane road, Daryl hanging out the open window, yelling, taking swigs out of a half-pint. She could see Damon get the bottle and take a long drink while Loretta, sitting in the middle, steered.

Then Ben motioned that he wanted a drink and reached his arm out to Damon, who leaned farther out and handed the bottle over. Ben drank, then Mona. She couldn't see how fast they were going, but the wind coming through the open window was blowing her hair all over. When Mona handed the bottle back she took a snort, as her father called it, and tried to hand the bottle to Chuck. He had his sleeve pulled back to see his wristwatch and had his pocket watch out too. "2109 and 2108 and forty seconds. I'm losing time," he said.

"Take a drink," she said.

"I can't remember when I wound last. It's really important to always do it at the same time, so the main spring wears evenly. My father wound at 0800 every other day." She nudged him with the bottle. Then Mona reached back and grabbed it from her and leaned across Ben to pass it on to Damon in the other car, Ben yelling, "I can't see, I can't see," and laughing his head off.

The place was more a roadhouse than anything else. A long bar and a band that played too loud. The ballroom was jammed with people, most of the men in uniform, their brass flashing in the semidarkness when they caught the light from the table candles. She danced with Ben, her brothers, and Chuck, kissed him long kisses as they slowly went around the floor.

Every time they ordered drinks, Ben would add some more from another bottle he'd bought. "Let me freshen your drink," he'd say. She couldn't be sure Chuck was enjoying himself. Sometimes he seemed to be in a trance, staring into space. Then he'd start checking the time again. He was probably tired; it had been a long three days. But not once during that time had she thought about school, her class. Not once, until this minute. She was proud of herself.

When Ben started talking about going to Reno to visit his aunt, they asked him to drop them off at the house. Her brothers and Loretta stayed. "Isn't it late to be visiting?" she asked Ben as he stopped in front. Mona was asleep in the front seat.

"It's 0123," Chuck said.

"She won't care," Ben said.

She explained to Chuck as they went up the walk, "His parents are divorced. He won't have anything to do with either of them. But he likes his aunt in Reno. I used to visit her when I went to school there. We drank tea and she made cucumber sandwiches for us. She must be his great-aunt, because she was old."

She just kept talking like she had to get all this information out. Her mother had left the light on over the stove, and she went in and turned it off, then felt her way back to the living room and sat down next to Chuck on the couch. He put his arms around her and they started kissing.

When his hand slipped up under her dress it felt natural, warm, comfortable, until she started thinking, Is my underwear clean? What was she supposed to do? She had always wondered why he hadn't tried anything, but she'd thought it would be her breasts first. She would have liked that better.

He had got his hand between her slip and dress and couldn't get anywhere, and he took it back out. She tried not to go rigid, but it wasn't easy. It was like watching a scary movie where you didn't know what was going to happen next. He was rubbing along her leg now, kneading like it was made of dough. Not hurting, but firm, sure. Then he touched her between the legs and she started hiccuping. Loud. Again and again. "Oh, excuse me," she said, "excuse me," her whole body recoiling in jerks and starts. But she couldn't stop.

Then she heard the Lincoln slow to go up the driveway and Chuck was sitting up and she was trying to pull down her dress, still hiccuping. He turned on the light and sat down in her father's chair, and she was leafing through a *Saturday Evening Post* when Damon and Daryl came through the front door.

On the way back, he drove. It was barely dawn, and it had started to rain by the time they got to Reno. She half dozed. She had got up at five-thirty, but her mother was already up, wearing her robe, to make the coffee and offer to cook breakfast, and then her father came out to hug her and shake Chuck's hand before they left. Her mother had kissed Chuck good-bye.

When she came awake again, it was really raining and the windshield wipers were going back and forth, back and forth, but it wasn't soothing; it started getting on her nerves. She felt cross. Her foot nudged the box lunch her mother had made for them. She reached down and felt around for a sandwich and asked, "Do you want one?" He shook his head and she unwrapped the waxed paper. She wasn't hungry either, but she took a bite.

When they passed the sign on the Nevada-California border she finished chewing, then swallowing the mouthful of tuna fish and bread and heard herself saying, "You think I'm cheap, don't you?"

He looked over in surprise. "No, no I don't."

"Yes you do. I never let anyone do that to me before. Never." Then she started crying. She was amazing herself. She never cried.

"Eat something," he said, and she started sobbing. "There's no place to pull over." She sobbed louder. She couldn't help it. Her whole body was wracked, she couldn't stop. She could feel the wet tears going down her neck under her collar.

"Don't cry," he said. "Don't cry. It doesn't do any good."

She was back at her desk, watching the kids, who were being good for the first day after Easter week, working on their reports. Like everyone else, she left the last hour for the easiest subjects. The kids were too tired to do anything important after the final recess. So sometimes she had some of the better readers read to the rest of the class, or they could work on their projects. Each was to pick a president and write a paper on his life, draw his picture, and make a map of his home state. It covered all the subjects and supplemented the fifth-grade U.S. history requirement. The kids seemed to like working with the old encyclopedias. She was amazed at how much work they put in on their projects.

That's not to say there weren't exceptions. Leroy, who had a morning paper route, was sleeping behind an open book. And Mary Maureen, who had insisted she was going to do both President Roosevelt and his wife but had started neither, was just reading a Nancy Drew, not even pretending to hide it inside another book. She'd had to yell at her three times today, "Snap out of it, Mary Maureen," when she sat there staring into space. She'd asked to be excused to go to the lavatory and hadn't come back for twenty minutes. And Avery, who'd finished his report and was helping Sharon look up things about Lincoln. Avery had chosen James Garfield, and when she asked him why he'd said, "Because he died so soon. So there'll be less to write," as if he were explaining to someone who didn't understand.

She would see how smart he was. He deserved the report card he got. He wasn't doing the work. And he wasn't going to pass. Maybe she should go over and tell Aunt May. That way she could get used to the idea. Just a casual conversation. Then maybe she could ask about marrying a Catholic. Her mother had caught her by surprise. "Are you serious about him, Elaine?" When she didn't answer, her mother went on, "If you are, you better consider what's in the future for any children you might have. I'm not prejudiced against Catholics. But I don't think your father would like it if his grandchildren had to go to Catholic school and couldn't belong to DeMolay or later the Masons, because they can't keep secrets, you know; they have to tell everything to the priests. I have nothing against them, but you have to consider everything. And it's not to say he's not a nice boy."

"I never thought of that," she'd said.

"Well, give it some thought, Elaine."

She had that very afternoon, when Chuck had taken her into the church on Good Friday. It was mysterious; it gave her a feeling that something unexpected or wonderful could happen. But then to see Chuck on his knees praying, it didn't fit the picture, the way she thought of him. She couldn't imagine him telling his sins to another man, or kissing a bishop's ring. She'd seen that in *The March of Time* a couple of weeks before at the El Camino Theater. Would he tell the priest what they did on the couch?

At three the buzzer went off and she jumped along with half the kids. Without being told, everyone started putting things away. "Remember, you have your spelling pretest tomorrow," she said. "And I should see your maps too, from your projects." She paused. "You're dismissed, class."

Chuck was waiting, got out of the car when he saw her coming, to open the door. Everything was back to normal. "Well," she said, "I'd better get home and write my mother; she was getting kind of worried." She didn't have to go on, she knew that, but when he asked why, she said it anyway. "She thinks we're getting too serious. And because you're Catholic, I'll have to become one, and if we have children they'll have to be raised in your church."

"Oh," he said.

"Would you only marry a Catholic?" she asked.

"I never gave it any thought."

She didn't know what to say. The silence was getting longer and longer. He started the car. Then he started talking as if she hadn't said anything.

"Before I forget, I'd like to invite you to a ceremony over at Mare Island on the sixth of next month. They're going to award some of us our decorations. They have a piece of the bridge from the *San Francisco*, Jap shell holes punched all over it, to show people, and they think they might sell some bonds at the same time. Just for a few hours on a Saturday afternoon."

"Of course, I'd be happy to," she said, wondering how she could turn the conversation back to what they'd started talking about. "Do Catholics have to go to church every day?"

"No, on Sunday only. You can go, I guess, but I never have. I stop in once in a while, just to pray, but not every day."

"I see," she said. When he stopped the car in front of the house, he got out and opened the door for her. Mrs. Hughes came out of her side of the house to sit on the porch bench. She couldn't say anything more, or try for a kiss, or a hug.

Chuck had the duty, so she walked home. For an April, it was hot. The heat made her think of summer and Carson City. Was she going up there in June, when school got out? She had no reason to stay. None that she could convince her mother with, anyway. What if she went and they shipped Chuck out?

She noticed Mary Maureen walking on the other side of the street a half-block behind, pretending not to see her, her sister Ruthie walking about five steps in front, carrying her coat, one sleeve touching the ground. A month ago Mary Maureen was confiding that she wanted to be a teacher. "You'll make a good one," she'd said. Now she was ignoring her. Was it possible to be a good anything? A good person?

Last night she'd got Chuck to come in, after the USO dance. She'd gone into the bathroom and unsnapped her bra and rubbed toothpaste on her teeth with her finger. It was like she was getting the sun in her eyes when he danced with her, some powerful spotlight that she had to close her eyes against, and then she became confused and disoriented. She always wanted to touch him, put her fingertips on the side of his neck and feel the tiny pulses of blood moving under his skin. She didn't care what he did to her; she wasn't going to hiccup this time.

When she came out of the bathroom he was sitting stiff in her new chair. She started turning off the lights as she walked toward him, leaving just the one over the stairs on, and she sat down in his lap. "Am I too heavy?" she asked.

"No, not at all." And then he started looking at his watches. "It's a lot later than I thought," he said. "At 2400 I have to be back at the base. We're having a lot of trouble keeping this draft of recruits together. It's always bad the night before they get shipped out. We want to give them a last liberty, but a lot of them don't want to come back. Well," he said, "I better get going." She had to get up first.

She started counting the squares from the corner to Mrs. Hughes's house on Cupid Row. When she got to the apartment, Mrs. Hughes was standing on the porch, waiting. She smiled at her.

"I want to talk to you, Miss Walker."

"Of course," she said. Had she lost another clothespin? Had she left a light on? She was following Mrs. Hughes into her side of the house when the woman abruptly stopped and turned back around.

"What I have to say, I'll say right here," she said, raising her voice. "I won't have it. I told you when you moved in, no men."

She tried to interrupt. "Mrs. Hughes, Mrs. Hughes, let's go inside."

"No men, that's what I told you." She was almost shouting.

"Let's be reasonable, Mrs. Hughes. I invited my date in after a dance." Mother Mitchum had come out and was standing on her porch, listening. Someone else was running by across the street, dogs barking. Avery. All she could think of to add was, "I'm twenty-three years of age."

"I tried to treat you as if you were my own daughter," Mrs. Hughes said. "I was never blessed with children, but I wouldn't want my daughter with a sailor after nine P.M. He didn't leave until after eleven. Think what I must think. Or the neighbors. Common decency is all I ask. A single woman should always be aware of her reputation. So there. I've said it. You do what you like." And she went inside and closed the door.

She got inside too. Didn't put up the shades. Stood there in the gloom and tried to catch her breath. She was breathing as if she were the one who had been shouting at the top of her voice. Now what? She would move. She wouldn't be talked to like that. But where? Eight weeks of school left.

On the walk to Edgemont she had been remembering when they'd played school as kids. She was the teacher and Daryl and Damon were the students and the classroom was under the dining room table. She couldn't remember what Mona had been. Was that why she'd become a teacher? She started across the playground, hurrying, a little late though the first bell hadn't rung yet, and noticed something was different. She wasn't sure what. Unlocked her classroom, hung up her coat, and put her purse in the bottom drawer of her desk. It was important to be first, to have a few minutes. It was so peaceful in the big room. Last week one of the subs had said in the lunchroom, "If it weren't for the kids, teaching would be a good job." She had laughed with everyone else. It wasn't the kids, though, she decided, but the theory that was wrong, that put forty-three people in one room for seven hours and expected them to change for the better. The first bell rang.

At morning recess, looking out the window of the lunchroom, she saw the boys on their knees, their rumps resting on their heels, pitching marbles at a line in the dirt to see who was first. It was marble season, that's what was different. Big circles of kids, watching or playing, were spaced all over the playground. No dogfights, no playing war. It was marble time now. Jumping rope was all year. So were tag and basketball. Tops were a springtime event too, but she hadn't seen any here. Baseball, of course. But it was almost mysterious the way the marble season suddenly began. She hadn't seen anyone yesterday with any marbles. Now everyone was playing.

She'd made her father include her when her brothers got marbles. She'd been only fair, losing most of them the first day. But she had liked the whole idea of the game, the aiming with your thumb and trying to hit the other marble out of the ring marked in the dirt, trying to make your own marble stay in for another turn. Had she been a tomboy? Other girls played. Agates were worth ten ordinary marbles. So were the clear ones. Steelies were worth five. She should have been a boy, she thought. She'd never liked dolls. Refused to play with them. Teddy bears were ridiculous.

A couple of days later, when the kids trooped in, the boys' front pockets bulging with marbles, she surprised them by asking, "Who's the best marble player in our room?" There was a silence while they thought. This happened when she broke the routine, said or did something different from what they expected.

When no one else answered, Mary Maureen raised her hand for the first time in weeks. She had changed. "Leroy is. He can shoot the hardest." Several voices agreed; other kids nodded their heads.

"How many marbles have you won this morning?" she asked him.

He looked embarrassed. Getting this attention was unexpected. "Eighty-two, Miss Walker," he said.

"That's good," she said. Where was she going with this, she wondered. She had a lesson plan to follow. She should be starting penmanship. "I used to play marbles," she said. They just looked at her with blank faces. She wasn't a teacher, she was a loony. "Please stand for the salute to the flag," she said.

Later, in the lunchroom, Mr. Allen and some of the other teachers were already talking about next year. She put her sandwich back in the waxed paper half eaten; she was getting tired of tuna fish. Would she be here next year? She hadn't signed her contract yet. She could get work in the shipyard, as a riveter, a welder, something. Wouldn't that mortify her mother: hair done up in a bandanna, slacks, carrying a metal lunch box. Ninety-five cents an hour for women, plus overtime. It would be more than she was making as a teacher.

She was falling into reveries lately. She wasn't sure what she'd do for the summer. Go back to Carson City and work in the shop? When she'd left, she'd left for good. That was a joke. Her mother picked out her clothes. All she'd ever bought for herself was a chair for her apartment, and she never sat in the thing.

"Mr. Allen, we have a little problem here." When Eunice spoke, everyone listened. She turned around in her chair. Avery was standing in front of her holding a shoe box in the crook of his arm, head down, his sailor cap full of marbles in his other hand. Face red, hair flopped down on his forehead, the tail of his shirt out. The white butcher string he used for shoelaces in his tennis shoes had broken so many times that the knotted ends fluttered up and down on the black tongues like thistledown as he shuffled his feet. It was like she was seeing him in a newsreel.

"We have a trickster and a profiteer here in our school," Eunice said, and she grabbed the shoe box and put it on the table.

"Do you want to explain, Avery?" Mr. Allen asked.

"He was taking all the other kids' marbles is what he was doing. Unfairly," Eunice said. "I've got to get back out there."

"Go on, Avery," Mr. Allen said in his kind voice.

"It's just a game," he said, and he pointed at the shoe box on the table. He didn't stutter now; did he only do that when he wanted attention? She could see when he moved that his pants pockets were full of marbles, and even his shirt pocket. And he had two men's socks full, tied through his belt. "If a person can roll a marble through that hole," and he pointed to the smallest of the three squares cut in the side of the box, "I give them twenty-five marbles." She noticed now the number 25 written in orange crayon over the first hole. "If they get through this hole, they win fifteen, and this one, ten."

"How far do you get from the box?" Mr. Allen asked.

"Ten feet," Avery said.

"Has anyone won twenty-five marbles?"

"Oh yes, sir, plenty of times."

"But a lot more have lost, apparently, by the look of your cache."

Avery looked down at the marbles in his hat. "I've been lucky," he said.

"Who gave you that idea, with the shoe box?"

"Where I went to school before," Avery said. "They did it."

"Do you realize that you're going to end up with all the marbles in the school, the way you're going? We can't have that, can we? Let's not use the shoe box anymore. Leave it on the table." Avery made a move to go. "And Avery, I want you to give ten marbles to everyone that doesn't have any that played your game. Do you understand that?"

That sullen look came over his face. "I understand, but they're my marbles," he said. "I won them."

Mr. Allen stood up. He wasn't smiling now. "No backtalk, Avery. Put your marbles in the box, if you can't follow instructions, and I'll give them out."

"That's not right. They're mine," he said, holding the sailor hat with both hands.

Mr. Allen's face was red now. "Did you hear me?" Avery raised his head, glaring back at him, and opened his mouth to speak, then crossed his eyes, mocking him. Mr. Allen slapped him hard across the face. The sound was too loud for the room. Something wet, spit or snot, sprayed across her legs as Avery fell backward, cracking his head against the edge of the oak table. Marbles from the cap went everywhere. She stood up. Mr. Allen was frozen, his hand still held out open, fingers splayed. It had happened so fast. Avery lay there like he was dead, eyes closed, blood coming out of his nose.

"He shouldn't have acted that way," Mr. Allen said to no one in particular. "Belligerent." The marbles were still rolling, as if the floor were tilting back and forth. She knelt beside him. He was breathing easy, as if he were asleep, his chest going up and down. She put her hand on his forehead and brushed aside his hair. His skin felt warm, as if heat were pouring out of him. She was reminded of a dog, a puppy.

"He's just stunned," Mr. Allen said. "I didn't hit him hard." He cleared his throat. "I'll be in my office if anyone needs me." He limped out. The other three teachers got up without a word and left too. One came back to switch off the hot plate.

Avery opened his eyes. She kept her hand on his forehead. "How do you feel?" she said. He tried to get up. "Stay still for a minute, hold your finger under your nose. That's it, the bleeding is almost stopped. Have you had a bloody nose before?"

"A lot of times," he said. "I'm used to them." He just lay there limp on the floor.

The first bell rang. "Can you stand up?" she asked. He sat up. Then she helped him to his feet. His nose had stopped bleeding. She watched as he untied the two socks from his belt and put them in the box. Then he dug out the marbles from his pants pockets. "After you're done," she said, "go into the lavatory and wash your face." He nodded. He looked like he was going to cry. She didn't want to see that. She started to leave.

"Miss Walker, you're not going to tell Aunt May I got punished?"

"I wasn't going to," she said.

He came back subdued and sat at his desk. She couldn't keep her eyes off him. He looked exhausted, like he was worn out from carrying all those marbles. Fragile, transparent, like he was made of glass too. She had to stop looking.

Mary Maureen

I always had to hurry up, so I took the shortcut back from the store, around the heart, skipping, but trying not to use the soles of my shoes too hard. There was no leather to put on another pair, like there were no more tires or tubes for my two-wheeled bike and it had to be put in the garage.

I was hurrying because we needed the sliced bread for my father's lunch. Grammy had forgotten again that we were out. She couldn't bake enough bread, now that there were four lunches to make every day. She sent me to the store, and I didn't have to take Ruthie because I had to get back as fast as I could.

I was passing Cupid Row, swinging the loaf of bread in a circle at the end of my arm and jumping over every other square in the sidewalk, when Miss Walker called. "Mary Maureen, Mary Maureen, will you give me a hand?" She was calling from the upstairs window. I waved and went up the stairs in two jumps and came down on the porch. Mrs. Hughes opened her door and yelled at me. "What do you want? You're shaking the whole house." Before I could answer, Miss Walker opened her door.

We moved the furniture. A small writing desk. The couch. "I like the change," she said, her hands on her hips, looking things over. "Put the coffee table in front of the couch." I did what she said. "That allows the rug to wear evenly," she said. I never heard that before. We didn't have any rugs but the ones Grammy made out of rags, and those were next to the beds so your feet wouldn't freeze on the linoleum when you got up in the morning.

"Want to do this for me? Make me a seam for my stocking?" She handed me the makeup pencil and put her foot up on the flat of the chair to the desk, pulling her skirt tight around her leg. I wet the pencil with my tongue like she said and drew the line from the back of her knee to the ankle. I knew that there was no more silk because of the war effort, so women shaved their legs and drew the seam line on so it would look like they were wearing stockings. Avery said they needed the silk for parachutes.

"Now this leg," she said, and she put her other foot up. Grammy wore white cotton socks held up by rubber bands at the knee. My mother wore slacks and you didn't see her legs. I did the other one, careful not to touch her skin on the calves. It looked like when we plucked the down off a chicken, blue-white with little holes where the feathers came out.

"Thank you," Miss Walker said when I was done.

"It was nothing, ma'am."

"Here, I have something for you." It was a cookie she'd made herself. Oatmeal, big as a pancake.

I ran when I remembered, but I knew it was too late. The Packard was gone. Ruthie was playing with ants, letting them run up her arm, next to the porch. "You're going to get it," she said.

I was already explaining when I opened the door that Miss Walker had stopped me, but Grammy yelled, "Where were you? I had to use last night's biscuits to make your father's lunch." She picked up her wooden spoon and I was backing away, but my mother opened the front door then. "Do you know what she did?" Grammy was still yelling. My mother looked surprised, like she was going to back out because she was in the wrong house. I slipped by her and got away.

I waited for the right time to find out. Not the day after that drunk man called Avery a Gorman, or all that week. Then I chose Leroy to help me make the PTA meeting poster in the back of the room while the rest of the class was doing their penmanship. He could print better than I could and didn't always need a ruler to make a straight line and could write in cursive without any trouble.

I waited again, back at the work table, getting the best crayons out and letting Leroy use the colors he wanted. And I mentioned, peeling the paper off the yellow Crayola, that he didn't look Japanese if anyone would take the time to notice close, and he remembered that day when the shipyard workers grabbed him and Avery. And we went on from there and he told me Avery's name wasn't Fontana, it was Gorman. His family changed their name after the father was sent to prison. Fontana was their mother's name. "Quit it," I said to him, "just quit it."

"It's the truth," Leroy said. I tried not to look too interested because that's when people stopped telling. Especially Leroy. He was contrary, worse than Avery. If you said my turn he'd say no it isn't. But if you didn't care, he'd let you.

"Why did he go to prison?"

Leroy stopped running the orange crayon down the *T* to look at me for a second to see how interested I was. "He killed someone." I must have looked like I didn't believe him, because he said, "My mother was there and saw it," then added, "so was Avery."

I got up and sharpened my pencil, took my time. Ground it all the way down to the printed NO. 2 SOFT while I watched Avery's back as he bent over his desk to write, his face almost touching the paper. Went back and sat down at the work table. Never asked anything. Just forced spit through my front teeth, waiting.

"Avery almost got killed too," he went on like I knew he would.

"Cross the *T*," I said; he'd forgotten.

"My mother was with his Uncle Johnny and Avery. They were in a bar over by Half Moon Bay. I never was there because I had to go with my sister to visit my grandmother. Avery's father came in then, my mother said, and pretended like he didn't see the three of them sitting in the booth. Just stood at the bar with his back to them but watching them in the mirror.

"Johnny slid out of the booth like he was going to the toilet and Avery's father turned around then and pulled out a gun from his waistband. I've been in that bar lots of times. When we went for abalone and mussels. Me and Avery kept the fires going on the beach." I didn't say anything.

"My mother said Johnny tried to joke his way out of it. Told his brother he was going to pay him back. Johnny must have cheated him out of his half. Then Avery's father cocked the pistol and pointed it at Johnny, and Johnny started laughing. He was always laughing. My mother said there was only three or four other people in the place besides the bartender, and when Chet pointed the gun everyone left. But the jukebox kept playing right along.

"My mother said she didn't think Avery's father would shoot. She'd known Johnny for a long time and there had been arguments before. But Johnny must have been worried this time because he grabbed Avery out of where he was sitting and held him up in front. 'Now, Chet,' he said, 'you wouldn't hurt your boy. I know you better than that.'

"Chet shot Johnny right in the middle of his forehead and blew the top of his head off. My mother had to wipe Avery off with a bar towel; he had blood and brains all over him. Then Avery's father ran out and they caught him later." Leroy finished the 6 O'CLOCK for the time of the meeting and went on, "My mother took me to the funeral but Avery didn't come."

"Don't tell anybody," Leroy said. I nodded. But Grammy asked me what I had been whispering to my mother after dinner, and I had to tell her too.

My grandmother said she wouldn't come if Avery came, but Mrs. Hughes said he always found the most mushrooms, so she came and he came too, walking behind, carrying his lard bucket with Ruthie.

The streetcars didn't come fast enough to catch you, and no one ever looked, crossing the rails, but we had to be careful when we got to the next sets of tracks because there were so many trains now. There was too much water under the trestle, so we had to go over the top to get to the mud flats. The three of us pretended we'd never been down here in our lives, Avery looking around as if we hadn't dragged the ties over this part of the track. He could pretend better than anyone I'd ever seen. He liked to say he was sent to keep Aunt May company until Sammy came home again and he got to stay up late and do what he wanted and him and Aunt May got along like two peas in a pod. Grammy said the only reason he was next door was because Aunt May was tricked into taking him. "He belongs in reform school is where he belongs," she'd say. And we could hear the yelling through the wall when he did something, and he was always doing something. But he didn't know he was going to be sent away if he didn't get better grades in school. I knew, because Grammy had been telling Aunt May that she wasn't doing Avery any favors by keeping him when he could be out working somewhere or selling newspapers if nothing else.

Just as we were ready to cross the tracks, a train came. It came fast, tooting its horn, and we ran back to the streetcar tracks. It was a trainload of soldiers that hung out the windows and cheered when Avery and then Ruthie stood at attention and saluted as the dozens of cars passed by.

Then we ran for it, the rails still vibrating from the train through our shoes, and got to the other side and between the barbed-wire strands that were stretched so you could loop them up. Then past the stands of eucalyptus that smelled like cough drops, to where the new grass had come up.

We spread out then, and the first time that Ruthie picked a toadstool, Mrs. Hughes and Grammy both yelled at her. She dropped it, fast. "That's poison," Mrs. Hughes said. Grammy yelled, "You'll turn purple and we'll have to put you in a hole in the ground and let the big worms eat you." The good ones were all over, and we started filling our buckets. Mrs. Hughes was picking miner's lettuce too, because Aunt May didn't like her and wouldn't trade winter cabbage. Grammy and Mrs. Hughes talked as they went along. Avery had filled his bucket and was helping Ruthie. He didn't even look, much less wander, over to where he had the railroad ties and the lumber hidden for his boat. You could see the way the canals turned like a twisted old jump rope all the way to the airport.

Trains kept passing, the noise or the blasts of wind making the leaves come down from the trees like knife blades. The mushrooms got sparse then, and we had to keep walking. Only Ruthie and Avery had full buckets, and he started helping me then. I didn't care if he did or not. He had laughed at recess today when Leroy pushed me down. Another boy crawled behind me and Leroy pushed me over his back. Avery laughed with everyone else. I wanted to kick him.

We had to go all the way down to the crossing to fill all our buckets. Cars had lined up to get by as soon as the train passed. When we got near, we could see the old car on the tracks. A man got out and opened one side of the hood and looked under. "It's a '31 Plymouth coupe," I heard Avery say to Ruthie, like she knew one car from the other. Then the man went back and opened the rumble seat and got some tools out and went back to the front.

I heard the horn of the next train; it was still way down the track. If the man heard the horn, he didn't move any faster, just kept working under the hood, stopping to wipe his hands on a red rag and light up a cigarette. We were close enough that I could see the green part of the Lucky Strike pack in his shirt pocket.

When the train pulling a string of boxcars was coming down the track fast, the noise so loud you couldn't hear yourself think, he wiped his hands off again and took four or five quick steps down the track and started waving his hat by the brim in a circle over his head to stop the train, stepping slow toward the locomotive.

I didn't close my eyes, but I didn't see anything anyhow because Grammy put her big hand over my face. When I pulled away the train had just hit the car and started pushing it down the track in front of the cowcatcher. There was so much noise: the train wheels braking against the rails, shooting sparks; the horn; and the sound the car made as it crumbled to pieces.

The train finally stopped and we all rushed back the way we'd come, toward the mud flats. Ruthie dropped her bucket; Mrs. Hughes picked her up. All of us running, Avery at the end. As I looked, he turned back and started running in the other direction, doubling back toward the middle of the train, faster, and I was yelling Avery, Avery, but couldn't stop because Grammy had my hand, and he disappeared under the train.

On report card day I didn't see Avery and he didn't come home. Grammy had already been over to Aunt May's to show her mine with all A's and all Excellents. When Avery finally came home we heard the shouting. "Stupid. How can you be so dumb? You dummy. Sammy never got an F in his life. Get out of my sight. Get out in the garden and loosen the soil around the potatoes. Get going. I'll decide if you're going to stay when I'm good and ready."

When I went out in the backyard and climbed the fence, I couldn't see Avery. He wasn't working. The shed door wasn't open; he didn't have any tools out. I got down and went back and down the street to the corner and then over alongside the railroad track.

The trouble was, Avery wouldn't listen. When Miss Walker would say something for us to do, he'd do the opposite. Read pages in our reader, he did his spelling. When we were supposed to do our United States history he'd do his arithmetic. Or draw battleships. He never listened. Or he played tic-tac-toe with Arnold, or fooled around with Leroy. You have to pay attention in the classroom. I told him that. He knew. He didn't want any help. They were going to keep him back in the fifth grade again.

I was going to have to run under the trestle, under the train tracks. The ties looked like a sewer grate way up in the air overhead, but you could see rectangles of the sky turning gray now that the sun was behind the Coast Range. There was no water, and I ran as fast as I could through the cement tunnel and out the other end. It was hard going through there when it was almost dark, but it was worse going over the tracks.

Avery had to be somewhere, and I walked all the way out into the marsh, and then all the way to the canal where the boat was. He had got the ties in the water, nailed together with two-by-fours.

He wasn't there either. I went where he hid the tools, but they were still there. He'd got the hammer, saw, and crowbar at the accident when the man got killed by the train. He had been a carpenter, it said in the paper, and belonged to Local 484. Avery got the nails, too, when he went back to pick them up. Everything in the rumble seat had spread out along the track when the engine crashed into the Plymouth. It was a miracle, Avery told me, because nails were so hard to get now with the war. My Grammy said the carpenter must have been crazy or drunk to think he could wave down a train that was traveling that fast. It took a mile for a train to even slow down, Mrs. Hughes said, much less stop, once the brake was put on.

It was getting darker now. He was going to have to go back where he came from. I knew that. Aunt May wouldn't keep him after this. She was going to phone for them to come for him. He should have paid attention, that's what school is for. Not just reading, writing, and arithmetic, but to pay attention.

I got through the barbed-wire fence again without catching my coat or braids on the wire. I slowed down walking because a train was coming; it was dark enough to see the light before I could hear the sound of the engine. I wasn't about to go near that trestle with those wheels coming down the track. Then I thought I was seeing things, but it was Avery, sitting in the middle of the trestle. That was the shape of his head, when he was wearing his sailor cap. It couldn't be, but it was him. I started thinking of the carpenter. I never saw him get hit, and didn't think about it much anymore. But it was like before, except it was dark and it was Avery on the tracks. He sat like he was at his desk at school, his legs dangling between two ties of the trestle, facing the train. I couldn't help myself. I kept getting closer. They never tooted the whistle on the train, just went fast on the straightaway. Avery told me once that trains could go a hundred miles an hour sometimes, if the tracks were level and they weren't pulling a lot of cars.

I couldn't yell out; it was no use anyway. The noise was already here, the train almost on top of him and his sailor cap, the light beam already past him and showing up the track ahead. I hoped he was happy now, smashed flat like a penny on the rails. I wanted to yell, Are you satisfied now, Avery, are you, but I couldn't open my mouth. There was nothing I could do.

The train went over him. Right over him. I started waving as if at the engineer or Pullmans full of soldiers, waving and waving to say good-bye to Avery. When the caboose's red light disappeared, I had to go under the trestle to get back to my street.

He was sitting down there in a puddle of water, laughing. Avery was. When he saw me he tried to stop. I couldn't believe my eyes. The carpenter had been cut in three pieces and ground up like a sausage, Grammy said.

"I dropped down between the ties. I thought I could hold on until the train passed, then lift myself back up," he said. "I've seen some big boys do it. But I couldn't hold on. You should have heard, Mary Maureen. You should have heard."

I wanted to give him a good kick in the pants and yell at him, You are a stupid boy. But I just stepped over him. He tried to get up, but he had hurt his ankle. When he got to his hands and knees I helped him up, but he limped. "I didn't see any sparks from the wheels because my eyes closed and wouldn't open again," he said.

I didn't say anything. It was like hearing a ghost talk. Avery should be dead. But he was alive. He was never going to learn. The train should have taken him.

Burn day was the third Friday of the month, and Avery always lit the fire for Aunt May. "With saving newspapers and everything else for the paper drives, they shouldn't have any trash left to burn," my Grammy always said. "Why do they have to burn and fill everyone's house with smoke?" Because the dried-up weeds, cornstalks, and the rest from Aunt May's victory garden were in a pile higher than I was, is what I thought, but I never said that, of course. "We used to haul that off," she'd say. She let us go and sit on the fence to watch because it was Friday night and we didn't have any school tomorrow.

Avery was standing out there leaning on his pitchfork watching the sparks rise up. There must have been a lot of green weeds in that pile because there was a lot of smoke, and it didn't burn fast. It got dark and Grammy came out to watch from the gate.

There was no wind and it hadn't rained for a week, but the fire wouldn't burn, and Avery started poking the pile with the pitchfork when Aunt May yelled from the back porch. At exactly 7:30 the streetcar passed, filled; no one seemed to sleep at night anymore. It was past dark now, but I could see the yellow-and-green car like a big butterfly trying to leave the ground, swaying, the bell clanging, sailors and people going to work hanging on, as it was starting to raise up.

The stars were out again, and I was looking up to see if I could find the Big Dipper when the air-raid siren went off. The streetlights went off at the same time the searchlights went on, and the night fighters took off at the airport.

Aunt May could move quicker than I thought. She was carrying a spade and she started shoveling dirt into the fire. "Run," she yelled to Avery, "run and turn off the lights in the house." I ran too, past Grammy, who went out to help with her washbasin full of water. I got to the house and turned off the lights fast, before they came, and let my mother sleep.

When I ran back, the fire looked brighter if anything. It had caught and was blazing, sparks going up to the sky for a mile. Aunt May was shoveling so fast sometimes she wasn't even getting any dirt, just some dust that blew away when she threw it on the fire. I remembered the front porch light then and ran back. You couldn't see it from the back, but you could see it from the street. When they patrolled, if they saw any light during an air raid, even through a blackout curtain, they started banging on the windows. The air-raid wardens would smash a light out if they could get at it. I turned off the porch light and went back.

Avery was shoveling dirt as fast as he could, and Grammy was scooping up dirt with her basin. I watched as she threw a load that fell mostly on her shoes, and the fire leaped up like she was putting gasoline on it.

"Get a hose, get a hose," Aunt May was yelling at Avery. The fire was in the wrong part of the lot for the hose to reach. Avery dragged it as far as it stretched, but it never came close. It was awful quiet now; the fire didn't even make a noise. The siren had stopped. I could only hear my own breath coming out my nose.

I thought of our hose in the wash shed, then ran past Avery and yelled come on to him. We ran though the gate; Ruthie was still sitting on the fence, watching. I unlatched the door and went in. It was too dark but I felt the wash trays and found the light switch and gave it a flick just to see for a second. First I saw Avery's face; he was holding his breath and feeling with the flat of his hand over his shirt pocket. Then I saw what he was looking at. Michael's big foot, hanging down from the trapdoor in the ceiling. It disappeared. I was still staring when Grammy came running back with her basin still half full of dirt.

"What are you doing in here?" she yelled. "What?" I couldn't think what I was doing there. I could still see Michael's size 14 shoe. Avery was trying to say *hose* but couldn't get past *ho, ho, ho,* pointing at the coil of black rubber hose hanging from a nail. Grammy turned off the light then as I grabbed the hose. And we were running again. The fire truck was already there, dousing the bonfire, and the air-raid wardens in their white helmets and armbands, the police with their clubs out, and two jeeps of soldiers with their rifles.

"It's still Friday," Aunt May was saying to the chief warden, "it's burn day."

"It doesn't matter what day it is; you're signaling to the enemy bombers." I always liked to watch things like this to see how they ended. When my mother argued with my Grammy and I'd have to go outside, hearing it through the door wasn't the same as seeing it happen before your own eyes. I would have liked to see when they found the carpenter who got run over by the train, too.

I didn't see Avery around anywhere and went back into the dark. He was laid out on his back, Ruthie was holding one of his hands, and the other was over his shirt pocket like he was saluting the flag. He didn't make a sound.

I didn't understand what was wrong until a soldier came by with his blackout flashlight that showed blue and I saw the pitchfork tine coming through the top of Avery's foot. Aunt May saw and started yelling, "I told him at least a hundred times, lean the pitchfork against the fence or stick it in the ground. A hundred times I told him."

"This is going to hurt you more than it's going to hurt me," the soldier said. He had the pitchfork by the handle. Avery was smiling when the soldier gave the handle a yank.

Daddy always included Aunt May and Avery, so they sat in the back with me and Grammy, and Ruthie got to sit in the front with my mother and father. The car was already out of the garage, and my father went back in to get the shovels and sacks. We were pointed at the wash shed. My mother looked distracted, like she was thinking what she had to do before she went to work, but this was Sunday so she didn't have to go to the plant, and my father didn't have to leave until five o'clock.

I was on Grammy's lap and could see her reflection in the window. She was looking at the wash shed door as if she could see through it. Avery was watching Abner, who was chained up and blinking at the sun. I almost forgot and touched my hair. Grammy had already slapped my hands hard twice this morning. She sat straight, and her legs were bony to sit on.

My father got into the car, adjusted his hat, and fired up the Packard. It was the same car he'd driven all the way from Tennessee to California, four times. It was old then and older now, but he kept it running. My Grammy said he could take it apart and put it back together in his sleep. He was handy. He could fix nearly anything, go over and repair Aunt May's sewing machine, go over when the toilet got backed up or the gas furnace wouldn't go on. Anything. "How much do I owe you?" Aunt May would say.

"You'll get my bill in the mail," he'd say. And they'd both think that was funny too. It was the only time she'd let any of us in her house except to use the phone.

My father was foreman now at the shipyard. Aunt May said to Grammy he'd own the place before he was through. I noticed he could never sit for long; he had to be up doing something. Fix the toaster so the bread would pop up higher. Or do two things at once, read the paper and listen to the radio. Or he'd tell stories about back home that were better than the radio. We'd all pay attention, even Avery. Especially when he was driving; it was as if the steering wheel was a knob on a radio and he was tuning himself in so his voice was clear enough for us to hear. He started one now.

"You remember back home when that girl had the spell? Her folks lived over behind the grain store."

My mother nodded. Grammy said, "In the two-story house."

"Happened last night at work. Welder had a spell, fell backwards off a scaffold. Not high up. Some of the boys got to him first, put the handle of a screwdriver between his teeth before he broke them all to pieces."

"That girl could talk as good as ever. It was just luck you were there, Dennis," Grammy said, "or she would have choked to death."

"What did you do?" Aunt May asked.

"I'd just come back from the hardware store for lunch. I had two pounds of eight-penny nails in my hand to start nailing boards on that rabbit hutch. She went down right in front of the house, on the sidewalk. I thought she'd just slipped or one of the other kids with her pushed her down. But she started to make that noise they make. I ran. I got her jaw open and could see she had swallowed her tongue. She was already choking. I couldn't have got it with, say, a four-penny or even a six. An eight did fine; stuck it right through and was able to yank it back where it was supposed to be."

"Her father came by later," Grammy said, "told me Dennis saved her life. Their name was Williams. The daughter's name was Clara. She couldn't sing in the choir after that, though; she'd get spit all over everyone."

Aunt May started laughing. "It wasn't funny if you were standing next to her," Grammy said, trying not to join in.

We all watched through the windshield as the car got to the top of the grade and reached Skyline Road and started slowing down. There were a few other cars ahead, and people standing around with their shovels. We were out of town and up in the hills, in the country. We were high enough so we could look down and see the blue water of the bay to the other side. The San Mateo bridge going across, Coyote Point covered with eucalyptus trees that looked like they were growing up out of the water. Then the airport runways. And Highway 101 cutting across the mud flats where Avery's raft was hidden. The tracks. San Bruno.

We got out of the car and stood around. This whole hillside had belonged to the Japanese flower growers, before they were taken away. Aunt May put one hand on my shoulder. Even with her canes and braces she had trouble on uneven ground. We waited until my father came back. "As far as anyone knows," he said, "we can go help ourselves." We were the first in the field, and we started digging. There were more gladiolus bulbs than you could count. Every shovelful of dirt filled the bottom of a bucket with them, some as big around as an apple. I emptied them into a gunnysack.

Aunt May turned over as much ground and as fast as my father. I could barely keep up. There must have been a whole hillside of field, and more and more people came as we filled our sacks. I could only half remember when the flowers were in bloom, driving by red, pink, white, and orange sections that looked like the design on the quilt on Grammy's bed. My mother had a little flower garden in front, and some in back, just by the porch and the drive and the back stairs. She got most of the cuttings and bulbs from Aunt May. But my mother never spent much time out there, and if I didn't cut some flowers, the mums or zinnias, we'd never have any inside the house. But I'd hear her talking about it with her friends from the plant. Ruthie and me would meet her at the streetcar stop sometimes and walk her home, and she'd be going on about her flower garden, the pleasure she got from it, as if it was all she did when she got home, instead of go to sleep. "You should see the roses," and she'd name them. But our rosebushes were in back and she hadn't been out there in months. I couldn't cut them because the aphids were so thick even the red ones looked white.

These glads were free, as many as we wanted. Aunt May wouldn't stop, even after everyone else was standing by the car. I stayed with Avery, who kept filling the buckets up when there were no more sacks. Then he cleaned a bulb off on his sleeve and took a bite out of the white pulp. I laughed at him. I didn't know if he was pretending or not. But Aunt May saw him too. "Don't play the fool," she yelled, and he spit it out. Everyone was looking at him.

My father came back a little ways and called out, "We're hardly going to have room for us, May." She turned over one more shovelful and we picked every one out. The Japs wouldn't care how many we took because they weren't here anymore to take care of the flowers. They were in prison now.

We drove back the other way, past the national cemetery. There must have been two miles of white headstones behind the fence and under where the big flag was flying. I didn't want to ask if they were from this war or not. But I got the feeling they were. They had to put the bodies somewhere. I couldn't help thinking of Sammy because he was in the Pacific. Aunt May must be thinking of him too. But at the same time I was thinking of Michael, like my mother and father must have been and Grammy must have been.

Michael had tried to enlist that Sunday when the Japs pulled the sneak attack on Pearl Harbor. We'd already eaten our oatmeal with raisins that Grammy put in on Sunday. He had been sitting at the table soldering on something, keeping the iron white-hot over the gas burner. My mother ran for my father, who was in the garage, in the pit working on the Packard. When he came in they started repeating again on the radio, "At 8:15 A.M., the first wave of Japanese planes . . ."

Sammy came in, then Aunt May. "Did you hear that, did you hear that?" Sammy kept saying.

"I'm going to join up," Michael said. He was going around looking for his shoes. We all used to laugh because Michael's feet were so big and he had the habit of slipping off his loafers wherever he was and then he couldn't find them. The joke was his shoes were size 14EE and should be easy to see.

"Now, don't go off half cocked here," my father said.

"I'm going to join up too," Sammy said.

"No you're not," Aunt May said. "You're going to work tomorrow." Sammy was on the first shift at Swift's.

"And you have to finish school," Grammy said to Michael. He was a senior and was going to graduate in June. Sammy had quit high school when we first came, to get a job. He was almost two years older than my brother. Michael had taught Sammy about radios, and both had their own call numbers and licenses. They talked to people in Brazil one night on their shortwave.

When Michael found his shoes—they were under the couch—it was my mother who said, "Do you know where you're even going? There's no place to enlist in this town." He listened to her, even if she wasn't his mother, where Grammy, who raised him, he never paid any attention to. You'd have to be told that he wasn't her son, the way he acted around my mother. Of course he didn't look like her, he had blue eyes and long arms, but he called her Mother most of the time, hardly ever her name, Dora. Grammy would always explain that Michael was my father's first wife's son.

"We can go to the city," Michael said. "The Federal Building has a place; I saw it when I went to get my radio license." Grammy started wailing then, and my mother had to take her upstairs.

After President Roosevelt spoke, things quieted down and I finished reading the rest of the funny papers to Ruthie. All the visitors went home. And Michael and Sammy, with their clothes in valises and a big lunch my mother made, took the streetcar to the city to enlist.

We kept the radio on all day. My mother ironed in the front room. Grammy stayed upstairs. And my father went back outside to finish putting the Packard together. Mrs. Hughes came over twice in the afternoon, once to tell us the Japanese had landed in San Diego, California, and another time to change that to she'd heard from an old neighbor that they were in Seattle and the Hawaiian Islands had fallen.

It got dark early in December, and we had our lights on by five o'clock. Had Sunday dinner just like always. My father had killed one of the old roosters and we had fried chicken, mashed potatoes, and gravy. My mother had made bread pudding too, my favorite. The radio was still on, something my mother never allowed while we ate, and we were going to listen to our programs if they came on later. An announcer kept coming on saying, "We interrupt this program . . ." and everyone stopped eating and turned to the radio until my mother got up and switched it off. We were almost done eating and thinking about dessert when the lights went out. My father was ready, because back in Tennessee they had storms and he knew what to do. He had a kerosene lamp lit in a minute, and a candle in the bathroom.

It was my turn to dry, but it was too dark for my mother to wash the dishes, so we just all sat down. There was no electricity and no radio. Ruthie wanted to play with her dolls, so I did, dressing and undressing them. It was almost time for bed when the siren went off, loud, at the airport. No one knew what it was for until Aunt May yelled through the wall that it was an air-raid warning. My father made me and Ruthie get under the dining room table. Grammy, who was in her room, tried to come down the stairs in the dark and fell headfirst the whole way. My father had to turn on the lantern. Her knee was already starting to swell up big. My father wanted to take her to the hospital, but she wouldn't go.

We never got into our pajamas; we slept on blankets downstairs. Even the trains stopped running. Except for when the siren went on again, or when airplanes came over, it was quiet.

I thought I'd stayed awake, but when Michael and Sammy came in at one o'clock I woke up for sure. "It was a madhouse," Sammy kept saying. "You couldn't get in the door."

"We gave them our names and addresses," Michael said. "They're going to let us know. I told the sergeant how many words I could send a minute, and he said the Army could use me."

Grammy's knee got better enough to walk on because of hot compresses and soaking it in Epsom salts. They never called Michael or Sammy. Michael went back to San Mateo High School and Sammy went to South City to Swift's every morning.

Michael kept saying when we heard the news on the radio, "If they don't take me pretty soon, it'll be over before we get there. We won't get our licks in." He crossed the numbers off the calendar day by day. When he did hear from the government, it was to find out he was too young and had to wait.

Sammy had bad teeth and had to have them fixed before they'd take him.

Michael fretted; he couldn't even sit still to fix a radio for the appliance store he worked at. It was almost the end of June when Sammy came over yelling, excited, that they were going to be taking boys from town. In a week's time both Michael and Sammy got their draft notices to report. One of Sammy's girlfriends' fathers was on the draft board. They grabbed each other by the shoulder and danced around the front room, shaking the whole house.

The night before they left, my dad took them uptown to Noonan's and bought them both a shot of whiskey. He must have talked to them there, but he was still talking to them when they got back home to eat dinner. They had drunk whiskey before. I'd seen them both sick as dogs. When we sat down to eat, Aunt May was invited too. My father changed the subject to the Army. When he told about the Army everyone listened, because he had been a staff sergeant.

"You boys have to understand that the Army is made up of men just like you, from the generals to the privates. And when an officer or noncommissioned officer tells you something, it's for your own good. They're not going to tell you to do something they wouldn't do themselves. If they tell you to dig a hole," and he tapped the handle of his fork on the tabletop, "you dig, because it may save your life. And you dig it deep too, as deep as you have time for. And don't you ever snicker, talk funny, or make signs behind an officer's back. Ever. Because they'll find out, and then you'll be in trouble.

"And don't lag behind when your officer says fix bayonets. You stay right up there, shoulder to shoulder with the other men in your platoon, so no one gets an enemy thrust in the back. It's natural to be scared with the noise from the explosions of artillery shells and the screams of the wounded, but you can overcome that. And you don't let your friends down; whatever you do, never let another soldier down. Because they're your family now, out there in no-man's-land. Your family. Do you understand that?" They both nodded. I noticed Sammy's eyes were red. "If you let your family down, that's the finish, the end of you as a man. You're not worth anything."

The next morning they left, and we all walked to the streetcar station and waved good-bye.

Sammy wrote from San Diego the first week, and Aunt May read us the letter. In the confusion after they were sworn in, he lost track of Michael. He was in boot camp in San Diego and was going to get into radio school. It was the Navy that took them both, so my father talking about the Army didn't do them any good. Later Grammy got a letter from Michael, who was in Louisiana.

I had the dreams. And then I'd wake up listening to the dark, my ear toward the wash shed. It was Abner. The sound he made when he moved and the chain clinked. In the daytime I couldn't look toward the shed anymore, or go farther than the big crack in the cement on the driveway. It was only when I woke up in the night that I could turn that way, and I always saw the shoe. Avery knew but he didn't say anything. He didn't look like he knew, but he did.

He let me come with him now when he worked on the raft. Let me nail when I wanted. Sometimes. Made Ruthie take off her shoes and socks so she wouldn't have mud on them when we went home. Took the new potatoes from the garden and showed us how to cook them over the coals of a fire. We ate them, burning our mouths.

I wanted to say something to him but I didn't have the words. Not about Michael in the shed. I hoped he'd ask me when he was ready to sail away. He'd have to ask me. I'd go. I'd go. It was me that found that wood for the deck and the cabin.

I went to the mud flats by myself now, just to sit down on the bank above the raft. I didn't care if my Grammy caught me; I just did what I wanted. Just like Avery. You could ask him why he did things and he'd just look at you like he did Miss Walker. "Answer me," she'd yell, her face turning red, everyone quiet now, watching the door to see if Miss Cameron was coming, or the principal.

I came and told him about the wood. I thought they were some kind of doors by the size of them. "Plywood," he said, "it's plywood." I had never heard of it. They were heavy, and we each took one end. He got Ruthie to go under and walk bent over to let the middle rest on her back. We got all seven pieces to the raft that way.

We started trying to measure them for putting on top of the railroad ties. You could bend them in half, but you couldn't break one. But the plywood cut easier than a board with the saw. We worked on that raft hard, and I never once even looked like I wanted to ask about going when it was finished. But he knew I wanted to go.

I couldn't pay attention anymore in class, either. Miss Walker was always yelling at me to wake up. She had me stand in the corner with my back to the class. Leroy kept shooting spit wads through a milk straw, hitting me in the neck, and the class laughed each time, all because I wasn't paying attention. I wasn't listening when it was my turn to read. And I didn't turn in my paper. And I left my arithmetic book at home. Avery didn't laugh. He didn't seem to notice. It was like I had caught the impetigo from him too, but instead of scratching my sores until they bled, I was pulling out my hair. Single strands that I'd curl around my finger and put in my mouth and eat. I couldn't stop.

I went over to Aunt May's when she yelled over the fence that we had a phone call. My mother was up, and Ruthie came too. Avery was standing there at ease; he had explained how to do it, his arms behind him, hands clasped and his feet fourteen inches apart, looking straight ahead.

My mother picked up the phone and listened. She wasn't pretty. Some of the other girls in my class had mothers who were. But not mine. She needed glasses because of the war work at the factory and squinted all the time now. She looked like she was always staring into the sun. She didn't wear lipstick or rouge. And when she used to wear the dresses Grammy made, you couldn't tell the front from the back. Now, with wool slacks and a shirt on, she looked like a little man. She forgot to comb her hair sometimes and it hung in rattails. And the big varicose veins on her legs she got carrying me and Ruthie got bigger from standing in the plant for twelve hours, and she had to put salve on when she came home. And her teeth: Grammy said, "Thank goodness the girls didn't inherit them."

"Dennis, I can't leave now; the kids are home. Your mother had a spell and she's laying down. No, we didn't have a disagreement." She listened for a while more, then hung up the phone. "That was Dennis," she said to Aunt May, who was sitting in her chair, her legs up on a footstool and a blue-and-white flannel blanket hiding them. "A refrigerator ship docked at the yard and has to be unloaded before they can repair the damage. He says there's forty thousand pounds of real butter they're going to throw over the side. I can't go up there, I don't have the strength, and then go to work after."

Aunt May was all dolled up like she always was. She used more makeup in a day than my mother did in a year. "What if Mary Maureen and Avery went up and took his wagon? On the streetcar," Aunt May added.

My mother looked over at Avery, who kept looking straight ahead. She didn't hate him like Grammy did. When we pieced between meals, she always gave him some if he was there. She put the purple medicine on his head when he got impetigo, after she shaved around the sores, then cut the top off one of her old silk stockings and sewed one end shut so he could wear it over his head. Avery always washed the vegetables for her and gave her the good ones, besides the ones that Aunt May wanted to trade.

"May, do you think they'll let him on with the wagon? Why not some shopping bags?"

"How much can they carry? If the conductor will let them on down here, he has to let them come back. Have you ever seen what a load he can put on that wagon?"

I had to change my dress, and my mother redid my braids. Ruthie was crying because she couldn't go. My mother gave me a nickel knotted in the bottom of my handkerchief to put in my pocket to phone if we got lost, and tokens for the streetcar. Avery combed his wave so it looked like Sammy's and wore his sailor cap on the back of his head. My mother walked us down to the streetcar station and lifted the end of the Radio Flyer when the car stopped, so Avery could pull it on from the handle, like they did it every day.

The car was empty; it was Saturday, only a few sailors. Neither the conductor nor the driver said one word. I was all ready to tell them I knew Mrs. Hughes, but it wasn't necessary. I sat down, but Avery didn't sit with me. He took a place farther forward.

When we passed the racetrack I could see over the rows of stables to the grandstand and the infield where the pond used to be. There were sailors running in squares, wearing their white T-shirts and blue denims, with their heads shaved. They ran in their groups, one after another, around and around the track. I thought of all the times I'd said, "Michael is in the Navy. My brother is going to the Pacific to kill Japs. Michael will be a hero. We have the blue star on the red, white, and blue field in our window, like Aunt May. Michael is in uniform." Michael is in the shed. In the backyard of our house. A deserter. Draft-dodger Michael. Grammy knows. I know. Avery knows. Does my mother? Does my father?

The last time I took the streetcar was last summer. Gladys was living in a stable at the racetrack. We went to the city because we had to shop. They were putting barbed wire up that day to keep the Japs inside Tanforan. From the streetcar I could see down past the fence into the rows of stables. The Japs were standing around the clothesline, and the mothers were taking down sheets that sailed like kites in the wind. The men were wearing jackets and hats and were smoking. And between where two rows of stables met, there were girls jumping rope. I saw Gladys, who was watching the streetcar go by. I started yelling out the open window, "Gladys, Gladys," waving my hand. She'd sat beside me in third grade, knew her multiplication tables up to twelve, lived up past the school, and I had gone to her birthday party.

My mother grabbed me by the arm. "Quit that."

"It's Gladys."

"Stop it, sit down now." Gladys hadn't waved back if she'd heard. The war had only been going on since December then, but there were still no school clothes to buy in the city. That seemed like years and years ago.

We rattled on up the Peninsula toward the city. You couldn't see the tall buildings. Avery was pretending he was alone. Not with me. "Avery," I said, not loud, "Avery," but he wouldn't turn his head back. I always thought the Peninsula was like the glass on a thermometer, where the red bulb at the bottom is the city, and the rest is down where we live. I always expected when we got there it'd be different, San Francisco. Different besides the buildings and all the extra people on Market Street. But it's the same people as anywhere else, and the big buildings are stone, and nobody lives in them. And it's not as fun because there's nothing to buy.

Avery was watching the barrage balloons like they were airplanes and you could tell one from another. They looked like big grubs to me. I moved up to the seat behind him. Whispered, "They look like flying grubs to me." He didn't answer or turn his head. He was pretending I wasn't there. I could see the little round scars on the back of his head where the impetigo was. He had others too, one long, the length of my finger, on his neck and some shorter ones, like wrinkles.

He had the Flyer between two seats across from us, and you couldn't even see it. His cap was on the seat beside him, folded like they do to keep the part you can see clean. Sammy showed us all the tricks when he came home.

Sammy wouldn't have become a radio operator if it weren't for Michael. He's the one that showed Sammy how to do it. Michael was making radios at my age, and had his license, the youngest in the state of Tennessee. There was no thinking about Michael. I would like to ask him something. Go into the shed and say, Michael, I know you're up there and not in the U.S. Navy. But then what would I say? And worse, what would *he* say? What would I do if he wouldn't answer? I stopped thinking.

We got off where we were supposed to and went the right way. It wasn't far. Neither of us had been there before, but there were street names in the cement at each corner. I walked behind Avery and his wagon. It was noisy with the traffic; you couldn't think. People were going back and forth. I could see the dock cranes, and we went faster. We waited for a green light to get across the street, one so wide that I couldn't see across it. There were big railroad boxcars going down the middle on tracks, pushed by a little machine no bigger than the handcars you sometimes saw on the tracks at home, with men pumping them. There were clanging bells and you could feel the ground moving under your toes. Avery took my hand when I couldn't move, and we ran when the light turned green, the wagon making a racket behind us.

Pop was waiting for us at the gate and picked me up off the ground like he hadn't seen me in a long time. He gave Avery's hand a shake, then looked over the wagon. He took us, walking slow now, around a big warehouse. Then there were the ships. Some were right at the wharf, so close you couldn't see them all, floating there like steel wedges. How could they float in water, if they were made of steel? There were others out in the bay, tied to orange buoys, all colored gray like a rainy sky with bows as sharp as knives. I didn't ask what kind they were.

I knew I was never going to go in the Navy, even if they were taking Waves now. I didn't even like to rinse off and get water up my nose when Grammy washed my hair. And she'd been yelling at me too because she said I was going bald from pulling hairs out of my head. How could I go on the raft with Avery then? There was a thought again. A raft has to have water to go anywhere. A person couldn't get away from that. But I was going on that raft when it came to it. I didn't care.

My father stopped and pointed. "See that cruiser there? It was half sunk at Midway, and it's ready to go back out to sea." The wagon rattled like the wheels were going to come off, going over the cables and hoses strung out like tree roots all over. He stopped again. "There's a Russian freighter that a tugboat brought in last week. Broke down in the Pacific. A sitting duck. It's almost ready to go."

"There she is," Pop said. You couldn't miss the butter ship. There were cranes taking nets loaded with boxes out of the middle. The refrigerator ship was tilted away from the docks so much it seemed like it might roll over. When we got closer I saw the gash in the side like a big rip across the front of your jacket. Pieces of wrinkled metal and pipes hung loose. You could count the decks like shelves in a cabinet. "Got rammed in a convoy, had to come all the way back alone. They saved it, ballast to port, and kept it from taking on water. That would have sunk her. Good captain. He brought her and the butter home safe," he said.

"What happened to the other ship?" I asked. I had to speak my thought or it would drive me crazy. I would have to know the answer before it would go away.

"It was a destroyer; they're designed to ram. Probably didn't even scratch the paint. At least it never came back here to be repaired." It made me think, if just another ship, hitting, could do this, what could a bomb do to our house? Or a bullet to your head?

The butter boxes were on wooden pallets, forty-eight squares in a waxed cardboard case with metal bands around. Pop loaded the wagon; he got four boxes on and one on top. Avery hopped around like he was doing the most work, holding the wagon still, shifting the boxes just so, giving them pats with the palm of his hand. As soon as my father said, "That'll do her," Avery whipped a length of clothesline rope he had ready over the top and tied and tied his knots.

We had to wait for my father behind a building while he phoned to make sure which gate we were to leave through. I looked around. Over by the time clock a white sheet was hung up on wires with big print across the top, THANK YOU THANK YOU, then row after row of people's names. Then at the bottom it said, YOURS TRULY, ADOLPH HITLER AND TOJO. There was another sheet farther on that said, ABSENTEEISM HURTS THE WAR EFFORT. I saw Leroy's father's name with *five days missed out of the month* after it, then two Gormans with eleven days each missing. I was surprised because I thought most of Avery's family was in prison. I didn't tell him I knew, and I never planned to. There were no Mitchums up there, of course.

I turned away when Avery looked back at me to see where I was. He was standing at parade rest now, which was like at ease, but stiffer, in front of the wagon. There were other signs and posters, some stenciled on the walls. LOOSE LIPS SINK SHIPS. GIVE BLOOD. BUY BONDS. I'd never seen so many people in my life, not at a Sunday ball game at the park or at the longest parade I ever went to, all working on the ships. Women too, grinding, riveting, drilling, carrying lunch boxes. Hanging from ladders while they welded, sending millions of Fourth of July sparkles down the sides of the ships.

I wandered over to where the gangplank from the Russian ship came down to the pier. There was no one around. The thick ropes that held the rusty ship sagged in the water like they weren't doing anything, as if the ship was stuck in the still, greasy water.

While I was standing there trying to make out the lettering in the ship's name, Avery came over, lifting the front part of the wagon over the cables. He couldn't stand it, not knowing what I was doing. "I've never seen letters like that," I told him.

"Maybe they were drinking, to make the letters backwards like that," he said. For some reason that made me laugh, and I was laughing when I noticed five big men standing behind us, wearing overalls, hats, and thick sweaters. We were standing in their way and I pointed for Avery. When he looked he got startled and lost his footing on a hose and fell backward.

The men were all smiling and one said something and picked Avery up like a doll. Held him out under the arms while another man picked up his cap and combed back his hair with his fingers and put the cap back on his head. One said something and pointed up at the ship. I didn't nod, and Avery was still hanging there, not moving, but a Russian picked me up and two others, one in front and the other in back, lifted the wagon, and we were all going up the gangplank.

I was so surprised I didn't know what to say. They carried us right up onto the deck of the ship and never put us down. The man who was carrying me had me like my mother used to carry Ruthie, my rump on his hip, his arm across my middle. They didn't put us down but carried us right into a room inside the ship that had tables and chairs and put the wagon up on the table and sat us on the edge, our feet resting on a bench. I looked over at Avery and saw he didn't know what to make of this either. I tried to pretend I didn't care. What was going to happen when my father came back and we weren't there?

More men came into the room and they were all talking. Another brought a tray with two white mugs of steaming tea and thick slices of bread and cherry jam. Avery started eating like he'd never seen food before, with no manners, filling his mouth full and then taking more bites like they might take it away. He was just showing off for them.

They had the wagon down on the floor and were taking turns pulling it around the table. They took Avery's cap off and looked at that and his army patches on his jacket. They brought more jam and bread, which was a mistake, because you couldn't fill Avery in a million years, the way he was acting. He started giving them marbles. His best ones, puries. He'd fish one out of his pants pocket and put it in one of their big hands. You'd have thought he was giving them rubies. One burst into tears and started hugging Avery, then me. Others kissed me too. Avery didn't mind. I'd never seen men like this before. One had my hand and was counting my fingers. Another was petting my neck. Half of them were crying now. They talked but I couldn't understand.

And Avery was kissing them back. I'd never seen him act like this before. No one ever kissed Avery, and I'd never seen him kiss anyone before, either. Michael wouldn't kiss my father. They shook hands.

Another man came in the room and started shouting. He had a beard and a white officer's hat. The room was so crowded I couldn't see the door. I knew Avery hadn't kept an eye on the butter. We were picked up again and along with the wagon got carried back down the gangplank and they put us on the pier, after kissing us a couple of times each. The others were at the rail, waving. Avery took off his cap and bowed like an actor and they started clapping and cheering. I got into the feeling and did a short tap dance, and they cheered some more. Then we headed back to where we were supposed to wait.

On the way back, I told Avery I'd never seen sailors like that before. "That's because they were women sailors," he said. I was going to argue but I thought about it first and decided he could be right. Maybe they were women. They had smooth cheeks and they felt like women when they hugged me. And when Avery took off one of the Russians' hats, the sailor's hair was in a bun.

"They have women working on the ship?" I said.

"Looks like it. They must want to help the war effort," he said.

We still had to wait for my father. When he came I asked him, "Did you ever see any of those Russian sailors, Dad?"

"They stay to themselves. Some of the men tried to invite them to the cafeteria, but they didn't want to go. They're good workers; as soon as the parts were milled for their engine, they put them right in. They're always chipping rust and repainting." I didn't know what else to ask. If they were women? It was too much to explain.

My father took us by a shortcut and we went out a gate where he knew the guard at the office. "No trouble at all, Mr. Mitchum," the guard said, waving us through. I had to think, does it make much difference now that my father is a foreman, when Michael is in the shed?

After my father had left us at the corner, I took ahold of the handle too and helped pull the wagon. This was Sammy's Flyer and Avery pretended it was his. How did Michael go to the bathroom in the shed? Why did this have to happen? He must use a chamber pot and Grammy must empty it when no one's looking.

Avery made me stop what I was thinking about when he asked, "What's your favorite sandwich?"

"Fried bananas." I never had one in my life before, but I read about it in a magazine. "But my favorite right now is pink pickle relish sandwich spread with slices of thick Spam on a drop biscuit. What's yours?"

"Wonder Bread with a coat of margarine, then you sprinkle a spoonful of sugar even all over. Then take the bread to the sink and lick all the loose sugar off. Then you eat the slice of bread upside down and taste the sugar on the top of your tongue."

"How many sandwiches have you had like that?" I asked him. He had to count on his fingers.

"Three." With ration stamps for sugar, and Aunt May the way she was, I didn't think he'd had that many. "I might have one tonight," he said, "and use this butter."

"I don't like the stuff," I told him.

We were going to have meat loaf for Easter. In the morning I ground the bread crumbs and peeled the potatoes for Grammy. It wasn't the same anymore. Except for Ruthie, we all knew where Michael was. Because I couldn't ask, I couldn't think about anything else.

The night before, me and Ruthie dyed eggs. Grammy knew how to make the colors out of beet juice, spinach greens, and brown onion skins. You couldn't get any regular dye or chocolate Easter bunnies. I asked to invite Avery but Grammy said no. My mother didn't say one word. Instead, Grammy told us parts of Michael's last letter from Louisiana.

My father was going to work at his regular time on Easter, so he slept late and my mother just sat and read the paper. We listened to the radio and played with my cutout dolls. Ruthie fell asleep on the floor.

Mrs. Hughes came over all dressed up after church to talk to Grammy. "Miss Walker went up to Carson City with that sailor." I had heard this all before, and seen too, but my mother said, "Excuse yourself, Mary Maureen, and go out and play." Grammy had seen first, before Mrs. Hughes, when Miss Walker got a ride home from school. Grammy watched from the front window without moving the shade. She wouldn't let me look, so I went upstairs to her bedroom and stood on her trunk to see out the window. He was just another sailor until I recognized him. He was the one Avery knew. His friend, who beat all those other sailors up with his club.

I went out through the kitchen and pretended to get a drink of water and grabbed the heel of bread and smeared butter on with my finger and then, quick, dusted sugar on that and put my hand with the bread inside the pocket of my dress.

Avery was still in the garden, watering down the ditches by the squash, using a shingle to keep the water flowing even. "Happy Easter," I said. He smiled like he did when he thought something was funny, and I told him I had something in my pocket. He led the way back to the fence where there was a lean-to of sweet peas, pink, purple, and red, going up white string nailed on the boards. We crawled in on our hands and knees. It smelled better than any perfume I ever smelled in my life.

I handed over the bread to Avery. When he realized what it was, he started squeaking, he was so happy. I didn't know I was doing it, no matter how many times I got my hands slapped, but I was pulling at my hair again, and Avery saw and just kept giving his head little shakes until I caught on and stopped. I was thinking what Avery had told me they did with saboteurs. The same thing they did with spies; they were executed by firing squad. I knew this already. Then, pretending like I didn't care what he answered, I'd asked, "What do they do to deserters?" He'd acted as if he didn't hear me, and ran off like he had to go home. They were going to shoot Michael dead if they found out. There were bees at the flowers. Hundreds. Thousands. It worried me, but Avery didn't seem to notice. It was colder behind the flowers than it was out in the sun. I told that to Avery.

"Look at the sun," he said. "Through the sweet peas, use this red one," and he reached up and spread out the bloom so it was as big as it could get, then lay back with his head against the bottom board of the fence, his eyes half closed, staring up at the sun through the flowers.

"I used to think you could go blind looking at the sun," he said, "and I would only watch until I saw the green and yellow spots. But if you use something like flowers, I used rose petals once, it protects your eyes enough so you can stare forever, and it keeps you warm. Do you believe me?" he asked. I knew he was teasing me. The sun was blood through the flower I was looking through. The longer I looked, the more everything became that color. Red air between my eyes and the flower. Then my eyelids too when I closed them down from seeing the melting sun. Even with my arms over my face, everything was still dripping blood drops. But I was warm now.

I looked over at Avery, who was still staring up at the sun through a flower, smiling, happy. Little tears coming down the sides of his face. "Mary Maureen, Mary Maureen," Grammy called, "come home right now."

I sat up and was dizzy; I couldn't see right. "I got to go," I said, crawling for the end to get out. "I got to go."

• • •

The day after Easter when I came home my mother was sitting at the kitchen table. It surprised me so much seeing her there and not Grammy that I didn't ask, What are you doing home from work at this time? Ruthie got up on her stool and I got out the milk and a cookie for each of us.

My mother didn't say anything when Ruthie started telling her about something. I interrupted, "Where's Grammy?" This was the first time I ever remembered not seeing her when I came home.

"She's in her room," my mother said. The house was too quiet. I couldn't hear her sweeping or making the beds or cleaning the toilet. I finished first and tried to be quiet going up the stairs. Grammy was laying out on her bed, one arm over her eyes.

"Are you sick?" I asked. "Are you asleep, Grammy?" I went closer. Her eyes were closed tight. I went back downstairs. Something I hadn't noticed before, my father's lunch box on the drainboard. I opened it and the red-topped Thermos dropped down on the sandwiches in waxed paper. Napkin. The two small oranges he liked. Cookies. "Where's Daddy? Mom, where's Daddy?"

Ruthie was blowing bubbles in her milk, tipping the glass too far and ready to spill it on her dress. I took the milk away from her. "Mother," I yelled.

"He's joined the Army. He quit his job and joined the Army this morning. He's on his way to Fort Lewis in Washington." She was looking at the table as she spoke.

At first I didn't know what to say. "No, he has to work. He can't go in the Army. He was in the Army before. He has to work now."

I ran out of the back door and looked in the garage. The old Packard was there. I couldn't believe it. I kept thinking of the troop trains of those boys passing on the tracks, waving, holding their caps. I couldn't imagine his face leaning out a window.

"How's your grandmother?" Mrs. Hughes called out, crossing the street and coming down the drive when she saw me.

"She's fine, ma'am."

"Caught her by surprise, all right, your father joining up. She was over visiting when your mother came running. I guess they tried to talk him out of it, but it was no use. He knew someone; he's going to be an instructor here in the States. I think it was very patriotic, if you ask me. They're taking men his age every day now. They drafted a man who had seven kids, I read in the paper. They need everybody; they're getting desperate. And your father volunteered. You should be proud of him."

I saw Avery listening behind the picket fence. He was digging up dandelions out of Aunt May's flower bed. He could get the long white root out in one piece, using an old table knife to loosen around first and then ease the root out.

I couldn't explain to Mrs. Hughes: if my father wasn't going to be here anymore, who was going to fix that Packard now, I ask you, or carve the turkey, or read the funnies to us on Sunday? While Mrs. Hughes was talking I saw Miss Walker come driving up in the U.S. Government car with her sailor.

The sailor got out first and went around and opened the other door. Took his hat off when he came over to talk to Mrs. Hughes. "Mr. Mitchum joined the Army today," she said.

"Well, what do you know about that," Miss Walker said. The sailor just looked respectful. "You'll have to get another blue star for your window, Mary Maureen."

"Yes, ma'am." I started feeling sick to my stomach. I didn't turn around but I heard her coming, the sound of her steel-tipped canes, and watched Mrs. Hughes stiffen and start to turn away. "Aunt May, Mr. Mitchum joined the Army today," Miss Walker called out.

"I knew something must be up with an admiral visiting the neighborhood," Aunt May called back. The sailor laughed. "I'd try and enlist in the Army myself, but someone has to protect the virtue of the young women in this country." Miss Walker was turning red. "You happen to have an extra cigarette on you, Captain?" He reached into the inside of his jacket.

"Oh, by the way, Mrs. Fontana, this is Chuck Sweet. He's going to be a chief petty officer."

The sailor said something the same time Aunt May asked, "You wouldn't know my son, Sammy? He's in the Navy."

"No, ma'am, I don't think so."

She took out three cigarettes, saying, "You don't mind? You can't get ready-mades anymore, with rationing."

"Help yourself, my pleasure." Mrs. Hughes was sitting on her porch now.

"Well, it was nice meeting you all," the sailor said, backing away. "I'll see you later." Miss Walker was going to say something but didn't and walked him to the car.

Aunt May gave a look over to Avery, who was almost hidden behind the pyracantha bush, and then turned back to me. "Don't do that," she said, and I pulled my hand from the top of my head. She started going back toward her walk.

Ruthie came out of the house and went over to where Avery was and just fell on her knees, getting green all over her dress from the grass. "Ruthie, you have your school clothes on." I went over and jerked her up. "You're supposed to change." She started bawling. "Don't you ever mind?" I yelled, and I dragged her back to the house.

Avery

You know who told me, you little liar?" Aunt May was trying to trap me in the corner of the front room, hanging on to the back of the couch, limping after me because she'd lost her canes. "Wait till I catch you," she kept saying. I kept moving around, ready to make a run for the front door or the one in the kitchen. I'd had Sharon sign my report card with Aunt May's name, so she wouldn't know. Mary Maureen's grandmother told Aunt May.

"You're going back," she yelled. "You're going back," and I ran for it. I could hear her yelling after me, "No one can get all unsatisfactories in deportment. No one. Sammy never got that."

I went out in the garden and started weeding where I left off, running the water in the regular ditches to the tomatoes. Ruthie came in, leaving the gate open so Abner could come in and dig, or some of the chickens to eat up the lettuce. I had to close that, then keep an eye on her. But I found a praying mantis and let her play with that.

Ruthie liked bugs, caterpillars, worms, any of them, just to look at; she never stepped on them, or ate the caterpillar like Mary Maureen said. She liked to hold the black-and-orange ones up by their fur and look at them close in the eye is all. Or she'd lay down on the ground, her cheek in the dirt, and watch them eat. Let them almost escape, then stop them with a twig for a while. She helped ants find dead things on the ground, picking them up on a leaf and carrying them over to where a dead fly was, or a spider. And best she liked sow bugs, lining them up to race. She did that for hours sometimes.

She let the praying mantis go and came over where I was thinning the carrots. Pull one, two, three, and leave a carrot. I found the longest red worm I ever saw and let her lace it through her fingers. She never stayed clean, that was the problem; then she got yelled at. No matter how many times you mentioned it, Ruthie, you're getting all dirty, dust yourself off, she always ended up filthy. And she always acted surprised; she'd look down at herself and start to sniffle. I did the beets the same way, and then the radishes. There was going to be a big crop this summer.

Aunt May wouldn't forget what had happened with the report card. But I wasn't worried. She wouldn't stay mad forever, or try and catch me unawares or when I was asleep. But she'd keep reminding me, telling me she'd send me back. But I knew she wouldn't. Not as long as I didn't do anything really bad, like when I tried to kill the teacher with the tack on her chair that time in my other school, or something like that. Who would do the garden? Before I came she had to hire it done. Or Sammy did some, before he went in the Navy. But he couldn't now.

"You're going to get it, Ruthie," Mary Maureen said, sitting on the fence. "Wait till Grammy sees you. Get out of that dirt." I pretended I didn't know she was there. Kept weeding away. "Ruthie."

She caught a grasshopper under her hand. Lifted it up and then clamped both hands together with him trapped inside. Then looked at it through the cracks between her fingers. She gave me a look.

"Avery, tell Ruthie to get up off the ground." I kept weeding. It was a job I liked. You could tell from the first tug if the whole root was going to come up with the top. Young new green dirt-bomb grass was easy, always came up with a hundred little white roots. Dandelions were hard, usually left part of the root. Milkweed too, even if the dirt was soft and wet. Wild oats depended on the ground too. Scissorweed came up easy. Aunt May liked bare dirt around her vegetables. "Everyone knows what happened, Avery. We could hear. Grammy said, 'What's that stupid boy done now?'"

She was smug, Mary Maureen was, as if nothing I could say back would ever make her stomach feel sick. I didn't even look over at the wash shed. And I didn't say anything. I kept yanking the weeds, leaving them in a straight row so they'd be easy to rake up.

Aunt May came into the garden, went straight over to the compost pile to see if I'd turned it. Down the rows I'd already done. "Move the hose," she yelled at me, "it's flooding." I jumped up and ran, bent the hose double to stop the water, and went and put it under the marigolds that kept the snails away. I went back where I was weeding, and she came down the row closer. I could hear the tips of the canes digging into the ground as she came.

It's not knowing, when you can't see what's going to happen next, that's the worst. On all fours, I kept pulling. Aunt May passed us, she didn't say anything to Ruthie either, and went over to the hotbox to see the seedlings.

I said good morning ma'am to Mother Mitchum, who was watching me from the steps, so I kept walking down the street. No one else went to church on the whole block. She'd tell if I went in the direction of the tracks and the mud flats. I had planned to head for the boat, work at getting the cabin ready. I kept walking farther away from where I wanted to be, knowing enough not to look back because she'd see. I knew she was watching and would never stop.

I went to the church; there was nothing for it. Sat in the last pew by the back door. Tried to think of something else. What I was going to do the next time I could get to the raft.

I wasn't noticing like I usually do. I had the biggest tinfoil ball in the class because I saw the tinfoil before anyone else did. Or coins: I had a mustard jar half full of the new 1943 steel pennies I'd picked up. It was me who found Mrs. Hughes's front door keys, and Mrs. Mitchum's watch crystal and Ruthie's tooth. But when it was people, I didn't always notice. Mass was almost over with and we were ready to leave when I saw the first-class. He had been sitting right in front of me the whole time. I tried to get out but there were too many people in the way. I had my hat pulled down. I don't know why, but I didn't like to see the same people twice, or let them see me again, if I could help it. I didn't want a ride home from him. And I didn't want him to remember me untying him upstairs at the USO. Or him to ever know that me and Mary Maureen saw him beat on those sailors that time.

"Hey, sailor, you don't wear your cover inside unless you're under arms." I pretended I didn't hear. Then my hat was lifted off. I had to turn then. He was holding it out to me. "If you're going to be a sailor, you better get with it. This is the second time I've had to mention this to you."

"Yes, sir," I said.

"And you don't *sir* enlisted men. How many knots can you do now? If I recall correctly, you were pretty good at taking them apart. I didn't remember that the last time I saw you."

I interrupted. "Forty now, with the double sheepshank." The people in front wouldn't move. The fat priest was standing by the door blocking the way, trying to shake everyone's hand.

"Avery, how come you're not an altar boy?" I didn't answer, but the first-class kept talking anyway. "I was one of the best at St. John's. I can speak Latin as good as you can speak English." I nodded. "And I took care of those deck monkeys that put me in the closet at the USO."

I could smell the whiskey on his breath when I turned to look up at him. It was hard to tell if he was full of bullshit or not. There were so many people who always exaggerated or put an ending to things by making one up. I couldn't tell about him. The only person I ever saw besides my Uncle Johnny who didn't was Mr. Mitchum. He did what he said he did. But that was before I knew about Michael. Mr. Mitchum must know who was in his wash shed. He had to know. They all had to know there was a draft dodger and deserter that belonged in prison in their own backyard.

The first-class was talking to the people around him now, who were all happy to see him in church and in the Navy and ready to fight the Japs if they happened to come to town. We'd been ready for the invasion for so long now I had almost forgotten about them coming. A lot of kids in my class where I used to live had their suitcases packed right after December 7, ready to evacuate. I didn't have a suitcase but I was ready.

The only ones who got evacuated were the American Japs, to the racetrack first and then back someplace where they couldn't get bombed. It never made any sense to me. Why were they letting them go first? They'd have a better chance with the real Japs than we would.

When we finally got to the door and I tried to duck around the woman in front who was talking to the priest, he caught me by the shoulder and asked, "What's your name? Why aren't you in my confirmation class?" I can forget sometimes and start to speak like the letters were all lined up on my lips and needed to be just pushed over the side. I never got past the A. *AAAAAAAA.* I dropped my hat trying, stuttering my whole body to say my name by trying to shake it out of my mouth. "You're tongue-tied," the priest said, pushing me past. I felt sick from trying, red-faced.

"Hey, Avery, you lost your cover." The first-class handed me my hat. I still couldn't move to get away fast, but he went down the steps and into the crowd.

When I came up from the garden, Aunt May made me hurry up and eat fast to go over to the Mitchums' to listen to the news. Without a radio we didn't know anything. She'd already eaten and sat across the table waiting while I chewed up my macaroni and cheese. It was hard to eat with any politeness with her watching me. She slid over my portion of the orange Jell-O with a dab of mayonnaise on top. Besides the pieces of peach and pear I had four grapes, which were the best things except for the two halves of a cherry in the can of fruit cocktail, in my opinion.

When we got over there, Aunt May got Mr. Mitchum's chair and I sat on the floor. He had gone out earlier to get some ice cream and invited two sailors and a soldier home for a dish. We listened to the news while we ate. They were polite. The sailors were going to fireman school and the soldier was from North Dakota. They didn't say much. All had good manners and didn't lick their bowls like Ruthie did and I thought of doing. But I would not shame Aunt May.

The news was so-so. They spent a lot of time on the North Africa theater, which had nothing to do with us in California. When they got to the Pacific, everyone listened to everything. We knew they were telling us only good news, with just a little of the bad, over the radio. If the censors wouldn't let the sailors even tell where they were or what they were doing, you know they made sure the radio announcers didn't say too much either. They were still fighting on

Guadalcanal. And the Japanese navy was hiding somewhere in the South China Sea. General MacArthur and Admirals Nimitz, Halsey, and King were all working hard.

When the sailors and the soldier excused themselves, we all stood up and said good-bye. We followed them out on the porch and then up the drive. Aunt May said Mr. Mitchum used to do this all the time, invite servicemen home, but now he was working seven days a week, almost. Before the war Mrs. Mitchum used to make home-cooked meals for the draftees that were stationed over at the airfield. I noticed none of the Mitchums looked over at the wash shed when we went back inside.

We tried not to miss going downtown Saturday nights after they let the sailors loose. But you had to be careful. No matter how many times we reminded ourselves don't get close, we always moved nearer and nearer. Not just for the tinfoil, but you had to be right at the exact spot where everything was happening to really enjoy yourself. The first time we went, Leroy went right up to where a circle of sailors were wrestling with each other and got the sleeve of his shirt tore off. Another time a second-class cook threw a beer bottle and missed and hit Leroy square in the forehead but didn't break the glass. But coming downtown to watch was better than going to the movies, in my opinion. You knew it wasn't true on the screen, that it was made up, but on payday night what you saw on San Mateo Avenue couldn't happen in any movie. I have to admit here I never got close if I could help it. Leroy was always saying come on, but I let him go ahead and pretended I was following, but not very close or not very far. Except once.

A chief who must have just got back from the Pacific—you could tell not only by the ribbons but because half his face was beet red but his forehead where his hat shaded it was white—got in some kind of an argument with some other sailors whose heads were still shaved because they were just out of boot camp. It takes a little time for these situations to come to a boil. I used to notice how they started when my Uncle Johnny would take me into bars before the war. With the sailors the middle part, where everybody's working themselves up for breaking someone's nose before you start hearing the bones break, was faster. But the ending was always the same.

The chief was doing most of the stirring, taking a few steps away, then coming back to make another point. He had three hash marks on his sleeve. He was just a little taller than I was and had a potbelly. "You swab jockeys think you know it all. I've used up more ink signing for my pay than you've seen of the Pacific Ocean." He was up on his toes but his face was at chin level of the closest sailor.

One of them got around behind—I couldn't tell if he was a second- or third-class seaman from his sleeve, but he wasn't rated—and hit the chief over the head with a length of pipe he had under his jumper. The chief went down but rolled away and was on his knees before they could put the leather to him.

I thought it was over and moved nearer to where Leroy was standing to see better instead of getting behind something. The chief reached under his coat and came up with a pistol, but bigger; the barrel was as big around as a potato. When the sailors saw, they started backing up.

"Come on, you bastards, I've got something for you here." When he fired, the shell came out slow enough to see, right by our faces, giving off little sparks as it passed. It went through the open window of a green 1938 four-door De-Soto, ricocheted around inside getting redder, then exploded.

The whole car turned yellow hot, then burst into flames. Leroy ran right out of his shoes like the heat had melted them to the sidewalk. The chief broke the pistol in the middle and was reloading. The sailors ran for it, ran into a bar and slammed the door closed. Leroy said I dropped to my knees and was praying, but I think I was just protecting myself like we did when there was an air raid, my head between my knees and my arms wrapped around my ears. It was the civilian owner of the DeSoto who stopped the chief from getting another shot off from the flare gun.

Leroy had to come back for his shoes, and he got me before the police came. We could hear the sirens as we ran. It was Leroy who noticed I had pissed my pants. But he never told anyone.

·

I couldn't keep Mary Maureen away, no matter how hard I tried. She was always there to help when I got away to go down to the raft and work. She had apologized for telling her grandmother about Sharon signing my report card. And I accepted her apology, too.

She had found two red rubber tire tubes, I didn't ask where, and brought them down. It was just what I needed to put over the leaks. The deck was made up of old boards I got when someone tore down their chicken house. When you stepped down from the bank onto the raft the water shot up through the knotholes in those boards like there was a bunch of whales squirting water underneath, and got you all wet.

Mary Maureen cut up the tubes and I nailed them over the holes and cracks. Especially inside the plywood cabin. I hated to see that wood get wet. The more we did, the more I got the feeling that I'd take the raft out of the mud flats. But my mind kept putting complicated ideas in the way. Should there be a sail? A rudder? If there wasn't, the raft would just drift where the current would take us.

I told Mary Maureen about it while she was measuring cardboard for the inside walls of the cabin. "If I find those things out," she said, "will you let me come?"

"Mary Maureen," I started out. I'd tried to avoid this subject because, just because. "I don't know where we're going to end up."

"It doesn't matter. I'll come."

"I don't know if this canal even goes to the bay. And there's a submarine net across the water under the Golden Gate Bridge."

"Then why are you building this raft?"

I didn't know what to answer. I noticed Ruthie was trying to catch the tadpoles in the water and was getting herself all wet. "Ruthie, come over here and help me." I gave her a roofing nail to hold and I concentrated on giving little taps until I was sure it would stay up without hitting her fingers.

The very next day Mary Maureen was waiting for me by the school gate after we were let out. I tried to walk by after patting Ruthie on the head. "Avery," Mary Maureen said, "I have something to show you." I pretended I couldn't hear. "Avery," she yelled, "listen to me or I'm going to tell about what's in the mud flats."

It had been a mistake to ever include her. But, my mind thought again, without her I would never have got the thing built. I stopped and let them catch up with me. "I want to show you something," she said, and we took off with her walking in front. I grabbed Ruthie's hand so she'd keep up. We kept going, then turned down an alley I hadn't been in for a long time. She stopped in the middle. "There's the mast," she said, pointing into a yard. It was an old four-by-four clothesline pole at least twelve feet tall. There was still a pulley dangling from a rusted hook. The mast was leaning halfway over, and the windows in the house were all broken out.

"And the canal goes into the bay," she said. "We have a piece of canvas in our garage for the sail. And I know how to put one together. I asked my father."

"You told your father about the raft?"

"No, just that I wanted to know for a school project. He showed me on paper, and he told me about the bay."

"We're going to need some rope too."

"I can get some."

"And we should make a rudder too, to keep the boat straight."

"Are you going to let me come now, Avery?"

I was already thinking, making plans on how to get the mast pole to the canal. I had to nod. I couldn't leave her out now. "When it's dark, I'll come back with my wagon."

"I'll help you," she said.

It was the next morning when I thought of the submarine net. I had to know. I had already done the shopping, and I had to finish the dusting first, but I could hear Mary Maureen playing jacks next door with Ruthie. It was driving me crazy, but I couldn't leave; Aunt May was talking on the phone and watching me.

I pretended I was going out front to sweep the walk and waved Mary Maureen over. "How are we going to get past the Golden Gate Bridge?"

"The nets are for subs and big ships. My father says the fishing boats pass right over, he sees them all the time." I felt such relief. I decided that certain kinds of thinking are good for a person. We were going to sail away. I said it aloud. "We're going to sail away, Mary Maureen."

What next? I had to wait until Grammy went over to Mrs. Hughes's to visit before I could jump the fence to the Mitchums' house. Mary Maureen had banged the wall when Mr. Mitchum was getting up. He already knew what Aunt May wanted. He was supposed to have asked someone in the office at the shipyards who to contact about her radio. But he kept putting it off. Aunt May didn't want to remind him anymore. "They're slow as molasses, those people from the South," she said. But she sent me over.

He was up polishing his shoes. I could see him through the open bedroom door. He never rushed, Mr. Mitchum, he did everything as if he'd forgotten what he'd started out doing. But he got the job done, if you were there to remind him. Mary Maureen was good at it, I noticed. He'd start changing the brushes on the generator before he went to work, and then stop in the middle to start something else: put tire-tread heels on Ruthie's shoes because she was always using them to brake on her scooter and you couldn't get rubber anymore. Mary Maureen would pipe up, "Pop, are you going to put the Packard back together before it's time to go?" He had to pick up five welders that didn't have cars. Then he'd go back to putting the generator belts back on. He did not hurry. And he was never late. But he kept everyone else on the edge of their chairs.

I'd already climbed up on the back fence five times to see if he was up yet. They wouldn't wake him, and no one could even make a noise around the house when he was in bed. They walked on tiptoes. He worked seven days a week, with all the overtime he could stand.

I went back over a couple times more while he drank his coffee. Aunt May kept sending me back after I'd report. He was up. Shaving. "Tell him we could listen to the late news to know what's happening to Sammy in the war zone."

I went back but didn't say anything, just stood in the kitchen at ease. Mary Maureen poured him more coffee. Ruthie sat at the table, playing with her oatmeal. Mrs. Mitchum was already at work on Saturday.

We all followed him over the front way to Aunt May's, and he knocked on the door before opening it and said, "I think I can straighten this problem with your radio out, May, if I can use your phone to make some calls."

"Go ahead, Dennis."

"I talked to one of the security people who used to work for that department, and he told me what to do."

Aunt May got up so he could sit down in her chair nearer the phone. She slumped over and held on to the sideboard. He gave the operator the number and then talked to somebody at the Odd Fellows Club. I couldn't follow that because I had to watch Ruthie. She knew better, but she'd break something, or steal. You had to keep an eye on her all the time. She was in the first grade but didn't act like it sometimes. Aunt May didn't like her in her house.

Then it was to the American Legion. "Tell them it was my husband who was Italian and my father was a deacon in the Presbyterian church for years," Aunt May said. She had made some real coffee she'd been saving back and went out to get Mr. Mitchum a cup. Then he made his last call.

He started out loud from the beginning. "Goddamn it to hell, what do you think you're doing? Her son's fighting for this country." You could hear him all the way over to where Grammy was talking on the sidewalk, because she was knocking on the door in the next minute, calling out, "Dennis, Dennis," and I let her in.

When he got off the phone that time he stood up. "They're going to keep the binoculars because they're Navy issue, but the rest you can have back. When I come home tomorrow, I'll stop by the Federal Building and pick everything up."

He was as good as his word: we had the Zenith back in its place against the dining room wall the next day. It had a few scratches on the cabinet but it played as good as ever.

I had to know. I had to see if Michael was in the wash shed. Who else could it be? But I had to know for sure. I couldn't look from Aunt May's roof or the victory garden lots behind the fence. There was no view from the sidewalk unless I stood on my wagon, let it coast going by on the sidewalk, and if I did that more than once, Mother Mitchum would be out on the porch with her broom handle.

I had to think. I had to think. I walked around the whole square block once, then twice, getting down behind the hedge on my hands and knees in front of the Mitchums' house the second time. I couldn't see. And Abner was on the end of his chain, sniffing the air for me.

Why did I have to know? If you know something, it can help you. It can make things better for a person. Make you stronger than just your muscles. Not that there are thirty-two presidents, or twenty-two missions in California: that means nothing, because almost everyone else knows that too. So you know it and that's the end of the matter. But knowing where Aunt May keeps her money or which mushrooms are poison or why Mrs. Hughes never goes downtown past the Purity store or why Sammy always needs the allotment money the government sends Aunt May: it's all useful. It's knowing that can turn into ideas. That can be good for you.

Mrs. Hughes and Aunt May got into it years ago before I came. It was over Mrs. Hughes's oak tree and the wind blowing the leaves into Aunt May's yard, killing her flowers. Mrs. Hughes didn't have flowers, had cement in front where the lawn would have been, and one big hydrangea plant up next to the front porch. And of course the oak tree that hung over the whole house like a big hand and arm in the winter after the leaves came down. Aunt May said the leaves poisoned the soil so nothing would grow.

I didn't do Mrs. Hughes's shopping but I cleaned the oak leaves out of her rain gutters and put some shingles back on the porch roof. She held on to me from the attic window with a rope. She paid me two bits for that. I gave her vegetables too, when Aunt May wouldn't know. And she spoke up for me with Miss Walker. I knew that to be true because the teacher said, "You have a real admirer in Mrs. Hughes." But I never said anything about the time I saw Mrs. Hughes get caught taking a packet of rubber bands from the five-and-dime, when you could still get them. The clerk must have been married to a sailor because I'd never seen her before or heard anyone talk like that. I was in the store looking over the marbles. They had some pure and clear as water and some blue and red ones. I never stole, but it wasn't because I didn't want to. But it was my idea that you could get what you wanted in other ways. I never passed a bakery that I didn't want to run inside and before anyone could stop me eat up a whole tray of jelly doughnuts, or slide along the floor and just get my head into the case and eat with my teeth, not using my hands, or go through the skylight at night when there was no one there and eat pies and doughnuts until I blew up and died. But it was easier to go over and maybe sweep the steps on Mrs. Hughes's porch and wait her out. And she'd open the screen door and hand me a nickel and I'd go buy the jelly doughnut.

If I could see all the way to the airport from Mrs. Hughes's attic, I could see the Mitchums' wash shed from the roof over her kitchen. I had shinnied up there before, plenty of times, and she wouldn't hear if she was in her bedroom.

The thought was good, but the problem was, I had to be careful. I couldn't be seen by anyone. Not the Mitchums or Aunt May. Especially not Miss Walker. I was trying to stay out of her way so she might forget me. So I didn't go over to Mrs. Hughes's when she was there, or even walk by the front of the house if I could help it now.

I had walked home a block behind Mrs. Hughes after she was caught. She'd started crying when the clerk yelled at her, "I saw you put them in your purse." Bawling was a good idea and usually worked. Leroy could make more water come out of his eyes than your regular faucet does. I couldn't do it. I could never cry, no matter how hard I tried. The clerk let her go, just made her pay for the rubber bands.

Mrs. Hughes was waiting at the corner for me. "It was an accident," she said first. I looked up into her eyes like I always did to see how smart a person was. If you have shiny eyes you're smart. My eyes were shiny. Mrs. Hughes's weren't. Neither were Mary Maureen's. And through the eye hole you can see what a person is made of. Like they are windows, your eyes. An old woman where I used to stay told me that. She lived in a garage and I visited her there. She was smart but had had a stroke. If Mrs. Hughes wasn't smart, she was clever enough. "Here," she said, getting her coin purse out of her big leather hand-bag, "take this for being a good boy," and she handed me a quarter. I took it all right. The five-and-ten clerk didn't stay long, her husband must have got trans-ferred, because in two weeks she wasn't there anymore. I went over and reported that fact.

If Michael was in the shed, he had to eat. There was water in there, but he needed food. Someone would have to bring him his supper. I could lie up on Mrs. Hughes's kitchen roof and wait. I just wanted to see. And then I could think. Then these ideas would have shapes. Michael would have a shape.

Aunt May was still resting when I came back from mass, so I couldn't turn on the radio. I looked at my *Aeronautics Aircraft Spotter's Handbook*. When I heard Ruthie calling I hurried back out, put on my shoes, and went over. It was too early for them to eat Easter dinner yet.

Mary Maureen was sitting on the back stairs. "We're going to make a kite. My father said you can help if you want." I knew she or Ruthie had asked for me.

Mr. Mitchum had talked about kites before. The ones he'd made when he was a boy with his father, and the ones he'd made later. He never mentioned Michael. The only one who did was Grammy, who wanted everyone to listen when she got a letter from him.

I had never made a kite myself. I bought one once, but I must have not put it together right because the paper tore and the stick broke before I ever tried to get it off the ground. You have to have someone that's done it before, who knows what they're doing. Even with a store-bought kite, it's hard. There were more directions than in *The Blue Jacket Manual*. I had watched some kites in the sky before: I knew it was possible. I wondered if they were going to let me in the Navy, sometimes. In the end I smashed the kite I bought, crushed it round and tight like a ball, and forced it down a big gopher hole. But I kept the string.

"Avery," Mr. Mitchum said, "I wondered if you'd show up. It's kite-flying time. Do you feel that March wind?"

"Yes, sir."

"It's just the right kind," he said. "Gusts like that will take a kite up faster than you can let out the line." He had sat down on the back stairs with us and was scraping the one stick smooth with the blade of his jackknife. From where we were you couldn't see the wash shed, but as loud as he was talking, louder than he usually did, you could hear from there.

"I did some government work last night," he said. "They had a saw in the carpenter shop and I cut some scrap up. Look at this," he said, and he bent one of the sticks almost into a circle, stopped short at a big C. "Red fir," he said, "it's got give. Never saw anything like it back home. Wait until the wind gets behind this kite; it'll bend these double."

He took the other stick from Ruthie and made the notches in the ends for the string. He marked the middle of the stick and balanced it on the dull end of his knife. It went to one side and he took a couple of curls off that side.

It was a true miracle the way he could make things. Some Sundays they talked about how they needed a miracle to raise enough money for new vestments for the priest or an altar for the church or something for the bishop or the Pope. They never mentioned what Jesus did when he was a carpenter or before he started to become God. That's when all those church miracles started rolling in. But he must have made a lot of cupboards and stools before he ever could turn one loaf into a whole mountain of bread. I'd seen Mr. Mitchum turn a stick into ten pinch clothespins for Grammy, or take new growth out of an old willow down the street and make a bentwood chair, just go ahead and make a chair as quick as that, that you could sit on a couple of hours later. Then he made a table to match.

He put the kite together just like I always thought it should go. The tissue paper must have been saved from Christmas because it had Mary Maureen's writing, To Mother and Father, in black crayon. The sticks made a cross and he made them stay together with a wire. Then he threaded the string through the notches and laid that on top of the paper that we were holding against the cement on the driveway. Then he cut out the shape in the paper, leaving extra to fold over the string.

He did it all like the thought was so strong even his hands and fingers knew how without being told, and he kept telling us; the sound of his voice made you listen. "This is important, to keep the seam fold directly against the string without any play, or good-bye kite. It'll fall apart on you every time." He used tape he got from the shipyard to seal the fold over the string. "Now," he said, holding up the kite, "we need to make the shape that'll scoop the air. He cut off a length of string from the reel and tied it lengthways on the up-and-down stick and pulled it into a little curve. Then he tied another piece on the crossways one, so tight that it made the stick curve more than the lengthways one. The kite was almost as tall as I was. I realized I had a lot of questions I'd like to ask, but I didn't want to try. He saw me looking closer at the reel, like one you used when you went fishing, but bigger. It was all wood and set in a box.

"My father made it for me," he said, "when I was Ruthie's age, out of cherry-wood."

I was getting so excited I couldn't stand still long enough to ask anything. But why wouldn't that paper tear in the wind?

He thought of everything, had a tail already cut out of what looked like an old sheet, longer than Abner's chain. That dog was watching us close, just waiting for one of us to take a step closer so he could start snapping his teeth. Mr. Mitchum let us tie the little pieces of cloth on like bows. "It'll act like a rudder and at the same time like a kind of ballast to keep it in balance," he said before I could think of the question.

Last he attached the string from the reel onto the line that made the sticks bend. He had all the ideas a person could have on a kite. As soon as he lifted it off the ground the kite came alive. It leaped a little, waved back and forth, wiggling the tail to see if it was ready.

He just stood there looking around as if the sky was too crowded with airplanes or zeppelins or Jap fire balloons or something and we couldn't start quite yet. Even Mary Maureen was hopping around. But he waited, holding the kite like a big shield in front of him. "Dad, Dad," Ruthie kept saying.

Then, instead of going out in the street where everyone I'd ever seen flew their kites, which was the best place once they got over the telephones wires, Mr. Mitchum went out through the gate past Aunt May's garden plots and across the street next to the streetcar tracks.

Ruthie carried the tail. I carried the box with the spool of string. And Mary Maureen and Mr. Mitchum each had a part of the kite. It shuddered like it was trying to get away. He kept saying, "Hold it now, hold it." I could feel the wind hard on my face.

I couldn't help myself and tried to say, "Don't let it go, Mary Maureen, Mary Maureen." But I couldn't get it out. I got the stutters, I was so worked up. But no one seemed to notice.

"This is the most important part," he said. "This is where things go wrong no matter how good your kite is made. This has to be done perfect." He told us again what we were to do. I saw then that where the wash shed joined the side of the garage there was an air vent, with little slats of wood going crossways with spaces in between, for the air to circulate. If someone was in there they could see out.

I held the kite up over my head as far as I could put my arms up, just like he said. Ruthie still held the tail ready to throw it up in the air when I let go. Mary Maureen was at the next telephone pole with plenty of slack around her feet and holding the string between her thumb and forefinger so we could see. Mr. Mitchum yelled, "Run," and Mary Maureen took off. I stretched the kite up on my toes and my fingertips. I could see the string looping less and less and then the tug at my hands, Mary Maureen running. I didn't want to let go. I wanted to hang on and let the kite take me with it up in the air. Away. Away. The wind took the kite from my grip and Ruthie whooped as the tail whipped across her face as it was taken up. We both were jumping up and down watching the kite rise, take the slack line all the way back to Mr. Mitchum, who let the reel spin free as the kite went up.

The tail was whipping back and forth like you do on a swing with your legs to gain height, the point wiggling its way slowly, cutting through the soft sky as if it were made of water. I felt my heart and it was trying to leave too. It thudded against my hand like it was going to break through my skin. The kite kept going straight up. Getting smaller but more graceful. Driving itself like it was getting pulled up. For the first time I thought there might be a heaven, like a street you could learn to find. The kite could get there, I thought, if there was enough string.

The kite finally stopped, the big loop of string invisible after the first few feet out of the reel. The kite stayed fixed in the blue sky like an arrow, the long tail beating back and forth, the movement levering the kite where it was. It was the highest I'd ever seen one.

There was still some string left in the reel but most was played out, holding the kite where it was. My neck hurt from looking up, but I couldn't stop from trying to keep the kite in sight. It was as if it might disappear if you stopped looking. Mary Maureen held the line but it wasn't necessary. The kite couldn't move, stuck fast there in the blue sky. "Go get some brown paper bags," Mr. Mitchum told Ruthie. She ran fast.

I had gone to mass this morning in the fog because the drugstore was closed and there was no other place I could sit down. The church was full. Easter is worse for that than Christmas. I could stand it until the monsignor came out to give the sermon. Then I got up and gave my seat to someone and drifted out through a side door. I didn't want to go work on the boat in the fog, so I climbed up on Mrs. Hughes's roof for a short stay. I had been keeping a lookout for a while now. He never came out at night like I thought he would. Never once, watching, anytime. Just after dark Grammy would go in with her basket of clothes, turn on the light, and you could hear water running in the wash trays. Then she'd come out carrying a bucket full of the clothes she was soaking, the door wide open the whole time. Early in the morning when it was still mostly dark, she'd go again with the bucket, turn on the light, and start the wringer, but close the door. Then she'd go back to the house to make breakfast. I couldn't stay for long on the roof; in the daylight someone would see me. I'd slide down the drainpipe and go back through my bedroom window. He had to be in there. I'd seen his shoe.

Ruthie came back out of breath, her stomach pumping in and out. Neat as ever, Mr. Mitchum lay the bags on the ground and cut squares out of the middle with his knife, about the size of school paper. "Watch this," he said. First he took out a pencil and wrote something, then he tore the paper down the middle to the center, then fitted it on the kite string. He placed the paper as high as he could reach, so I couldn't read what he wrote. Instead of looking at the kite now, we watched the brown paper.

I thought nothing could surprise me, not in church or at school or here on our street. I was watching too hard to notice what the paper was doing. "It's moving," Mary Maureen said. "The paper is moving." She pointed. I went over to where she was standing. I lined the paper up with one of the poles that held the streetcar wires up and watched. It looked like it moved past that. Slow, but it moved, and kept moving right up the line. "What makes it do that, Pop?"

"I don't know; my father showed me that when I was your age. It might be some kind of vibration from the movement of the kite that draws the paper up."

I held Ruthie's head steady so she could see the paper move. Then she took the pencil first and wrote her name and I put her paper on the line. It started going up too.

Then Mary Maureen got the pencil. "What shall I write?" she asked.

"It's a message you're sending. I used to think it was telling the kite something," Mr. Mitchum said.

She wrote and I didn't look and she handed the pencil to me. I wrote and tried to give the pencil back to Mr. Mitchum but he was staring into space like Aunt May does. I asked her once, "Do you see anything?" She did it so often I thought she must be enjoying herself. "Do you have to know everything?" she said. That was just her way. She was teasing me. "I learned to do that when I was sick. I'd pick something, or it would just appear, something from when I was a girl, in the swimming club, something that made me happy. I got so good I could do it for hours, seemed liked months, sometimes. But when it ran out I had to come back to where I was, lying in the iron lung."

However it was the messages moved, they moved right along, Mr. Mitchum's in the lead by a half block. Then our three coming up, spaced a few yards in between. I never tired of watching the kite. Ruthie was already on her hands and knees playing with a blue-bellied lizard. Mary Maureen was picking at her hair, wrapping a strand around the end of her finger and then putting it in her mouth. Mr. Mitchum was still staring over his garage.

I heard Grammy start calling for them. I noticed then that the sun had gone down. But the sky was still as blue as if it were noon, it was just that there was no center left. Only the flowers knew and were rolled up, the California orange poppies along the railroad rocks like fractions of sunlight, the sweet peas like marbles against the back fence. No one moved.

I could see Grammy now at their back gate, the fence boards almost black without the sun. I looked up at the sky now. Mr. Mitchum's message had arrived; you couldn't tell it now from part of the kite. The other three were almost there.

Grammy called out when she spotted us, "Dennis, Dennis." He shuddered like the kite did when it wanted to go up, and looked around him like he wasn't sure what he was doing here. Waved his arm back and forth over his head to Grammy, who went back through the gate when she saw.

"Let's go, girls," he said, opening up his knife with his thumbnail, and as I watched, he cut underhanded the string that was going invisible up to the kite. I was so surprised I never even tried to say anything. Mary Maureen kept looking back at the wooden reel, then at the sky. The string was gone. But the kite was still there in the same place; you could see it like before. Nothing changed.

"Come on, Ruthie," he said, reaching down to take her hand, "we have to go home." He started walking away, Mary Maureen going ahead of them. I grabbed the reel and tried to hand it to Mr. Mitchum. "No," he said, "you keep it for us, Avery. Keep it for me while I'm gone." They all walked away across the street and through the garden lots. Mary Maureen shut their gate with a bang.

I ran up the bank to the tracks and stood on top, jumping in the air trying to reach and grab the string if it was still there, low. I kept trying, jumping and jumping. I couldn't catch it or it wasn't there. It made me out of breath. But I could still see the kite the other three messages had reached. I hid the reel in a drainage pipe and tried to figure out which way the wind was blowing. You couldn't tell with a wet finger or your tongue. I could never tell which way if the wind blew my hat off. But the Japs knew; they could send their firebombs over on the wind currents.

I moved along the track, trying to keep the kite in sight and not stumble. It got dark. Then darker. I thought I could see the kite still at times, making that wiggling motion, the tail coiled like a corkscrew.

The wind seemed to be blowing toward the mud flats. I had to try. I cut off the tracks and through the fence past the eucalyptus trees. The full moon came out and kept moving, faster now. I knew there was no chance that I could catch the kite but I had to try.

I kept going, running against the gray clay on the mud flats through the tunnel under the Bayshore Highway, listening for the sound the wind made slapping against the tissue paper kite. It had to come down somewhere. This was the farthest I'd ever been. I stumbled, got my feet wet up to my knees, and lost my sailor cap, but I kept going. Until I reached a big fence that I couldn't go around or climb over because of the rolls of barbed wire on both sides on the ground. The airport runway must be on the other side, but I couldn't see. Up high on the fence was a sign with a big skull and crossbones and I started stepping backward.

The moon was as bright as a light bulb in a room. I couldn't pretend to see the kite anymore. And there were no sounds. I could see the lights where our street was and started going in that direction. I wasn't watching for it, but I found my sailor cap on the way back.

I knew when the sixth-grade messenger came into the classroom and handed the slip of paper to Miss Walker that I was going to the office. Then she called me up to her desk. I could run for it, get out of the classroom and off the school grounds before they could catch me. But I went to her desk. She handed me the note. *Please send Avery Fortana to my office.* And initials.

"I didn't do anything," I said before she could ask what I did. She looked like she was the one going to the office. Since they took my marbles away, Miss Walker had been helping me. When I finished my President Garfield report fast, she said I should pick another president to get a better grade. And I chose Jefferson because she acted like she wanted me to. "He's my favorite," she said after I picked him for my second project. But he had been president for eight years, not the six months President Garfield was in the White House, so there were a hundred times more thoughts in the encyclopedia about him. But I tried, and she helped me. Stopped at my desk to read what I wrote, and made corrections. When we went to the library she had me check out a book about his life.

"Leave your hat here," she said, and pointed at her desk. It was folded and through my belt. I did what she said. But I didn't wear it at school anymore; I just carried it around. I didn't want to be in trouble anymore. She whispered, "Be good now; just go up there and be polite. No back talk. I don't know what this is about. Go on now," and she handed me the slip.

I had to wait in the other office with the secretary, who said, "Sit over there." I sat on the wooden chair, my feet almost touching the floor now. I didn't mind. I knew how to remember good times. Drinking a strawberry milk shake. Thinking of all the flowers coming up in the springtime and Aunt May telling me about them. Or working on my boat. I had the practice.

When Mr. Allen called me in, I wasn't nervous either. My heart was beating, because I'd found I could feel it in my thumb too and didn't have to look for it on my chest, and my eyes stayed put because I pretended I was looking at Aunt May's iris that were just blooming.

"This is just a visit, Avery; don't think you were sent for." I made my mouth smile for him. "I want to help you, Avery; that's my job, helping students in school. You probably haven't had it in your speller yet, but *principal* is spelled PRINCIPAL. P-A-L, the principal is your pal." He laughed. "That's how you tell that word from the other *principle* that you use in math." I tried to smile again. "I'm your friend; I want what's best for you.

"You're having some difficulties doing work in the fifth grade, and this is your second year there. So I thought I would ask the superintendent, Mr. Enoch, if he knew of a school that you'd like better. And there *is* one, in South City, that would like to have you. And it's not all sitting at a desk and fooling around with books all the time. They have projects, games where you might take big barrels of screws or nails of different sizes and sort them out. It's all for the war effort. And they have a baseball team and other sports there." He stopped and wanted me to say something but I didn't.

"I want you to have a future, Avery. What do you want to be when you get big?"

"Join the Navy, Mr. Allen, sir."

"This will help you become a better sailor. I promise you. In fact this school is like the Navy; you live there, in clean dormitories. Everything is taken care of for you."

"Thank you, Mr. Allen, but I don't want to leave the street where I'm living now. But I appreciate your offer."

"You're not going to get promoted, Avery. How would you like to spend another year in the fifth grade when all your friends go on to the sixth? How would you like that?"

It's something extra when a flower smells sweet. Daffodils and narcissus do, and you can lean over them and take a deep breath and fill yourself with their sugar.

"How would you like that? Avery? You don't have to answer. But all I have to do is get permission from your guardian. I wanted to be your friend, Avery. I wanted to make you a better citizen, so when you went in the Navy we could all be proud of you."

I picked the biggest narcissus and put it in Aunt May's dictionary, the thickest book. It pressed fine, and after a month it still smells as good as when it was in the garden.

"Go back to your classroom, Avery. I'm tired of looking at you."

Miss Walker asked me to stay in at recess and I told her. "He knows you're improving, Avery. I said you could do the sixth-grade work, that I want you in my class next year if I teach sixth. Don't be so concerned, now; go out and play. I'll talk to him again. There's been some mistake."

I trusted Miss Walker. She had come over twice to talk to Aunt May, to tell her I was doing better and was a big help to her as paper monitor and was doing one of the best reports in the class. Aunt May didn't say anything about it, and I pretended I hadn't heard through the door.

I went outside and sat down on the benches where we ate our lunches in good weather. I felt so tired, like I had been running around and around the heart until I couldn't take another step.

But everything happens so fast that you don't have time to understand why. It's all surprise, like the wind gets knocked out of you and you can't breathe. Mr. Mitchum joined the Army. Mary Maureen had to tell me three times before I would believe her. Then I asked Ruthie. Then I had to ask Mrs. Mitchum.

Anything can happen, I've always known that, good or bad. I could be here today and gone tomorrow. But I wanted to be here, if I had to be somewhere.

The last time Leroy would go downtown with me at night, we found a bar with the back door pinned open and we went right in through the kitchen. Everyone was busy and we pretended we were looking for someone. "Is my uncle here?" I asked, low, and no one heard to answer.

We had both been in this place before; it wasn't anything new. We'd been in most every bar one time or another, between my Uncle Johnny and Leroy's mother, and my other uncles and their friends and Leroy's father. They used to treat us, put us up on a stool, buy us a Coke with a cherry in it. But that was before the war and everything changed.

The place was jammed with sailors. There was a pool table, and the players barely had room to use their cues. The trouble with being inside, you were trapped if something happened. Walking around outside was bad enough; you didn't see as much but you could get away. There was more tinfoil on the floor here than in the street, but it was usually wet and always made me think of spit.

I started picking up the empty packages of cigarettes like I really didn't want to but had to help the war effort. I put the packs in my bag without separating the foil from the paper. The sailors were thick; it was like being in the back of a clothes closet behind all the coats and shirts. It was that dark, too. But here there was smoke and the music from the jukebox you couldn't understand. Five bartenders were trying to keep up. The noise gave me a headache, but I found a dime and some pennies. It was going to be a good night.

There were a couple of civilians at the far end of the bar. The two of them had suits on, and one was holding out a picture in a frame and spitting on it. I got closer and could hear the furniture store owner who tried to give me the yardstick saying, "Now, now." The one that spit yelled back, "It's his goddamn fault, the son of a bitch." I kept picking up, and found another dime. I knew better than to get closer and not mind my own business, that the bartender would yell at me if he saw. But I moved near enough to see the photo the next time he spit. It was of President Roosevelt. And I recognized the man that was spitting. He owned the big liquor store. His son had been killed. The fourth from the town so far, I read in the paper.

"It's not just his fault," the other man said. "We all wanted the Depression to end. We all wanted to make some money." He was drunk too. "And we did.

You made money; you made good money from this war. Roosevelt didn't do anything that we didn't want him to." The other man didn't listen and spit again.

You never saw many women in the bars anymore. A lot worked, and the sailors, if they were married, didn't bring their wives before they shipped out. Tonight there were a few dancing, one at the bar I remembered from before. And when I started picking up near the booths, there was one wearing a sailor's cap, sitting with her arm around a sailor's neck. Helen, Leroy's mother. A second-class aviation metalsmith was whispering something in her ear. She was laughing and ready to take a drink out of her Tom Collins glass. There was another sailor on the other side, his head resting on the back cushion, asleep. A sailor behind her in the next booth was leaning over, trying to get her attention to offer her a cigarette out of his pack of Old Golds. There were several others standing by the booth, trying to talk to her.

I watched. I hadn't seen her since the trial. She hadn't had to testify because they decided it was just manslaughter, not murder. All my brothers and sisters had seats in the front row next to the jury.

I found Leroy. "Let's go," I shouted into his ear, "I've got enough." I showed him my bag full. I could see his pockets were stuffed. He understood but didn't move until I took him by the arm and we went out the front door.

I could see the clock under the bank sign when we started walking; it was almost 9:30. It didn't make any difference when I got home. Aunt May wouldn't know; she went to sleep early. I started watching Leroy then, because he wasn't answering when I was talking to him. When we reached the alley where he turned off, I couldn't think of anything to say. He'd seen his mother. "Let's come back tomorrow night; the sailors get their twenty dollars for the month. Look what I found, I got two," and I tried to hand him one of the dimes, but he wouldn't take it or look at me. Just shook his head and started off in the direction of his street.

Ruthie and me made butter, but Mary Maureen wouldn't help at first. Once was enough, she said. I was over there so I helped. Mrs. Mitchum was still up, and she got the big crock bowl down for us, and I opened the end of the package and dropped the two pounds of white margarine into the bowl. Then we got the potato mashers and started mixing while Mary Maureen poured the powdered coloring in. We mashed it and mashed it.

"I'm not going to look," Mrs. Mitchum kept saying, but she did when Ruthie got it in her hair. I had it all over my knuckles. She was making us fudge if we made the butter. When we were done it didn't look like the butter I remembered, more like pale lard.

We had already used up the real butter that we'd got from the shipyard.

Aunt May traded hers for tobacco, but I got a scrape from one end of a brick for a sandwich. The Mitchums shared with everyone: Mrs. Hughes, Miss Walker, and the women who worked with Mrs. Mitchum. If they could have, Mary Maureen said, they would have sent some to their friends back in Tennessee.

We sat at the kitchen table politely taking turns reaching for a square of fudge out of the pan, no one making a hog of himself. It was so good it made all my teeth ache. I let the first piece just melt on my tongue. Mary Maureen called Grammy to come down from her room but she wouldn't. She said she had a headache. When I was there now there was always something wrong with her.

Mrs. Mitchum told us she'd read where the government was coming out with oleomargarine in a plastic bag with the dye in one corner so you never have to touch the butter. You could take turns like you were squeezing a bean bag and hand it to the next person. But she hadn't seen any yet in the stores. I said that Sammy had told me they get all the real butter they wanted in the chow hall. It was only fair that those that were going to die should have a good meal. Mrs. Mitchum got up and put the pan of fudge on top of the refrigerator and said the girls had to go to bed and I had to go home.

It was always the good times that brought on the others. Especially when I couldn't sleep. I'd try to think of something else, but the dead things would start appearing. Or the black dog that bit me on the chest over my heart and hung on until I got him off and then came after me howling, and I kept running and running.

It was never the blood, or me thinking it was me that was shot dead instead of Unk, that time that I screamed. I screamed and thought no one would hear me because I was on my way up in the sky, until Leroy's mother put the towel in my mouth and yelled, "Stop, Avery, stop," and I knew I was alive. It was the eye, the sea lion looking at me, that gave me the trembles, not old Johnny's laugh, or when I hear him saying, "Don't take everything so serious, Chet, I'll pay you back. Sit down and have a drink. I'm buying; now that's an occasion." He laughed again a lot and was laughing when my father pulled out the pistol, slapping his knee, "Oh my oh my, Chet, you never knew how to take a joke."

We used to get up in the middle of the night when there was a minus tide, and I'd go back to sleep in the back of the car on the way to Moass Beach. Johnny liked abalone steak better than anything in this world. He got the ones that were undersized, no more than six inches across the shell, because they were young and you didn't have to beat the life out of them with a mallet to get them tender enough to chew. Unk used a leaf off the springs of a Cadillac, they had the best steel, for a pry bar to snap the abalone off the rocks. He'd grind one end to an edge and drill a hole in the other to run a line through to tie to your belt, then mark a notch at nine inches for legal size for those that needed that. His friends would come into the garage and he'd give them away like they were calendars after New Year's. "I got to keep busy," he'd say to Helen when he'd start grinding on another pry bar and she wanted to close up and go downtown.

Unk got me up that morning like he always did by lifting the end of my cot and dropping it back on the floor. That knocks the sleep right out of your head, and I got dressed and got into the back of the Plymouth. There was a minus-two tide. I woke up once more when he stopped at the top to put some water in the radiator. As good a mechanic as he was, he would not take the time to fix his own car. It was always stranding us somewhere. He wouldn't fix the leaks in the radiator; he'd rather let the car get heated up and have to stop. That's what Helen told him all the time.

We got to the cliffs, and it was not only dark, but it was drizzling. No stars, no moon, when it was like this. The dark you can get used to, but not the slow wetness that starts on your face and soaks you through. You could hear the booms of the surf as the tide went out, and then the crack, like a rock on a tin roof, of a rifle shot.

We got everything and walked the path down the cliffs to the sand. Picked our place near some rocks that shielded us from the wind, and I started dragging back the driftwood. Unk sat down and put on his thick socks first, then his knee-high rubber boots. Helen said what she always said, "What good are those boots? You always go in over them and they get filled." He never answered, he didn't like to dispute over things like that. But once he said, "I never leave for this beach without thinking this time I'm going to keep my feet dry. Maybe today will be it."

"Well, one of these days you're going to drown, because you're so hard-headed." We got the fire blazing so he'd be able to see his way back, no matter how far he went out.

With two gunnysacks, ripped so they fit over his shoulders, one on each side, and smoking a cigar, Unk went out on the smooth rocks. We followed until the seaweed got too slippery and he started feeling around the bottom of the boulders for the abalone. Then we went back to the fire and I dragged more wood up and Helen threw it on the fire.

We hadn't seen any other cars where we parked, but the cliffs went on for miles, and by the number of rifle shots we knew there were more people down for the minus tide. I couldn't hear them barking, but the sea lions were out there too, gobbling the abalone like seven-hundred-pound vacuum cleaners. Unk saw one once, eating the meat out of a shell, he said, like it was a bowl of oatmeal. They weren't shot at because of that, though; people just killed them. I'd seen it plenty of times: men using the hoods of their cars up on top of the cliffs to steady their aim, potting the sea lions lying out on the rocks in the sun.

What amazed me was after, when the tide brought the bodies in. Big dead blobs of fur half buried in the sand, the birds and flies all swarming over the worst stink you could imagine. You couldn't get close. But a week later you wouldn't find a trace. And I'd look, always mistaking the heaps of floating brown bulbs of seaweed that you could pop with your heel for one of the bodies.

We took a walk, after we got enough wood, to see if we could find anything interesting, like those glass floats or nice-looking seashells. The sun was coming up, and we could see through the morning fog. Helen found a brass lantern on part of a buoy from a fishing boat. I let her find everything, even if I saw it first. I was busy burying all the birds with a stick. There were always a lot. Seagulls mostly. A duck that Johnny called a helldiver, and a lot of other little ones that I never knew the name of.

I thought it was just a lump of seaweed, because there was no smell, but it was a sea lion. I'd never got up close to one. But Helen went right up and gave it a kick. "Come on, look," she said, so I had to go. You couldn't even tell where the head was, it was so round. Helen started walking around it. Then I saw the sea lion's eye. It was looking at me, looking straight at me, and it blinked. "Here's where it's been shot," she said, "there's a big hole." The sea lion was still alive, but I couldn't tell her that. "Cut me off one of its whiskers, Avery, and we'll have a toothpick for Johnny." I was backing away already. "Avery, take my fingernail file and get me a whisker. He won't bite you." The eye was watching me. I wanted to run for it but I couldn't. And I wanted to saw off the whisker too. But it was the eye that made it hard. I got up close and started using the file, back and forth back and forth, not looking. The whisker came off, thick and hard as a wire, and I handed it to Helen. I never looked again.

When Unk came back, both sacks full, he could hardly walk, his boots were so full of ocean, and even his cigar was wet. We got the boots off first, and he got warm by the fire. I took one sack at a time up to the trunk of the car.

Then we went to the restaurant and had our buckwheat cakes and eggs. Everyone was happy. Helen had given Johnny the whisker and he had it in the corner of his mouth when my father came in.

When I opened the front door to the knock and saw Mr. Allen and he said, "Avery, is Mrs. Fontana in?" he never gave me a chance to think. He stepped around me. Aunt May was in her chair and never had time to cover her legs.

He started talking about the school in South City and he had a paper he wanted her to sign. I was so surprised I never closed the door. Then Miss Walker came in and they started arguing. "You were supposed to wait for me to decide."

"Last month you said you didn't want him in your class next year."

"I changed my mind. He's improved."

"I'm the principal."

"And I'm his teacher; it's supposed to be up to me."

"Not anymore; the superintendent has decided. I'm here as a courtesy to Mrs. Fontana." And he looked down at Aunt May, who had her eyes fixed on the extra-thick part of his black shoe. "He's your responsibility, Mrs. Fontana. We all want to help him, but if he causes any more trouble we're going to have to expel him permanently. Then, because he's underage, there would be a hearing. And you'd have to testify against the state. And pay all the expenses, as his guardian.

"But if he goes to the other school with your permission, you won't have to worry. We all want what's best for Avery." He was holding the paper on his notebook, his fountain pen uncapped in his other hand. She took the fountain pen first.

"May," Miss Walker said. And I ran.

Out the back door, making it crash as hard as I could against the wall. Then the screen door. Through the open gate. I turned to run along the back fence, but didn't turn off when I came to the slant rows of sweet peas. I kept going, crashing, kicking, swinging my arms as if I were fighting, feeling the pull of the string and stretch and snap, the flowers sticking to my legs, arms, and around my neck, but I kept going.

When I got to the sidewalk I stopped, breathing hard. I saw the vent over the wash shed and was going to wave good-bye but started running again when I heard a streetcar coming. Over the streetcar rails and up the loose rock and down the railroad ties. A Navy blimp passed low overhead like a gray cloud. I could see the cabin and maybe some of the crew looking out the window as plain as day.

I turned off the track down the bank toward the mud-flat side and slowed to a walk to get through the fence and started trying to decide, stepping over the new crop of mushrooms. No more thinking, I was done with that. I would sail away out of the canal to the bay. The boat was built enough for that. The mast wasn't up yet, but I didn't need a sail. I'd float away.

When I got to the place where I could see the raft and the canal, I knew. I knew all along there wasn't enough water. The railroad ties on the bottom of the boat were all up, all showing. The boat was stuck in the gray mud. I wasn't going anywhere.

When your ideas are impossible you have to stop using them. When you can't think of anything good. When your ideas have no shape or color. You have to stop it. It was only when you did things without thinking before or after that sometimes worked. Trampling Aunt May's sweet peas. That made me feel better by the minute. When Mr. Mitchum cut the kite string he was smiling to himself.

I am Avery. *He could do anything. It was only a matter of making his hands or his feet do the work. He didn't need to get any ideas. He didn't need to think anymore.*

Just his hands and his feet jumped to the raft, and the green water waved against the bank. Then opened the cabin door. He hadn't brought the food he'd been hiding in the shed. But he didn't need it. There were plenty of mushrooms and he'd eat them for dinner. Hands picked up a rusty lard can and feet went back the way he'd come, to the grass by the eucalyptus trees.

What a day. Have supper and then a good night's sleep. I can stay a long time on the raft. No one knows I'm here. And I have plenty to eat. I can stay here until I'm old enough to join the Navy and they'll give me a uniform and new shoes.

There were a lot of mushrooms. He started picking. He watched his hand snap the stem off at the ground and put it in the bucket. When he came to the first toadstool he let his hand do what it wanted. Then another and then another. His legs carried him back to the boat.

He sat with his back to the cabin wall, the door hooked closed. There was still enough light flashing through cracks to see and he took his hat off. A thought tried to get through. What had he written on the message to the kite? He couldn't remember. There was no heaven, just like there was no water in the canal to sail away on because there was no rain. Just like there was no more school. No more sea lion eye. No more mustard sandwiches. No more going back. And no more. No more.

His fingers told him so. And they pulled a white string off, stuck to his shoulder, with eight sweet peas, and put them across his legs. He watched his hand take the first mushroom and he chewed. They were better with salt. His hand took another. He closed his eyes. His hand took another.

But his thoughts wouldn't stop right away. He knew the message to the kite now. He hadn't known what to put down that day. Hello, he had written first and then another Hello. The three other messages were on their way up; he had to hurry, and he wrote, Whoever's up here don't worry, Avery Gorman. He signed his old name so they'd know who it was. The kite must be waiting for him now.

Chuck

Since Easter Sunday when he got back from Nevada it had been one thing after another. He couldn't catch up. There had been three knifings, a shooting, a civilian almost stomped to death. The sick bay was full of injured sailors. The brig was over capacity and they were sending forty prisoners up to the brig on Treasure Island. He'd stopped counting after three hundred on the number of courts-martial this month. And he was letting most go, if he could, for minor infractions. Van Beek was chewing him out daily over something, blaming him every time some civilian got his car stolen or his tank siphoned of rationed gas or his daughter got her rear end pinched at the movies or a family woke up and there was a drunken sailor in the porch glider and another sleeping with their dog.

They had put the worst bars off limits, the ones where they jackrolled the sailors, watered the whiskey, and the prostitutes were all clapped up. The bar owners yelled bloody murder, as if everyone's right to fleece the military was in jeopardy. When they cut liberty back from 0400 to Cinderella liberty, back to 2400, Van Beek got a call from the lieutenant governor of the state. By the time he got there the XO was pacing, and every time Van Beek tried to tell him what was going on he'd interrupt himself with, "Those sons of bitches."

He was standing at attention; Van Beek never gave anyone at ease. "The sonofabitch told me I was going to have to learn how to get along. That we all had to do our part in the war effort. That he was getting complaints about the way I was handling the situation," Van Beek finally got out. "What the hell do they think this is, anyway, a goddamn circus we're running here? We're losing twenty percent of the boots the way it is now. I have more men in sick bay than out on the rifle range every morning. There's so many injuries in that town, it's getting worse than the War Zone. Given enough time the Axis will win this war because we'll run out of eighteen-year-olds.

"You're going to have to get your ass in gear, Mr. Sweet. If they ream me, you're going first. Beef up your shore patrols, and before any sailor goes out the gate I want every goddamn one of them to know that if they offend a civilian or injure themselves they are going to pay. Set up a lecture for all the recruits: no one leaves this base until they understand that while on shore liberty the U.S. Navy is responsible for their personal behavior. And they will act accordingly. Get it through their thick heads they're government property." He was yelling again.

"You know what that turd said?" Van Beek lowered his voice, stopped pacing to point at the phone. "We all have to make sacrifices, and I'd have to learn that. Him being a public office holder, he'd learned that the hard way. And he said he better not be receiving any more phone calls. Mr. Sweet, I hope the Japs do land and go up to Sacramento and stick their bayonets into those politicians' fat bellies. I'll show them where the highway is. This is not a war, Mr. Sweet, it's a circus, and the spectators in the stands have taken over. The animals aren't allowed to do what they were trained for. Why are you still standing there, Mr. Sweet? We have to get busy. He promised me he'd come down here himself with his friend the admiral if we couldn't accommodate the civilians who are suffering during this war, what with the deprivations of rationing and no proper respect."

Now every morning he stood in front of three platoons of recruits at a time and started reading the regulations. They sat at ease in the old racetrack stands, happy to be resting. He knew it wasn't going to make any difference what he said. He had never listened to any you-better-not speeches either. "If you are caught intoxicated or abusing civilians or their property, fighting, yelling, spitting, or using foul language while on liberty, I personally and the U.S. Navy in particular will see to it that you never, never see the other side of the front gate again as long as you are here." He had ten of the biggest men from the permanent staff that pulled shore patrol standing behind him, wearing all their gear. "See these men? They're going to be out there waiting for you to fuck up. And when you do, you'll be sorry, I guarantee that."

He could be anywhere and his mind would wander somewhere else. Anywhere other than his desk. Elaine giving him another French kiss. They made him nervous. He'd never had anyone do that before. If a whore had tried, he'd have washed his mouth out with soap. He'd be worried about cankers for weeks.

Carson City. He'd lost five checker games to Loretta. It had thrown him off, spending those three days with Elaine's family. Elaine was like her mother. Who was like his own mother? Molly wasn't like her. Maybe it didn't matter anymore.

He had fit in up there just like he belonged. He kept thinking they were going to find him out, somehow realize that he couldn't even remember living in a regular house. At St. John's he'd had a bunk, and before that there were rooming houses where he'd slept on a pallet on the floor. On ship it was a hammock. Here a single thin mattress. With the Walkers he'd had a good bed, box springs and mattress. It was too comfortable; he couldn't go to sleep. Ben came in saying, "You still awake?" He wanted to pretend he was asleep; he could smell bourbon across the room. "You want a snort?" He still didn't answer. "Jesus, I'm pooped. Ever try and tear off a piece of ass under a front porch with a bunch of spiders watching you?" He had to laugh; he couldn't help it. "With the goddamn English it's worse," Ben went on. "They won't lay down. I must have screwed standing up in every doorway in London."

"That's true?" he asked. "I don't get it."

"Somebody told me once it was because they thought they wouldn't get pregnant that way. But, Christ, I put on four rubbers once, one at a time, to show her, and she still wouldn't fall over. I hope there weren't any black widows under there. I love Mona. Elaine has all the personality in the family, but Mona is okay too. Her brothers are the two biggest assholes in the state of Nevada. Draft dodgers."

"They're at West Point, aren't they?"

"That's the best place in the world to hide, play soldier; the war will be over before they leave New York." He could hear Ben lie down on the bed, then the sound of him swallowing from the bottle of bourbon. "How come you don't wear your ribbons if you rate them? You made me feel like a shithead later on when Elaine told me."

"Those little clips in the back fall off and the pin sticks me in the chest."

Ben laughed. "You're a character. Sure you don't want a snort?"

"No, I'm on the straight and narrow here."

"Don't let this family fool you; it's not perfect."

He didn't answer, rolled over on his other side. Ben started breathing evenly like he was asleep until he said, "I did kiss the runway when we touched down, after our ninth mission. I kissed the tarmac. I kissed it three or four times, I was so happy to have made it back from that last mission." He paused again.

In spite of himself he was waiting for Ben to go on. He knew his own story and had heard a lot of others. But they were all different. Like they'd happened in different wars, not to different people. In a different time. "What happened?" he asked.

"The searchlights picked us up, right off. It was still dark, early morning. You couldn't see anything. But I was looking, making sure their night fighters wouldn't sneak up on us, when their antiaircraft batteries opened up. You could see the flashes from below and you'd wait for the shell to reach the plane and explode. I had worked myself up about the flak so much during an air raid on my last pass in London, I'd stolen the hubcap from a car. Bent the sides in like a cup to put between my legs, I was so worried that the shrapnel would come up through the plane and take my cock and balls off. The other waist gunner, who was new, had heard the same stories already and was standing on two flak jackets for the same reason. Are you still awake?"

"I'm awake."

"Then it stopped; we were just flying, taking it easy, seems like for an hour, but it's longer. The sky had lightened up; it was going to be a clear day. The pilot announces we're approaching the target. We get all tensed up again, looking to see what the Germans are going to do. I feel the bombs go; the plane kinda lifts itself after the weight drops. We turn around easy; the whole formation heads back. I'm already thinking ahead to tonight, cold beer at a pub near the base, when, bang, I feel something hit me hard enough to knock me down and there's an explosion. I keep telling myself I have to get up, get up and shoot, but I can't. I can hear the other crew members calling my name but I can't answer. I'm just laying there thinking I'm a dead man now and how unfair it was I was killed in my prime.

"I came to at the approach to the runway and sat right up. My head hurt so bad I thought I just came off a three-day drunk. When I sat up, the copilot, who'd thought I was dead because I was covered with blood, fainted, fell right over and got a big gash on the top of his head.

"I got right up to help when the wheels touched down. I still didn't know what happened. I just had this terrific pain in my shoulder now that was making me sick. There was an ambulance waiting and I insisted I could help carry the stretcher for the other gunner. Because there were a lot of people around and I was always a show-off, that's when I got down and kissed the asphalt. But the pain made me pass out and they ended up taking me in the ambulance too. I had a compound fracture of the collarbone.

"What had happened was, we were hit and a piece of shrapnel came through and took the other waist gunner's leg off at the shin. His boot with his foot inside came across where I was standing and hit me in the chest. How do you like that? All three of us were in the same ward. We worked it out. You sure you don't want a drink?"

"No thanks."

"I'll let you get some sleep now. I'm tired myself. I don't know why I came back here; I have no family but an aunt in Reno. Habit, I guess. And Mona too, of course. She's reason enough. Damon and Daryl will find out for themselves. I wish I'd gone in the Navy."

He tried not to think of Elaine so much, and when he did, he forced himself not to think anything dirty. He wasn't going to ruin this by doing something he was going to regret. He hadn't even had a normal date with an American woman, much less got serious about one. Elaine probably told her mother everything. He wasn't sure why people worried about Catholics so much. The priests tried to enforce all those rules against sins, but he didn't know anyone who obeyed them. That's why they had confession. That was an old joke. He'd gone to confession off and on while he was in the Navy. After the *Arizona* was sunk, he went once. But not since. He'd stopped that part of the business. If he sinned he'd take care of it himself. He didn't need a priest to tell him he needed to say a hundred Hail Marys. He would find his own grace. He did on the raft. By not giving up, by trying to save the others. But he'd been the only one to survive. He hadn't prayed then and he hadn't confessed since. His father was the Catholic, but when he was working it had been his mother who got up on Sunday to take them to church, when she was home. She had never converted as far as he knew, but she'd go with them, pray, do what everyone else was doing.

He had to show Elaine respect. He was thinking that, but at the same time his mind's eye was fixed on Elaine's breasts. The way they strained the button on her black suit coat. He'd like to nudge the button loose with his nose. She wasn't that kind of girl, the way she acted when he tried to get in her pants up at Carson City. He was going to have to use more self-control.

If he wanted to prong a woman, he could pick one up in the bars. He'd never seen so many whores show up in such a short time. Even when the whole fleet was in, there wasn't this ratio. It meant more trouble, naturally. No matter how many there were, the boots would want to fight over them. Marry them and the rest of it, make out a government allotment, put their name on the insurance policy. But what was surprising was the high school girls and younger showing up where they could be picked up by a sailor, wherever the boots congregated up in the city: at Playland, out by the beach, the Sutro Baths, on Market Street. In the Orient you could always get young girls if that was your inclination. It had never appealed to him. He liked the older ones that spoke a little English so he could talk to them, make them laugh, before they went upstairs. He had never had the nerve to try to pleasure a whore, after he'd learned how with Jeanette. This war had turned everything upside down. Those young girls were fucking for kewpie dolls that a sailor won for them at the carnival at Playland. A ride on the roller coaster, a hamburger and Coke. He had heard too many stories not to be sure some must be true.

He got a chance to go into town late, too late to phone Elaine that he was coming. He went to the USO because he knew she'd be there. He timed it right; the band had just finished playing and she was walking back to where the women stood to be asked to dance. He took her by the arm when she walked by. "Come with me," he said.

"Chuck." She looked pleased to see him. It always surprised him. "I thought you weren't coming."

"Come on," he said. She didn't say no, or anything about the rules, as he led her to the door and put her coat over her shoulders. They held hands as they went down the stairs through the mobs of servicemen and out to the car. She didn't say anything until they were driving. "Where are we going?"

"I'm taking you on a date. I've never taken anyone, and I want to practice on you. We're going to dinner first."

"It's ten-thirty; I don't think anyplace is open. And I ate four doughnuts already in the last hour and a half. Glazed ones, they were so good."

"Gluttony is a sin."

"You're a sin," she said, sitting close to him and starting to kiss him on his neck.

He kept driving, put one arm around her shoulder. "Have you been to the Pacific yet?" he asked. "Because that's where we're going."

She didn't remember at first, but when she did she laughed. "In fact, I have; last week when we went up to the park to see the aquarium we took the fourth, fifth, and sixth grades up by bus along the Coast Highway. I've been to the Pacific theater."

They walked along the hard sand. The fans of water spreading out on the beach as the tide came in looked smooth as glass in the full moon. He didn't want to get too close. "Come on," she said. She was slipping off her shoes. "It's not too cold."

"I think I'll stay right here." He sat down on a piece of driftwood. He wasn't afraid of the salt water.

"If you walk with me I'll give you a kiss." He shook his head. "Two kisses." She laughed when she said that last part. It was that sound that got him to his feet. He kissed her, missing her lips, kissed her on the mouth the second time. "You have your shoes on," she said. He didn't understand; he was running his hands up her back under her blouse, down over her skirt, holding her as close as he could. "You're wearing your shoes," she said. He looked down, surprised. "Come on, let's get out of the water."

On the way back he drove barefoot. She had rung out his socks and put them over the car heater. "I don't know how to act," he said.

"I like your dates," she said.

He was half asleep at his desk, his eyes closed, when he heard the music. He had been up half the night again, trying to make sure the thirteen hundred recruits made it up to Hunters Point to embark without anyone getting away. The band must be practicing on the parade ground, the sound carried by the wind, it sounded so close. "Stars and Stripes Forever."

At one time he would have got up and walked to wherever the band was, get closer, not just to hear but to see them play. It gave him such pleasure. And he'd offer, "I'll rest you," to a tuba player or baritone, his favorites in brass. Of course, he was better at the clarinet or bassoon. Sometimes the bandmaster would let him.

Brother Ralph insisted they be versatile, not just one-instrument players. Adapt your musical knowledge to the whole family of instruments. He had tried. Except for the strings, he could get by. They were the hardest. When someone got sick at St. John's, he'd volunteer just for the practice. He marched down main streets in every town in western Montana playing everything from the trombone to the flute. Any parade, Fourth of July, Armistice Day, Labor Day, rodeos, holy days, any day, and St. John's Marching Band would be there.

He'd won second place in the state finals for the bassoon. There was a senior, a girl whose father was a music teacher; she'd won first. There'd only been four entries in the whole state. They had laughed about that. He'd talked to the girl after. "You're good," she said, "keep practicing." He'd always remembered that. But she had been much better.

When he enlisted he was going to put down bandsman; it didn't mean you would get it but there was a chance, with his experience; Sonny had got to be one. Would things have turned out any different? The recruiter had talked him into putting down baker. "You'll be working inside when it rains," he'd said. "No foul weather like the deck crew. You don't want to be a bandsman; everyone makes fun of them. They're candy-asses. Their sisters all end up whores."

Bakers were all crazy. It was getting up at 0300 hours every morning that did it. You never completely woke up or went to sleep. That's where he screwed up. He could have been anything with the war. They were making men officers with his time. But he had no high school diploma. And worse, he had bad time. Almost six months in the brig. Busted down. Insubordination. Fighting. You name it, he'd done it. No rate. But the Navy didn't care; they let him reenlist, and he struck for yeoman. If the brothers had taught him to play musical instruments, Miss Clay had taught him to type and spell.

That's where he got rated and that's where he became a kiss-ass. With the chiefs. With the officers. He got used to not having to stand watch. No mess duty. He became a passenger on the ship. Spitting over the side, watching the buildings in the harbor get bigger and bigger, thinking of the cold beer he'd be drinking. He made up the duty rosters. He had no trouble after he became third-class. He drank his drink, dropped his anchor in all and sundry female ports, and went back to the ship. A good sailor.

They allowed him time to play with the band when they practiced. On the fantail usually, after noon chow. Sit in when they needed an orchestra ashore for an officers' dance. Fill in on Sunday mornings when somebody was in sick bay or'd got liberty to play for church services. On the *Arizona* that Sunday, that's what saved him.

He got up out of the chair. He was always tired, even when he got a night's sleep. Restless. How did he end up a master-at-arms, a policeman? He wasn't doing anything. That's why he felt out of sorts. No exercise. Nothing was the same anymore, and nothing was different when he made chief. He'd been waiting years, and it didn't mean anything. Not after the first day.

It meant a uniform with fewer buttons, a different tie and cap. Van Beek had been funny. "Congratulations, Chief. It took me fourteen years to make that rank, and you do it in half the time. You must be twice as smart." It was the first time he'd been given at ease.

"I bet you can't roll out a gross of cinnamon buns in an hour or type eighty-three words a minute either," he'd said back. Van Beek had laughed. He'd never thought he'd be kidding around with a lieutenant commander, and this one in particular.

There was no ceremony; a runner delivered a nine-by-twelve white envelope while he was making out the duty roster. It was the official notification that he was a chief petty officer. He read it again, again, getting more pleasure each time. He looked around the office for someone to tell. The Salt was on patrol. The others weren't even rated yet; they wouldn't understand the significance.

He'd only seen it happen twice before the war. One was a brown-nose kiss-ass radioman and the other a signalman who was a good sailor and earned the rank. At the first port, Subic Bay, he'd bought drinks for anyone that came in the bar from the ship. The radioman had offered but no one took him up on it. The signalman had moved into the CPO quarters and that was the last he'd ever seen of him. There could be no friendship between the ranks when you got that high up. And it was the way it was supposed to be. No one was going to listen very carefully to an order given by someone they'd shared a bottle or a whore with on shore the night before. It had to be that way.

He'd already got a uniform tailored, his hash marks on the sleeve, the new rating. Hanging on a hook behind the door. He couldn't help himself; he had to put it on. It was like dressing up as an Indian at St. John's. It was better. He didn't look at himself in the mirror but he felt unusual. Conspicuous, like he was impersonating a chief.

He had to go back out into the office but he couldn't get himself to turn the handle. He just stood there with the knob in his hand, listening to the strikers talk and type. Men coming to the counter for passes, or for permits to bring their cars on base. Coming off leave with stacks of orders. He went out the back way instead, to the CPO mess. It was still early for supper but the place was full. Chow hounds. Being waited on by stewards. Eating as if they were to go on duty in thirty seconds. Most of them fat, with ratings he'd never seen before. He sat down and was brought a plate of chow, the same food the recruits got, but it tasted better. This mess had its own galley, its own cooks, cooking for three hundred rather than three thousand.

He got back to the office. No one said anything. The strikers nodded when he passed their desks. Salty Randolph was back, brought him something to sign. No comment on the new uniform and his new rank. He went back to his cubicle and got to work. When he checked his pocket watch it was 1540. He thought of Elaine; he could go pick her up from school.

Kids were coming through the school-grounds gate like it was the narrow end of a funnel, then spreading out again over the sidewalks and streets in front of the school. He had to stop at a crosswalk until the kids thinned out before he could drive on. He had planned to surprise her in her classroom, but when he got into the school, she wasn't there. The janitor in the hallway told him there was a teachers' meeting that would last until five. It was too long to wait. He went back out to the car. He hoped the janitor would remember to tell Elaine he'd been there.

He hadn't been to town in the daytime for weeks. He made the turn onto Main Street, going north back to the base. The place looked so peaceful in the sunlight. It seemed abandoned, only a few people coming out of the drugstore on the whole street.

When he recognized the two little girls that lived near Elaine, he slowed down to see what they were up to. The older one was trying to hit some boys on the back with her lunch box. The younger was kicking them in the legs and screaming.

The five boys had sticks and were poking them up into a tree like they were trying to get down some fruit. The tree had white flowers; Elaine had told him it was a magnolia tree. He was going to drive on when one of the boys turned around after getting a crack on the head with the metal lunch box and pushed the older girl down, then tried to drop on his knee in the middle of her stomach.

He was yelling out the window before he could stop the car. When he got out, the boys dropped the sticks and ran. It must not have knocked the wind out of her, because the bigger girl got up, picked up her coat and lunch box, and begin shouting up the tree, "I hope you're satisfied now. I got my dress all dirty."

He looked up too at the same time that Avery came down the trunk, let go of the last limb, and landed on his feet on the sidewalk. The kids froze, staring, when they saw him standing there. "Does anyone want a Life Saver?" he asked, reaching into his pocket. He knew he had some because he always got a roll if he knew he was going to see Elaine.

The little girl put her hand out as he peeled back the paper, but her sister grabbed her arm. "We can't have any, thank you, it will ruin our dinner. We have to go home."

"Here, Mary Maureen." Avery started unbuttoning his shirt and took out a stack of comic books. She thumbed through them, counting.

"Thank you, Avery," she said. "I knew you'd do what you promised." She walked off, with the little sister following.

He was still holding the Life Savers and offered one to Avery, then took one himself. He looked back up in the tree. "You having a little problem with those other kids?"

"Not exactly," he said. "They were just trying to get the comic books off me." Once he got talking right, it came out in a rush. "We had a paper drive Saturday. Anytime I saw comic books or something Aunt May might like, I'd put them aside, or if I was fast enough, those magazines with the pictures of women in bathing suits for each month. My uncle gave out calendars with the same women. But everyone was after them. The big boys wanted them all. I brought the comic books to school to give to Mary Maureen. I waited until after school, but the seventh-graders knew I had the pictures and the comics; one of them had been on the paper drive. I owed Mary Maureen because she helped me finish my work in the garden so I could go on the drive. I always find the most comic books; she knows that." He stopped talking and looked closer. "You made CPO," he said.

"In fact I did."

"Congratulations, Chief Petty Officer."

He felt awkward for some reason, stood up straight, then remembered he had some extra CPO patches in the pocket of his coat. "Here," he said, handing one over. "You been squared away lately?" he said, for something to say.

"I try, most of the time. But things don't turn out like you expect."

"You have to obey orders, Avery; that's why they make them. If we don't follow the regulations, we just might as well be a mob."

"Today I was showing Leroy one of the pictures I got, and Miss Walker saw and took it away. I didn't know they were dirty. That they would expel me for that if they caught me. I know she's trying to help me. I was collecting them because my uncle liked them."

"Why didn't you give them to your uncle?"

"He's not around here anymore." The kid reached into his inside jacket pocket and pulled out a roll of papers and handed them over.

He opened one double page out. It was some magazine he'd never heard of before. The blonde was a looker, dressed in a red swimsuit, posed with a little saying: *July's a patriotic month. Let's celebrate it right. In case you're out of fireworks, why here's some dynamite.* "What do you take for them?" he asked.

"You can have them."

"No, I couldn't do that."

"Cigarettes."

"You're too young to smoke; you'll stunt your growth."

"For Aunt May; she smokes."

He felt around. He had almost a full pack of Lucky Strikes and a few in another pack. Avery was watching. "Here, take these." He handed over both green packs.

The boy started backing away like he might change his mind, saying thank you a couple of times. When he got to the sidewalk he broke into a run like someone was chasing him.

When he was sent for by the XO he thought it was going to be an everyday bullshit session. He and Van Beek were getting along better now, both taking turns telling their before-the-war sea stories. For some reason they both started with Caribbean ports and were on their way to the Orient, as if they were saving the best whores for last.

He went through the open doorway into the office, his clipboard under his arm, reaching for his cigarettes, shaking out another Lucky from his pack to offer the XO. And because he'd just come from outside he had his cover on. He didn't notice at first that there was someone else with the XO, who was sitting at his desk, until he glanced to one side and saw the gold stripes on the officer's sleeve. He tried to get the cigarette out of his mouth, his cap off, and stand at attention all at the same time.

The XO and the captain both laughed. "As you were, as you were," the XO said. "The smoking lamp's lit, the smoking lamp's lit. This is Captain Mills, who's come to visit us from Washington, D.C."

Instead of acknowledging him with a nod, the captain stepped closer and put out his hand. It surprised him so much he was slow to put out his own. "It's a pleasure to meet you, Chief."

"Thank you, sir." He looked too young for the rank.

"The captain here has come to see you, Chief, and I'll let him speak for himself."

"As you know, Chuck, this war costs money, and that's why we have bond drives. To give you an example, most people don't know what a battleship costs. Something in the neighborhood of one hundred four million dollars, and a carrier costs almost as much. The American people are generous when it comes to supporting their fighting men, but we need even more money. We've found it doesn't hurt for them to listen to the men who have been there, who've seen the blood and gore of battle. The people at home must never forget the sacrifices that are taking place on their behalf, and they in turn must do their duty. That duty is to buy bonds," he ended in a whisper.

The XO started clapping. "I've known Buck here since he was an ensign fresh out of Annapolis. He gets better the higher he goes."

"Thank you," the captain said, taking a bow. "Thank you. The skinny is, Chief, there's a dedication coming up, a memorial to the USS *San Francisco*, and you're going to be at the ceremony. The XO here says . . ." He started laughing. "I can't get over how Van Beek has almost caught up with me, when five years ago he was a chief like you."

"If this war lasts another couple of years, I'll pass you, too," Van Beek said. They both laughed as though they had practiced together before.

"Anyway," the captain said, "we'll give you your decoration or something and you'll give a short talk about your experiences. What it means to the sailor at sea to have the complete support of the American people, so step right up here and buy bonds. We need you." He pointed his forefinger at the XO. "We'll take your money. I should have worked in a carnival." The XO laughed. He tried to join in, but it came out in a grunt.

"It's not easy to speak before a crowd," the captain added, "but it can be learned. On the other hand, it has to look and sound authentic. No one is going to buy a bond from a snake-oil salesman like me. But they might from you. We'll have to see. Some fighting men have that something, and some don't. Just think about it for now. The best pitches are short, no more than five minutes, but three can be plenty.

"Well, that covers it," he said. The XO stood up fast. "Van Beek, it's always good to see you. I'll be in San Francisco for the next couple of months. Come up and see me, but you better phone first. And you, Chief, I expect great things from you." After shaking hands with both of them, he went out.

The phone rang, and as the XO was talking, he watched the gray staff car pull up outside. A third-class opened the back door for the captain and then drove off.

The XO put down the phone. "What do you think?"

"I can't speak in front of anyone."

"It's easier than you think, and like Buck said, you can learn. He phoned and asked if I had any talent, and I told him about you."

"I wish you hadn't. I don't want to do it. I'll go to the ceremony for the dedication. But I wouldn't be any good at the bond selling."

"First, Chief Petty Officer Sweet, you don't have a goddamned choice. Second, you're not being asked, you're being told. It's not up to you, it's up to what the captain decides. Third, I don't like a bellyaching whiner."

He was standing at attention now. "Yes, sir."

"Good. Don't ever forget who you are, and what you are, but most of all, where you are." The XO was shaking his finger at him like Brother Ralph used to for him to stand and solo. "And I want you to try, too, Chief Petty Officer, and hard, to do your best. If I think you're not giving one hundred percent, I'll assign you to fleet so fast you won't have time to pack your seabag. And that's just for a start," he shouted. He paused, took a breath. "Now, forget all that I just said."

When he was dismissed he went back to his office. Sat there telling himself, It's no use thinking of all the things that you should have said. Or done. What could he have done but stand there and take it? He was getting too finicky, way too used to this easy life. He didn't want to go back to sea, but he was a sailor. He didn't want to sell the bonds, but he had to follow orders. And there was a war going on. Remember Pearl Harbor.

Before, no matter what happened, he'd never considered getting out of the Navy. Never. Never. Becoming a civilian, getting a job. Going back to Montana, working for the railroad. The shipyard here. He had another two years left on this enlistment. Then they wouldn't let him go until the war was over. He couldn't desert. Where would he hide this time? When he'd run away from St. John's he'd only lasted four or five days, and that was in the summer. Because he didn't want to play the bassoon. He'd come back starved on his own, taken his strapping, and then they fed him.

The Navy was his home. He had to keep reminding himself of that. But he'd done his share. Everyone thought that. What was one person's share? Who was to decide? They'd caught an AWOL Marine buck sergeant who'd had the silver star with a cluster and was wounded two times on Guadalcanal, and that's what *he* said: I've done my share. But he was still given five months' brig time, busted to private, and sent back overseas.

He got his hat and went outside. It was better to think in the open. Past the slop chute. He drank only beer now, and only on the base: he'd sit there in the CPO club and sip, bullshitting with the other chiefs. No hard stuff. He didn't want Elaine ever to see him shitfaced, out of hand. It wasn't the Indian blood; that didn't make him better or worse. He didn't need a drink now; he needed to think.

What could he say for three minutes before a crowd of people? He could yell for an hour at the recruits without even having to think or write down anything, just stand there and scare them to death enough so they wouldn't tear up the town. It was too easy. The worst part about the speech was he might have to tell what happened on the raft to sell any bonds. But how was he going to decide on which version?

It had become routine, coming to town, stopping at the church first, just to sit, rest, think, wait until it was time to pick up Elaine. A Catholic church was peculiar when you thought about it. It was usually the biggest building in town, bigger than a battleship, and maybe used once a day for a couple of hours, a few people coming in like now to pray or light candles, while the non-Catholics suspected the worst with this dreadnought in their midst. The nuns and priests inside going at the old slap-and-tickle—Ben had said the English used that expression for harpooning the whale. And all the Catholics' loose change going to the Pope, who was provoking the general run of parishioners— wops, greasers, Polacks, and Irishmen—to have too many children and overload the school system. One of the teachers at Elaine's school had told him that.

He checked the time; he had sixteen minutes. It only took four from the church to her school. He should think better thoughts here. No one was sup- posed to know what you're thinking anyway. Life was just a story. No, life was just a bowl of cherries.

That reminded him of one of his sea stories he was going to have to tell Van Beek sometime. When he was an apprentice seaman a month aboard ship, a third-class bosun's mate had asked if they wanted to have some fun, him and a couple of friends. He'd gone along. They went below to one of the big heads, a metal trough, twenty feet long, with seawater running through, seats placed at intervals to take a dump. Half a dozen sailors were seated over the trough, doing their duty. The bosun's mate had some newspaper and he balled it up, then struck a match against the bulkhead and handed it to him, nodding toward the paper. He put the match to the paper and the bosun's mate put the burning paper in the trough.

They watched as the running water floated the burning paper down toward the sailors sitting there. He hadn't understood fully what was going to happen next until the first sailor jumped up cursing when the flame seared the hair off his ass. The bosun's mate was gone and they were left standing there. He was still holding the match. They ran too.

He had told that story to Salty and some of the others, drinking coffee, taking five. None of them had laughed. He'd tried to explain why it was funny. None had even been aboard a ship yet. They couldn't understand anything. They just looked at him.

They spent all their time trying not to look like sailors. Let their hair go too long. Didn't take pride in their shoeshines or the creases in their jumpers. Grew mustaches. Some had civvies hidden somewhere and put them on like they weren't in the Navy on liberty.

Once he became a sailor, he was a sailor. Even before the war he'd worn his uniform whenever he went ashore. He was proud to be in the Navy like he was proud to be a member of the St. John's orchestra. But now this Navy wasn't the same Navy he had joined. These men weren't sailors. Old Randy had to think which was which when asked what side was port or starboard. They weren't making the best of the situation. They weren't sailors. They weren't anything. And they were everywhere. The old Navy was gone.

That's what he thought. But Van Beek mentioned that five of the men in his section had put in for transfer to the fleet. At first he was indignant. The

XO was insinuating he was losing the personnel because he was too hard on them. And he was pissed because he'd spent all that time teaching them their jobs. Now they wanted to leave. He tried to sound casual when he got back and approached the Salt. "What's this I hear, you're jumping ship? You asked for a transfer," he added louder, when Randy didn't look like he understood. All the talking around them stopped.

"I want to get at the Japs," Salty said.

One of the strikers was listening who'd put in for a transfer too. "What about you?" he asked him.

"My brother is on an LSD. I thought I'd like to serve with him."

Another piped up, "I didn't enlist to visit California." Everyone laughed.

After that, he looked differently at them. That's when he started getting the cinnamon buns every morning, bribing the bakers with liberty passes, and telling his men sea stories they didn't understand. When the first kid got his orders for sea duty, he made sure a seaman first-class stripe was on his sleeve. And he warned him what to watch out for. Don't listen to the sea lawyers. Don't borrow any money, especially at five for ten. Wait until the eagle shits for your own cash. Keep your hair short and your mouth shut. He went over his personnel file, beefed up the kid's experience as a yeoman striker, added to his proficiency scores. Made sure his allotment to his mother in Vermont was current. When he saw the red tag of a non-swimmer, he felt sick. The kid hadn't learned in boot camp. He was going to the South Pacific and he couldn't swim.

He took the whole section over for some suds at the CPO club when the first one left. Randy had got the kid a silver ID bracelet with the kid's name and serial number on front, and on the back, TANFORAN SWABJOCKEY CLUB. They all contributed. This war wasn't going to last forever, he kept telling himself, watching them drink the cold beer. But sometimes it seemed like it might. Or long enough to get everyone killed.

He had got a letter from Myra last Thursday. Sikes had finished his training at the submarine school in Connecticut. He hadn't been stationed on the East Coast but was serving on a newly commissioned sub. He was on a shakedown cruise and was coming back to the West Coast. She might come out if Sikes got any leave before he was shipped out.

Subs were death traps. He didn't remember much after the sub picked them up from the raft. He was semiconscious, raving for water, his tongue so thick in his mouth he was gagging. They put him in a hammock over a torpedo, and his hand kept grazing the cold metal side as the boat rocked, getting under way. A corpsman was spooning lemon water down his throat. The engineering officer came in and wanted to shake his hand. He didn't understand anything. He was never sure he was off the raft while he was in the sub. The other survivors were talking about what happened on the raft. He could hear the boat's bell sounding the half hour. That started making him feel safe. He half-remembered men coming in to the compartment to look at him, the other survivors dying before they got back to port. The sub's captain wrote him up for a decoration. He tried to explain that Commander Cord had done it already, after the *Arizona* sank. He didn't want any more. The medals were a curse, a reminder of what had happened. They weren't recognition for a heroic act—being alive was enough— they were a sign your days were numbered. He wouldn't wear the ribbons. No. Your family will be proud of you, the submarine captain had said. He didn't have a family. They had done so much talking on the raft about families, friends, and shipmates, mothers and fathers, the rest of them. That's what killed the others. Some tried to swim home. That's why they gave up and he didn't. The fish were his family, the sharks that came to feed were his brothers and sisters. Stop. Stop. Hail Mary full of grace. He had to stop thinking these thoughts. He was safe here.

They weren't going to send him anywhere. If it meant giving a speech, he could do that. Probably. He looked at his father's railroad watch. Another four minutes. But Van Beek was trouble. He liked to fuck over people just for drill. He'd seen him. Didn't make any difference, officer or enlisted man. If he could get away with it, he'd try it on anyone, yelling at some scared lieutenant jg, "If the Navy wanted you to have a wife they would have issued you one," as easy as he chewed out an enlisted man.

It was time to pick up Elaine. He snapped his father's railroad watch closed, crossed himself, picked up his cover, and genuflected as he left the pew.

He tried typing out what he had so far, but the speech didn't sound right. "Ladies and gentlemen, officers and men, we're here today to honor a ship, the USS *San Francisco*, with a memorial." He could see himself standing up in front of a crowd at the site overlooking the bay where part of the superstructure was to be placed, a slight wind blowing off the water, the smell of brine and salt in the air.

He'd heard so many speeches since the war started that it was going to be impossible not to sound like them. As soon as you mentioned war, war zone, war effort, warships, home front, patriotism, and sacrifices, you were repeating the same speech.

The XO had called him in the next day as if nothing had happened. There was no chewing-out. Van Beek told a sea story about Hong Kong, where as a third-class he and some other sailors had had a rickshaw race down a Victoria street, how he'd beaten on his driver's head with his cap until he pulled ahead and won the race.

Then he'd had his turn and told his Hong Kong story about the rickshaw driver who'd tried to roll him and another sailor from Florida by flipping the rickshaw backward as they were going up a hill so their heads would smash against the pavement. He'd been knocked out, but his shipmate had rolled with the movement and was able to get up and kick the shit out of the driver. Then, at the very end, Van Beek had said, "By the way, Chief, I expect to have the first draft of your speech on my desk by Friday."

"Yes, sir," he'd said going out. The bastard.

"There is not a man in the United States Navy who isn't ready to sacrifice his life for the good of his country," he typed. That wasn't true. He'd seen ships leaving Pearl where some of the sailors had to be dragged aboard. If he'd had any sense he'd have stayed in sick bay after the *Arizona*.

"But your ordinary sailor needs the equipment, the tools to fight back with. It costs one hundred four million dollars to pay for one battleship. Your sailors are ready to use that ship against the Axis, to fly the planes and shoot the guns so you folks will be safe. To go to your jobs, churches, and sit at home." He must have heard that before somewhere. Word for word. Everyone was going to know he hadn't written this. It must have been at the hospital: the orderlies used to grab him because he couldn't get away very well in his wheelchair every time an officer came into the ward to speak, so there'd be an audience.

"Now it's your turn, my friends, to support our fighting men. Buy bonds. Think of your sons. Think of your friends and neighbors. Think of yourselves." He'd have to read it to Elaine, see what she thought.

As he was typing the second draft he realized where he'd heard some of the words before. St. John's. But it wasn't about the nation supporting the war. It was God who wanted people to give. "Sweet Jesus needs cash," another student had whispered to him as he passed the collection plate during mass one time. When dumb tourists would come by to see the famous school, the brothers would give the same kind of speech. He hadn't remembered that. The school had needed money to build more classrooms. Buy a big yellow bus. Or just plain food. A dollar, a single greenback, will feed an Indian child for days. Who will take the responsibility for feeding this child for one quarter of a month? A hundred-pound sack of potatoes will feed ten children for a week.

But everyone was up against it during the Depression, which seemed to have disappeared with the war. People had so much money now they didn't know what to do with it. There wasn't anything to buy. No cars or houses. They might as well buy War Bonds.

But at St. John's it was the photos and the orchestra music that did the trick. Maybe during his speech he ought to pass around photographs of dead sailors that had been floating around in the Pacific for a week, while he whistled taps. They'd buy bonds then.

Had he ever mentioned to Elaine that he was half Indian? He never told anyone if he could help it.

He'd let the speech rest awhile; he'd think of more later. It was time to pick up Elaine. He checked his pocket watch too. It was amazing, in a way, how he didn't think of the war anymore. Who was winning or who was losing. He'd stopped reading the papers. They censored everything anyway. You never knew what was going on, and it was better that way.

He walked right into the school, said hello to the secretary; they all knew him. Elaine was at her desk, grading papers. Spelling tests. He came in behind her and tickled her on the back of her neck and she jumped. "Oh, you startled me," she said, taking his hand. "I'll be finished in a minute." She was going down the rows of words and making red checks against the errors, then tallying up and writing the scores on top.

"How'd Avery do?" he asked.

"He didn't come to school today, or yesterday either."

"He must be sick, then?"

"Day before yesterday," she said, still grading the tests, "I had an argument with Mr. Allen at Avery's house, and he ran out. When he didn't come to school yesterday I asked Mary Maureen and she said he had a cold. But Ruthie came up during recess today and told me Avery was hiding somewhere. He didn't come today. I don't know what to think." She put her pencil down and rubbed her eyes. "It's all so complicated. I might have led Mr. Allen to believe Avery should be held back. And then Mr. Allen went ahead and decided he shouldn't be promoted to the sixth grade. But I had changed my mind. I wanted him in my class next year; that's what we were arguing about. I should stop and see Aunt May again." He didn't understand why she looked so upset.

He gave the world globe a spin when she stopped talking, looking for places he'd been. None in Europe or Africa. Up and down both sides of South America, Australia, New Zealand, through the Panama Canal nine or ten times. Iceland, he'd been to Iceland.

"Are you ready, Chuck?" she asked. "I'm tired," she said in the car. "I don't think I'll go to the USO tonight." He was glad. He didn't like her dancing with all those sailors. That made him smile.

"What are you thinking?" she asked.

"About you," he said, and that made her smile. "Do you want to stop for a root-beer float?" He didn't have to ask twice.

As they sat in the booth across from each other their knees touched, and neither of them moved away. He showed her the speech and she read it through twice before saying, "I like it."

"The only trouble is it's too short," he said. "I timed myself at a minute fourteen seconds. I need at least three minutes."

She read it through again. "You're going to have to develop your ordeal on the raft. Not just mention it." She looked at him then. "You never talked about that before."

"It's not important," he said. "I had forgotten about it until I put that sentence about it in the speech. The XO suggested that."

When she finished her float he tried to talk her into having another one. "Look at me," she said, "I'm gaining too much weight now. People will think I'm pregnant." Her face turned as red as he'd ever seen it, and she got up to go. "I didn't mean it like that," she said. He couldn't think of what to say.

When they turned onto her street he saw the old lady on the corner. Kids. The other woman with the crutches came out of the house next door. Elaine had introduced him. The only one he knew for sure was Mrs. Hughes, who was standing by her front porch. Is this the way it was? A neighborhood, families? "I'll go over and ask about Avery," Elaine said. She came back to the car almost running. "They don't know where he is. He's run away. He's been gone since the day before yesterday." He got out and went over to where the women were standing.

"Did he take any food?" he asked the woman he remembered was Avery's aunt.

"I don't think so," she said. "I've looked everywhere. I phoned. I can't get ahold of anyone. They don't answer. But I know he wouldn't have gone back to his family. I told everyone he was sick. I thought he'd come back on his own. He's such a wild boy."

The two little girls came closer. "Leroy, his friend, told me once that Avery had a boat in the canal," the oldest girl said. "Ruthie knows where it is because Avery drew a map once of the mud flats and showed her."

"I could find it," Ruthie said.

"Maybe I ought to take a walk out there," he said.

"He'll be back when he gets hungry," the girl's grandmother said.

"I'll go with you as soon as I change my shoes," Elaine said.

Mrs. Hughes came up. "Did you find him?"

"He was supposed to help her in the garden." The grandmother pointed to Avery's aunt. "And look how it turns out; she has to look for him. The worry of it all. You either send him where he came from, May, or put him in a home. I wouldn't take him back if I were you. He's not to be trusted."

"I'll go have a look," he said.

"We'll go with you," the older girl said. "I know a shortcut."

"You hold hands when you cross the tracks, Mary Maureen; you know where that carpenter is now."

"I'll be back," he said to Elaine, following the girls.

There was a path through a vacant lot. He followed, the girls almost running, the older leading the way. Fine spring grass the color of new peas was coming up like fur over the black ground. He wasn't thinking anything. Across a street, down and up the rock bed for two sets of railroad tracks. Ruthie automatically started tightroping on a rail, tiptoeing like a trapeze artist, arms out, her sister holding a handful of her skirt so she'd balance. When they came to the trestle they went down the slope under the tracks, stepping on dry places in the cement causeway. "My father used to work for the railroad," he said, but neither girl answered.

A big windbreak of trees ahead, behind a barbed-wire fence. He knew where he was by the sound of the planes taking off and landing. Another path to the fence, the older girl holding a strand up and putting her foot on the lower. He passed through first. They made noise going through the dried leaves and dead branches under the stand of trees. He'd never seen this kind up close, but they were planted everywhere around the base.

Now he could see the airport. The hangars, the conning tower, rows of fighter planes. P-38 Lightnings. It was a couple of miles away. Between was flat ground, mostly dried gray mud, with a canal of dirty water. He felt his feet already sinking in the soft mud by the canal, enough to leave prints. This was a strange state, California: no seasons, no weather, strange trees.

The girls stopped, looking, he didn't see at what until he came up. There was a raft in the water, tied to a piling on a footbridge. Written on the side of the cabin in white chalk was USS *Arizona*. He got down and pulled on the line and brought the raft in closer to the slippery bank. The older girl yelled out near his ear, and made him jump. "Avery, I know you're in there. You better come out." He couldn't tell if the kid was or not; the inside of the cabin was lined with cardboard. He couldn't see an opening. "Avery," she shouted again.

"Hold on," he said. "How do you know he's in there?"

"Because this is where he hides when he gets in trouble. And there's nowhere else for him to go. And Aunt May warned him . . ."

He went down the bank, getting the gray mud over the toes of his shoes. The raft went down with his weight, the water sucking up between the boards and then releasing, flowing down again. With that sound he was lost at sea again. He felt around the cabin, looking for the opening. "There's a door; he's in there," the older girl said.

He found the doorknob, an empty thread spool nailed onto the plywood. He pulled on the knob but the door wouldn't come loose. There was something holding it from the inside. He could smell something rank.

"Avery," he said, "we have to muster topside. Come on. Open the hatch." There was no movement. He couldn't hear anything. He walked all around the cabin, but he couldn't see in. At a knothole he poked his finger through, but there wasn't enough light to see.

"He's in there," the girl said.

He got irritated. "He's not in there." Then he heard a noise, a cough. He gave the side of the cabin a kick, then another, but it held. He tried lifting up on the plywood roof and it gave, the nails squeaking as he raised the sheet and then flipped it over into the canal. He reached in and unhooked the door.

The boy lay on his back, chalked-faced, green-and-black fluid trickling out of his mouth. There was puke all over his chest and the deck. He was holding on to his white cap with both hands. By his side was a coffee can of mushrooms. The smaller girl pulled her skirt up over her head and held it tight against her face. "No worms, no worms," she screamed, jumping up and down.

"You ate the toadstools, Avery, yes you did. Oh my, oh my," her sister said as he reached down and picked him up, then started running. Didn't wait to see if the girls followed. Just ran. Never stopped until he reached the corner, gasping out of breath, and saw the women up the street. He heard the girls behind him shrieking, "Toadstools. He ate toadstools." He started running again. It was Elaine's landlady who grabbed the kid's head and put her fingers down his throat, and more stuff came out all over her dress. She took him and pressed his stomach against her bent knee, and it came out like a geyser.

He ran and opened the door and slid across and got the car started and she was right behind him, pumping his stomach with the flat of her hand and getting more out, wiping his face with the end of her apron.

He took off fast and it wasn't until he reached the corner and had to look to the right that he saw the two little girls sitting in the back. He looked at them again in the mirror as he leaned on the horn and went through the first stoplight. Ruthie had her eyes closed and hands into a steeple, her face wet and swollen, red. Her sister had one of her braids in her mouth and was chewing as if she were eating a mouthful of hair.

He went up there as often as he could. Sometimes just to the hallway, looking through the open doorway. Avery looked too small in the hospital bed. His breath came in short bursts like sighs that you had to listen to closely to hear.

He'd brought Aunt May here that first night. There wasn't a hospital in town; the closest was at the base and he'd driven right through the front gate, honking the horn, the Marines jumping out of the way, the car reeking of bilge. As soon as the corpsmen took the kid, he got another car to take Mrs. Hughes and the girls home. No one said anything the whole way. Then he asked the aunt if she wanted to come back with him and see Avery. The girls had taken him into her house when no one answered the door.

"I wasn't planning on it," she said. But she got her coat and canes then and hobbled to the car. So did Elaine that first night. She sat next to him, stiff, looking straight ahead.

"What's wrong with him?" the aunt asked, as he was helping her up the stairs to the second floor.

"They can't tell. They think he might be paralyzed, if he kept any of that poison down."

"Paralyzed," she said. "I wouldn't wish that on anyone. It's better to be dead." When they reached the floor she was winded and they stopped. Elaine was still holding her by the elbow; he had the other and the two canes. "I don't like hospitals," she said. "I spent too much time in them. Never knowing if I was ever going to get out or not." When she got to the door she told him, "I can't stay long." Elaine took her up to the bed. "I hope you're satisfied now, Avery." She gave a loud sniff.

He went down to find Jack, the corpsman he'd talked to before. "There's no change. Like I said before, it depends on how much he ingested and how much he spit up again." Jack had three hash marks on his jumper but was only second-class.

"Keep an eye on him for me," he asked.

When he got back to Avery's room, Aunt May was waiting in the hall. "I'm ready," she said. Elaine was still standing by the bed, looking at Avery.

He offered to take any of the neighbors that wanted to go. The two little girls were always ready, but their grandmother wouldn't let them. Elaine didn't want to go again. "I feel responsible," she said when he asked why. He couldn't make her understand that part was over; whoever was to blame, it didn't matter. You had to start again. "This didn't have to happen," she kept saying. "I should have seen. I should have understood." He just listened to the end. He'd never seen her so upset. He noticed no one ever mentioned suicide.

His speech was approved first by the XO and then by Captain Mills. He had practiced timing himself until he could reach the last word and say thank you just as the second hand clicked for the one-hundred-eightieth time. He could get up there and give a speech. It wouldn't kill him.

He'd got a handful of Navy patches and had them sewn on the back of the smallest-sized foul-weather jacket he could find, then hung the jacket on the wall where Avery could see it from the bed when he woke up, along with a new sailor's cover with A. FONTANA stenciled on the inside. They were still feeding him through tubes. He seemed to be shrinking; he looked about half the size he'd been. Watching the boy from the doorway, sometimes he lost track of the time. It didn't seem fair that a kid that age could die. He hadn't ever had any fun in his life.

He found himself coming by at odd times. When he got off watch at 0400 he'd take a walk over to the sick bay. Shoot the breeze with Jack if he was around. There was no improvement.

It was going into the second week, and he'd already taken Elaine home from school, when he found himself back in her neighborhood. He had meant to go back to the base but started driving around and saw he was at the curve of one of the heart-shaped streets and followed it around until he came to Cupid Row.

Aunt May waved him over when she saw the jeep. "I finally got hold of his family. I told them what happened, but they didn't seem too interested. Never even asked what hospital, and I forgot to tell them. Probably worried who's going to have to pay. I don't have any money," she added.

He didn't know who was going to pay either. They had Avery's name down as his dependent, Avery Sweet. "We can go, we can go, our mother said. We can go with you," Ruthie came yelling, skipping down the sidewalk.

"Good," he said, "let me go see if anyone else wants to go." He didn't even approach Aunt May. He walked over to Elaine's. He didn't want to put her on the spot, but he had to offer. Mrs. Hughes came out; she hadn't gone back after that first time. "Would you like to go see Avery?" He knew she wouldn't go if Aunt May was along. "Just Ruthie and her sister are coming." She took off her apron and reached through the door to grab her purse. Elaine came to the screen door. "I have papers to grade," she said, looking ready to cry.

They sat by Avery's bed. Ruthie took his hand and played with his fingers. Mrs. Hughes talked about her husband's last illness. Mary Maureen had brought her school report, "President Roosevelt and Eleanor," and she read that for all of them. They lasted twenty-three minutes before he said, "Would anyone like to go over to the CPO club, where they make the best ice cream sodas in the U.S. Navy?" Mrs. Hughes said she'd go too, once the girls did.

"I don't know about the rest of you, but I could stand another." There wasn't anyone in the club this early, just the Negro messman cleaning up. "Who's going to join me?" he asked. "My treat."

"I will, I will," both girls said at the same time, raising their arms as if they were in school.

"I might as well," Mrs. Hughes said.

"I heard someone went back and cleaned up Avery's boat," Mary Maureen said. "Leroy put the boards back on, he told me. When Avery comes back he'll be pleased. He was going to take it out of the mud flats someday, he told me that a lot of times. Float into the bay. There's a lot of nails in that boat."

"Avery knows sixty-one knots now," Ruthie put in.

"You two finish your dessert," Mrs. Hughes said.

Mary Maureen

I talked on the phone to my father. Aunt May hit on the wall with her cane and we went over. We all took turns. My mother went first and last. I talked after Grammy, then Ruthie. My mother was the only one not crying. They surprised us and sent my father to New Jersey and then from there they were going to ship him to England. He was going to do secret work there for the invasion. He called from the dock before he got on the boat.

He told me to be a good girl and to mind. Not to be sassy. And get good grades in school. Take care of Ruthie. I didn't get a chance to tell him about Avery, that he was in the hospital after eating a toadstool, and Aunt May said he could come back if he lived.

Ruthie was bawling so bad no one could understand her; my mother had to take back the phone. Grammy kept saying, "You take care of yourself, Dennis. Don't worry about anything; everything will work out just fine."

My mother had to go to work; she thanked Aunt May for letting us use the phone like we always did. "Anytime," she told us, "anytime."

Aunt May didn't like hospitals and never went but once to see Avery. Grammy didn't go at all; she just didn't like Avery. Miss Walker didn't go again either, but it was because she had a lot of work to do at the end of the year.

I went as often as Chuck would take us. Sometimes Mrs. Hughes and my mother went too, especially after Avery woke up. It was important to keep up with the rest of the class. I brought him assignments and gave him his spelling tests and the rest of it. He had plenty to do; there were women who came in and read to him, and they gave him games and made him cookies. He always shared with me and Ruthie. I didn't tell him someone took the plywood cabin off his boat, after we'd put everything back, and then it must have been the railroad that took their ties back. There wasn't much left.

I got to push his wheelchair down the hallway and outside the ward. He could walk but they didn't want him to try yet. Chuck had taken him to lunch at the CPO club. Three weeks he'd been there in the base hospital, and Grammy said she hoped the taxpayers of this country never found out.

I don't know what I expected, with my father gone. Michael to come out of the wash shed? Maybe. But he hadn't, as far as I knew. Sometimes I wished I could just ask Grammy, Is Michael in there or not? He was in there. But why? That's what I wanted to know. Why?

Sammy wrote he was getting married to a Hawaiian. Grammy said that's all we need on this street. I found the place in my geography book, but no pictures of the women. Aunt May didn't say anything. She was always working in the back lots now. Mrs. Hughes said Aunt May's victory garden had gone to hell. She tried to get me to work, but I wouldn't. "You're not going to get any more vegetables," she yelled at me. "And you're not going to get any more eggs," I said back. Grammy made me go over and apologize. I did, and Aunt May accepted.

My father wrote us from wherever he was. Each of us got our own letter. He put Miss Mary Maureen Mitchum on the front of mine. He said it's damp where he was but he was getting used to the climate, and that I'm to watch the chickens don't get out and Abner doesn't bite anyone. He sent me an English pound note.

Avery had to rest, but he was coming back for sure. He looked awful, Mrs. Hughes said the last time we went. He looked to me smaller than Ruthie. They were going to let him keep the navy blue pajamas and purple robe, plus all the books and toys. He could go back to school, but he had to take it easy, Chuck said.

When Chuck came over to see Miss Walker he had things for us. He gave Aunt May two cartons of cigarettes and Mrs. Hughes a pound of coffee. Grammy, he got her needles for the Singer. Me and Ruthie he gave gum or Hershey bars. He gave my mother a bottle of lotion from the PX for her hands. Miss Walker got anything she wanted.

When Avery came back we were all out in front. My mother gave him a big hug. Mrs. Hughes gave him a quarter. Ruthie tried to kiss him but couldn't reach high enough and got him on the neck. Grammy stayed where she was, washing; it was Monday. I said, "Welcome back, Avery," and he thanked me. Aunt May came out when she heard all the commotion and patted him on the shoulder. "How do you feel now that you're back?" Mrs. Hughes said.

"FFFine," he got out. He wasn't supposed to come back yet, so it was a surprise when he stepped out of the government car on Monday. Chuck came around and got a white canvas seabag out of the trunk with all of Avery's stuff inside.

Avery was standing straight, turning his head around, looking for changes on the street. Aunt May's garden was all abloom. The trees had leafed out since he was in the hospital. The vacant lots had weeds up to your hips. But everything else was the same as far as I knew.

Miss Walker came out, pretending to smile like she does before she tells us, "If that's the way you want it," and the whole class is punished because of one person disobeying. "Welcome home, Avery, welcome home." Avery tried to say thank you. He still looked like he was sick; his eyes were too big for his head now. She went on how the class missed him.

If I looked careful I could see Grammy watching between the shade and the curtain. She wouldn't come out here no matter how much she wanted to know what was being said. She hated Avery too much. "It's the first time in history the devil rejected anyone," she said. "But he took his uncle, and with any luck they'll electrocute his father." My mother told her to hush. But she was right; Avery's father had caused some trouble in the prison and there was going to be a new trial. Leroy showed me in the paper. And when Aunt May wrote his family, the letter came back marked No Longer at This Address.

Miss. Walker was bending over like she does at your desk to help, and in that kind of voice asked Avery, "If you're feeling well enough, would you like to go with Mary Maureen and me to the city and see Mr. Sweet receive a medal from an admiral? Would you like that?"

He answered clear as day, "It would be a pleasure, Miss Walker, to accompany you and Mary Maureen."

"Fine, fine," Miss Walker said, stepping back quick like his voice was coming from a radio program. She had put her hand on his shoulder. I always thought she acted like she was afraid of Avery. She'd nearly jump out of her skin when he'd come up and speak to her at recess. She had surprised me, asking me to go, the day before yesterday, in front of Grammy and my mother, who was coming down the sidewalk from work.

"She'd be more than happy to," Grammy said.

"It's dress-up," Miss Walker said.

"She'll be clean, with her good clothes on," my mother said.

Chuck took Avery's seabag up on Aunt May's porch and had to leave to go back to the base. My mother and Aunt May were talking. I told him then, "Avery, I've got a surprise for you," and I opened the brown paper bag for him to look into. He couldn't help but be happy. The bag was half full of tinfoil, already peeled, for his ball. I got it over at the streetcar stop, went there every day while he was in the hospital.

"You have the biggest of any of them. Some of the kids brought theirs to the school. You have until next Friday. You're going to win, Avery, I know you're going to win."

"Thank you, Mary Maureen," he said, walking backward up the walk to Aunt May's house.

Of course Ruthie wanted to go too, but Grammy said no first. Avery told my mother he would take care of her, but my mother thought Miss Walker might not like it because she didn't invite Ruthie. Avery said he'd bring something back for her, and gave her a stack of his special funnybooks to read while we were gone.

Avery looked nice in his blue sharkskin slacks and white shirt. I think he got them when he went to his father's trial. The tie was Michael's; my father gave it to him.

He had come over to our house right when he first came to Aunt May's and wanted my father to tie his tie for church. He didn't know any knots then. The tie he had was old and stained, and my father got him one out of the closet, washed his hands at the sink, and sat back down on the kitchen chair to put Avery's collar up, me and Ruthie watching. Since Avery saved our eight-cylinder motor from burning up, they both talked about tools and cars all the time. Avery would say, "What we need here is an Okie end wrench," and my father would laugh like it was the funniest thing he ever heard. And then my father would say something like, "No, this is going to call for a sky hook," and Avery would start giggling, holding his sides like someone was tickling him. Ruthie would laugh too, but she didn't know what they were saying any more than I did. After he got his collar up all the way around, he tied a double Windsor knot in Michael's tie for Avery and said he could keep it.

When he wrote he always asked after Avery, and my mother always mentioned it to him. When I wrote my father—my mother gave me the envelope and the airmail stamp to lick on—I said cheerful things about school or the family, my report on the President, or something Ruthie did. I never said, Why did you leave us here alone? And is Michael in the wash shed? You're supposed to be the father; why is Michael in there? We all have headaches from the worry of it. And you're not here. How would you like it if I were over there and you were here? I'd just like him to know what's going on here on our street, and I thought of ways of doing that every time I walked down to the corner where the big olive-drab mailbox drop is. Instead, I'd write that Ruthie can say the alphabet backward now, you just have to ask her, and Avery made her a one-person jump rope for showing Mrs. Hughes. And I would write, Avery wore Michael's tie to the bond drive.

He had that tie on, with the same knot my father tied, he told me. He showed me how he could just loosen it and then cinch it up after he put it on. He had stopped wearing his good clothes to church a long time ago, so I hadn't seen him dressed up much. And his shoes, I think Chuck gave them to him, because they were black ones like the sailors wore but were too big and he had to stuff paper in the toes. He had a clean handkerchief. They must have cut his hair at the base, because it was short and he had no wave yet. I had my red corduroy pinafore on and a white blouse. Grammy had washed my hair and braided it. My good shoes and anklets were on my feet.

Miss Walker came out and down her steps where we were waiting. "Don't you both look nice," she said. I knew I did because I had looked a long time in the mirror at myself. Miss Walker always looked nice; she had on her brown suit and light green blouse and white-and-brown pumps. But she always put too much lipstick on, and it was on her teeth.

We were the first on the gray Navy bus that was going to take us up to the city. It stopped for us on the corner where the bank was. It was Saturday anyway, and it felt like a Saturday because you were free from what you did on other days, school and chores. I thought of the weekend as the S days. Sillytime. You were supposed to clean on Saturday and go to church on Sunday. But Grammy did housework all week, and we didn't go to church because my mother was an atheist.

I was so excited I couldn't sit still. We all sat on the same seat because the driver said there were a lot of people going to San Francisco for the ceremony. Miss Walker sat in the middle and put her arm around my shoulder when I started to fidget. We started whisper-singing Row row row your boat gently down the stream merrily merrily, me and Miss Walker. Avery looked sick still, but I thought he hummed.

The bus kept stopping and a lot more people got on and the seats started to fill up. Then I saw one woman was crying and others were red-eyed and had handkerchiefs in their hands, and their kids sat still, sad, like they were sick with a stomachache, and we stopped singing and I knew who they were from the pins on the women's coats. They were gold-star mothers. Someone had died in their families, sons or brothers or husbands had been killed in the war. Miss Walker already knew, but when Avery understood he got wide-eyed and stiffened like he was sitting at attention. Two little boys and a girl sat behind us, all smaller than Ruthie, and I said, "You three look just fine in your good clothes," and they grinned and nodded at me.

"This will be a historical event," Miss Walker told us. "They're going to read a speech by the President of the United States." I knew that and said, "I'm going to memorize it and put it in my paper." Avery just looked out the window.

Miss Walker had surprised everyone when she asked Aunt May out on the sidewalk if Avery could come. Everyone treated Avery different now, but since Avery came back she acted like he couldn't hear, because she was always repeating things for him, writing on his papers when he didn't understand, and calling him to her desk to explain again. She was treating the whole fourth reading group like that. She even made Sharon stay in from recess, something I wouldn't have done because Sharon could make white foam thick as toothpaste come out of her mouth and nose if you made her do something she didn't want to do.

When we got off the bus there was already a crowd and you could see the street was blocked off at the other end by men in uniform. There was a big stand with chairs and red, white, and blue bunting. There was a band playing their instruments, bright as the sunlight on them, and a color guard with all the service flags. I was so worked up I couldn't make myself listen to the band playing away.

Miss Walker said something but it was too loud to talk and I couldn't understand. Avery was looking around at the crowd like there were too many people. There were more people than at a parade. But I could see better now. Along one whole sidewalk were flatbed trucks, loaded with Army things we saw on the long trains that went by behind the house. It was like going down the rows at a carnival; there was just too much to see. And the people: Miss Walker took our hands before we all got lost. But she was looking in the wrong direction from the exhibits. "Miss Walker," Avery said, "here's a one-thousand-pound bomb." We had been discussing one day in class which planes carried the biggest bombs. It was like the ones in the newsreels, but not dropping away from a plane. This one cabled down on the flatbed was as big as the Packard. Printed in yellow paint on one side was AIRMAIL DELIVERY TO TOKYO, IN CARE OF GENERAL TOJO. There was a midget one-man Japanese submarine captured at Pearl Harbor. The crowds were getting thicker. There was a 1939 four-door Chrysler painted olive drab, full of bullet holes, more than a hundred when I counted. Someone behind us said, "I could get it to run." When we got up close to read the typed card on the car it said, "Lost on Bataan and recaptured on Guadalcanal." There were rifles and antiaircraft guns. A new American Sherman tank with 75MM cannon.

I saw Chuck first. He was in front of another flatbed near the reviewing stand in his perfect uniform, standing at ease, talking to a group of people. I showed Miss Walker where he was, but she couldn't see, so I led the way. He didn't see us come up. He was explaining, "Those are shell holes, ma'am, in this section of the bridge of the USS *San Francisco*," pointing, for a blond woman who was slim and wore smart clothes. Avery asked then what size the Jap guns had been. Chuck noticed us then, of course, but pretended he didn't. "The largest, sir, must have been at least from a six-inch gun," he said, winking at us. "The others could have been anything. Shrapnel. Fragments. That one is most likely from a two-inch gun."

"Were you on board the ship then?" the blond asked.

"Yes, ma'am."

"What did you think, while all this was happening to your ship?"

"I didn't have time to think," he said.

The microphone made a noise and a voice asked, "Can I have your attention, please. This is Captain Mills of the Twelfth Naval District. As you can see, we've brought plenty of interesting displays to show you what your War Bonds buy for our fighting men. Please join us now for our program, which I'm sure you'll find interesting. A special address will be read from the President of the United States, Franklin Delano Roosevelt." Everyone went quiet when he said that name. He paused, then went on, "There is no limit to the number of heroes this war has given us. Today we have selected four brave men, one from each branch of the service, to receive from Admiral Ross the decorations they've earned for extraordinary valor. One of these men will speak about his own personal experience; that will be Chief Petty Officer Sweet, from the U.S. Navy. And we have Army Air Corps Lieutenant James, who has shot down five Japanese Zeros; Sergeant Zacky of the United States Marine Corps, who has lost three limbs, blown off by a land mine, but is still serving his country; and Army Corporal Lohman, who has already been awarded the nation's highest decoration, the Congressional Medal of Honor. These men have given their best, and now they ask you to show the same generosity of spirit and buy bonds: build up our war chest to defeat the Axis powers. Now the Twelfth District band will play our national anthem."

"The Star-Spangled Banner" started. Chuck snapped to attention and so did the other servicemen around us. I stood still, and so did both Miss Walker and Avery, with our hands over our hearts.

When that was over the band played "Anchors Aweigh." People started milling around again. Chuck squeezed my hand and pulled on my pigtail. "I'm glad you could come," he told me, and he shook both my hand and Avery's. Miss Walker brushed some lint from his lapel and Chuck checked his watch. "Eleven hundred," he said. "I better take my seat. Wish me luck."

"You're going to do fine," Miss Walker told him, and he rushed off. "This is exciting, isn't it, children?" I wasn't listening. I watched Chuck walking across the reviewing stand, his shoulders back, the other servicemen saying things to him. The whole street behind us was jammed now, with more coming. It was getting warmer. The music stopped.

The government official went first, and read the speech. President Roosevelt had known the admiral who was killed on the USS *San Francisco,* and said this war was killing our finest men, but they would be remembered forever with this memorial to a gallant ship and crew. It was a short speech and didn't mention either Eleanor or Falla.

After that the four servicemen stood up at attention at the front of the stand, the color guard holding the flags that were flapping from the breeze coming from the bay. The old admiral was handed an open box by another officer, and he pinned a medal on the chest of each of the men, who saluted back.

Chuck was last. He had his hat pulled down so far on his head his ears stuck out. After he got his medal and saluted, the crowd started the applause. Miss Walker looked so proud her face was red.

The admiral sat down and the other man got up. "Ladies and gentlemen, officers and men, I want you to listen closely to the next speaker, a man who not only deserves your attention but has earned that attention. Chief Petty Officer Sweet."

"Thank you, Captain Mills." A formation of Coast Guard patrol planes passed overhead, drowning him out. He kept trying to speak over the noise. I told Avery in his ear they were PBY-5 Catalinas, and he shrugged his shoulders.

". . . none of us ever minded standing at our battle stations for hours, sometimes days if necessary, ready for the next attack. There is a saying in the Navy, 'Hurry up and wait.' And that's what you do in the war zone. You wait to defend this country against the Axis powers. But we all do that in our own way.

"On December 7, 1941, at 0815 hours, I was serving aboard the USS *Arizona*. That was my home for almost eight years. The Navy is my life and my career."

Me and Ruthie had heard Miss Walker and Chuck practicing this speech through the screen door, sitting on Mrs. Hughes's smooth cement front walk, playing jacks. Mrs. Hughes was sitting on the porch bench pretending to read the paper, but she couldn't see without her glasses. I knew the speech by heart, or as well as Miss Walker. The problem with the speech they wrote was the people at the base wanted to make changes all the time. He'd come over and they'd want this in, or something about that. He gave up four or five times, but she didn't and kept at it.

"The Japanese attack on Pearl Harbor sank my home. I'll never forget that, or the eleven hundred of my shipmates that are still serving aboard that ship and will for all time. I survived to serve on the USS *San Francisco*, the ship we're honoring today. I was blown overboard and spent eleven days on a raft, waiting to be rescued.

"I never had any doubts, not one, that the American people would come through. I knew that they would build with their own strong hands and strength of will, both the men and women of this country, the ships and the planes that it took to find me in the middle of the Pacific Ocean. That you would continue to do your part, just like the men dying in this war are doing, even as I speak.

"But we have to go beyond that, what we have done together, the work and toil, the shooting and the bombing, to support the war in another way. It costs, ladies and gentlemen, one hundred and four million dollars today to build a battleship. A home for fifteen hundred sailors to protect this country. A dreadnought that can shoot a shell that weighs a ton a distance of twenty-six miles.

A battlewagon the very sight of which will make the enemy cower underground like the rats they are.

"But how much sweat and how much time will it cost the American people? That's up to you to decide, just like it's in someone else's hands when this terrible war will end. You never let me down. I survived because of your generosity. And now I'm going to call on you again. Please buy bonds. If you've already bought, buy some more. If you haven't, please help. It's up to you to decide whose turn it is to make the next sacrifice. Thank you."

Miss Walker wasn't the only one who was sniffling: my nose was running like a faucet and tears were running down my cheeks. The people started clapping and yelling, the band started up playing. Chuck was waving to the crowd and the admiral was shaking his hand.

While Chuck was talking with his friends, we wandered to some of the exhibits. Miss Walker had to read every single little notice they had put up to tell you what something was, when you could see for yourself. There were rows of rifles, wired onto a board, and bayonets, hand grenades, pistols from all the countries at war. Cases of Army patches under glass, and then medals, and we looked at everything.

Avery didn't always talk to strangers, but he did to an older boy with a jacket covered with pins. He wanted something, and he was trying not to let on that he did. He tried to keep a smile on his face, like he had no cares in the world, but because he had been so sick, his head looked like a skull. I watched Avery talking a blue streak, and they were trading, closed fists out. He got something and the boy got something.

"What did you trade?" I asked, because with Avery it could have been anything. He had more marbles, more comic books, and a bigger foil ball than anyone else in the school, probably in the whole city; his pockets were always full of things he'd trade with. "Nothing," he said, and that was all he'd say. It wasn't money because neither of us had any. My mother didn't give me any because my father was in the Army now and we had to pay for the house. Aunt May never gave any to Avery, not even for church now, because when Sammy got married they cut her allotment in half.

They were giving out "Buy Bonds" pins, but you had to buy a war bond. There was a long line in front of the booth where they were selling them, people holding their money in their hands, their purses open, waiting their turn. There was a short line to sign a petition to never have another war. People were reading the paper but weren't writing their names.

There were lines for everything now, especially since my father went away. We were always at the grocery store, getting in some line, all of us except my mother. Then me, Ruthie, and Grammy would walk home with the week's food, carrying the bags in front of us, Ruthie always dropping something. Sometimes the bottom of the bag would fall out for me or Grammy. Avery offered to go with us with the wagon or loan us the wagon, but Grammy wouldn't allow that. My mother could drive a little but the Packard wouldn't start anymore. My mother took Avery into the garage because my Grammy wouldn't and he looked it over for a while. He said he thought the battery was dead, but there was no way to get another. So we walked and waited at the meat counter for our pound of hamburger. Avery was lucky, he and Aunt May sometimes just ate sandwiches for dinner. They had sardines and crackers for Friday because Avery was Catholic. When I was walking those blocks around the heart, resting my grocery bag on the top of fire hydrants, I wished I was a Catholic so I wouldn't have to lug all this flour, molasses, and cans of Spam, all heavy stuff.

There was an ice cream stand and one for hotdogs and Cokes and another for snow cones. Orange was my favorite, and we used to have them all the time, before. Avery didn't even know what they were. He liked ice, and we watched the woman scoop a paper cone full of little diamond slivers and then squirt your favorite—raspberry, green, or orange—over the top.

I stood near the stand, fanning myself with the program and breathing with my mouth open until Miss Walker noticed too and offered to buy us one. We all took orange. I always forgot and took a big mouthful of ice because I knew the syrup was on the bottom by now and I wanted to get there as fast as I could, but I started to get a headache and had to spit the ice back in the cup. Me and Avery watched Chuck sneak up on Miss Walker and put his hands over her eyes. "Guess who, guess who," he said, as if she didn't know. But she couldn't answer with her mouth full of ice. She gave him a bite out of hers. He was still wearing his medal. Miss Walker had her arm around his waist. "How did I sound?" he asked.

"It was better than the President's," Avery said.

"I don't know about that," he said.

"I'm proud of you," Miss Walker said. "It was wonderful."

"These are good. I'm going to get one."

"What did your executive officer say?"

"He didn't come. But it doesn't matter what he thinks. It's what Captain Mills wants."

Chuck got green, the worst color. Green jelly beans, you can have them, too. Vegetables. It would be all right with me if there was nothing green you had to eat in this whole world. My paper cone was soggy when I got to the bottom, but the pool of orange syrup was there and hadn't leaked out.

"I better shove off," Chuck said. "They want us to stand by the bond booth to shake hands. I'll phone you when I get back tonight. Maybe come by, if it's not too late." And he kissed her on the lips.

"See you later, shipmate," he said to Avery. "Glad you and your girlfriend could come." Avery's face didn't turn as red as mine felt. "I was just teasing you, Mary Maureen." And he patted the top of my head.

We had to catch the Navy bus back to San Bruno. There was a crowd and we had to wait for the second bus. Avery had got a stain on his white shirt and Miss Walker was wetting her handkerchief with her tongue and trying to get it off. I was tired and when we finally got on the bus I fell asleep nearly the whole way.

We got off at the bank again and started walking down Main Street. A soldier driving a convertible saw Miss Walker and yelled out "Hubba hubba," and waved. I didn't understand and neither did she. It was a foreign language but he was an American soldier. "What did he say?" she asked us. I didn't know. Avery knew, you could tell by his face. He shook his head.

"Come on, Avery, you're downtown all the time." He whispered to me. "It means you're good looking," I told her. "Hubba hubba means you're attractive." She didn't look like she believed me. I didn't know if I believed it myself. You couldn't tell what words meant anymore. It was the war. I knew if I tried to look it up in the school's big dictionary it wouldn't be there. *Jitterbug* wasn't. It was like they were always making up things to complicate the situation so you wouldn't know how close the Japs were to California. Who was *Kilroy is here?* Where was Tojo? This war had twisted our street and the whole city, just like an earthquake had happened and changed things. My father was gone and Michael was in the shed. And there was a Navy base at Tanforan. But how were they going to change things back to the way it was before? Where were all these sailors going to go? Or Avery, for that matter? Would Miss Walker go back to the desert where she came from? Or maybe the war would never stop; then would everything just keep getting more and more different and strange until nobody you knew or yourself was here anymore?

Grammy said Armageddon was coming as soon as the Germans built enough long-range bombers to fly to New York City. She read that in the paper she got from the Baptists. "It will be the beginning of the end of the world," she said, "when they start dropping the bombs on the Empire State Building."

But I said, "It's the people that will never be the same. They can build the building again, if there's any people left, but what if something happens to President Roosevelt? He has been President my whole life. Where does that leave me then, or Ruthie?"

"I don't know his name," Grammy said, "but they have a vice-president."

Ruthie couldn't remember Michael, that he would never eat oatmeal, and had to have dry cereal. I was quizzing Ruthie on things. Grammy was mopping the kitchen linoleum. I tried not to mention Michael when she could hear because she looked like she had something stuck in her throat and couldn't breathe very well when I said it. This time she mopped herself out into the dining room where she couldn't hear me.

I took Ruthie to the front porch when we were alone once, when I had everything ready. I had cut things out of the paper and the magazines Avery gave my mother. And I started showing Ruthie. Just a few seconds, hold the photo up to her face, and she'd have to decide. She thought we were playing school. I started slow; she knew the movie stars because we went to the El Camino Theater and she knew General MacArthur, Admiral Nimitz, and Admiral Bull Halsey. They were easy because their pictures were everywhere, like George Washington's or Abraham Lincoln's. She knew Avery when I showed our class photo. And the President in dark glasses and a hat and without a cigarette holder. And she knew Michael and Sammy in their swimming suits over at the ocean. I showed her a picture of an Army warrant officer. And she didn't know her own father anymore. "You don't know Daddy," I said. "Look." He had his uniform on and his sharp axheadlike overseas cap. A piss-cutter, Avery called it. Ruthie started sniveling when she saw I was right. That's how things had changed with this war. A daughter doesn't know her father. The war had twisted everything. And he had been gone only two months.

The three of us walked around the curve of the heart to get to our street. But I was in no hurry. I stopped to see a whole flock of planes zooming and zipping over the airport like flies. We all tried to guess from recalling the aircraft spotters' book. But it was hard. Birds were easier because they sooner or later stopped somewhere. Planes never did, in the sky. Miss Walker stopped, her body turning, her hand up to shade her eyes like she was saluting.

"The one with the wings like a seagull has to be the new Corsair," she said.

"Thunderbolt is what I think," I said. Avery had his hand up but I don't think he was looking. "A Stuka has those kind of wings too."

"It's not German, it's American, and besides, it has no gun in the rear cockpit." We started walking again.

Guessing planes was like guessing families. How they looked alike and how they looked different. It was easier the older you were. My father with his sandy hair looked like Grammy, who had white hair, but they were both tall and big-boned, with blue eyes and the same nose. Ditto Michael. He was the image, Grammy said, of her own father, my great-grandfather. And I looked like all four of them, same hair; mine was blonder, but it would darken, Grammy said, and I would be tall. And then there was my mother, who was dark, brunette, fine-boned, and short. I was going to be taller than my mother. And Ruthie was going to be a dwarf, because she was like my mother but even smaller. Both had thick, curly hair. "Thank God you didn't get your mother's teeth is all I have to say," Grammy would tell Ruthie. She had nice teeth now that her permanent ones were coming in. You wouldn't know that Ruthie or my mother were part of this family if you had us all walk down the sidewalk five minutes apart and you had to choose. And now that my father was gone, the change in my mother was more than I could bear. Was she always like this, and it hadn't come out because there were so many of us that were the same? It was like my mother, who looked so different, had to start acting different too, until we weren't going to even know her or remember the way she used to be. She sat in the dark now without the radio going, when before she couldn't wait to go to bed. She came in and sat down, ate what Grammy had got for us on the table, then sat in the soft chair until late at night. Sometimes when I got up in the morning she was still there, her eyes wide open. She didn't like to comb or wash her hair anymore, but sometimes she at least let me get the rattails out with a brush. And she never was a talker, but now she didn't have anything to say at all.

And the worst was, Ruthie was starting too, just sitting there in the dark with her. Or in our bed, not going to sleep, because I could tell her eyes were open. Then I couldn't drift off. "Good night, Dora," Grammy would say going upstairs, but she wouldn't get any answer from the front room where it was pitch black. How were we going to change back after my father came home is what I wanted to know.

I told Avery one time how I thought everything was so mixed up I couldn't keep it all straight. He said the war had kept everything the same. "Look at the cars," he said. "Before the war I could barely keep up with new models to guess. But now I know every car I see. I can tell a Plymouth from a Dodge just from the rear end a block away now. I've had time to memorize all the differences, because they're not making any new ones now. So I know every single car on the road."

I never thought of it that way. When we got to Miss Walker's porch she thanked us for coming and we thanked her for taking us. I tried to slow-walk, heel to toe, the rest of the way, but Avery wouldn't wait. We came to my house first and there was nowhere else to go but inside.

Chuck

At first just getting through the speech was such a relief he didn't care about anything else. To be able to stand up there in front of those people and just get his voice to come out of his mouth was enough. It hadn't got any easier after the first time. The words didn't matter; what he said was incidental to getting through all the three-by-five cards Elaine had written the notes on for each section of the speech. He was always surprised when he came to the last one and there were no more words to speak.

He was aware sometimes of people's faces looking up at him, watching, as if they weren't only hearing what a battleship cost but were able to know what he was thinking too. About the raft, the feel of the sandpaperlike skin as a shark rubbed against your legs, slid past your body. The way the big fish wiggled their tails when they had a mouthful of someone's flesh and were trying to pull away.

The applause and applause. He was so tired after he gave the speech he fell back in his gray metal chair panting, his arms trembling, until he finally started to relax and knew it was over again. By that time the admiral, Richard, who had fought with Dewey at Manila Bay in 1898, had got up to say his piece.

Next was the Air Corps lieutenant, who wanted to be called Ace, and referred to the bond drives as the Holy Roller Show. The admiral called him a Bolshevik when they argued. "You're going on report, Lieutenant," he'd say.

The Marine sergeant followed Ace. His legs had been blown off just above the knee, and the fittings for his prostheses stuck out through his trousers as though he had pockets full of coins. He'd gesture at the crowd with the hook at the end of his arm where his left hand used to be. Then the last was Ronald, an Army corporal who'd been decorated for killing more than a hundred Japs on Guadalcanal. He always ended his speech with "I can't wait to get back at those little yellow slant-eyed bastards."

Traveling around the West Coast bases on the bond drives was an eye-opener. Before the war, there were always interservice rivalries; he'd heard that when the Army was getting bombed at Schofield Barracks at Pearl, they were making calls to the Navy headquarters to knock it off. But now the draftees didn't care what branch of the service they were in; they just counted the days till they were civilians again. The old Navy was wooden ships and iron men; now it was iron ships and sissies, the admiral said.

"You need those myths," Ace said, "or you wouldn't get anyone in the U.S. of A. to believe in patriotism or manhood or the cause. If people didn't believe a Marine was tougher than a soldier or sailor, what would happen?"

"They would all join the Army Air Corps and be shitbirds like you," Sarge said, thumping his artificial feet against the floor. They were in their hotel suite in Long Beach, dressing before they were driven to the shipyards. Ace and Sarge were drinking from water glasses full of bourbon. The admiral had a glass too, but was sipping. Ronald didn't drink, and he didn't dare take one before a speech.

"Why do we need a Marine air force, a Navy air force, and an Army air force?" Ace went on. "Because you have to believe each one is different, each branch has to be separate, even in the air. Just think of the duplication, the cost to the American taxpayer."

"They all have different objectives, you Bolshevik shitheel," the admiral shouted.

Sarge made a ring with his thumb and forefinger around his lips and made an obscene noise. "Ooops, I thought I was in the officers' club."

"You're going on report, Sergeant, I won't have it."

The admiral was always yelling, "Why can't you be more like Chief Sweet?" which made the others howl. The one time he'd had too much to drink, he'd taken Ace and lashed him upside down to the fire escape outside their fourteenth-floor hotel room after the admiral had passed out.

He knew this wasn't going to last. Ace was getting too far out of hand. Captain Mills was already talking about breaking in another Air Corps officer. "It's not easy," he heard Mills tell the admiral. "We have to have the right mix or it won't work."

He'd been gone six days on this rally and all he could think about was that it was 0710 now and in eight hours, at 1520, he could go into town and see Elaine. He was supposed to have the time off until they left for Portland. But as soon as he got to the gate, there was a message from the officer of the day that he was to see the XO immediately.

"I am asking as a favor, Chief, do what you can. We're on the rocks and breaking up," the XO said. Van Beek had developed a tic. His cheek flinched and made his right eye blink. And he kept picking up the same stack of papers and tapping the bottom end to straighten them. "I didn't know how good I had it as a chief. Buck phoned to say you're TAD, but I'm asking please, just go read the report on the rape." The phone rang. "Every time that thing rings now, it's someone chewing my ass out."

"Yes, sir," he said.

He was never sure whether Van Beek was acting or not, but he went over to his old office to take a look. "It's past that we're breaking up; we're sunk and sitting on the bottom," Randy told him. "Besides what happened last night, court martials are up three hundred percent, AWOLs a thousand percent. But this rape is going to make things worse. The civilians are going to want someone to pay."

"You made second class, congratulations."

"They had to give it to me after you left; I'm the only one who knows where everything is," Randy said.

He went around the office shaking hands. Most of the men he knew; he introduced himself to the new ones. Then he went back to his old desk and started reading the report. After the first few paragraphs, it was hard to concentrate on what he was reading. The words were making him flinch. He shut his eyes. This shouldn't happen here. This was what the Japs did to the Chinese and the Nazis were doing to everyone. He had to force himself to pick up the report again.

Randy brought him a cup of coffee and a stack of cinnamon buns. "I've kept up the goodwill of the bakers," he said. When the phone rang, Randy picked it up and listened. "We'll be right over," he said. "She's out of surgery and might come around," he explained. "Base hospital. We better go over there."

An orderly took them to the room. The girl had been beaten up; her face was so swollen her eyes were slits, and there were big lumps on her forehead. Bandages covered the stab wounds, four in the throat and six in the upper chest. Her nipples had been burned black with a cigarette lighter with the USN rope and anchor on the side left at the same.

He had seen worse, men trapped, burning to death, screaming, crying for their mothers, begging for someone to shoot them. But the twelve-year-old girl lying there affected him more. She looked so innocent. This should never have happened. She should have been safe.

The parents came in, the mother sobbing, the father blowing his nose in a white handkerchief. The girl didn't move, didn't speak, if she was able. A detective from the sheriff's department and a couple of the city cops came into the room. He waited outside in the hall for the detective.

"I read your report," he started out as the detective stepped past him.

"Happy days are here again, a sailor who can read. Can you think? Now, that's the question. Have you figured out who the victim was yet?" The detective kept on walking down the hall.

Randy came out. "That was Lou Schwartz. Louie has a perpetual hard-on for everyone, and sailors in particular."

"I remember him," he said. "Are the city cops going to be any help?"

"You know better than to ask that, it's Louie or nobody, or whoever did it confesses, and I don't think that's going to happen." As they were standing in front of the sick bay an ambulance pulled up and a couple of corpsmen slid a Marine out the back and lifted him onto a gurney. His head was covered with blood, dripping like someone threw a can of paint at him. Randy went over to find out what had happened, while he got the car.

"He was on the back gate and a car pulled up, civilians, and he thought they wanted directions, but they grabbed him by the necktie and started hitting him with baseball bats. They looked like shipyard workers, he thought," Randy told him.

Later in the day he drove into town. There wasn't a sailor anywhere. Store owners started coming out on the sidewalk to watch him go by. He put a nickel in the slot and got the local paper from the rack. He read through the front page thinking, We're still winning the war. The war news was always good. It was only when you visited the hospitals and saw the sailors, or went to the shipyards and saw what the ships looked like that had been in the Pacific, that you knew. There was nothing about the rape.

He stopped the jeep in front of City Hall. The police station was in the back. They must have drafted the best ones, because the city police that were here now were a sorry lot. "We got five in the back cell," a sergeant yelled as he passed. "You better get them out of here before it's too late."

He ignored the sergeant and stopped at the open doorway where Detective Schwartz sat behind a borrowed desk. Louie had only one eye, which was why he hadn't been drafted. He had heard him before; the first time Schwartz had explained how President Roosevelt had known the Japs were going to bomb Pearl Harbor and let the massacre occur anyhow to get the United States in the war. The second time he'd blamed the Navy generally and all sailors individually for his wife running off with a second-class radioman. But Louie used the same screwball logic to catch criminals, and he was the best in the bay area. There was supposed to be a list of police departments that wanted his help; Sikes had told him that.

He was going start out with "We're going to have to work together, Lou, let's try and get along." But then Louie pretended to notice him for the first time and said, "Some of the neighbors of that girl have shotguns and have declared open season on any of you Crackerjacks that are in town after dark." There was no use answering; Louie wanted to argue. He went back to the big holding cell and got the key ring off the hook. All five boys stood up when they saw his uniform. "I'm real glad to see you, Chief," one said. He got them all in the jeep. Then he went back inside with the cigarettes. Louie was loaned to the city from the sheriff's department for the investigation; that was something, at least. It was another couple of days until he flew to Portland for the bond drive. He just had to pretend he was doing something. There was no need to go overboard.

The detective looked up this time and then went back to writing. He put the two cartons of Camels on the desk. Louie looked up again and put down his pencil. "I stopped smoking for the duration." He grinned. "But I appreciate the bribe. I'll pass them around."

"We'd like to catch whoever did it. If he was a sailor, so be it."

"*If?* What else could he be? Would a dog tag be enough for you?" He stretched his arms. It was hard to tell which eye was glass. They both looked fixed, unable to move off center. He should have brought a bottle of bourbon; Louie looked like a secret drinker. The skin on his cheeks was ruddy and swollen. "We've had rapes before, you know; sometimes the jockeys would get too enthusiastic with the local bar women. But that was easy to sort out. The racing officials, unlike the present occupants of the track, understood that it was very important to cooperate with the city."

He cut him short. "We went through all the records, and no one at the base has ever been accused of committing that kind of crime, or anything similar."

"So, Mister Detective, what does that mean? It was a first-time offender? Or possibly, now, just possibly, most rapes aren't reported, or if they are, the cops don't do anything, so how accurate are those records?"

"I don't know what to think."

"You know what the chief of police thinks? There's no such thing as rape. The woman is always culpable. Do you know what that means, sailor, *culpable?* Excuse me, Chief Petty Officer Sweet."

He didn't get angry; that was what Schwartz wanted. He tried to think of a definition. "It's like you're at fault."

"Close enough. The chief's approach, which is held by many people in our profession, is the needle-and-thread theory. Ever try and thread a needle if the needle's moving? Thus we have 'All women are culpable.'"

"But that was a twelve-year-old girl."

"Right. It's not unheard of that twelve-year-olds fuck, the chief of police would say. She was provocative, showed her panties."

"She was beat up asleep in her own bed."

"The chief would say that is beside the point, or she told someone where she lived."

He wasn't going to get angry. "What do you think?"

"It doesn't matter what I think. It was a scum-sucking sailor who assaulted the victim is what I think."

"All I want to do is find out. If it was a sailor, we want to catch him too."

"*If, if* again," Louie was yelling.

And he was yelling back, "You know what *cuckold* means, you civilian piece of shit?"

Louie jumped to his feet. "Get the fuck out of here, sailor."

A half hour after he got back on base, Captain Mills called to say that they were invited to a bond rally in Chicago because some movie stars weren't able to make the date. "Chicago, the big time," he shouted over the phone. "Do you know what this means? We're getting a chance to compete on the main circuit. Scratch Portland; we're going to Chicago."

"Yes, sir," he said. It was a relief in one way, getting the hell off the base for a few days, but Elaine was in San Bruno, and he was beginning to think of a lot of things he'd rather do than giving this speech over and over. Even in the war zone there was a chance to loosen up sometime, be yourself, stop thinking, stop being scared, lie out on the steel deck and look at the stars. Here he was rushing around like a chicken with its head cut off. He had this daydream where he was kissing Elaine for such a long time he almost fell asleep. It was only with Elaine he could relax, be himself. Try and be funny, make her laugh in that goofy way she had.

Furtive moments, she called them, when he jumped the steps two at a time to see her for an hour. They'd neck, unable to even eat a sandwich and keep their hands off each other, and he'd be gone again for two or three days. It was the first time in his life he'd ever had someone waiting for him. He thought of himself like a magnet that could zip to Elaine no matter how far away he was. Both his mind and his body. They would embrace after an absence as if they were trying to meld together.

It was just another trip, Chicago. Both Sarge and Ace fell in love two or three times with women Mills sent up to their hotel rooms. Ronald wasn't interested; he worried a lot about his family, writing letters to his sick mother. Sarge was already calling him queer. The admiral said he was too old, but took one of the women into his room after Ace passed out.

He'd already told them he was saving himself for his marriage. What can you expect from a sailor? Ace said. He wasn't sure why he refused. He tried to think it out, flying back from Chicago. He usually didn't pass up such opportunities. It was the idea of Elaine. There was something in his mind that made him think it was unfair. Not only to her? It made him uneasy was all. What if he caught the clap? He'd have to work out some reasoning.

When he got back to the base he checked in with the XO's yeoman and went over to the office. Randy wasn't there. He got out the file on the rape case. There was nothing new. He had wondered if anyone had checked with the state to see if any rapists had been let out of prison lately. He didn't even know who to phone. He found a Sacramento phone directory and looked up all the state offices. He explained what he wanted. According to the file, the girl had regained consciousness and didn't remember anything. She wanted to go home. She couldn't identify anyone.

Even though he liked to see the look of disbelief on Elaine's face, he didn't tell her about the others on the bond drive: the seventy-eight-year-old admiral, or Ronald the soldier, who threw a coffee cup in an argument at Sarge the Marine, who chased him around on his leg stumps trying to brand him with an iron, or Ace the flyer, who stole hundreds of blank fifty-dollar bond certificates and signed them with the Secretary of the Treasury's name and gave them out to kids and to people who worked in the hotels. Just their names. It was too complicated.

He was back, and he couldn't get enough of Elaine, but he had to maintain his self-control. She wasn't some floozy. She was off limits. Why was this so different from how it had been with Jeanette? Elaine was a virgin from a good family. He had never met anyone like her before. That was the problem. He didn't know how to proceed with her. He just couldn't see himself on top of her. Time didn't work like it was supposed to. One thing didn't follow the next. The hand on the knee didn't always lead to the other on a tit. And she didn't move his hand, she just watched as if she were getting ready to scream. It was unnerving.

Coming back after a couple of days away on a trip somewhere, he'd be all steamed up, wanting to know what that first glimpse of her would be. The space between her bent elbow and her side, down to her hip. The smooth slope of her calves. The way her hair sat on her shoulders and back. Elaine herself. He was lucky to find someone like her, to have her waiting for him. Sometimes the Elaine he kept seeing in his imagination was so vivid it was enough.

He'd pick her up at school and she'd shout Chuck! when she saw him, stroking his arm, standing so close he could feel her breath on his face. He was always the one who stepped back. It wasn't the proper place to be hugging and kissing someone. She didn't care who was there.

Sometimes there were kids there. "Hello, shipmate," he'd say to Avery, who had half a lemon and was going over all the desk tops, bleaching off all the ink. "Ruthie, Ruthie." He'd pick her up and pretend he'd plucked off her nose, show her his thumb between his fore and middle fingers, and she'd feel her face to see. Or he'd chase her up and down the rows of desks. He never felt he could tease Avery like that; he looked too serious. And that stutter: he didn't want him to have to speak. It was like watching someone get tortured.

Elaine was always talking about her students. He couldn't keep most of the names straight. Mary Maureen was disappointing Elaine now. But Avery was going to get two A's, four B's, and the rest C's. "You're going to be a scholar," he told him. Elaine nodded, beaming, as proud as Avery was.

She was always startling him, anything from sticking her tongue in his mouth to the way she could eat ice cream. One time she had a strawberry milk shake on the way home from school, a marshmallow sundae after they picked up Dora and the kids on the way to the movie, and another milk shake on the way home. He couldn't get used to French kissing; it always made him jump. She'd put her tongue in his mouth and he'd be so uneasy he'd freeze. He couldn't respond, get his own tongue to do anything but lie there.

Was he supposed to mention love sometime? He had missed too many things; he didn't know what he was doing. He didn't know what he was supposed to be feeling about Elaine. He wanted to fuck. But that wasn't love. He wanted to take his finger and wipe the lipstick off her teeth, rub both her hips at the same time with the heels of his hands.

Had he ever loved anyone? His mother. Had he told Jeanette he loved her? He had loved his mother. And his mother had loved him. He understood that now. They had been talking before a rally, feeling each other out. Ronald had said he was half Cuban. The admiral was all American, he said, and Sarge added "American as an asshole" and went on report. Ace was German and Dutch. Sarge, Swedish and English. "I'm half Blackfoot Indian on my mother's side and Welsh on my father's," he'd said. No one made a comment. It was the first time in the Navy he'd admitted on his own he was half Indian. And to himself that he had a mother he loved.

Did he love Elaine? Did a boner when you thought of her mean you loved someone? He didn't know. Would he like to marry Elaine and live with her for the next fifty years? He had to think about that. But when he did, it always came back to how awkward he was. He didn't know how to treat a woman. What to do next.

They had just left a movie in Broadway Burlingame, and going back to the car, he unlocked the passenger side and stepped aside for her to get in before shutting the door. She started to bend her knees to get inside and he scooped her up off the ground into his arms. He was holding her close like that, she was looking up at him, and he didn't know what he wanted to do next. He just held her as a few other couples passed, going to their cars.

"I like this," she said. "Am I too heavy?"

He hadn't felt her weight. He put her back on her feet. "I wanted to pick you up," he mumbled. It was like that; he didn't know why he was doing things or what he was feeling when he was with her.

• • •

Going on the bond drives was getting worse. Although he kept trying hard not to think about the raft, he found himself hanging on to the side, up to his neck in the Pacific, when he spoke. Sometimes he'd stop in the middle of a sentence, remembering what had happened while they were adrift, and then jolt back, off balance, to continue his speech.

When he returned to Tanforan from the Los Angeles rally, it was pandemonium. He hadn't thought it was possible for things to get worse. Sailors were deserting by whole squads. Three suicides in the time he was gone. They'd caught a gang of sailors dressed as naval officers committing armed robberies in the east bay.

"We're just keeping records," Randy said. "The history of May 25. We can't stop anything or catch anyone. We're just here to keep score."

"What does the XO say?"

Randy just shrugged his shoulders and shook his head. Randy only told him the funniest ones. "When you were gone, a whole section of Seabees on the permanent staff were caught wearing Wave uniforms and sneaking through the barracks at night. Wigs, makeup, the works. Sneak in, then run out. The recruits kept reporting it but no one believed them. It went on till the Seabees were doing whole Broadway show routines before they were caught. They had bought the Wave uniforms themselves and explained they needed the practice before they auditioned for an overseas show tour. They're all up for undesirable discharges."

The sheriff kept sending tickets to the unit—passes to the ball game, this time—and some tickets to an American Legion dance in town. When he showed them to Elaine she wanted to go to both. He hadn't expected that; he thought she would say the ball game. "You just miss the USO," he said. He meant it as a joke.

"I enjoyed going there to dance. I thought I was helping," she said, and he changed the subject. There were all these forbidden topics that stopped the smiles. Her brothers at West Point. He didn't want her to go to the USO because of the goddamn sailors. Was he jealous? But she never hesitated to bring up the Catholic business. He never understood why that was so important. He went to church because he used to go when he was a kid. That's all there was to it. A habit.

He went early to pick her up for the dance, just to be with her longer, but she wasn't dressed yet. She rushed around getting herself ready, came out of the bedroom wearing her robe, holding up two sweaters, and asked, "Which one?" She did it with three scarves and a pearl necklace and a brooch.

He went out to talk to Mrs. Hughes. As soon as Ruthie saw the car she came running to see what he had for her. He'd remembered a pack of gum for both sisters. Mary Maureen came over but hung back a little. "You're going to spoil those kids," Mrs. Hughes said.

"You want to go to the ball game Sunday in the city?" he asked Mary Maureen.

"I have to ask my mother."

"Ask her, see if she wants to come." She ran across the street. He knew Avery was watching from somewhere; he was too shy to come across the street. He tried to include him, but the kid never came around unless he caught him in the open. "Ruthie, go see if Avery wants to go to the ball game. I have a ticket for you too, Mrs. Hughes," he said.

Dora came walking over. "Come to the ball game, Dora, I've got tickets," he said while she was still on the other side of the street. "They're so desperate for players the two of us might have to play a few innings to get the game over with." She laughed when he teased her, behind her open hand. "Ask your mother-in-law. There's a doubleheader, but we don't have to stay for both games." She always had some excuse for not going. "Come on, the girls will get some fresh air. See all those deferred-from-the-draft ballplayers."

"You sure you don't mind all of us?"

"The more the merrier."

Elaine came down the stairs. "How do I look?" she asked Dora. "Does the skirt match the blouse?" She hadn't put on either sweater.

"You look lovely," Dora said.

Ruthie came running back. "Avery can go," she said.

"Good. This Sunday, then."

As he opened the car door for Elaine, he thought of the little girl who had been raped, just a couple of years older than Mary Maureen. Maybe evil was everywhere, like polio, just waiting to cripple the next person. Elaine was still putting on her makeup in the car. No wonder she got it all over her teeth.

The Legion hall was full of uniforms. He was surprised, but why shouldn't it be? There was a regular bar at the back of the hall. He thought he had been in here once; he must have been drinking. That night he met the conscientious objector? But that had been in another bar. Whatever had happened to him? he wondered. He kept thinking of things he wished he'd told the CO. Things he remembered now. On the *Arizona*, he'd been part of a 20MM antiaircraft gun crew. Because of that, Commander Cort had made him a gun captain on the *San Francisco*. He did his regular master-at-arms duties, but when general quarters sounded he ran for the gun mount.

They'd been at battle stations the whole night. He was sitting in the gunner's place when an enemy twin-float scout plane started following the convoy. The *San Francisco* was escorting supply ships to Guadalcanal. Everyone was edgy, tired: besides being on alert for thirty hours, they'd seen the *Wasp* torpedoed, go up in flames a few days before. They'd helped pick up the survivors as they jumped off the deck of the carrier. Keeping his eyes on the plane, he reached back for his canteen, unscrewed the cap.

He watched mostly out of boredom as the Japanese plane came in closer to the convoy. The scout planes never got in range; they just shadowed the convoys and radioed back their positions. He didn't think they were armed. An AA battery opened up from the destroyer ahead before the plane was in range, but the damned plane kept coming right into the flak. More batteries started firing. The plane started smoking and in a gentle glide arced across the horizon and landed parallel to the passing ships. It happened fast; the plane skipped across the surface of the water like you'd skip a flat rock. He watched the pilot open the cockpit and pull himself up and out onto the wing of the plane. The plane was settling, the pontoons already submerged. The pilot took off his aviator's cap and held it to his side by the strap. The plane was only a hundred yards away, if that. All the firing had stopped. It was so quiet you could hear the bow slice through the sea, the hum of the engines. He kept thinking some-one should lower a boat, rescue the man. He could have information, intelli-gence. But he knew there was no stopping, not in a convoy, not even for one of their own men; they'd leave him to his fate. He took a sip of warm water. They were passing close enough for him to see the faint smile on the pilot's face as he stood on the wing. He looked like he was going to wave with his free hand.

Then a thirty-caliber machine gun started firing from the ship astern, kick-ing up spray around the wing. Then ship after ship cut loose. A loader was hitting him on the shoulder, yelling, Fire, fire. He held on to his canteen with both hands. As he watched the whole area turned to foam and spray and smoke. When the firing stopped, the plane and pilot had disappeared. He couldn't tell where they'd been. The ship's crew was hip hip hooraying, cheering, yelling, pounding empty shell casings on the steel deck. He noticed a third-class from another battery take off his helmet and get sick over the side. He'd like to find the CO and tell him about that.

He danced close to Elaine in the semidarkness. She had to know he liked her. He had to take some other step. Steps. He got her a whiskey sour and nursed a beer. The orchestra played slow numbers that you barely had to move to. They turned on the lights for the dinner.

Some of the Legion members had their own uniforms, somewhere between a policeman's and a mailman's. A lot just had piss-cutters on their heads, but with medals pinned on and patches. One wore a Spanish-American War cam-paign hat. They were all older, from the wars before. Was he going to be like them, think back on his service time as the best time of his life? Dwell on that for the next fifty years in reunions and the rest? There were a couple of men in World War I army uniforms, puttees, stiff collars to their jackets. It was amaz-ing that they could still fit into their uniforms.

Elaine seemed to be having a good time talking with the other women at the table, sitting with her back straight as she ate her roast beef and potatoes. He was doing what everyone else did, and it wasn't bad. This was how civilians lived. He could manage this life.

They left early. It was Elaine's idea to park by Coyote Point, overlooking the south end of the bay, near a grove of eucalyptus trees that hid the Merchant Marine School. After a few kisses she put his hand between two buttons of her blouse. At that exact minute, two blue air-raid-warden flashlights appeared at the window. A voice demanded to know what they were doing in a restricted area. He took Elaine straight home, though she'd suggested driving over to the coast.

He wasn't his fun-loving self last night, he thought, waking up. He could have driven over to the coast. The bond-drive team was going to Benicia to give their speeches to some ammunition workers; they'd be back tonight. He was thinking about that and at the same time that he would like to give Elaine some flowers. And put a note in: I love you. It was better to write something like that than say it aloud. It had more permanence.

He had to hurry if there was going to be time for everything. He got a jeep, drove over to the officers' housing area, and picked a bunch of roses out of the front-yard gardens. Drove into town. It was 0547 when he got to Cupid Row. He was going to leave the flowers behind the screen door when he noticed the light was on. She opened the door wearing her robe when he opened the screen door. "I couldn't sleep," she said.

"I was just leaving these for you. I was thinking about flowers and I thought I'd bring over some," he said. He hadn't expected her to be up. He felt for the note and put it up his sleeve.

"I was thinking of you too." She didn't seem to feel this was awkward. Why did this always happen?

"I have to go," he said, "but I might get back early tonight. I'll phone." She was nodding, holding the flowers and his other hand too. "And we have the ball game Sunday," he said. She leaned forward and kissed him. She hadn't brushed her teeth yet. Then the thorns from the roses were sticking him in the chest. When he pulled away, one of her breasts slipped out of her robe, and they both looked down at it. She casually fit the robe back around it, shaking her shoulder at the same time as if it were trained to behave better.

"Maybe tonight," he said.

He drove fast up to the city to get there on time, thinking he could have reached out and touched that tit, just to see if the skin was as soft as it looked, feel the texture of the bumpy brown circle and nipple.

The admiral was there, of course, waiting in the lobby of the hotel. He looked the way an officer should: tall, with silver gray hair, his shoulders still square and erect. Ace and Sarge hadn't come in yet. Ronald was stationed at the Presidio, and he came in next. Captain Mills was trying not to look worried. He was still thinking of Elaine, in between speculating what would happen if they didn't show up. Sarge had come in without his prostheses for his legs once, drunk, his empty trouser legs dragging behind him. Mills had filled him with coffee and propped him on a chair behind the mircrophone for his speech. When they finally came in this time, a couple of minutes apart, both Ace and Sarge were cold sober.

When it was his turn to speak again for the second shift at Benicia, he started using hand gestures instead of holding on to the podium as if it would get away. He knew the words by rote now, and had left the cards in his pocket. He wouldn't need them anymore. He was so confident that when he started going back to the raft he was able to keep going, the words flowing, flowing like the feeling of water; he was on the raft again, as sure as he was breathing. He felt the coating of salt on his face that burned his eyes when he blinked.

He kept sailing farther and farther, 1200 hours, remembering every detail of the first day. The second. Third. The sailor who insisted he saw his ship directly under the raft. Everyone started putting their faces into the water to look. He could see a shape down there, but it had to be hundreds of fathoms deep here. They kept looking.

Then someone spotted a shark's fin and fired his .45 until it was empty. The shots seemed to bring more sharks. In a matter of minutes there were more fins than you could count. The men hanging outside tried to get up out of the water. The decking was crisscrossed boards suspended by ropes from the oblong balsa frame. With the extra weight, the raft started to submerge. The sharks fed at their leisure. He was lucky for the first attack; he was in the middle. But he shouted his own song with the rest: I'll practice my bassoon ten hours a day. I'll go to mass. I'll have the roster typed by 1100 hours. Please. Please. Then it was over.

There was still no water to drink. It was still hot, the sun burning the men who'd lost their shirts red. Some were babbling. Some tried to drink the sea water. The sharks came back like they were visiting a floating meat pantry. Meatlocker. How about an arm? A head? Here's a whole side of flesh; anyone like ribs?

He had thought when the ship started getting hit that that was the worst, the shells going through the bulkheads around him as if some giant drill press were at work, tearing holes through the steel. Flashes from the turrets that lit up the whole ship. The smell of black powder. Explosions. Then he was falling and thought, I'm on my way to hell, and he hit the water and automatically started to swim. He didn't understand what had happened. Had the ship blown up? Were they sunk? He kept swimming in the dark, still hearing the guns, seeing the flashes in the distance. The water was covered with oil.

He saw the rafts, men yelling ahoy ahoy, and thought, I'm saved, I'm saved, when they pulled him aboard. It got cold that night and he sat on the rim of the raft, the loose decking gurgling as it slapped up and down with the motion of the waves, the water up to his knees. It's just a matter of time, they all agreed, before they rescue us.

It rained on the seventh day. A downpour. He filled his mouth full again and again. At 1300 that day they heard a plane. Someone had a signal mirror and flashed that until the sound disappeared. They'd heard planes before, but never that close. There wasn't a ship in sight. He'd got someone to stand on his shoulders to see better while he straddled the rims of the raft. They agreed all those ships had to be somewhere, and they must be looking for survivors.

When the sun went down it was cooler, and he roused himself from the stupor he was in during the day. There would be talk then. "I had a whole bunch of bananas, hundreds, in gun turret number three. It was the coolest part of the ship. I brought them aboard green enough so they'd last awhile for me and my buddies. The damn ship is right under us again. If we dived we could bring up some of those bananas."

They all looked over the side. At night the sea would light up as if the night sky had reversed itself. The stars, millions, were in the water for them to count. There was more light the longer you looked. He saw what looked like at least a six-inch gun, broken, pointed at an impossible angle. He heard himself yelling, "I see the turret." All he could think about was the bananas. He'd eat the skin too, not waste anything. He unbuttoned his shirt. "No," the gunner's mate said. "My ship, my turret, and my bananas. I'm going."

"I would have given them to you," he said. There was a splash and they all waited. "It's too heavy a burden for one person," someone said, and there was another splash.

He could see as plain as day the two sailors going down, swimming into the open hatch. They waited topside. He could taste the bananas. He liked them more green than yellow. The natives always came out to the ships with fresh fruit for sale.

"Those sonsofbitches are down there eating all the bananas," someone said, and there was another splash. He wasn't that hungry anymore, he thought. He had his own problems trying to keep track of the time. He marked the day on the strips of hard canvas wrapping that covered the balsa ring. The hours were the most important, to keep count of the time. He started calling out every hour on the half hour and logging it in: 0400, 0430. The time had to be recorded; that was the most important part.

He was blinking his eyes, his leg hurt where the shark had bit him, and he came back in front of the audience at the arsenal. Ace was hitting him with Sarge's crutch to get him going again. He picked up the sentence where he'd left off, and the audience let out its breath.

They were back at Tanforan in the XO's office by 2340. Captain Mills was talking. "We're exceeding all expectations, Sweet, do you realize that? I don't want you to get tired out, now. Anytime you're not scheduled to speak, you're to take it easy. Anything he wants, Van Beek. For a start, get some tailor to measure him for a uniform. That government issue stinks. He looks like he's in the Merchant Marine." The XO was writing it down on a pad. He was trying not to stand at attention while they were looking at him.

"You should hear him, Commander, not a dry eye within a mile. I cry every time, and I've listened to dozens of his speeches. He just keeps getting better and better. He's as good as any of them, better than Franklin. The audience hangs on every word when he pauses; you have to know what comes next.

"You have a car, gas, right, Chuck? I want him on a food-and-lodging allowance too. Anything, Chuck. You let Van Beek know."

"Yes, sir."

Mills went out. The XO was rubbing his eyes. He had promised Randy he'd go over to the coast on a raid. They were to leave the base at 0300. He had time to snooze for a couple of hours before then. "I'm going home," the XO said. "Do you still think this is better than the fleet?"

"Much better, sir."

Randy was there when he got over to the office, looking over the stack of complaints, phone messages, even a telegram about Saturday-night trouble. He helped sort them out. One hundred one cases of clap reported from sick bay, most attributed by the sheriff's department to one place over on the coast. He didn't feel sleepy or tired, just relaxed, now that the three speeches he'd had to give were over. He was ready to go.

The convoy moved out at exactly 0300: two buses, one full of SPs and corpsmen, the empty bus to bring back the drunk sailors; four jeeps; a pickup truck full of equipment. He waved the vehicles past and got in the last jeep.

It was the buoy bell that woke him up to see the ocean, blue, flat to the horizon, with no bottom, without sides or a top, and no holds, nothing to rest on. He wasn't afraid anymore, but he was going to be sick, the way the driver was going down the switchbacked sides of the hills, speeding up, then braking at the curves to speed up again on the straightaway, waiting for him to say slow down.

He didn't say anything, as if he didn't know or didn't care that they'd drop a thousand feet into the ocean if they lost the brakes. He hadn't been over this road before. California was an island. The Pacific made it different from anywhere else. You could either see it, smell it, or hear the sound of the surf any-where you were in the whole state. They were passing through and under groves of eucalyptus trees. It must be the state tree, there were so many, and planted everywhere.

They came to houses, little towns, truck farms. He recognized an artichoke field. He had never seen the plant until Avery told him what it was in Aunt May's garden. California was a different country, not just a state in the rest of the nation.

He saw the first place and signaled to the driver to stop in front of the bar and restaurant. "Let us go in first," he told the rest of the men. "Just watch this one. We don't want to hurt anyone, if possible. It's easy to get carried away." Randy was grinning at him when he said that. "We just want to get our sailors out of here in one piece." What was it he'd read? There were sixteen million men and women in uniform now? It made him tired to think that, more than staying up all night.

It was 0407. They were ahead of schedule; it wasn't light yet. He opened the door to the bar. Four men, sitting on stools. A bartender, leaning his elbow against the shelf of the cash register.

"Good morning. We got a call," he started out. They let him go on. "Two sailors, disturbing the peace."

"You took your time about it. I phoned just after two," the bartender said, walking around the bar, unlocking a door at the side of the room, flipping on a light switch in a storeroom. The first sailor was sitting with his back against the wall. He tried to get up but couldn't get his legs under him, and Randy stepped in and gave him a hand. The second sailor was lying on his side, and he shook him by the shoulder until he rolled over onto his back. His face was caked with dirt and blood and there was dried vomit down the front of his jumper. "He'll wise up now; he got a good going-over from some of the boys," the bartender said.

"Get me a wet towel, please." He was trying to find the sailor's pulse on the side of his neck. "Roll call," he said to him. "Drop your cock and grab your socks." The sailor groaned. He picked him up under the arms and dragged him out into the bar. The bartender came back and let the wet towel drip on him some before saying, "Here." He squeezed one end and tried to wipe some of the crap off his face. "Fall out, sailor. Topside." The sailor started sucking on the end of the towel. "Get me a glass of water."

"Do I look like a goddamn nurse?" The four at the bar laughed but the bartender went and got one. The sailor got most of it down. He checked for his wallet. His watch was gone too; just a white ring where it had been on his suntanned wrist.

Randy came back and they got him to his feet and moving. "The other one's been jackrolled too," he said. He and Randy went back into the bar, leaving the front door propped open. One of the customers had a smirk on his face. He waited, listening for the buoy bell again. "Sir," he addressed the bartender, "those two enlisted men have lost some of their personal gear. Would you have any knowledge of that?"

"You're lucky they're alive. Get the hell out of here now."

"You heard him." One of the men got up off his stool. He clubbed the closest off his stool and then jabbed the standing one in the solar plexus and he fell over backward. The bartender was reaching for something, and he swung the baton, missing his head and smashing a bottle full of beer. He vaulted the bar and grabbed the bartender from behind and took the cocked pistol away from him.

"I'm going to make some calls, put this place off limits, maybe take your liquor license too." He saw Randy had taken care of the other two; all four were standing with their faces against the wall. "Give me their gear now."

"I don't know what you're talking about."

"Without their liberty passes and ID cards they'll have a lot of grief." The bartender just looked at him. How many times had he done this? What did he usually do next? He couldn't remember. He picked up the old brass cash register and tossed it over the bar onto the floor. The thing rang and the drawer opened, spilling coins out on the floor. "Get their IDs."

"I didn't take them," the bartender said, but he reached under the sink and came up with a brown paper bag. There must have been twenty wallets inside, besides watches, rings, even dog tags.

"Thank you, sir," he said. "The money now. Those boys are just out of boot camp, just got paid for twelve weeks. Two hundred bucks will cover it, I'd say."

"They didn't have that much on them."

"Get it. Now."

He asked Randy to drive the jeep slowly with the two sailors in the back. The hurt one had the dry heaves and they kept stopping to let him lean outside. "We didn't do anything, Chief, nothing," the boot said. "We were having a good time drinking and dancing. There's a lot of good-looking women over here. We'd heard that, so we hitchhiked over here. The bartender told us that after twenty-four hundred things got rough and there were a lot of bad characters around then, and we'd be smart to let him have our watches and wallets. He seemed like he was okay, so we did. But when we were ready to go and wanted them back, he said he didn't know what we were talking about."

"We're shipping out; we've got our orders," the boot went on after a while. They passed a place where you could see between the sand dunes to the ocean again. They all looked. It was so smooth and blue; how could it look so serene? "But the worst," the boot said, "was one of the girls let me do it out back on the roof of a rabbit hutch, and I didn't bring a pro kit or rubbers, and our lieutenant said if any of us got a venereal disease he was going to write our mothers."

"Don't worry; we'll stop at the VD station. Relax now, enjoy the view of the ocean. You're going to be in the middle of it in a few weeks, and all your troubles will be over."

The convoy stopped out along the roadway. The whorehouse was down the road; they could just see the roof of the place. "We walk from here," he said. "The idea"—he raised his voice so all the SPs could hear—"is to catch all the sailors in that place so the corpsmen can check them out." He noticed a third-class in front had a .45. "Randy, no guns. Put that in the jeep." And he pointed. He remembered the pistol he took from the bartender, and put that in the jeep too. "These sailors are on our side. We don't want to shoot them; we just want to check them for clap. As you know, we're in the Navy, and it's the sailors we're really here for, but it would be nice to have the corpsmen look at the women too. I want to emphasize that the civilians are not in the military service, and because the sheriff's department did not send anyone, we have to respect everyone's rights. Whores are civilians too."

He should have worn his boots. His shoes were full of sand by the time they got near the house. Randy was giving orders as if the place were a fortified position. It reminded him of the involved snowball wars they used to have at St. John's. Forts, rows of snowballs ready to throw. A flag sometimes. Their hands, faces and feet freezing. Getting ready for the fight was always better than the fight itself, when you had to use up your snowballs that took you hours to make and you never hit anyone.

Randy blew the whistle and the searchlights went on. There were people everywhere, running in different directions, trying to get out. He'd once seen a hawk drop down on the chicken run; as soon as the leghorns saw the shadow they went crazy trying to get away, throwing themselves into the wire and against the walls of the shed. He was thinking of St. John's again. It went in spurts; it had been months, and he hadn't given the place a thought, and now it was all he could think of. The mind was funny, more capricious than what fate had in store for a person. *Capricious, cuckold, culpable.* As second-class yeomen they'd all looked up words in a big Merriam-Webster dictionary to use in reports to make it easier on men who were facing disciplinary action.

"Sweet, what does *expectorate* mean here?" an officer going over the court-martial list asked.

"The seaman sneezed on the chief, sir."

"This should be a captain's mast at most, then, not a summary court."

It had gone on for three years before some officer reviewing the court martials came on board the *Arizona* and started yelling, "Do you sea lawyers want to get locked up too?" It was human to err.

"Chuck, come on," Randy said. "The corpsmen are setting up. We got everyone except for the taxi drivers waiting for the sailors. They took off across the beach in their cars." He was daydreaming all the time now; he had to pay attention to what he was doing. "We got twelve whores, ninety-one sailors, a pimp, and the madam." He was going to be twenty-six on his next birthday. More than a quarter of a century. That was a long time.

The women were all in one room waiting their turn, the madam telling Randy she ran a clean house, the pimp smoking a cigar, looking indifferent. A gang of SPs were trying to look in the open doorway where the whores were going to be checked. He went over to them. "The house is secure," he said, "but I saw a lot of footprints in the sand going away from here. Go see if anyone got away. There's a seventy-two-hour pass if you catch any sailors that slipped out." They took off double time. He knew where they'd spend that pass, or their next liberty, for that matter.

This whorehouse had a lot of lace doilies on the furniture and lamps with colored glass shades, like someone's home. The furniture was leather stuffed with horsehair. Two corpsmen were sitting behind a table, ready to take samples from the first whore. She pulled up her dress, showing her bush, and cocked one leg up without resting her foot on the table while the corpsman took a sample and spread it on the slide. The other corpsman had a microscope ready and labeled the slide before putting it in the holder. The next woman stepped up.

He shut the door. The sailors they'd caught were out on the porch, going through a short-arm inspection. The sun was coming up. He could see down the beach toward the mountains they'd driven over. It was a long way for a piece of ass, but he'd gone farther.

He was tired now, and they had gone to every place on the list. He would get back in time to shower and pick up Elaine and the heart people and drive out to the ballpark and sit in the May sun with his arm around Elaine, drinking cold beer and eating hot dogs.

Elaine

Almost everyone at school thought that Avery had eaten the toadstools by accident. "Poppycock," Mrs. Hughes said. "He knew, no matter what time of the day or night it was that he picked them. She drove him to it, that cripple." Aunt May said, "What can you expect, with his family?" She didn't know what the Mitchums thought.

"Paper monitor, please pass everyone one sheet." At least she'd got the school some paper when she went home over Easter. Her father had loaded up the trunk of the car with reams. They had been down to using rolls of butcher paper, cut into squares with the paper cutter. The shortages were getting worse. There was no Kleenex or toilet paper in the stores now.

She went back to her desk and started to fill in the register. It was quiet, for penmanship period. When she looked up again, Mary Maureen had her head down on her arms. Next year if she was here she'd make sure she wasn't living near any of her students. It was enough that she had them all day. She shouldn't have to deal with their personal lives too. Mrs. Hughes had told her this morning that Mr. Mitchum was in New Jersey or someplace, ready to be shipped out. What a situation. She had never got a chance to talk to Dora after Dennis left. What must it be like for her, two kids, working all the time, having a mother-in-law living with you, your husband and son in the service?

What would she do if they sent Chuck overseas? She didn't want to think about that now. What if she got pregnant? How could she? You had to have intercourse first. But she had asked Mona, just in case, though it was more, she realized later, to show Mona she was having fun too than really to find out anything. Mona pretended she was an old hand. "Douche, even if it isn't your fertile days. Servicemen get free rubbers, make him use them too." She couldn't be pregnant. He hadn't done anything to her. Besides, they'd had an argument over nothing. She had gone to the USO when he had the duty. Danced once, when some soldier kept after her while she was working behind the counter.

Chuck had phoned Mrs. Hughes and then phoned her when she got home. "You said you weren't going anymore."

"Well, I got tired of staying home."

He hung up on her. The next day he didn't come to the school to pick her up. Two days later he phoned to apologize. She'd promised she'd never go again and started to cry, in front of Mrs. Hughes, loud, wet, inconsolable sobs. What was wrong with her?

The recess bell rang. She looked around, startled at the sound. For a minute she didn't know where she was. The class was waiting to be excused. She couldn't think of the words. She nodded, smiling at them. "Go play," she said.

No one in the lunchroom had mentioned what had happened to Avery, or even that he'd been gone, now that he was back. She didn't think anyone knew. She had told the secretary that Avery was ill, was in the hospital, and that was all. And she told herself that for whatever reason he ate the toadstools, he wouldn't do it again; he'd been too sick.

She was taking a big bite out of her jelly sandwich and reading the *San Bruno Herald* when Eunice and then Mr. Allen came in. They all nodded at one another. She and Mr. Allen were civil to each other, but it didn't go beyond that. Not after their disagreement at Aunt May's. He never stopped to talk when she had yard duty, or included her classroom when he made his rounds, as he called them, to say hello, say something to the class about the school bond drive, whisper to the teachers the latest gossip about the Association's plan to ask for a raise in salaries next year.

She was scanning the Purity ad when Mr. Allen said, "What would you like me to tell Mr. Enoch now, Miss Walker, about your star pupil? You've insisted he isn't slow, mentally retarded, as some of us thought. Shall we conclude now, knowing he's attempted suicide, that he's deranged?"

Eunice laughed. It didn't register: she knew what he'd said, but the words didn't connect with anything she was thinking. "Excuse me?" she said, and he repeated almost verbatim. How could this have happened? He used to think Avery was a good boy. She remembered that time. Now he couldn't leave him alone. How could things have reversed themselves so? Maybe it was because Avery reminded him of when he'd lost control, that time with the marbles, and that was why he couldn't stop. She was defending Avery now. And herself.

"You must have more information than I do, Mr. Allen, but whatever a student's situation, the state wants us to try to educate them. That's why we're here, I thought. As teachers, not to judge them."

He didn't say anything more, and Eunice changed the subject to the new workbook series for next year. The newspaper in her hands was shaking. She tried to go back to reading, but it was impossible. At first she was outraged that he would keep harping on Avery. Then she wondered if she was to blame. Then she thought her answer might be right, though she had never put it into words before. No matter what, they had to try to teach each kid. They had to try.

It was just an impulse when she invited Mary Maureen to the ceremony, then Avery, when Chuck brought him home, but Chuck was pleased. "I need all the support I can get," he said. He was too nervous about the speech. They had gone over it so many times he had it letter perfect. She never let on, but she was amused at the way he worried about this speech, as if it were the most important thing in his life. Usually he was so assured. Maybe it was his military bearing, shoulders back, standing straight, that gave the impression he said exactly what he thought. She loved his chin.

She took a long time to dress, primping in the mirror behind the door in her underwear—skivvies, the sailors called them. She didn't look like a pinup in a bathing suit on a calendar. Her upper legs were too big. But she had nice skin, a nice complexion. She didn't use rouge. If she needed a little red on her cheeks, she'd take a touch of lipstick off her lips and rub it in. But she had to keep her lipstick off her teeth; it made her look like a clown. She put on her best pair of stockings for the occasion, with only a hole at the toe and one she'd closed with clear fingernail polish above the knee.

It shouldn't have been a surprise that both kids looked so dressed up. Why was she so fussy? She could have offended Dora, trying to be sure Mary Maureen wore the right clothes for the occasion. It was warm when they got off the bus. She could already feel the droplets of perspiration forming on her chest and beginning to roll between her breasts and down her back like single raindrops. She wanted to look her best for Chuck, to be perfect for him. Not damp and soggy, with her upper lip wet.

She was so proud of him, sitting up on the platform. She'd have liked to point her finger for the people standing around her and exclaim, "That's my boyfriend. My fiancé." But he hadn't said he loved her yet, much less asked her to marry him. She wished they hadn't brought the children. She'd have liked to go to a movie after, someplace dark, and just neck with him, sitting in the back row so no one would see, through a double feature.

When she heard her name, it startled her and she jumped. It was Eunice, with an older man, gray-haired, wearing a jacket and tie. She was introduced, but in the confusion she didn't get his name.

"I thought that was Chuck who spoke. What an inspirational speaker. I'm going to buy a hundred-dollar bond." Eunice giggled. Just then Avery came up. When he saw Eunice he stopped dead, and when she looked over at him he slipped back into the crowd. She thought Eunice would say something, but she didn't, she just drifted away to the exhibits with her friend.

Now, why should she feel both good and dread that she had brought Avery?

It should be easier to understand your very own feelings, like identifying aircraft that you could see well: a Flying Fortress could only be a B-17F. Thoughts were like shooting stars: now you see them, now you don't. But it was worth the look of surprise on Eunice's face.

Every time she thought of her mother now, what always followed was, Chuck is a Catholic. How had the two become joined like that? She couldn't take religion seriously anymore. It was like a sorority at college; women belonged because their mothers had, or for social reasons, or they liked all that rigmarole of being sisters.

Her mother thought you shouldn't marry a Catholic because they made too many concessions to their church, and a spouse would have to follow the rules too. Her mother never got anything straight, though. She thought of asking Mrs. Fontana, who didn't seem to have changed much for the experience. Her husband had been Catholic; she would know.

She took her time walking home from school, going over what she was going to say, but Aunt May wasn't out working in her yard. She wasn't able to get herself to go up to the front door and knock, like a normal person, a grownup with any manners.

The next day she went to school along one side of the heart and came home along the other. She felt it might be lucky. Her mother had phoned last night. Why was religion so important? It wasn't to her, but it was to her mother, who kept making comments. "Your father thinks you're probably going to mass now. Catholic women have to have all those babies, you know."

Maybe the best way was to invite Chuck to dinner, if he could get away. Cook something nice. She could do a pot roast, with potatoes and carrots. She had the ration stamps for meat, though it was unlikely there would be any to buy. Forget that part. Perhaps over a good meal they could discuss religion. She could start out asking What did the Catholic Church demand of non-Catholics if they fell in love and wanted to marry a Catholic? Was that subtle enough? Why was it these perfect scenes you thought up just for pleasure never came close to what happened?

She *was* lucky. Aunt May was in her front yard, yelling at the Mitchum girls for drawing their hopscotch game on her sidewalk in front of her house. "It's public property," Mary Maureen was yelling back at her.

"I'm going to tell your grandmother on you." Avery wasn't anywhere around. Mrs. Hughes was sweeping her walk. The mailman was coming down the street with the afternoon delivery. Was there anyone else near? As it turned out, they didn't have to be near. Aunt May had to be deaf: not only did she misunderstand the question, but she answered in such a loud voice everyone in San Bruno could have heard. How close was Dora, coming home from work with her lunch bucket? What she'd asked was simply, When you married your husband who was a Catholic and you weren't, what did you have to do?

"You just lay there and spread your legs," May bellowed. "I was always dry, so he'd have to spit on the end of his pipe. That's what he called it, laying pipe. Before he was a scavenger he worked as a laborer for a plumbing contractor. He was sixty-three when I married him but he was Italian and hung like a bull. He never let me alone until he had his second stroke when he was seventy-four. Hello, Dora, I was just telling Elaine the facts of life."

"Mrs. Fontana, I asked you what it was like to be married to a man who belonged to the Catholic Church, what were your obligations as a spouse, I mean." She wanted to crawl in a hole and die. It was too late to run or say I have to excuse myself, walk away with dignity, pretend she was just passing by and hadn't heard. The worst was, May had put an arm around her waist for balance, two old friends, talking intimately. Dora looked distracted and passed by with only a hello.

"Oh, oh," May said, "now I understand you. We never went to church. We went to see some priest, when he asked me to marry him. Some old man. They spoke Italian so I didn't know what they were saying. Went back and forth, until Newton went out to the car and brought back two gallons of the dago red wine he used to make back then. He gave the priest a ten-dollar gold piece too, and we signed some papers, I think.

"When Sammy came, I can't remember whose idea it was to baptize him. Probably one of his nieces. I was so proud of that baby, that I could have had anything to do with making something so beautiful. We went back to the same priest. And we paid him another ten-dollar gold piece but no wine this time, and we went into the church and he sprinkled some water on Sammy.

"Then we didn't do anything until Sammy was seven or eight and one of Newton's nieces, who were always sticking their noses into our business—he used to live with them when he was a bachelor—said we were raising Sammy like a heathen, and he should be taking his first communion. So I got up and took him to catechism class. It was after eight-o'clock mass and taught by a fat nun who had a wart on the end of her nose and bad teeth, all rotten in front. She scared Sammy and he used to carry on something awful."

"Is that your phone ringing, Mrs. Fontana?"

"Avery is in there; he'll get it. Where was I? So one Sunday morning—we'd stayed up late Saturday night playing pinochle, and him laying pipe every chance I gave him—I didn't want to get up and take Sammy to church. When he yelled at me, 'Take him to mass,' I yelled back, 'You're the Catholic, you take him.' He rolled over and went back to sleep. And so did I. That was the last time Sammy went."

She wanted to get away from there, but she had to know, to be sure. "You didn't have to became a Catholic?"

"No, that's all foolishness. That's the Irish priests that believe that. They can't screw, so they say that to keep others from enjoying themselves. I was born a Presbyterian and I'll die a Presbyterian. But when my Sammy went into the Navy, they put a C on his dog tags. He told them he was one. What difference does it make, anyway? We're all Americans."

"I never thought of it that way," she said. She couldn't get loose from May's grip.

"You have to put something. The boy in front of him said he didn't believe in anything, but they wouldn't go for that. They made him put P for Protestant. So Sammy said C. And the officer said someday the boy would thank him. Sammy found out later when you're killed they put your dog tags lengthways between your teeth so they can see what religion you are and they can call the right kind of preacher."

"Well, it was certainly nice talking to you, Mrs. Fontana."

"Come back when you have more time. Bring over that sailor. I'm not like that old prude you rent from, life is too short. Have yourself some fun while you can. You can bet I did. You might mention I'm almost out of the cigarettes he gave me. I'll buy them for what he paid for them."

"I'll mention it to him," she said, gaining the street and trying not to run.

He wouldn't say where they were going but started driving toward the city, up Sneath Lane past the military cemetery, which seemed to be getting more and more white headstones, as if they were mushrooms popping up after a rain. Those boys under that grass, like Chuck or her brothers. She made herself stop thinking about that. No one was going to die. The last low rays of light tried to pass through the grove of eucalyptus trees along the south side of the narrow road, but it was almost dark in the cemetery. She found herself trying to count the headstones and closed her eyes to stop.

"Penny for your thoughts," Chuck said.

"They're not worth a penny," she said. "Did you know all those trees were imported from Australia? Mrs. Hughes told me that they were planted everywhere when she was a girl, put up as windbreaks. They're no good for lumber, though."

She guessed where they were going when she saw the lights outlining the roller coaster. Playland. It was like a big carnival, with rides—she could see the sign TUNNEL OF LOVE and a Ferris wheel now—and food stands, game booths, that seemed to go on for a mile. There were mobs of sailors carrying cones of pink cotton candy, and she could smell popcorn.

She was surprised when Chuck didn't stop. They went right by and farther up the hill and parked at the side of a big glass-domed building. It was dark, and the lights inside made the place look like a gigantic lampshade. They were closer to the ocean now: she could hear the surf pounding against the rocks and feel the vibration through the car.

"What will it be, swimming or ice skating?" he asked. She wasn't sure what he was talking about. She liked to swim; she had made it across Topaz Lake once. It had been so cold. "Let's swim," she said. She would dive to the bottom of the pool, away from the school bells and the sirens at night.

She waited for Chuck to come around and open her door. They would rent swimming suits; she could already feel the scratchy wool against her skin, the kind they always had at public pools. Then she remembered her menses: she couldn't go swimming.

Her mother had waited until Mona finally got hers too before she gave them the speech her mother had given her. They were driving somewhere, and she was leaning over the back of the front seat, listening. She was thirteen and her sister was fifteen.

"You can have babies now. The home for unwed mothers is full of girls your age that didn't know when to say no," and she spelled for emphasis, "N-O. Old enough to bleed is old enough to butcher. You have to be your own mothers now. I can't be with you twenty-four hours a day. Your virginity is the only thing that separates you from an ordinary streetwalker. And don't think you can just forget about it or keep it a secret if you lose it. People will know, they'll find out. Even if you don't get pregnant or catch a horrible disease, it'll be written on your face. The way you look. The way your eyes see and what your lips say and the way you walk. It will be an open invitation for every man, and you won't be able to refuse."

"Let's go ice skating instead," she said. "You don't mind?"

"No, no, I was hoping you'd say that." He opened the trunk and got out a peacoat and watch cap. "I don't want you to catch cold. I used to come here to Sutro's whenever the ship put in at San Francisco." He was talking a mile a minute as they went inside.

The building creaked and swayed. The glass dome was clear and as high as the sky; looking up was like being inside a diamond. It must have been five stories tall, all made out of panes of glass. He bought tickets. She couldn't stop looking up, her neck back so far it hurt. When you looked down on one side, you could see the rink through a window, see the small skaters circling like puppets and hear the faint music. The building was immense, as big as the Cow Palace, bigger. It was like seeing a fairy tale come to life.

"What does the pool look like?" she asked. He took her by the hand and led the way down some stairs to a gallery. She leaned over the rail, amazed. There were six different pools, steam coming up as if they were on the boil.

"I used to come here and swim," he said.

"Alone?" she asked, smiling at him. He didn't understand her implication. "You didn't bring a girl?"

"No," he said, "by myself. I spent all that time at sea living at close quarters, a year sometimes, looking down at all that water. Then I'd come here and swim in that salt water they pump in from the same ocean. It was like swimming in a big bathtub where the water's the perfect temperature. I couldn't get enough of it. Each of the pools is warmer or colder, the way you like it. You can go from one to another. We didn't have anything like this in Montana. The river sometimes, in late spring, before it got too shallow. I used to like the ocean."

It was cold on the ice-skating side. He laced up her skates, fitted the wool watch cap over her ears, buttoned her coat. It felt comfortable to be cared for, waited on. They skated arm-in-arm around the rink. Most of the men were in uniform. There were only a few other girls. They stopped for hot chocolate, sitting close. The music was too loud unless you were on the ice.

She decided this was her life and she was happy. She was more than a schoolteacher when she was with Chuck. He was so handsome. She leaned over, and not sure what she was going to do, she kissed him on the lips. They were both surprised. He pulled away first.

They went back on the ice. Her feet hurt now, but they went arm-in-arm around and around, blowing out big breaths of steam. His face was as red as a beet. She told him that after he slipped and went down on one knee and she helped him up and over to the rail. He kissed her hard then, with people passing. Someone whistled.

They stopped at Playland, got hot dogs, ate them walking past the lines of sailors waiting to go on the rides, across the street to the seawall. Watched the white-crested waves come in, one after another.

He bought her a candied apple on the way back to the car. She held it so he could take bites too as he drove. She wished they'd never reach her street, that they could just keep driving, that the night and the time would last.

It wasn't easy staying home every night waiting for him to call, listening to the radio while she read the paper or wrote letters; he ought to understand that. Her brothers were always writing, and she corresponded with several other cadets, friends of theirs, too. She could keep busy if she wanted to.

Once she got settled in and knew it was too late for Chuck to come, a sort of calm came over her and she turned off the radio and put on her robe and started wondering what to make for dinner.

She thought of the silence as kindly, and it didn't bother her to hear Mrs. Hughes through the wall, talking to herself as she worked on her squares for the quilt or ironed. It wasn't intelligible but she could understand some of the words: Mrs. Hughes's dead husband's name, Richard. Something about the streetcar line. Something that sounded like a jump rope rhyme: Wash on Monday. Iron on Tuesday. Mend on Wednesday. Shop on Thursday. Bake on Friday. Clean on Saturday. Sunday go to church. "Red hot pepper," she said aloud after. That's what she and Mona yelled when they jumped rope and went faster and faster, one end of the rope tied to the garage-door handle.

Once you got used to the sound of your own voice, talking to yourself was a comfort of sorts. Now, after eight months living by herself, it was hard to tell the difference between her thoughts and speech, if she was thinking to herself or speaking out loud.

They had got off the subject in the classroom today. She was doing that more often now, not following her lesson plan, skipping whole periods of solids. She was going over their president reports with each kid. She was mostly trying to explain that each sentence was a complete idea and you had to compose each one carefully when you were writing for someone else to read and understand. "What's a word, then?" Sharon wanted to know. She was sitting in an empty seat next to Sharon's desk. She had to think. "A symbol for something." The whole class was listening. "If you say *dog*, it's not the same as a real dog. It's in place of a dog. I never thought about this very much before," she admitted. Other kids asked questions. She knew they were just trying to keep her going, so they wouldn't have to do their math, but she tried to answer. "What's a paragraph?" Sharon asked.

"It's a group of sentences that can develop one idea or can connect ideas. What's another word for your report on Theodore Roosevelt, Sharon?"

"A biography." They had gone on with questions and answers, all the kids, until the afternoon recess bell rang.

Eating dinner alone was complicated, making just enough for one person with no leftovers. She tried to stop herself from snacking, so she made a point of cooking a meal. She missed butter the most. Her Sunday dinner tonight was sauerkraut, potatoes, and wieners. The canned sauerkraut was okay but the wieners tasted like they were stuffed with sawdust.

Chuck had offered plenty of times to get her food or sundries from the base. But she always felt like there was something wrong, taking things, that if everyone else had to go through the shortages, she should too. She hoarded extra cans of tuna when there was any to buy. Toilet paper. When the sign said limit of two, she took three sometimes. But having someone able to get you things that no one else could have was different; it was like going to the head of the line in front of everyone else and whispering to the butcher and coming away with meat. She didn't like using salt or baking soda to brush her teeth, and all she'd have to do was mention to Chuck that she was out and there wasn't any in the stores, but she couldn't make herself ask, say *toothpaste*.

The Sunday-evening programs would be coming on pretty soon. The

Mitchums always invited her over to listen with them at eight o'clock; Dora had sent Ruthie over earlier. She could leave a note for Chuck, if he happened to come.

Fudge, she had been thinking about it all day. She could make a batch and bring a plate over. She had some walnuts already shelled, and she got out the cocoa and the end of her sugar. There wasn't enough, and this was supposed to last her the whole month before she could get any more. It would have to be a half recipe.

Outside in the street an empty can was going end over end, banging to a stop against the curb. The neighborhood kids were playing kick-the-can. She went over to the screen door and watched for a minute. The streetlight had just come on but it was still warm enough to leave the front door open. Mary Maureen was standing on the manhole cover in the middle of the street, guarding a small dented can between her feet. It was almost summer if it was time for kick-the-can.

She watched again as the fudge cooled before she poured it into the greased pan. Mary Maureen was still it. She suddenly started running toward the vacant lot across the street, then stopped, looking from the height of the curb to see if anyone was hiding in the grass. She went loping back. She was going to be tall like her father, Dennis. "I see you, Ruthie, one two three," she yelled, jumping over the can for each number. "You're it."

Ruthie came out of the tall grass, both her socks loose around her ankles, her stomach sticking out, her curly hair full of stickers from the weeds, scratching at the mosquito bites on her forearm. Mary Maureen was already running to hide. Ruthie just stood there staring into the darkness, probably afraid to leave the can. The iron manhole cover caught the light from the street lamp and looked like a pool of oil. She took a few steps, then trotted to the gutter, her left foot turned, ready to get back to the can. As she watched from the screen door, a shadow came moving fast from the opposite side of the street. Ruthie must have heard something. She turned, ran, but the can was kicked high in the night air. "Avery," she yelled, "it's not fair." And then the can came down. Avery ran past and into Mrs. Hughes's yard. Mary Maureen had appeared behind Aunt May's fence. Someone else stood up behind the hydrangea in the front yard.

Ruthie picked up the can and went back to the manhole cover. Tapped the top, calling out, "One two three, here I come, ready or not," and stood with one foot on the can, arms akimbo. Never took one step away. "I'm always it," she called out. No one answered. She stood there until Mary Maureen yelled from somewhere, "You're supposed to find us."

"If I leave, you always kick the can."

"You're not going to get to play if you keep this up."

Ruthie wandered a little on her tiptoes, trying to see better. Then ran back fast, yelling, "Ally ally out free." Mary Maureen's voice yelled out, "You have to catch us. We're not coming out until you find us."

The night air was still. It was dark now. Not a light came from the houses around; everyone had their blackout curtains down. Ruthie reminded her of herself in Carson City. She had been the youngest on the street until her two brothers were old enough to play. "Ruthie, come home," Mother Mitchum yelled. She'd better hurry; it was almost time for the programs to start. The fudge should be cool enough to cut into squares now. She got one of her mother's good plates. She'd remember to bring it home tonight so it wouldn't get chipped. She needed to put some waxed paper over the top. Lipstick. The note for Chuck.

There wasn't enough fudge to go around twice. She hadn't known Aunt May and Avery would be there too. "What a short batch," Mother Mitchum said. "How many cups of sugar did you use?"

"What the recipe called for," she said. They had given her the best chair, almost in front of the Philco radio. They always had to demonstrate their old-fashioned respect for a teacher, and she always found it touching. Everyone was ready; the lights were turned off except for the one over the stove in the kitchen and the one on the radio dial, which stared back at them like a green eye in the semidarkness. Dora had made coffee, real coffee, for the occasion. She tried to sip it, not drink it down in one gulp. The kids were stretched out on their stomachs near her feet.

When the doorbell rang, it gave her a start. "That could be for me," she said, putting her coffee cup down, hoping Dora would offer her another cup.

"Turn the porch light on," Dora said. She found the switch and the yellow light came on. When she opened the door she saw it wasn't Chuck. A well-dressed man wearing a suit, hat, and overcoat stood in front of the screen door. There were several more men behind him. "We're inquiring about the where-abouts of Michael S. Mitchum, ma'am," he said, as if he were reading it off a paper. At first she didn't grasp who that was. Then she understood, Mary Maureen's brother. Before she could answer, Mother Mitchum was behind her. "He's not here," she said.

"We know that statement to be false," the man said, and he tried to open the hooked screen door. It was all happening so fast she could only watch in amaze-ment. Another man she hadn't seen moved in front and with his pistol barrel slashed the screen down the middle, lunged through, and grabbed her by the arm. "We'll find him," he said. Mother Mitchum screamed. Other men started coming through the torn screen, but it was still dark in the room, and they were tripping over things and cursing over the noise Mother Mitchum was making.

One of the men was playing a flashlight around the room, yelling, "Shut up, we're FBI agents." Someone found the lights and turned them on. Everyone was openmouthed in surprise except Mother Mitchum, who stopped yelling and had her apron up over her mouth. Mary Maureen still had her ear turned to the radio as if she were listening. Ruthie was whimpering, holding on to her mother's dress. Dora had a faint smile on her face. Aunt May was looking from agent to agent, stiff-necked, like an old bird. She didn't see Avery; he must have been hiding behind the tablecloth under the dining room table.

"You're hurting my arm," she told the agent.

"You're lucky I don't twist it off. Where is he?" and she felt a sudden pain in her shoulder and she started to fall forward on her face, but he grabbed her by the collar and pulled back. "Somebody better speak up; we don't have all night."

She could hear the other agents banging doors, going through the house, the crash of glass. Abner started barking then, loud. More yelling outside; then a shot and then another one. Abner stopped, but then other neighborhood dogs started barking. No one said a word in the front room. The agent had her arm behind her back by the wrist. Daryl had done that when they were kids until one time she'd kicked him good. She felt tempted. Instead she yelled, "I don't know what you're talking about."

"Goddamn it, you better talk, sister. If I have to arrest you all, I will. It's a federal violation to harbor a government fugitive."

"I don't live here," she said.

Another agent came up. "The garage and shed are padlocked."

"Bring in the MPs, let them do some of the work. Kick those doors in. Do I have to tell you your job?" He let go of her arm and she hopped away behind Aunt May's chair.

"My son is in the U.S. Navy," May said, but not in her loud voice.

"Is he now?" the agent said.

They could hear the banging then, and the agent went out. They all just looked at each other for a second, then followed. Two soldiers in white helmets were cracking boards on the garage door with their rifle butts. Another two kicked in the panels on the shed door and were playing their flashlights inside. A soldier drove down the driveway in a jeep, positioning the headlights and spotlight to illuminate the whole section of backyard.

She didn't know what to think, didn't completely understand what was going on; it all was happening too fast. Where was Michael? She'd never met him; he'd been gone when she came in August and had never got leave. Mary Maureen hadn't mentioned him when the kids talked about their relatives in uniform, until her father joined up.

She thought she'd better go home. This was more excitement than she needed. The nerve of that man, taking her arm like that. She looked over her shoulder and saw that the whole neighborhood was standing on the sidewalk. They must realize I didn't know anything about this, she thought. It was obvious he wasn't here. There was some mistake, like when they took Aunt May's radio. She wasn't Italian. But the unusual part was, Dora hadn't said a word in protest. Nothing. As if she too were waiting to find out whether or not he was here.

She felt something brush her skirt and looked down and saw Ruthie by her side and took her hand. Avery had Ruthie's other hand, and Mary Maureen was in front. She didn't know who started walking first, but she moved along too. She knew she should go home but she was going in the opposite direction.

It was all noise and confusion, yells, bangs; it sounded like they were tearing the garage apart. Soldiers were yelling into walkie-talkies; voices full of static replied. No one stopped them, they were out of the light, when Mary Maureen slipped the gate open and they all went through. Ruthie was holding tight enough to hurt her hand. They were in Aunt May's victory garden. Mary Maureen stopped and they stopped behind her. In the dark the lots looked as long as a football field. She looked back and saw a soldier on the garage roof, poking his bayonet through the shingles. She looked where Mary Maureen was looking and saw the louvered vent under the eaves of the shed fall out and two feet appear in the opening. None of the children said anything. Did they know Michael was a draft dodger, a deserter?

"There he is, there he is," someone behind them shouted. A group of soldiers with rifles ran past them. "Don't shoot him, don't shoot him," someone else was yelling. Two of the FBI agents couldn't find the gate in the fence. One was kicking up his leg and pulling himself over. A soldier tried and dropped his rifle.

Aunt May limped past them with her canes. They stood their ground. She couldn't see any more movement from the vent, if he'd come out or not. There was some light from the streetcar stop, but not enough to see past the shadows. She noticed the soldiers had stopped to the right of them and weren't any closer to the back of the garage.

"The sonofabitch is here somewhere," a sergeant behind them yelled. "Fix bayonets." A police car pulled up at the curb on the street between the garden and the streetcar tracks. Another car came down the street the other way with its siren on. The soldiers were forming a line across the garden. Aunt May started yelling, "Get out of my green beans." The sergeant told her to shut up. "You shut up, you imbecile," she yelled back.

A streetcar started coming down the tracks, full of sailors; seeing all the excitement, they were all on one side, hanging out the windows, hooting and waving at the police and the soldiers. Four more jeeps pulled up behind the police cars, and a voice amplified by a megaphone called, "Give yourself up now or face the consequences." It was silent for a moment. One neighborhood dog howled. She pulled Ruthie closer to her and brushed her hair away from her wet face.

Nothing happened. Then the sergeant behind them bellowed, "Move out," and the soldiers started coming across the garden. There were crashes in the dark, curses as the soldiers took giant steps through the vegetables, their rifles with the long bayonets held at the ready.

Then a movement darker than the shadows ran from the back of the garage, bent over. She saw him at the same time the policeman on the sidewalk fired his pistol. "Cease fire, cease fire," the sergeant yelled, "cease fire." The bullets hit the back of the garage. "You'll hit us." Two other policemen started shooting. She could hear the bullets pass over her head. The muzzle flashes were orange, the color of the crêpe paper that was hung over the ceiling in the USO at Halloween. The soldiers all fell to the ground.

The figure kept running, long legs taking huge strides, across the street and toward the streetcar tracks. She could see him plainly now because of the light at the stop. The overcoat he wore was open and flapped back like a cape. The soldiers started getting up all around her in the garden.

The sailors on the streetcar were yelling for him, rooting, as he ran toward the trolley, its bell ringing, lit up like a carousel. Michael grabbed the front of the cow catcher, swinging his long legs up clear of the ground. The soldiers and police were running after the streetcar yelling, the sailors jeering back. The conductor and the motorman surely couldn't see what was going on with so many passengers in the way.

Just before the car left the ring of lights from the stop, Michael fell. The streetcar gave a lurch but kept going. The sailors were all yelling now for the car to stop. She saw Aunt May was standing nearby, with Mother Mitchum and some soldiers. Then everyone started moving down the rows of strawberries toward the tracks.

She could just see over the sailors that were around the figure on the ground. One of them was putting a tourniquet above his knee with his neckerchief. But the rest of his leg wasn't there. Mother Mitchum tried to reach him but a policeman pushed her aside and handcuffed his wrists together.

She only saw him for an instant before more people came up and got in front. He looked so young. Like Damon. But Damon would never do this kind of thing. He was at West Point, serving his country. This was awful, but she shouldn't feel sorry for him. There were plenty of boys around who'd been hurt worse than that, and they were doing their duty. If she felt sorry for anyone it should be Dora, having a draft dodger for a son. Everyone in the whole family must feel terrible about this. She could hear a siren from a long way off, the ambulance, coming to take Michael away.

Mother Mitchum asked, "Then where's his leg?"

One of the policemen said, "He won't be needing it anymore where he's going."

But Mother Mitchum started getting louder. "Where's his leg? Where's his leg?" Some of the soldiers began looking around the tracks with their flashlights. "He's got to have his leg." She looked around. She didn't see Dora. She hadn't seen her since they were all in the front room. That seemed like days ago. She'd been worried about her mother's plate getting chipped. I hope the FBI broke it, she thought. She didn't see either Mary Maureen or Avery now. Ruthie looked like she was all cried out, drained. She picked her up and held her tight, Ruthie's chin resting on her shoulder.

The streetcar was still stopped down the track, lit up; the sailors were still on, yelling to the conductor let's go, let's go; the conductor was talking to a policeman, who was writing something down in a notebook. She had to step back when they brought the gurney to put Michael in the ambulance. Someone behind her murmured, "They should have let him bleed to death." Mary Maureen was back, trying to shush her grandmother. "Grammy, be good." She hugged her around the waist. "Be good." Some of the sailors were helping with the gurney. People were milling around. She could feel the track rocks through the soles of her shoes. They shut the doors of the ambulance and it pulled away. "Where are they taking him?" a woman asked. "To prison," someone else said. The bell dinged on the streetcar and the sailors started running, jumping on, whooping it up like they were chasing it down the track.

Ruthie was asleep. She tried to shift her to her other hip. The jeeps were leaving; most of the police cars were gone. She turned to go back and almost ran into Avery. He had Michael's leg, cut off below the knee, holding it upright from the bottom of the shoe at a slight angle so the drips of gore would fall away from him. The cut-off part of the pants leg still covered most of the brown sock, and the shoelaces were still neatly tied on the biggest shoe she'd ever seen. "It was caught under the streetcar, Miss Walker. I crawled under and got it out."

"Grammy, Grammy," Mary Maureen called out. "Here's Michael's leg."

She had to finish the letter to her mother. "Chuck is well. He took me out to dinner yesterday to a place in Lomita Park where they had black-market steak on the menu. I hope it wasn't horsemeat. He is scheduled to give his speech, which is a great success, to more shipyard workers and the like. The owners of the steel mill he spoke at last week gave him a gold pocket watch with the inscription, Defending the American Way.

"Chuck is not so sure now that he likes this new duty. Even though his talks are breaking records at the bond rallies, he is dissatisfied sometimes.

"The way I see it, the workers invest their money in the war effort to build tanks, airplanes, and ships, the tools our soldiers and sailors need to fight and defeat the Axis. They in turn are assured jobs so they can take care of their families.

"But Chuck says some of the ships they build are death traps for sailors, and the people who benefit most are the owners of the shipyards and the steel mills. They're the ones that put on the big banquets after he gives his speech.

"He says the wages of the men and women who do the work are frozen for the duration, like the food prices, but the contracts between the government and the businessmen are negotiable, and the plants and factories that the government has built and paid for will go to the owners after the war. Someone is getting rich, he says, but not the working man. It's all confusing, and he gets upset when he talks about the bond drives." That was putting it mildly. She'd tried to change the subject, but he'd asked her last night, "Who gets the hundred and four million for a battleship? And who inherits the eleven hundred dead men that were on board the *Arizona* when it went down?"

"Don't read that last part to Dad," she wrote.

"I only hope it's true that the first year of teaching is the hardest. I never want to go through this again, ever. I'm glad you're looking around for me up there, but as much as I'd like to be with you all, and this place does have some drawbacks, I know I'll miss it if I leave. I'm not talking about Chuck now.

"The people have been very kind to me here, the neighbors and the friends I've made. My colleagues at Edgemont. I've learned a lot in eight months. I've enjoyed my time here very much. The summer is still up in the air, but I've been talking to the superintendent, and he has an idea that sounds interesting. I'll write more on that when I have more information."

I'm going to finish this letter if it kills me, she thought. "The neighbors are still talking about the Mitchums and the son who was hiding in the wash shed. It not only made the two local papers but was in one of the city papers also.

"No one can understand how he could hide in the wash shed all that time and the family not know. Mrs. Hughes says the whole family must have known, but no one knows who turned the deserter in to the FBI. There is a lot of speculating on that. There is supposed to be a reward. Whoever reported Michael deserves a medal, in Mrs. Hughes's opinion. I feel really sorry for his stepmother. And his grandmother has not recovered yet.

"Chuck is taking me out again tonight. He's TAD, Temporary Assigned Duty, to the bond drive. He gets a couple days off every once in a while but is mostly traveling up and down the West Coast. But if everything works out, we may drive up sometime after school lets out and see everyone for a few days. It'll be nice to get home.

"I've been faithfully writing Daryl and Damon, and when they write back they sound like they are happy and doing well at West Point. Mona never writes, as you know, so it's hard to write to her. I never hear what she's up. to anymore, and you, Mother, hardly mention her in your newsy letters. Tell her from me I miss her. I miss you all. LoveXXXXXX, Elaine.

"P.S. There are only twenty-six school days left, not counting the last half-day when promotion certificates are given out."

Avery

*I*f I came back alive it was because my stomach loved me and didn't stop work when the toadstools came down, sent them right back up. And I still had my ideas when I was lying there: What if the old popes are in charge somewhere along the line, or a president, or even Betsy Ross? Thoughts like that could bring anyone back alive.

I remembered what Mr. Mitchum said when we read in the paper about someone who shot himself rather than answer his notice from the draft board. "It's a coward's way out. Dying is not the worst thing that can happen to you. It's the way you die that counts." I wondered if in England he was seeing the same Germans he did in the First World War.

Being dead was better than sleep or daydreams. It was all peace. I never thought of the sea lion or yardsticks or before during the days they said I lay there on death's door. It's not a place, not like the church heaven they tell you about where you have to pay to get in with goodness or Hail Marys. You just leave this world of sorrow along with the things you like, butterscotch sundaes, orange Popsicles, and Ruthie and Mr. and Mrs. Mitchum. And that's all. If you're lucky you leave someone like yourself here, like maybe Unk left me, to enjoy what he liked. There are no harps or pitchforks. That's all here.

When Leroy's mother brought him to see me, she told me that I wasn't going to die and I could hear her as plain as day. I had been listening a couple of days before I spoke or opened my eyes. She said my family left; the people who owned the house made them leave. And she thought they went out of state. That meant the county couldn't send me back. Mary Maureen had said Aunt May's vegetable garden was going to ruin with so many tomato bugs, snails, slugs, and earwigs you had to watch where you stepped. Even whitefly on the stringbeans. I had her where I wanted her. She wouldn't let Mr. Allen send me to some school. She needed that garden. And I wasn't going to forget anything when I got back to the street either. If Grammy hoped I'd die, I had plans for her. If Aunt May wanted me to work, she would have to share more. I would get to listen to my programs and have more privileges and keep my bedroom door closed and no more vacuuming. I couldn't stand the humming of that machine anymore.

And Miss Walker was going to pay, I guaranteed myself that, and the principal, Mr. Allen, and Miss Cameron. It was my turn as far as I was concerned. You have to get even in this life or how could you get ahead? I thought it all out, lying there.

This was not like telling myself that I was never going to stutter again. Because that was up to my tongue. I had nothing to do with that, so I stuttered. But maybe not always. Maybe I could be kind to my tongue. Not bite it or burn it with hot stuff or eat those mustard sandwiches. Maybe it would like a little sunlight. I could stick it out and let the sun make it well, like it dries out scabs and heals scratches and gets rid of colds. Not eat things that turned it purple, like beets. Or maybe it didn't like to get frozen with ice chips from the iceman. I could experiment.

If my stomach was my close friend, my best friend was my heart. We had been through a lot together. It kept beating when I was dead; the soul is inside there. That's why there are so many heart attacks: people kill their souls by doing something and they die when their heart stops from disgust.

Mary Maureen came and told me they had cut Aunt May's allotment again since Sammy married the Hawaiian. Mary Maureen saw the picture; both Sammy and his wife wore flower necklaces and she wore a grass skirt, and the name of the bar she worked in was on the cover of the photograph folder. It couldn't be worse, her Grammy said.

"And Grammy doesn't want you to come back," she told me. "She says you're nothing but trouble for the whole street. She's always at Aunt May not to let you. She thinks you've been sneaking around our place and inside the garage, trying to steal our food that we're hoarding. She's ready to call the cops on you, she told Aunt May." We'll see who's going to call who, I thought.

I dug the hole straight down by the zucchini, where anyone in the shed could see from the air vents. I kept going until most of the shovel handle disappeared and I had to scoop out the bottom with my cupped hands. I had to stop when the bottom started filling up. It was the bay water coming in. It always made me wonder if this whole place wouldn't be better off if it were underwater.

This was a surprise; it took both hands to manage my tinfoil ball, carrying it out from the house, resting it against my stomach. I had forgotten how heavy it was. Or maybe I was still weak. I waited until Aunt May went to sewing circle.

I had given this a lot of thought in the hospital. In fact, the idea was like the foil ball, it kept growing until I had to do something. And I decided no more, no more. If anyone wanted my tinfoil, let them find it again. I was through giving anything away. I was through with a lot of things.

I dropped it in with a splash and started shoveling back the loose dirt. I tried not to think of all the gum wrappers and cigarette wrappers I'd picked up, how I'd peeled off the foil and slapped it together with the rest to make another layer as thin as dried skin, and another. But I would miss the looking most, trying to find the next layer, the thinking where to go next, searching the town. Now only one other person in the world would know where my foil ball was, I thought when I put the shovel away, and he would never tell.

I went back in the house. It was warming up outside, but the inside was as cold as usual, mainly because Aunt May never opened the blinds. I didn't know if it was so people wouldn't see in or we wouldn't see out.

I had to compose myself, let my new friend, my tongue, know it was going to have to work. When the operator asked, "Number, please?" it had to do its part. But I couldn't depend on my tongue yet. I had my hand on the receiver but I couldn't move. Sammy's photo on the radio watched my every move.

We didn't write Sammy much anymore. But sometimes he wrote, for money usually. He thought the rest of Aunt May's allotment check should be his too. He was stationed in Honolulu now. He said he was going to stay there when the war was over.

I saw the shoe and I saw the leg. They had to belong to Michael. But all the time I spent on Mrs. Hughes's roof I never saw any sign of him again, or of Grammy going in there with food, or lights on at night, nothing. But I saw other things. Miss Walker, almost naked. She looked just like anyone else. With Chuck waiting in the front room. I could hear them laughing sometimes, having a time. Breaking the commandments. What if the principal knew? Or the priest at Saint Bruno's, who was always going on and on about adultery like that's all he ever thought of besides dinner? Or Eleanor Roosevelt? Or the police chief? What would they do to Miss Walker? No one cared what sailors did. They could do what they wanted and nobody ever said anything.

I had to straighten out things. And quick, while Aunt May was at sewing circle. Let those that deserved to be punished, pay. Everyone had to do their part to help the war effort. To destroy the Axis.

I'd heard the car come down the street slow, first almost stopping at the Mitchums' and then at Aunt May's. You can tell when one doesn't belong on a street. Then old Mrs. Mitchum started wailing, loud. I got down the ladder from my lookout on the roof fast. It was the Western Union car.

I could hardly breathe when Aunt May opened the front door and the messenger removed his cap and handed over the telegram. There were a lot of people in the street watching now besides Grammy, Ruthie, and Mary Maureen. Miss Walker was standing next to Mrs. Hughes on their porch. The people who had just moved into the duplex on the other side of the Mitchums were there, and the milkman delivering his route stopped to watch.

She took her time opening the envelope, like she was expecting it, and read it once. She must have noticed the people watching then because she opened the screen door again and yelled, "Sammy is just fine," and added so only I could hear, "Why don't you mind your own business?" and shut the door again.

"Change," she told me. "We're going to the city."

I was wearing my leather aviator's cap I'd found in somebody's garage on the paper drive. It was sheepskin lined and had a set of goggles you could pull down. The woman said I could have it. I took off my leggings too and my Navy jacket I got at the hospital and put on my school clothes and combed my hair. There still wasn't enough grown back to make a wave.

I had to almost run to keep up with her all the way to the streetcar stop. I didn't ask, just waited her out. On the radio programs a telegram meant somebody died. We got our seat and the bell ding-donged and she handed me the telegram. *Mom, send $900.00 or I'll get in trouble with the Navy. This is serious. I'll be able to send it back in a month. With interest. Love, Sammy, Honolulu, Hawaii.* I didn't say anything.

"I don't want the whole world to know about this," she said. She knew better. I waited for more. "I'm going to have to ask," she said.

I'd been to the hock shops before with an uncle to get his tools out so he could go back to work after a wingding. Uncle Johnny never thought much of that. "He may be my brother, but any man that would pawn his personal work tools has no pride," he said.

We got off in a neighborhood I'd never been in before and started walking. All the houses were built the same way and painted the same color, with no front yards, and all the garages were underneath the second story. "I used to live around here when I was your age," she said. She slowed down as if to be sure where she was and then went up the front steps. The door opened a crack after she knocked twice. "Do you remember me, May Lawrence?" The door didn't move any wider and her voice changed. It sounded more like Miss Walker's when she asked us please, please quiet down and get your readers out. After that she started writing something and handing over some papers through the crack in the door, and then she put a big wad of greenbacks in her purse and we were going back fast the way we came.

"No one has to know about this either," she said. "Since I was a little girl that family has loaned money. I had to let them hold the mortgage to the house, and I'll pay so much back every week until Sammy sends me back the money."

We got off on Market Street and she went into the telegraph office and I waited outside. Everybody walking by was a sailor. I could see the big clock on the Ferry Building and knew where I was from that. When Aunt May came out she didn't walk so fast as before. It was getting dark by the time we got back to our line. The barrage balloons hanging in the sky looked like little moons that were waiting to light up. She fell asleep and I watched for our stop. I was glad to get back to our street.

Aunt May started acting funny after that, like she couldn't remember things. She wouldn't start dinner until I reminded her, and then she'd forget again. I'd make her a cheese sandwich and cook her some soup from a package and bring the food on the tray. She wrote Sammy two letters and never asked me to write anything to go with them. She didn't yell much anymore or care if I dusted and vacuumed, so I tried to keep everything tidy. She didn't want to go out in the yard either, to supervise. "What's the use?" she said. She had got a letter from Sammy but didn't show it to me.

I could do what I liked; I had her where I wanted her now. But it scared me. When she talked it was about going to the home for cripples and losing the house. The bills, and then losing the house again. "It's me they're going to put in a home; you have your legs to run with," she said once.

I found Sammy's letter when Aunt May fell asleep in her chair one night. It was in the metal box that I was to grab and take with me if we were bombed. I had looked in it before and found out from her birth certificate she was fifty-nine years old. I had to read the important part of the letter three times before I believed what it said. It didn't seem like it was in his handwriting, or if it was, it wasn't his words. "I owe it to myself to take this opportunity," he wrote. "I feel the $900.00 belongs to me because the government took a percent out of my pay to send you that money in the first place. Shirley and I are going to use the money to invest in her brother's bar. It's a sure thing, the way the Islands are booming. I know you will see things my way when you think it over. And later if you still feel I owe you the money, I'll pay you back double. It was the only way I knew you'd pay me what you owed me."

I worked as hard as I could trying to get that garden to grow. I could trade the new peas for homemade bread and the early squash to a woman who worked at Armour for hamburger, but no one wanted to pay money for vegetables.

This was the start of the picking season, but I didn't know what direction Visalia was or Bakersfield, where the crops were, much less how to get there on my own. Someone always took us before. We sat in the dark to listen to the radio to save electricity, with the volume turned low, as if we didn't want anyone to know we were there. I put my name in with the paper distributor to deliver the morning papers and asked around at the restaurants to wash dishes, but they said I was too young or too small or they didn't need anyone.

The worst was watching Aunt May. She acted like she was already in the Home for Cripples, looking at the wall for hours at a time and then when she snapped out of it talking to me as if I were Sammy.

I got some lawn-mowing jobs and worked with a smile on my face like I could cut grass all day, and three of the people told me to come back. You need your own lawn mower for that business or they don't take you serious. The loan money was to be there by Saturday each week, and Sunday was when we'd get the first call. It turned out that when you were late you just owed more, triple the next week.

I went back to the woman who gave us the blood-red carnations and reported that ours had buds already and I asked if she might have any work. I helped her clean her windows, each of us on one side of the glass, using newspapers and vinegar. The printers' ink made the windows look so clear it was like they weren't there. I washed her Chrysler and cleaned out her rain gutters. She told me to come back too.

When I was with Uncle Johnny I mashed my finger; there was a big cut just below the knuckle. I washed parts in solvent and it always burned, and when I whacked it accidentally it hurt. Sometimes at night I'd wake up and feel it beating, like my heart slipped down there into my finger for a rest.

Then I noticed the red line that went down the side of my hand and up my right arm. I wasn't sure what it meant and didn't say anything. Just watched it sometimes, as if I could see it move. Then I started marking it with my ink pen at school each day as it went toward my elbow. Then I got the shakes so bad I couldn't stop and Unk took me to a doctor he knew, and he told me I could have died if the red line had reached my heart. He cleaned the cut on my finger out good and gave me some sulfa tablets to take. The red line kept moving for a few days, then stopped at my vaccination scar on my upper arm, but stayed for a while so I could keep watch before it faded.

When the FBI came for Michael, it was like the blood poisoning again; I kept thinking somewhere there was going to have to be an end or I was going to die. Who would have thought Michael would make a run for it against all those policemen and soldiers? I just watched each minute, like it should end, but it wouldn't. It wouldn't stop. Stop. Stop.

It was the exact same leg as the one we saw in the wash shed that time of the fire, me and Mary Maureen. It was still warm when I worked it out from underneath the streetcar where it was caught in the springs by the heel of the big shoe.

I never thought that was the end, that everything would go back the way

it was. Nothing ever returns. They couldn't put Michael's leg back. I thought
they could, but it was impossible. It was a matter of what was going to happen
next, because of this. You have to hope, and if that doesn't work you have to
pretend. You have to wish and make the promises. It was like the doctor's telling
me the red line would go away now. But it didn't, it stopped, but the cut never
got better until Uncle Johnny used a white-hot soldering iron and closed it for
good. Then the blood poisoning line disappeared.

But I tried. I tried to remember everything. I hid the neighbors' and Mrs.
Hughes's papers as soon as they were delivered, before anyone could read the
article about Michael. I could only imagine what was going to happen next.
And it did. Leroy gave Mary Maureen a clipping. She told me what she was
going to do, and it was too late when I found out; the letter was sent already
and in the post office pickup box down the street. I had to get it out by the
time the mailman came to pick up the mail.

I couldn't reach in the mailbox door; they had put a flap so you couldn't
put your arm down while it was open. My arm was too big anyway. I got Ruthie
and the wagon to stand on. I boosted her up and held her by the legs but she
was scared: it was dark inside and she couldn't reach far enough. Then we tried
a wire clothes hanger and tried to hook the envelope but we couldn't.

There was only a half hour left before the mailman came, and he wasn't
allowed to give the mail back. And once I asked, they'd remember that. We
tried again. I lowered Ruthie inside again until I almost lost my grip on her,
and when I pulled her back out the door snapped closed on her arm and she
started to whimper and I yelled at her to stop. Everything was going wrong. I
had no time to think.

"Go home, Ruthie; take my wagon and leave it by the driveway." She just
looked at me, trying not to cry, and put her arm she hurt inside the bib of her
overalls.

"Ruthie, go home now." She went, but she walked slow, and I had to hurry.
There was no time. I needed some gasoline. It was broad daylight and people
were passing by. There was no time to go back and try to siphon some from the
Mitchums' Packard.

I started running up the alley, looking into the garages. The first open one
was two-story, and I looked around. Everyone kept gas in cans because of the
rationing at the stations, and kerosene for lamps, with the blackouts. There was
neither, and I ran for the next and was almost through an open window when
someone started yelling and I had to run for it. But there was no time. I couldn't
get into the next few, but the one after that was open. I grabbed a fruit jar of
thinner that had paintbrushes soaking in it and left them behind and took a
gallon can of something that smelled like gas. I had to hurry.

I wished I was taller and that I had kept the wagon but I knew better than to wish on a star. A lot of the liquid spilled down the outside of the mailbox but I was lucky; there wasn't anyone around. I had the kitchen matches already, because even before I went and got the wagon and Ruthie, I knew it might come to this. Maybe I hadn't tried hard enough.

I liked fire all right. Starting. Setting the small flame of a match against something. Seeing the fire take hold on a sheet of paper, the way the flame would kind of hesitate, not sure if it wanted to burn the newspaper up, as if it had a mind of its own. Sometimes it didn't, because stacks of newspapers never burned very well in the hottest of fires. You could kick a black, charred bundle of papers apart and the newsprint on the paper in the middle would be good enough to read.

I held the door open and started lighting the matches and then dropping them in. One after another. Nothing happened. I was jumping back each time I dropped a match. I propped the door open with a stick for air and let the matches burn halfway down. Still nothing happened. I should have got paper and started that and dropped that in, but now there was no time. When I dropped the third to the last match in, the metal mailbox blew up with a noise like a bomb had been dropped. The sides puffed out, the lid blew up along with a sheet of flame as tall as the telephone wires. The outside of the box got so hot the paint burned off.

When I got up, there were two old men watching me from across the street. I walked away. There was no use running in a situation like this. You might as well take your time. I put my hands in my back pockets and whistled my way down the sidewalk.

I didn't know Ruthie had broken her arm when the mailbox door closed on it. Grammy had to get a woman down the street to drive her to the South City hospital. They put a cast from her wrist to her elbow. I didn't know until she came into the garden to let me sign the cast the next day. She didn't tell anyone how she broke her arm, just that she'd fallen but not how or who she was with or what they were doing. I had told her a lot of times I'd take her to see the big goldfish someday, and I promised again that we'd go across town to where I used to live and see the pond. When I could get up the nerve, I told myself.

"I'll remind you, Avery," she said. She always said that. Ruthie looked like one of those little angels in a church picture when she was happy. I expected to see wings coming out her back.

"Thank you," I said. She knew I said that for not telling, and because I hadn't listened when she said her arm was hurt, and made her walk home alone. She never mentioned any of that. "We're friends," I told her. "We'll always be good friends. Unk used to say you're a rich man if you have two or three friends in your whole life."

Ruthie was in the clear, but it was risky for me to think that about myself when I knew that the business wasn't over yet. That I wasn't so clever to have tackled that mailbox in the daytime. And I had Michael's leg to think about, besides the sea lion's eye and the rest, from then on. I kept wanting to look and see if the poison was moving again, twisting up my arm. The worry of it all.

I promised myself that I wasn't going to do anything else. That I had to stop. I didn't want to get even. I didn't want anything else to happen. I wanted everything to go back the way it was before. I wanted Aunt May to be herself. I couldn't make her yell no matter what I did. At least the Mitchums acted pretty much the same after Michael was caught. Grammy I didn't see so much of, but Mrs. Mitchum went to work and came home like before. Mary Maureen was doing things just to spite me, so I tried to ignore her and pretend she wasn't there, but Ruthie was always the same, always trying to be cheerful. I promised her I'd make her my partner if I ever got a home delivery route. Mary Maureen was too smart for her own good, as far as I was concerned. When I tried to explain something to her she told me I was too stupid to listen to. That she would do anything she wanted. So I stopped talking to her, or she stopped talking to me, and I didn't go over to the Mitchums' anymore. There was no one to invite me. Grammy would just yell at Ruthie if she asked, and Mary Maureen wouldn't open the door if I knocked.

When I least expected, they came for me. When I thought it was over. I went to school Monday and the two cops came and got me and drove me to the station. They took my fingerprints and tried to scare me first. I was in trouble and would be put into reform school the rest of my life. It didn't fool them for long that my name was Fontana now and not Gorman. A sergeant came in who recognized me.

They told me stories about my family for a while. How they had brought them to justice. And then they asked me why I blew up the mailbox. Did I know it was a federal offense? The FBI was in on the investigation because they thought I was a saboteur.

The cops always want you to confess. If they had a hundred witnesses and had you in a *March of Time* newsreel they still wanted you to say *I did it*. They liked that more than anything else. So I didn't say anything, like in the war movies. I would have given my rank and serial number if I'd had any. They knew my name now.

I was sitting in the chair and the sergeant came up behind me and pulled me up to my feet, yelling, "You little bastard, you better start talking to us. We have witnesses, goddamn you," and he shook the spit out of me and dropped me back in the chair. The two old men that were passing when the mailbox blew up looked at me through the doorway. It turned out they knew me. They recognized me, but I didn't remember them from before. They must have been in the bars when Johnny came in; he always gave the old guys a big hello and would buy them a draft, kid them, maybe even play dominoes or a hand of pedro. "We're all going to get old someday," he'd say. They knew I was a Gorman before the sergeant said, "Is this the Gorman, the little sonofabitch here, you saw blow up the mailbox?" They never even came into the room for a closer look. "I never saw him before," the one with the white carpenter's hat said.

"He doesn't look like the one to me," the other said.

"You said you saw him go into the house on the next street."

"He doesn't look like him. I could have been confused about that."

I sat there some more. The chief came in, who I had never seen except inside police cars. He just looked at me for a while, and then he said, "Do you believe in God? Then you better tell us the truth." And then the sergeant wanted me to confess again and was going to see how much I could take, knocking me out of the chair, then yelling like a crazy man, "I told you to sit in that chair," and I'd sit back down and he'd knock me to the floor again, until Randy, Chuck's friend, came in and made them stop. They let him take me out and he gave me a ride back to school.

It was Miss Walker who made me feel bad about the mailbox. She didn't ask or say anything. Randy had told me she phoned for me and all. I didn't know what to say anymore to her. I tried to do what she said after that. It's terrible when someone trusts you and you let them down. You can't see it happening in their face, but inside there must be the same pain that you feel, and you know you can't make up for it. When the poison gets to your heart it doesn't care about the right or the wrong of it. It's going to kill you anyway.

Sharon told me about her birthday before she brought the invitations, who she was going to invite, and who she wasn't. Not Leroy, because he wasn't nice to her. Mary Maureen, because she chose her to help take the Nazi flag around the school. She had a whole list of kids. I asked for Ruthie; she never got to go anywhere. Sharon said she would.

When we got the invitations for the Saturday, May 1, they said her father was going to come and pick us up at our homes and take us back. Mary Maureen got Ruthie's invitation too; I saw Sharon hand it to her with her own. But when I asked Ruthie a couple of days later, she hadn't got her invitation. She wanted me to go with her to meet her mother at the streetcar stop. Mrs. Mitchum listened when Ruthie had me explain everything as we walked, and then she asked me to come in the house.

It's not as bad when it's not going to be you that gets it, but you can still feel the dread. Mrs. Mitchum took her bandanna from her hair and called for Mary Maureen to come down to the front room. I stood by the door, resting my elbow on the knob. I hadn't been in the house since the Michael. Grammy came out of the kitchen when she called, a long time.

Mary Maureen came downstairs, and when she saw me sh coming next. "Where's Ruthie's invitation, Mary Maureen?" h—

"I don't know anything about it. I got one is all."

"Don't stand there and lie to me, I won't have it. Go get the other invitation."

"She's too young to go and she's not in our class. I won't go if she goes."

"Where's Ruthie's invitation?"

"I burned it over the stove."

"You'll go to plenty of other parties, Ruthie," Grammy said. Ruthie didn't put her lower lip out and start to cry like she did sometimes. She just watched her mother. "All right, then, Mary Maureen. Ruthie is going to that party and you're not. You just get used to the idea."

And that's the way it was when Mr. Lemke drove up in his Cadillac for me and Ruthie, standing out in the front wearing our best clothes with our presents for Sharon. Miss Walker was talking to Mrs. Hughes and waved when she saw who was in the back of the big car.

Sharon sat in front with two kids, counting us, and there were six more on the backseat. I asked Mr. Lemke how fast the car would go and he said a hundred twenty miles an hour. I could believe it too; that V8 was purring its way down El Camino Real passing all the other cars like they were standing still.

We kept going south down the peninsula between the biggest eucalyptus trees in the state of California. Lomita Park, Millbrae, then Hillsborough. That's where we turned off. I didn't know Sharon lived here, or why she was going to Edgemont if she did.

I had come here with Unk to work on cars. Sometimes they'd send a car with a chauffeur and we'd sit in the back like millionaires too. Biggest houses I ever saw, bigger than you can imagine, bigger than the school.

There were no sidewalks, just the blacktopped street. Everyone was shy as we passed houses that looked like castles behind their trees and shrubs. So I spoke up. Miss Walker told me once, I said, that when she was home and a little girl listening to the radio and they'd say the Grand National was at the Cow Palace, she thought people in California put their cows in big castles. Everyone enjoyed that.

I was still holding Ruthie's hand because she was a little nervous. But she looked like the icing on a cake. Grammy had put white shoe polish on her cast to make it look clean and she was wearing a pink dress and had a pink bow in her hair. She kept touching it all the time to check if it was still there.

When we turned into the drive we didn't see the house because it was covᴊ with vines in front except for the windows and the chimney and parts of ᴊne tiled roof and the great big wooden front door. I told Mr. Lemke he didn't have to worry about getting bombed; his house was camouflaged. He said he'd never thought of that, and that he'd have to look the next time he flew over. When I told Miss Walker about the party, she said she had thought Mr. Lemke was a marine engineer at the shipyard but had found out he was the director of the company.

We went inside and they took our presents and put them on a table. We met Mrs. Lemke and Sharon's sister and some of her cousins. We went out in the backyard of the house and there was a swimming pool. I'd never seen one before at someone's house. At Sutro's and Fleishhacker's, but not so you had your own and wouldn't have to pay.

A woman came around with a tray with punch, and I took one for me and Ruthie. She was still being shy and I made her let go of my hand and drink her punch. When someone asked what happened to her arm I said for her that she fell while jumping rope, and she nodded.

I looked at that pool a long time. It was amazing that someone could swim anytime they felt like jumping into the water. Mr. Lemke showed us all around the place. The side lawn was bigger than Aunt May's two back lots put together. He took us to the big five-car garage. He had his own shop in a special room. The welder was new. He had his own compressor and generator and hand tools, some that I never had seen before. He started up the metal lathe and I set the chucks and made some adjustments. Unk had this same exact one.

We played games, pin-the-tail-on-the-donkey and some others. We played croquet. Hide-and-seek. Croquet, I'd never seen the game before. We must have eaten five different times before Sharon blew out the candles and cut the cake. Sandwiches, nearly any kind you wanted, hamburgers and hot dogs. I never saw so much food.

We sang "Happy Birthday" and wore little hats and got whistles and balloons. Sharon opened her presents. She said thank you each time to us. I gave her books with her name inside on a bookplate, to Sharon Lemke, the best reader in fifth grade, from Avery Fontana. Miss Walker had helped me pick them out: *Heidi*, *The Five Little Peppers and How They Grew*, and the one I had read before, *The Call of the Wild*. Ruthie gave her a scarf. Miss Walker had paper and helped us wrap them up.

I asked Sharon had she always lived here, because she wasn't at Edgemont last year. She said she moved from Connecticut and started school in San Bruno because they were staying in a hotel in the city and thought that's where they'd live. But when she moved here to Hillsborough she kept on going to school at Edgemont because she wanted to. "Did you live in a house like this in Connecticut?" I asked her.

"Bigger," she said. "We owned a island before that." I couldn't imagine a bigger house.

I knew I would never live in a house like this. I couldn't even picture me doing that. How much would you have to save at a dollar an hour, what a welder at Mr. Lemke's shipyard was making? Your whole life, probably, for just one of those closets or that swimming pool. If money wasn't everything, Unk used to say, it was a good start.

I talked too much. Mr. Lemke took us into the library to show us what kind of ships his company made. There were models in glass cases, some even had sails. Big liners and liberty ships too. When I saw the name Matson Line, I said, "Ruthie's father used to work there." And Ruthie talked and told everyone Mr. Mitchum was a foreman but was in the Army now, stationed in England. Then Mr. Lemke asked me what my father did. Everybody knew, after Leroy told Mary Maureen, and she called me dummy and whispered I was a bastard. Unk left me the garage when he died, and the bank leased it to Lloyd to pay the mortgage, but that didn't mean Unk was my father, or that on that day over on the coast the gun was aimed at my head but missed me and hit Unk. I had my mouth open, ready to say something, anything, but I couldn't. I stuttered for him. I'd never done it on purpose before. It made me sick. I wanted to reach in and grab my tongue and pull it out by the roots. I kept it up until he said he would show us his office there at the house where he had more models.

I hadn't been to many birthday parties, but it was the first I ever heard of that you got more presents than you brought. All the girls got linen handkerchiefs and the boys leather wallets. The prizes you won for the games were better than the gifts we gave. I got a fountain pen and pencil set for winning at croquet. Ruthie got a prize for pin-the-tail, a silver bicycle for a charm bracelet.

One of the maids said we could have sugar cubes if we wanted, when someone asked, and I filled up Ruthie's dress pockets and my shirt pockets. Then we got a ride back to our street. It was better than going to Playland, Ruthie said, when she thanked Mrs. Lemke and Sharon. For me it was like visiting someone else's daydreams and getting to stay as long as you liked.

M Mary M aureen

I knew this was going to happen. I knew it. You can't expect to break the law and get away with it for long. My father should have known that. He was always telling us to respect the flag, the law, policemen, bike rules, your family, and all adults. Now look what happened.

Oh my. Oh my. Michael's size 14EE shoe. I had to sing now, my father's song for the U.S. Army. Over hill over dale the caissons keep rolling. I couldn't remember the song right but I had to keep singing. The caissons keep rolling along. I wasn't there. Nothing happened. I was asleep the whole time. But I couldn't sleep. I had to sing.

Avery was waiting for us the next morning like nothing had happened. I had fixed my hair with barrettes so it hung down in front so nobody would see my face. Ruthie skipped the whole way to school like she couldn't wait to get there. Miss Walker never said anything either and she was there in the front room when they came for Michael. No one in the whole school so much as mentioned what happened but everyone knew. I could tell that.

I almost forgot, myself. It was like it didn't happen. Except when we came home again. The door to the shed was off and Grammy wouldn't come out of her room. Avery came over and we got the door back in its frame and one hinge nailed on enough to keep it closed. He said we should hurry and get everything done before my mother came home.

The screen on the front door still had a big rip that we couldn't fix right. Avery held the two sides together and I tried to sew them with some twine. It wasn't a good job because the screen was stretched. Ruthie asked Avery while we were working if they could put Michael's leg back. Avery said he had heard that they could when he was in the hospital.

After we tried to fix the screen, Ruthie remembered Abner, and we went looking for his body. She found him where he had crawled after they shot him in the guts. What a mess he was, and stiff as a board. Avery couldn't talk, he had the stutters so bad he was shaking, but he made the motion to me we'd bury him and he got the shovel from Aunt May's shed. He started digging in the back lots away from the garden and close to our fence. It was a good place because the afternoon sun would stay on the spot for hours just the way Abner liked it.

I think Avery was more afraid of Abner dead than alive. He wouldn't touch him or get close. I had to take him by the tail and drag him to the hole by myself. His front teeth were broken off where the soldiers had smashed them with their rifle butts. I understood why. There was a piece of a soldier's canvas legging in his mouth, that I got out with a stick. He must have got a good hold and wouldn't let go. I swung him in the hole, but he was so stiff he wouldn't go down. I took him out and Avery had to make the hole bigger. Then he fit. I made Avery wait until I could run and pick some of my mother's roses, and I put them through his collar. I wanted to drop in his favorite dish, the only one he'd eat his dried dog food in, which was a 1931 Buick hubcap, too, but Ruthie wouldn't let me. Then Avery started pushing the dirt in with the side of the shovel, Ruthie and me stamping it down every once in a while so we'd use all the dirt and nobody would know where he was. We thought of putting up a marker later when we were done but I knew we never would.

We went on like before, my mother going to work, me and Ruthie going to school, Grammy staying home. And we could pretend Michael wasn't in the wash shed like before, but now he really wasn't. He was up in a hospital somewhere above Sacramento where the government put him. We couldn't visit but Grammy could write and so could he and we received his letters. Grammy read them to us just like before.

We had the sewing circle like we always did. Before, we had it on Friday, baking day, so whoever brought dessert, it would be easier on them. Then my mother had to work and women moved away and we had it on Sunday. Not every week, like before Pearl Harbor, just sometimes. But making the quilts got everyone interested again.

For the last six months we had been making twelve-inch squares for quilts, holding the material in embroidery hoops for the stitching. They were going to be war quilts; everyone got to sew the name of their relatives serving in the armed forces on their squares, or like Mrs. Hughes, she was stitching the names of the services including the Coast Guard and the Civil Defense, plus the names of the countries on our side. You could put anything you wanted if you had the room.

My mother did my father. Aunt May, Sammy. Me and Ruthie practiced mostly; my mother showed us how on scraps. Ours were to be included if we got good enough. And Mrs. Hughes said I was almost there. Miss Walker's square was half for the Army, for her brothers Damon and Daryl, and half for the Navy, but she didn't have Chuck's name on that section yet, so she had an anchor on one side and a cannon on the other. Everyone said it was pretty.

I practiced stars, both five-point and six-point, and the insignia for the intelligence corps that my father was in, and the jeep he got to drive around, now that he was a warrant officer. The stars were too hard, but I was going to put the jeep in my square if I got the chance.

Ruthie would go out to the back stairs, and if Aunt May was inside sewing, Avery would be there waiting. That boy thought he could sew. He did what looked like Abner but it had six or seven legs and big sharp teeth like a saw. Ruthie could sew better. But we always shared our dessert with him.

Aunt May didn't always come because of her legs and other reasons. When she didn't, Mrs. Hughes would come. They never came at the same time. We always had it at our house now, because it was easier on everyone. It couldn't be at Aunt May's because she didn't bake and Mrs. Hughes wouldn't go, or at Miss Walker's, who was new to the club, because Aunt May wouldn't go there because of who owned the house. So it was at our house, and everyone brought refreshments when it was their turn. Aunt May would bring graham crackers or ginger snaps from the store. I didn't mind, I liked things to be different, but Grammy would mutter and make comments after everyone went home.

She was still making her square with Michael's name and *USN* just like the government didn't have him in a prison hospital up north. And she was adding the outline of the state of Tennessee with NATIVE BORN inside. No one said anything; she just kept sewing. Everyone was to make as many squares of the design as there were members of the sewing circle, so everyone would have a quilt with the others' work. Me and Ruthie would get my mother's and Grammy's when we got older if we didn't learn well enough to do our own.

I showed Avery Grammy's square and he just looked at it without making any comments. I knew what Mrs. Hughes was saying because I heard her through her screen door when she was talking to a neighbor on the phone. And Avery knew what Aunt May said. I took some of Grammy's squares and was going to put them in the mailbox on the way to school. Let the government worry about them, I thought. I couldn't stand it anymore. But Avery stopped me. "The state of Tennessee looks just like a radio," he said. "It's too good to give to them." He was right; Grammy was the best sewer in the whole circle. I put them back.

Miss Walker always brought cupcakes in little paper molds with a lot of frosting on top, thick. My mother brought applesauce cake, which Grammy made because she didn't have time. And Grammy's was ice cream she made in our old wooden crank freezer. It took some work beforehand, but we all took turns. She didn't want Avery to help, but she didn't stop him from cranking the handle, and she set a dish of ice cream out on the porch for him. We wouldn't have had any without him, because Grammy had arthritis and my father wasn't there. But he had made a quilt frame before he left for the Army, and it was getting to where we were going to set it up for the first quilt, with a white flannel sheet for the backing and cotton for stuffing. The squares were in red, white, and blue and you had your choice of thread color, too; Miss Walker's mother sent a whole shoe box full.

Just as I was forgetting all about Michael getting caught, there was a big article in the paper, on the front page. We never got the *Herald* after my father left, but Leroy, who was delivering the afternoon paper now, left the article on my desk. Even before that, I knew something had happened because of the way everyone was looking at me. I put my speller over it, and then when no one could see I slipped the clipping into my dress pocket. I knew what I had to do.

I asked Avery if he had seen the paper. He knew already. And he knew Mrs. Hughes was going from door to door up and down the whole block, telling what kind of people we were, showing everyone a clipping someone had given her, saying the whole Mitchum family should be locked up. But she would still come to our house to work on the quilt as long as Aunt May wasn't there.

This was all my father's fault. He should never have left and this wouldn't have happened. He could have explained to the government like he did when he got Aunt May's radio back. Why was Michael in the wash shed in the first place? He had no business there when he was supposed to be in the Navy. My father knew better when he joined the Army than to leave us behind alone.

Now Michael had no leg and everyone knew that he was a deserter. On this street, in the whole city, if not the state. I was the sister of a traitor. And we kept him hidden for all that time. It didn't matter if I said I didn't see him. Poor Michael. Poor all of us.

Avery. We got in an awful disagreement. Avery and me. He tried to tell me my family wasn't to blame for anything. My father. "It's easy for you," I told him. "Your father is a convict. You have nothing to lose, saying that." He never got mad, which got me mad, him trying to talk to me like I was Ruthie. And I started yelling and told him to get off our porch and never come back. "I can do what I want," I kept yelling until Grammy came running. Then he got off the porch. And I was going to do it too, no matter what he said. He thought he was so smart. He couldn't tell me what to do.

Leroy won our room's award for the biggest tinfoil ball to help the war effort. Then we had to wait until assembly to see what he'd do in the entire school contest. I had seen some of the big boys carrying their tinfoil to school and they needed both hands. But so did Leroy.

Ruthie, me, and Avery had walked to school together that morning. He didn't run off like he used to. In fact he didn't run anymore. He did everything like his brain was somewhere else and his arms and legs could only move at half their speed. He waited on Aunt May's step if he came out before us and he let Ruthie take his hand anytime and would have probably carried my books if I was so inclined. But we had our argument and I didn't want anything to do with him. Grammy was right.

Ruthie would do all the talking, chattering away the whole ten blocks. When we got to school he didn't run with the other boys or lie down to spot for Jap balloons and American airplanes. He sat out on the bottom of the ramp, right below where the yard teacher stood. On the first day when he came back from the hospital everyone talked to him. "Avery, you were sick?" or "You had an accident?" Leroy called him stupid for eating a toadstool. But after that they left him alone, because he was too different, except for Sharon, or Arnold, who might talk to him before running off to play. At recess you were supposed to play. But Miss Cameron, standing twenty feet away, never said a word to him. He got up when the bell rang like it was just his clothes moving and went into our room and sat in his seat.

He hardly moved and he didn't go to sleep like he used to from staying up half the night downtown. But it was worse; he acted like he was daydreaming the whole time. When Miss Walker asked him to read, he stuttered but he acted like it was happening to someone else. He'd stop, take a breath, and go on. And he didn't try to be funny. He just kept reading. No one laughed either when he got spit all over himself or someone else, trying to get a letter to come out of his mouth.

In a couple of days it was like he wasn't there, except for Ruthie, who came over to sit beside him for lunch unless one of the teachers spotted her. Before, he was always courteous if he wasn't teasing you, but now he was even more polite, as if he was going to be the most polite person in the whole school, if not the state of California.

And he never got mad at anyone. Never caused any trouble that I saw, either. Two sixth-graders went up to him when he was going to sit on the ramp at lunchtime. First, one stopped him to ask something while the second got down behind him. They must have been new kids, because of the base. And then the first pushed Avery over the second one's back. Avery fell backward, hard against the cement, onto his side like he was asleep. His lunch sack ripped and his apple rolled out. He didn't do anything. Just lay there, not even looking surprised where he was. Then one of them kicked his apple into the wall and they went off laughing. He got up slow, went over and picked up the apple, and put that and his lunch into the trash can. Then went back and sat down on the ramp.

Before, it didn't matter how big they were, there would have been trouble for those boys, because Avery just didn't push or shove back when someone did that to him: he'd bite you or kick back or butt you with his head, and he could get you in a stranglehold around your neck with his arm, or worse, he did the scissors with his legs around your stomach until you said uncle, or he'd never let go and squeeze your guts right out of your ears. He just sat there now. But the most surprising thing, that made everyone in the class stop what they were doing to watch, was he did everything Miss Walker told him to.

On that Friday morning when he came out and he didn't have his tinfoil ball for the room contest I didn't mention it, because we weren't talking and I didn't want to know where it was. We went to school and Miss Walker weighed each ball on a scale on top of her desk. Nearly everyone had one. Mine wasn't very big but it was bigger than others. Sharon almost won; her father got a lot from the shipyard for her.

"Leroy is the winner," Miss Walker said, and he was jumping around, happy to have the most of something in the class. I knew how it felt because I once had the most valentines, back in the second grade in Tennessee, so I knew he was happy. He liked the attention. And so did I; two weeks ago I'd given a talk to every class in the school, because my father had sent me a Nazi armband with the swastika on the red cotton material, an epaulet with pink piping with a captain's bars, and a German flag. He got these things from prisoners he interrogated in England that had been captured in North Africa. My father promised my mother after he was sent to England that he wouldn't go any closer to the front lines. They wouldn't let him anyway, because of his age, unless he put in for a transfer to the desert. "England is dangerous enough," my mother said.

When we got the souvenirs, they were half mine and half Ruthie's, I took them to school for the class to see. Miss Walker said the whole school should see them and asked Mr. Allen. He agreed that I was to go to every room, and show what my father sent. I wrote out what I was going to say, and Miss Walker helped me.

Then Miss Walker said I should ask someone to assist me in holding up the other end of the flag. It was as big as a tablecloth. I was getting ready to choose one of my friends when she said I should take Sharon. I didn't think I was hearing right. We both looked over to where she was sitting, the only girl on that side, behind Avery's empty desk, drawing like she always was when she was supposed to be doing something else, wearing her pink angora sweater and white wool skirt and pink socks and patent leather shoes.

Miss Walker was looking at me and I was looking back at her too. She had been harsh to me lately, because. Because of what happened to Michael? I didn't know. She brought me up to her desk and called me lazy. Gave me a seventh-grade reader after I finished the sixth, which was supposed to be the end of my reading for the year, and told me next year she was going to put me to work. I should be doing more and a lot better. The worst sin in this world is wasting any talent you have, she told me. I didn't know what she was talking about. Just because I got enough on those tests they give every year that the man came down from Sacramento to talk to me didn't mean I liked schoolwork or I wanted the eighth-grade math like she was always suggesting.

She repeated, "I think Sharon would be a help." I knew you weren't supposed to hope bad things or they might bounce and happen to you. But I was wishing Sharon would have a fit and scare half the school out of their wits. "Go ask her," Miss Walker said, who couldn't even put her lipstick on right and got it on her teeth. I didn't even speak to Sharon, much less want to ask her for help now.

I think Sharon was as surprised as I was, and she accepted. Miss Walker let us start in our room for practice. We held out the flag while I read from the card, "This was flying on top of a building in Tunisia." And when I got to the bullet holes, Sharon would put her finger through them, and point to what we thought was blood. And she put the armband around her arm to show how it went, and the same with the epaulet. The class clapped afterward, which surprised me. And we started going to the next room. Sharon would remind me of things I forgot, or add things. After the first class, I forgot she might have a fit any minute. Mr. Allen saw us in Miss Cameron's room and said we should go to every school in the district, and he would see the superintendent.

On the day we marched out for the assembly, Miss Walker had Leroy walk in front of the class with her. He was so proud, carrying his tinfoil up over his head, the rest of us chanting Leroy, Leroy, Leroy, until Miss Walker said to stop.

The principal, Mr. Allen, was there, standing on the second step of the slide so we could see him, waiting for the classes to arrive. Miss Cameron was behind a table with scales, ready to weigh the tinfoil. All the class winners stood in a row, waiting their turn. There were some big tinfoil balls. It was hard to tell.

I noticed Avery just standing there at ease, his arms behind him, his fingers laced, looking up to where big white clouds were sailing through the sky like they had propellers, in perfect formation. He never bothered to look when Mr. Allen checked the weight again from Miss Cameron's paper.

All the students were quiet, the teachers standing in front of their classes. No one moved. It was like lining up for the class picture. Then he wrote something down on the paper and climbed back up on the ladder and made a joke. "Just one of these would make the whole tail section of a Black Widow bomber." And we all laughed. "If all of these," and he pointed to the foil balls, "fell on Tokyo, Emperor Hirohito would get more than just a bump on his head. He wouldn't have a head." We all cheered. "Without further ado, I want to announce our decision. The winner of the largest collection of tinfoil is Leroy

Smith, from Miss Walker's fifth-grade class." Did we yell and jump! Even Miss Walker. The principal put his arm around Leroy's shoulder. Each of the other class winners was given a certificate by the school secretary, and Leroy got a twenty-five-dollar war bond. His tinfoil ball would stay on Mr. Allen's desk until the War Department sent someone with a truck for the whole school's tinfoil. We marched back to our room. I wasn't the only one who knew that Avery's foil ball was bigger than anyone's, but no one said a word. Not Miss Walker. Not even Ruthie.

Right before the bell rang for lunch, a note came for Avery to go to the office. We all went out; it was a nice day to eat outside. While we were outside, the police took Avery away. I didn't see it, but I heard they took him right out of the school, two of them with their guns. No one knew what for, but I know Miss Walker tried to find out, because when I went to the office because I had a headache she was on the phone talking to someone at the police station. Leroy thought his father might have escaped and was coming back to kill Avery because he was a witness against him at the trial.

The next thing we knew, he was back. When we came in from lunchtime, he was sitting at his desk and Miss Walker was sitting at hers, both of them head down, doing their work. No one dared asked him; it would be no use anyway. Avery wouldn't tell you what day it was even if he knew, much less what happened with the police.

Grammy was ready to go back to Tennessee until the war was over and my father and Michael came home. "Between the jailbirds and the sailors on the street, we're not safe in our beds." I knew who she was talking about, but my mother made no comment about leaving, one way or another. My mother still sat in the dark by herself. When I asked her what she was doing she'd say, I'm thinking. But I was always afraid to ask what. We were down to four sitting at the same table, pretending we weren't in the same house together, until Grammy slapped Ruthie hard across the face and tried to take her pin away. My mother yelled so loud Mrs. Hughes said she could hear her all the way over at her house, "Don't you ever touch those kids again," and she picked up Ruthie, who was still crying and had both hands on her sweater holding the pin so Grammy couldn't get it away. Ruthie wouldn't say where she got it, and that only made Grammy madder. Ruthie loved that pin more than anything; she wore it on her pajamas at night too. It was just an Air Force insignia, a silver propeller and gold wings, that they wore on each lapel of their uniforms.

I knew where Avery got it, too. From trading with that boy at the bond drive where Chuck gave his speech. And he gave it to Ruthie. She thought she was so clever. Grammy knew who gave Ruthie that pin.

After that, Grammy did start looking at train schedules, but it was hard to get tickets, she said. "Who is going to take care of us if Grammy goes?" I asked my mother when we were going to the store. "You can take care of yourself," she said. "And I'll have Mrs. Hughes keep an eye on Ruthie. If she wants to go, let her go back to Tennessee."

I don't know how hard Grammy tried, but she kept the schedules by her chair to look at when my mother came home from work. Grammy didn't lay a hand on either of us after that. She wanted to sometimes, but I always reminded her what my mother said.

When I heard the knock that morning, my mother was just getting up, and she answered the door to Avery. I wasn't asleep. I'd been lying there feeling my nightgown wet on my back, and I kept thinking I was dreaming I was wet, but it was Ruthie's cold pee sticking the cotton cloth to my skin. I could hear my mother, her bare feet on the linoleum walking across the kitchen floor, making it squeak. The faucet. The rattle the glass top of the percolator made when she set it down on the gas burner. Then the knocking on the door. I knew it was Avery; he never knocked hard because Grammy would say he was trying to break the door down, and always just once. I heard my mother going into her bedroom, the sound of her putting on her chenille robe and her slippers to answer. I could picture her eyes half shut, her uncombed hair. Ruthie's face, that was next to me.

I was up by this time, stripping off my nightgown. I could kick Ruthie. I tried to dress as fast as I could, but by the time I got there to the front door they were both gone. I went over to Aunt May's in my bare feet, with nothing on my mind but to find out who phoned. Then I thought of a talk I had with Avery, before he was in the hospital. We were sitting on the front porch and he was trying to fix Ruthie's roller skates—she never kept anything good, a wheel was always coming off or the front or the back was slipping or she'd break the strap—when Chuck came by for Miss Walker. "They're in love," I said. "Sammy's new wife's folks own a bar in Honolulu," he said. Ruthie was letting two ants crawl up her arm. Quit that, I told her. She got up, and carrying her arm away from her dress, she went down the driveway where I couldn't see her.

I hadn't given love a lot of thought before, and I had to think it over. I loved my father most, then my mother, Grammy, Ruthie, and Michael. I shouldn't include Michael. I used to love Michael most. I knew a girl in the sixth grade who loved General MacArthur more than her own father. A lot of girls loved movie actors and singers and people on the radio. Ruthie thought she loved Red Ryder, even though I kept telling her he wasn't real. How can you love somebody that's not there? She didn't want to understand. It'd be different for him, but I asked Avery who he loved most. He put his head down like he was thinking it over too, but he never answered. He was a Catholic so I asked, "The Pope?" He shook his head. Grammy thought that both Mussolini and the Pope were together fighting the Allies. "Aunt May?" He shook his head again. I knew he had a mother but I didn't want to ask him that, or his father, who was in prison. I was ready to say the Virgin Mary because I knew the Catholics liked her, when "Martha Washington," he said, clear as day. He was kidding me.

I knew I smelled, but there was no time to dress and wash too. My mother was listening on the phone when Avery let me in. She stood with her one hip out like her body was out of joint. One end of the phone was pressed against her ear and the other she was looking into as if she could see the voice.

Avery knew, understood what had happened. He had that look on his face that he was caught. Aunt May was still in her bedroom behind the closed door. She called out when Avery let me in, "Now what? Is there a regular meeting going on in my front room, or what?"

"It's Mary Maureen," he called back.

"Am I going to have to get up?"

My mother put the phone down. She looked as if she were wondering how she had got here. I noticed her robe was ripped under the arm enough that you could see her blue nightgown. "Thank you, Aunt May," she called out.

"Any time, Dora."

I followed my mother out. Avery tried to say something as we went down the walk, but it didn't come out. My mother turned and smiled at him and he stopped trying. No one had said it, but I knew my father was killed.

Words aren't enough. They don't mean anything, unless you can see or do something different that makes you understand. We found out Saturday. It was on Monday that I started to believe. I wasn't going to school, because my father had died. Neither my mother nor Grammy carried on a lot, but my mother didn't go to work and Grammy stayed in her room Saturday and Sunday. Then on Monday washday she didn't even get up from her bed.

We all stayed inside the house, behind the pulled-down shades. No one suggested we turn on the radio or do our homework or make our bed. Monday afternoon me and Ruthie went out on the back steps to sit. I had read to her out of my reader all morning. There had been two more phone calls, and just my mother went over. I stopped reading each time while she went over to Aunt May's, neither one of us speaking until she came back. Then I read some more.

Ruthie acted like she didn't understand. She wanted to play, jump rope, get her cutouts and pretend. I told her no and made her sit and listen to me read. Go outside in the backyard, my mother said. So we did. I wished I could go to school. I had gone every day so far this year, the only person in the class that was eligible to win the perfect attendance certificate. I missed school in general. I noticed the time on the clock. Milk period. Reading. Lunch and recess. Avery would come home pretty soon.

Ruthie was playing down on the cement driveway. She had about forty sowbugs going over twigs and little bridges she had made. I had mentioned three times, Dad is dead. Mother had told us when we sat down for our oatmeal Saturday morning. "Your father was killed yesterday in North Africa." The government would let us know the details.

"I thought they were supposed to send a telegram," Grammy said.

"I don't know about that," my mother said. "They phoned."

"Maybe they could have made a mistake." My mother didn't answer.

I watched Ruthie as she tried to put too much oatmeal on her spoon and it fell before she got it to her mouth, onto the table. She picked it up with her tongue. She had no manners.

On the back stairs I told her again, "Dad is dead, Ruthie; he's never coming back anymore." She was on her stomach, moving the rolled-up sowbugs around with her fingernails. "Did you hear me?" She looked up with her dumb face. "He was blown to bits, probably," I said. "Into little pieces."

She wasn't listening; she didn't want to listen. "He's dead," I shouted. I got up and went over to where she was looking up at me, and I started stamping on her sowbugs, squashing them flat on the cement. "Dad is dead, Dad is dead, do you understand now?" I was coming down, jumping rope, my feet happy, up and down, up and down singing, "Dad is dead."

When the government sent the medal, my mother wouldn't look at it. Wouldn't let Grammy have it either. She put it in the back of her dresser drawer. When she was at work I got it and took it out of the box. There was a picture of President Washington on the front of the heart. I took the ribbon off and got a string to put it around my neck.

When I went to school that day and sat in the classroom, everybody was still looking at me because of Michael. No one had ever said anything worse than calling me names: *Jap spy* and *Tojo is your boyfriend*. But no one said anything about my daddy, but then no one said anything when he was alive, either, though Miss Walker gave me extra graham crackers at milk period for a few days. Except Avery. He said he was sorry and looked sorry about a thousand times. He always waited for me and Ruthie now and walked us home from school. He always had sticks of Juicy Fruit when we asked. He took us to the matinee and we sat through the double feature and got out in the sunshine and we couldn't see, were blinded in the eyes. Then he took us right into the creamery and treated us to a Coke.

There was no more going to the mud flats, but he always had something in mind. The library, he took us there; it wasn't too far. He and Ruthie checked out books. I didn't need any. Before, he wouldn't play with me at recess when the other girls played jacks or hopscotch, but now when no one else wanted to play hopsctoch with me, he would play. I could lag my square without missing, it was my best game, and jump to the seven and eight doubles anytime I wanted. I could beat him every time. And I made sure we played all the recess. That was the best part; I let him make a fool out of himself. If he wanted to act like a girl, I'd help him. If he wanted to spend his money on us, that was okay too. It made me sick to look at Avery. It was worse than when Ruthie broke her arm that time and he acted like it was his arm, going around sad, asking Ruthie if she wanted a Popsicle or a ride in his wagon. She was so clumsy she was lucky it wasn't her neck. She couldn't walk without falling down or shut a drawer without getting her fingers caught.

The medal looked like a locket shaped like a heart around my neck. I wore it inside my dress so my mother wouldn't see at home, but by the time I got to school it had bounced out. Leroy saw it while I was jumping rope and wanted to trade, a big gold Air Force eagle the officers put on their hats and a fountain pen that needed a point. "If you want," I said, and was trying to get the string off from around my neck when Avery came up. "No, Mary Maureen," he said. "No."

"Mind your own business," Leroy told him.

"You"—Avery said, and started stuttering. Leroy started mimicking him, "KKKKKK." And Avery was really tongue-tied. Red-faced. I tried to hand the heart to Leroy and Avery tried to grab it away. Leroy pushed Avery in the chest and tried to kick him. Then Avery jumped him, got him down, and pinned him to the ground. A lot of kids came running. Then Miss Cameron blew her whistle and came over and made him let Leroy up and sent Avery to the office.

He didn't come back the whole day and everyone said he wouldn't get promoted and would have to stay another year in the fifth. That meant I wouldn't have to hear him stutter anymore next year. I had to yank Ruthie off the school grounds because she wanted to wait.

Mr. Allen drove up later and let Avery out in front of Aunt May's. When Mr. Allen saw us he waved, he knew everyone by name, then drove away. Everyone on the street knew who gave Avery a ride. But when Ruthie asked, "Did you get a whipping?" he shook his head.

"He just talked to me," he said, "and made me do my homework in his office. He wasn't even there; he had to go somewhere else most of the time." He had walked up so close I could feel his breath on my face, and he stared at where the heart used to be but didn't ask. I had traded the locket for the eagle and pen and got a gum eraser besides from Leroy.

Avery got a battery somewhere and put it in the Packard. It was hard for me and Grammy to know when he was around anymore because Abner wasn't there to bark. I didn't like to go in the garage anyway; it felt like it was haunted, like Michael might still be there in the wash shed. Avery and Ruthie did all the work. My mother wanted to pay him, but he wouldn't take a penny.

It wasn't just the Packard; he got the aphids to leave my mother's roses too, squirting soapy dishwater on them. He mowed the little pieces of lawn and pulled all the weeds out, then clipped the hedge so the sunlight came in the window in the afternoon.

All my mother would have to do was mention something and Avery was right there. When her heel came off and the shoe man said it couldn't be fixed anymore, Avery took it somewhere and got it repaired good as new. Ruthie and him would meet her at the streetcar stop after work and carry her lunch bucket home and talk and laugh like they were having a great old time.

Once the car would start, my mother got in it and drove to the store and used the car to go to work. If she wanted to take a drive down to the park in San Mateo where the shipyard picnic was held, we went, the four of us in the front seat, down El Camino Real.

We still had the ration stamps for gas from before, and we used them up. We went to Fleishhacker's, the biggest pool in the world, for swimming. Avery had never been before and couldn't swim anyway. But I remembered from Tennessee, and my mother could swim like a fish. Ruthie caught on fast.

When Grammy started talking about going back to Tennessee again, my mother wouldn't answer. Then she told Grammy she was going to stay in California, where the wages were good and you could do what you wanted.

"Dennis would want us to live in Tennessee," Grammy said, and they argued back and forth. Then one night my mother shouted at Grammy, "Any time you're ready, I'll take you to the train station." Grammy didn't mention going back so often after that.

Avery didn't know as much about the Packard as my father did, but he tried, I'll give him that. He knew where to put the oil in and how to patch the tube in the tire. And read street maps: we could go anywhere in the city or down the peninsula. We took rides to the San Francisco Zoo and to the Egyptian Museum in San Jose. I wondered why the cities where people lived who worked in the steel mills and shipyards had Spanish names and the places where rich people like Sharon lived, Hillsborough and Burlingame, had regular people's names.

Sometimes I got my way and we didn't bring Avery along. It was always my mother's idea or Ruthie's. To me it was like bringing Abner along when he was alive: a lot of extra trouble and inconvenience. Avery wasn't part of our family.

Because I skipped fourth grade, I never studied the California missions or made one with clay in class like everyone else. I always wanted to see one, what adobe bricks really looked like, and my mother found out where one was and we went up one Sunday on her day off. She drove the Packard up to the city and we found the place with Avery reading the map. People were coming out of the front doors and I didn't know what to do. Avery led the way right into the place, showed us how the Catholics put water on their foreheads and made the sign of the cross. Inside there were still a lot of people. It was dark except for the racks of candles, and some bigger ones up on the altar. My mother and me had our scarves over our heads, and Ruthie had Avery's unironed and probably dirty handkerchief on hers. We wandered around. There were still people in the rows of benches, praying, and a lot of coming and going of others.

The place made me think of Halloween. Dark, the jack-o'-lantern people in costume, dress-up, carrying candles. There were a couple of priests in robes and some little boys in dresses. No Indians. I half expected there might be a few left, but there weren't any. The place made me hungry for candy.

When Avery knelt down to pray, Ruthie had to too, monkey see monkey do. They whispered back and forth. I could hear some. I knew who they were praying for, and I knew how much good it was going to do.

Elaine

Avery had changed. Or maybe she understood him well enough to know what to expect. They were friends. She trusted him. But when two policemen came in through the classroom door at lunch and went right to where he was sitting and pulled him out of his desk by his arm, she was so startled she couldn't react. "What did he do?" she finally managed to say.

"This is none of your business, ma'am," he answered.

She'd had enough of that with the FBI. She went running to the office and phoned the police station and asked to talk to whoever was in charge. The assistant chief of police told her, "You have to be a relative or an attorney before we can give you any information on the suspect."

"I'm his teacher, and I want to know what he's supposed to have done."

"He blew up a goddamn mail collection box, that's what he's done."

"Maybe you're mistaken. What day was that? I live across the street from him. What evidence do you have?"

He started swearing. "Don't play policeman with me, lady," he yelled.

She phoned a city councilman she'd met at the USO; he donated the doughnuts from his bakery. His wife woke him up and he said he'd phone the chief. "He's an eleven-year-old boy," she told him, trying to keep from getting excited. She phoned Aunt May, but there was no answer. The police must have gone there first. While she was calling from the office, Mr. Allen opened his door several times to see if she was still on the phone. The hell with him. Eunice came in and pretended to look on the secretary's desk for something. She called the base on the chance she could get Chuck, but he wasn't there. She talked to Randy, his friend, who said he'd take the patrol jeep down to City Hall and see.

She went back to her room to wait. She kept telling herself she had to do something, but she couldn't think of anything else. She could go down there, walk to the police station. Just then Avery came into the room, moving stiffly, leaning forward as if he were pulling his wagon with a heavy load. He stood by his desk, looking at her, and tried to smile. One side of his face was swollen, the eye almost shut, the lip puffy. She was going to cry if she didn't speak. "You still have the final copy of your president report to hand in," she said. He nodded and sat down in his seat and started writing.

Later that afternoon the chief of police phoned her back. The secretary came for her. "What do you mean, questioning my men about a case we're investigating for the government?" he started out. "Do you know that Gorman family is a bunch of criminals? They have rap sheets as long as my leg. Don't you ever phone a councilman and complain about an investigation again."

"Avery isn't responsible for what his family's done in the past," she got in.

"Don't talk back to me; you listen here. There were witnesses who saw him around that box, so don't tell me. He belongs in juvenile hall."

"Then why did you let him go?"

"We're continuing the investigation; he'll wind up in the state pen just like his father, I can guarantee you that. In the meantime, you better watch your p's and q's, miss, or you'll regret it. I can have—" She hung up the phone at the start of his next threat.

She walked home with Avery and Ruthie after school. She wanted to treat them to a soda, but Avery had to work in the garden. She and Ruthie had one. When she got home, Mrs. Hughes said the police had been across the street and Aunt May had been yelling at Avery for the last half hour. She thought she'd just make it worse if she went over there and tried to explain to Aunt May. And what was there to say? She hadn't asked if he had done what the police chief accused him of, but he hadn't denied it.

Eunice took her aside the next morning in the lunchroom. She spoke in her teacher voice. "You're too familiar with your pupils, Elaine. You'll never get them to obey. It just doesn't work. You need to maintain discipline, Elaine, if you have any plans of staying in the classroom."

"You do it your way and I'll do it mine," she said. Eunice nodded as though she hadn't heard, and was about to go on when someone else came into the room.

Eunice was always talking down to her. She hated it. She kept going over the conversation that whole evening, the retorts she should have answered with, and what she was going to say the next morning. She was so incensed, she was furious when she stalked into the lunchroom before school that day. But Eunice wasn't there yet. She said good morning to five or six other teachers and sat down and waited.

Eunice came rushing into the room just before the bell rang, calling out, "Surprise, surprise," holding up her left hand with a big diamond engagement ring. "He took me up to Coit Tower last night and popped the question."

"How romantic," the new first-grade teacher said. Irma was a year younger than she was and had started teaching at Edgemont after Easter, when the regular teacher came down with pneumonia. They walked toward their rooms together. She'd forgotten already how upset she had been. Forgot all the things she was going to say to Eunice. Irma was Ruthie's teacher now. She was a natural. The atmosphere in her room was amazing, the kids all paying attention, enthusiastic. Ruthie had held on to her hand, the time she visited Irma's room. Mary Maureen was sullen now and refused to do anything, but Ruthie and she were good friends. She came over to the apartment and they had oatmeal cookies and milk together nearly every afternoon.

She thought sometimes that Irma was such a good teacher because this was just something for her to do until the war was over and she went back East. Irma didn't care what other people thought; she did what she liked. She had graduated from one of the women's colleges back there and had come to California because her father was rich, a dollar-a-year man who did something for the government. They were friends, but only at school. She'd introduced Irma to Chuck once when he'd come to get her. Later she'd commented, "Isn't she attractive?" He seemed surprised. "She's got no chin," he said, "and she sounds like Eleanor Roosevelt." Eunice had never offered to go into *her* classroom to demonstrate her theories on discipline. Eunice was wary around her. Mr. Allen couldn't do enough for her. "Oh, you'd like to change the desks for tables so everyone can sit together? I'll have Leo do it tonight." She wasn't jealous, but she wished she could be as persuasive.

Mrs. Hughes didn't seem to care so much anymore, but Chuck still parked around the corner so she and the neighbors wouldn't see the car. He never stayed long enough, in her estimation, sitting stiff in her new chair, his hat on his knees, looking as if he were ready to leap up and make a run for the door.

Was there something wrong with her? Did she have BO? She bathed once a day, really lathered the soap, wore perfume. Bad breath? She brushed her teeth three times a day and right before a date and sucked on Life Savers whenever he took her out. She used foot powder.

She'd been in a silly mood, for a Sunday night. She hadn't seen him in nine days, and to celebrate he had taken her up to a restaurant in the city. A party at another table insisted on paying for their dinners because Chuck was in the service. It had happened before, and it always embarrassed her a little. Driving home, she'd leaned over and kissed one of his hands on the steering wheel, crushing her breasts against his arm. He didn't seem to notice.

When they got to her apartment they tiptoed up the stairs, but it wasn't necessary to avoid the squeaks because Mrs. Hughes's radio was going full blast. She went into the bathroom. What if I took off all my clothes and walked into the front room naked? she thought while she was peeing. Could she do that? She kicked off one shoe, then the other. She could. She kicked off her underpants, still sitting on the toilet. Stood up and unbuttoned and dropped her pleated skirt. She looked at herself in the mirror, wearing just her sweater and blouse. She wasn't attractive, she decided. Not like Mona. She didn't have that look that made men want you. That made them reckless. The come-hither look. The look that drove men wild. She could see herself down to her knees in the mirror. The beard between her legs looked unkempt, as if it needed a perm. Why did hair have to grow there? Was it necessary? Women were at such a disadvantage. They were always the chaste bride and never the bridegroom-chaser. That didn't make sense, but she didn't want to straighten it out in her mind.

She didn't want to be a man. Her mother did. She was always saying, I should have been a man. She'd always assumed she'd get married. Have a husband. She had a hope chest; both she and Mona had one. When Mona was a junior, one of her admirers made her one in wood shop. Her mother had paid him to make her one too, out of red cedar. The wood was supposed to protect your linens from moths. Her mother had bought them dozens of sheets and pillowcases at white sales. Towels. For your hope chests, she'd say, coming home with shopping bags from Reno department stores.

Living away, she could really appreciate her mother more. It was as if the distance first gave her a list of all the slights and wounds her mother had inflicted on her but also an opposing list of all the times she had tried to be fair. Give good advice. Don't be serious when you get to high school. It's just puppy love. That's just hot pants. Both Mona and she pretended to be shocked when their mother was crude. For her part, she *was* shocked. She didn't want anyone putting anything inside her. But Mona wasn't shocked.

She flushed and pulled on her underclothes and skirt. Washed her hands. Thought of putting on fresh lipstick but decided the heck with it. Going back through her bedroom, she noticed her drawing pad. To put herself to sleep last night, she'd started drawing her own feet poking out where the blanket had come untucked.

She looked at the pad. Her feet were rather pretty. They weren't ugly like most women's feet—no corns or misshapen toes from wearing shoes that were stylish rather than comfortable. She went back into the front room and said, "Why don't you take off your shoes and socks? I'd like to draw your feet."

"Hold it," he said. He was trying to fix the band on her wristwatch. It kept coming off the watch. It was some kind of elastic that you couldn't get anymore at the stores. He was always after her to wind it and take better care of it. Her parents had given her the watch when she graduated from high school. "It's a twenty-four-jewel Elgin," he kept telling her. "It'll last forever. They don't make them like this anymore." Sometimes she thought the only time he willingly took her hand was to see if she'd remembered to wind her watch. Now that he'd repaired the band, he had his pocket watch on one knee and was looking at his aviator's wristwatch to set the Elgin. I love him, she thought, I love him.

When he reached down and untied his shoelaces, she was surprised at herself for asking, and surprised at him. He sat there, more self-conscious than before, with his bare feet on the floor. She sat close on one of the wooden kitchen chairs, drawing. He had three long curly hairs on the top of the big toe of his right foot. She laughed when she put them in. "What's so funny?" he asked.

"Nothing," she said. "Could you pull up your trouser legs a little so I can get your ankles? It'll balance the picture." He pulled up his black trousers at the knee an inch or two. "Let me," she said. She got down and gave the cuffs three big rolls up.

His legs were both hairy and bony. There was an awful scar on one calf. She wanted to ask but didn't, but she drew it in. "What would be nice would be if I could get some of your upper body too. Then I'd have your legs and feet opposite your arms and hands. It would make a symmetrically balanced drawing."

He did it, got up and took off his jacket, folded it carefully and rolled up his sleeves. "Maybe if you took off your shirt," she said, drawing wild strokes on the pad. He did that too. First his tie and then off with his shirt. "I forgot your tattoos," she said. She'd already included them but wanted something to say.

She flipped to a fresh paper, started a new sketch. She put the feet in first, upper legs, and kept going, trunk and head, sitting there in her new chair without any clothes. She was going so fast now the pencil was doing all the work. It was like the subject was fixed in her eyes and they drove her fingers. And Chuck appeared on the page.

"Let me see," he kept saying. "Let me see." He made a grab for the pad and she let it go. He turned red. Red as a tomato. She waited.

"You have the rooster and pig on the wrong feet," he said, looking down to be sure. She had forgotten the wristwatch he wore on his ankle too. He was holding the big pad over his lap and chest like he was as naked as the drawing. She had to grin. Her sailor.

What had she expected? He got dressed and left. Was she too aggressive? She was pacing. Then she felt hungry and made herself a jelly sandwich.

When she finally went to bed, it was after one o'clock. She needed her rest. Her sleep. But she couldn't. Her eyes wouldn't stay closed. What had she done wrong? Wasn't she delicious? Delicious? She meant desirable. She must have got that from a magazine. Sugar and spice, that's what she was, and everything nice, that's what she was made from. She was delicious.

• • •

She took the roll. "Mary Maureen? Mary Maureen?" No answer. She was never tardy. Her only student with a perfect attendance record. She called out again, though she could see her seat was empty. Did she expect her to appear out of the cloakroom? "Please take out your spellers, class." The sounds they made annoyed her, dropping things on the floor, slapping the books on the desktops, fluttering the pages. Sniffing their noses, shuffling their feet, sighing out loud at the big tasks before them at school.

She walked all four sides of the room, then down the aisle past Mary Maureen's desk. She hadn't seen anyone playing Sunday morning or afternoon. She hadn't been over to the Mitchums' since the night the son was captured by the authorities. Mrs. Hughes was still talking about it. "I never would have thought that. Never. They were the best people that ever lived in that house. Mother Mitchum could whipstitch better than anyone I ever met."

She was going to have to put an *ab* in Mary Maureen's column for May 12. There was nothing for it. Avery would know where she was. "Avery, will you come up to my desk, please?" He got up slowly, his hair hanging down in his eyes, his shoes squeaking against the floor. A few heads came up to see, then went back down. He stood at the side of his desk, his shoulders slumped, his fingers on both hands fidgeting with each other as if he were frantically counting them again and again. "Yes, Miss Walker?" he asked. Was he making a face at her?

"Do you know where Mary Maureen is?" He actually looked over at her desk to be sure she wasn't there.

"Something happened," he said.

Why do they do this? she thought. "What happened?"

"IIIIIIIII," he started stuttering. He was doing it on purpose. She could feel the spit on her arm but didn't move it back.

"Avery, stop it." He clamped his mouth closed. She was trying to whisper but knew she was hissing. How did this always happen? She wanted to help him. He was ready to try speaking again. She felt them on her arm first, like raindrops, then saw that tears were coming down his cheeks. She looked around. It didn't seem possible. It was like one of the portraits of the presidents on the wall under glass had started crying. No, it was worse than impossible. His eyes were swollen and red. She didn't know what to do anymore. She reached for the top drawer but she had been out of tissue for a month. She got her handkerchief out of her purse and gave it to him. "Go to the lavatory and wash your face, Avery. Come back when you feel ready." He didn't move. He tried to speak again. "Go on, Avery." He almost ran out.

Sharon was watching, making no pretense of doing her work. "Are you daydreaming, Sharon? You're supposed to be doing your spelling." Sharon got out of her seat and came up to her desk. Brazen. Where did she get that assurance? Was she becoming too familiar with Sharon too?

"Miss Walker, Avery's upset because Mr. Mitchum was killed. That's why Mary Maureen isn't here today."

"Thank you, Sharon. You can go back to your seat now."

It was the first time that someone she'd known had died in the war. What a strange, hollow feeling. Dennis was dead. He was flying a kite at Eastertime. How could someone so tall, so angular, just disappear, allow the space he'd filled to close up empty?

There was so much to do, this close to the end of the year. She'd got behind, rushing home yesterday after Sharon had told her Dennis had been killed. She still didn't want to believe it. What must the family feel? She had found out Dora was only thirty-one, just eight years older than she was.

She and Mrs. Hughes had put their meat ration stamps together and she'd gone downtown and found a rump roast at the butcher shop. While that was cooking she baked a cake and Mrs. Hughes fixed a baking pan of macaroni and cheese, and they took them over.

Everyone was being brave. Grammy thanked them and asked them in. Dora was still at work. She looked at the girls for signs of grief. Ruthie looked sad, she thought. She held her on her lap and called her sleepyhead when she started to doze off. Mary Maureen still looked sullen and gave a smart-mouthed answer when her grandmother asked her a question.

She tried to hug Dora when she came in the door, but it was like trying to hug one of the porch posts. Dora stiffened and held her arms to her sides. Mrs. Hughes kept the conversation going, commenting on everything from the weather to the afternoon serial. Avery wasn't there, but Aunt May had already visited. They left when other neighbors rang the doorbell.

When she told Chuck that Dennis had died he said, "He should have known better."

"What do you mean?"

"You told me he was in the first war. And he reenlisted in this one?"

"So?"

"You have to be stupid to go through it twice, once you know what it's like. Especially when you don't have to. He wasn't regular Army. It's all a joke; the politicians, generals, and admirals could care less. He had to know that, since he served once. It turns into a bad joke when you die."

"You sound like Ben. You wouldn't go back, if they ordered you to?"

"I don't know what I'd do." They stopped talking and looked at each other. He was sitting on top of a desk, his long legs still stretched out. She had opened a drawer in her desk but had forgotten what she was looking for. "Do you think

I like giving those speeches?" he went on. "Do you think I enjoy getting up in front of all those workers and asking them to spend their money to buy more ships and airplanes?"

"Daryl always writes they don't have enough planes to train in."

"I don't care what your brothers say. I don't like asking those people for anything. Because more sailors will get killed out of it."

"Don't use that tone about my brothers." She realized she was mad and they were arguing.

"If they're so goddamned patriotic, why are they at West Point in New York instead of out on one of those islands in the Pacific or in the European theater, tell me that."

"They happen to be officer material, that's why."

"La-de-da, that's just what this war needs is more candy-assed officers from the academies."

"Don't you ridicule my brothers. Don't you dare."

He stood up glaring at her. He was just opening his mouth to say something when Mr. Allen came to the door. He had met Chuck before. "Look who's here, welcome home," he said, limping into the room to shake Chuck's hand. "Back at Tanforan?"

"Got in this afternoon from San Diego. It's like coming home," he said.

She stopped listening. She had almost called him a coward. That was the next thing she was going to say. Yell. When Mr. Allen left she got her coat and then her purse from the drawer. "I prefer to walk home," she said, going toward the door.

"Suit yourself."

She was still indignant. Walking home, she went the long way so she wouldn't have to pass the Mitchums'. The shades were down but Mrs. Hughes said Dora had gone to work again this morning. Neither of the girls had come to school, though. No one knew when the funeral was to take place. Not until the body could be returned, Mrs. Hughes decided. You couldn't have a ceremony without a body.

When she gained her apartment she felt better. She was home, inside. She wasn't going back. She'd signed the contract for the 1943–44 school year, but she didn't care. She'd work for her father. Anything was better than this. Who did he think he was, anyway?

The girls came back to school Wednesday. She went over to the primary playground at recess and pushed Ruthie in the swings as high as she wanted to go. Irma said Ruthie was doing fine. Mary Maureen called Avery a bastard, loud, after the bell rang and they were all in their seats. She called her up to her desk. "Do you know what that word means, Mary Maureen?"

"I know, and that's what he is."

"Don't you use that word in the classroom or anywhere else. Do you understand? Do you?"

"Yes, I understand."

The week went by just like it always did. She went downtown to do her Saturday shopping. Did her laundry in Mrs. Hughes's wringer, with her landlady supervising. She heard Avery's wagon go by, heading for Main Street. She saw Ruthie jumping in the air like she was doing some kind of a dance on her front lawn. She didn't understand what she was doing until she ran over, hands cupped, with two butterflies inside. She punched holes in the lid of a fruit jar and Ruthie put them in.

The sun went down and left the sky as pink as her new lipsick smeared across the horizon. She kept going back to the window for another look at the sky as she dressed after her bath. The color didn't dissipate; it stayed the same vivid pink. Like live coals in the fireplace after the flame went down. How hard would it be to duplicate that shade with oils? Maybe it would have to be watercolors. That pink. She was ready. The hell with him; she was going to the USO tonight.

She hadn't been here for a long time. What did she mean? She came every day to this hellhole. She went up the four flights of stairs fast, on her toes. She had heard the music from out in the street. There were sailors everywhere in the big room, more on the sidelines than on the floor, she thought in the semi-darkness. "Can I have this dance, miss?" a sailor asked. She didn't say I have to check in first, or I have to hang up my coat; she put her arms up like she was surrendering and they started dancing.

She told herself she wasn't going to think of Chuck; she was here to have a good time. Veronica saw her on the floor and came and got her coat, almost yelling to make herself heard, "Do you want to sketch tonight? Some of the boys were asking."

"Not tonight, I'm here to have fun," she said on the arm of a soldier. Slow dance. Fast dance. It didn't matter as long as they were moving around and around the floor. When one of her partners took a half-pint from the waist of his trousers and asked, "You want a snort?" she took a long one. She'd never allowed herself before; she'd followed the rules. Veronica had warned the hostesses about accepting drinks or presents, what the consequences might be. She was tired of always considering the consequences. But no one offered her another drink. She danced. Stopped to eat four sugar doughnuts, licking her fingers in front of everyone. She happened to notice the clock at 9:00 and again at 10:58. She didn't have to get up tomorrow. She hadn't wound her own watch since Tuesday.

She was jitterbugging, had taken off her shoes and in her bare feet was going as fast as she could move her legs. She'd never understood exactly what you were supposed to do, what the steps were, but the sensation, the gyrating movement, made her want to go faster. She could feel the sweat running down her back, flying off her face, getting into her eyes. The sailor was twice, ten times the dancer she was, moving like he was double-jointed, so fast she couldn't hope to keep up. When he slid her over his hip she went limp and between his outstretched legs she arched her back. The band got louder and the other dancers were clapping in a circle around them and the spotlight was in her eyes.

She couldn't get her breath when the music stopped. Her partner took her hand and bowed as the clapping got louder and people started whistling and stamping their feet. She didn't know who it was that grabbed her arm but thought it was to dance again; the music had started.

"You should be ashamed," Chuck said. "I could see your underclothes." She couldn't speak. He leaned toward her and sniffed. "And you've been drinking too." She was being led out the door and down the stairs. The fresh air made her feel how damp her clothes were. Wet. Sopping. She let him take her along, still trying to catch her breath. He was saying, "You promised not to come here. You're a teacher. Those men have only one thing on their mind. They're shipping out and don't care what they do."

They were alone in the primary playground. She was still out of breath and sat down on the end of the slide. Why had she been mad at him? The argument. He was going on and on. "Kiss me," she told him, "kiss me, you fool." He stopped talking for an instant. Then started again, "Elaine, I want—"

"Now," she said, louder. He bent down and was going to peck her on the cheek. She got her arms around his shoulders and took him down as she leaned back on the slide, kissing his mouth, his neck, his chin, his forehead. His chest. She expected the sound of the zipper on her skirt and felt her bare rear end against the metal slide. Her hips fit snugly between the two rims and he scooted her up until her heels were supported. Her eyes were shut as tight as she could keep them. She didn't want to see the dark.

She and Mona in the tub her mother sitting on the rim soaping the washrag. Wash your own rose her mother told her handing her the cloth. She started feeling her insides were being painted, stroke by stroke, brushstroke, showing her in detail what she was feeling. Pounding, pounding rhythmically, and it was her heels tattooing against the bottom of the slide, wanting to call out her pleasure trying not to let sound pass from her mouth. What was happening to her? Oh oh she felt like a velvet eggbeater was going inside her. She sighed and sighed. It was past wonderful, past past. Then the vibrations eased, the velvet thrashing slower going off in little fluttery recoils of goodness.

"I'm sorry, I'm sorry, I don't know what got into me. I'm sorry," Chuck was saying. She was so tired. Her maidenhead. Delicious. How could anyone feel bad after that? Who could say "What do you think of me now?" Cheap? Shameless? A whore? She'd like to say "Do it again." She started giggling.

"What?" he said.

"I don't know."

"I was wearing protection." She didn't understand, but then she did. That was good; she hadn't even thought of that. She was still lying on the slide; she felt her underpants lassoed around her ankles when she tried to move. She was still dizzy.

"I better take you home," he said. She stood up, pulling up her skivvies. Trying to get her clothes straightened, her blouse inside her skirt. Chuck was helping, pulling it around so the zipper was in the right place. She had to get her things, coat and purse. They went back up the stairs. People were passing, no one realizing anything different about her. She was no longer a virgin. No one exclaimed. She was saying good night good night.

They finally got to the car. Her head lolled on the back of the seat. She was so tired she couldn't hold it up. Neither of them spoke as they went around one side of the heart. "I'm sorry, Elaine," he said when he parked the car. "I lost control."

"There's nothing to be sorry about."

"Do you really mean that?"

"Yes, why would I say it if I didn't?" When she opened the car door the night air hit her and she didn't feel so tired. "Come on," she said, "I made some sugarless molasses oatmeal cookies." He got out of his side looking less worried, she thought.

She woke up stiff; her back was killing her. Chuck had flown to Long Beach late last night for a two-day bond rally. It was good it was Sunday. She had to move like an old woman just to get around the apartment. She had a nice soak in the bathtub and that helped.

Lying there, steam rising, looking down at her nipples and toes bobbing like buoys, she realized why her back hurt. The hard metal slide, that had to be the reason. She couldn't remember the act, that's how she decided to describe it for now, without thinking *me me me* like she was tuning up to sing. On one hand, it felt wonderful, and on the other hand, it was over. That part of the picture was painted; she had to go on. Go on to what? She didn't know.

But to think of Chuck made her weak, as if her legs were made of oatmeal and her heart, it was pouring, runny, like her fudge that didn't harden, seeping out every pore. She couldn't think straight anymore.

One potato two potato three potato four, five potato six potato seven potato more. My mother told me to choose this very best one and you are it. Chuck.

Turn the dirty dish towel inside out. Chuck. Wasting food helps Hirohito. Chuck.

She went back to school Monday feeling fine and counting the hours until Chuck came back. It was hard to pay attention in class. There were six days left in the school year. She felt a kind of sadness that the term would be over. Was she crazy? She had been waiting for this for nine months. There was going to be a June, July, and August vacation.

She had changed, but couldn't decide for better or worse, looking up and down the rows of kids. Mary Maureen was passing a note to Leroy. She couldn't tell if they had changed or not. She was smiling, looking over the students. Some of them noticed and smiled back. They were going to be together another year. The latest scuttlebutt was Eunice was going to become the principal. Mr. Allen was being promoted to district coordinator. She didn't know if that change was going to be better or worse. But she would be teaching the sixth grade, these students, next year. It wasn't such a horrible thought.

As the kids went out the door for morning recess she wanted to reach out and pat them each on the shoulder. Of course she didn't. Leroy passed, his pink wad of bubble gum behind his ear. He picked it off and plopped it into his mouth outside the door and started chewing. Mary Maureen went by, trying to untangle the gum she'd stuck behind her ear from the long strands of hair that had pulled out of her braid. That was why girls didn't usually park their gum there. She must have looked disapproving, because Mary Maureen smirked and said, "It's my gum," over her shoulder.

She ignored her. It was just a phase; Mary Maureen would come around again. She'd started out the best student in the class but now she'd stopped doing any work at all. She sat at her desk pretending, book open, but disrupting the other kids, whispering to them, passing notes, borrowing pencils, snapping her gum. Wanting to get a drink or go to the lavatory every ten minutes. Avery didn't go out for recess anymore; he stayed in his seat, sometimes working on his report or reading, sometimes staring into space. She never asked him why he didn't go out.

She got the first phone call after she put her purse down on the kitchen table but before she kicked off her shoes. "Telephone," Mrs. Hughes called. She was pretending to read the San Mateo Times, as if that could block out the telephone conversation two feet away.

"We found Mona," her mother said. She was going to say, I didn't even know she was gone, but her mother went on. "She was with a soldier up in Nebraska. She's ruined her life." She didn't know what to answer. She couldn't say anything without Mrs. Hughes knowing. "Your father thinks it's the war. I don't know anymore."

"Where did she meet him?"

"Reno, she went up with Loretta to shop. He started a conversation and the next thing you know Mona was telling Loretta to go back to Carson City alone because she was going to stay. He was waiting for a bus. We didn't hear from her for five weeks. And then it was a phone call and she wanted her last pay check sent to her in Omaha. Your father went up there but she wouldn't come back."

When she put the phone down and thanked Mrs. Hughes, her ear was numb. Her mother must have spoken for an hour. "Bad news?" Mrs. Hughes asked.

"Oh no, just some information I needed from my mother." She got away, put on her robe, and had just finished heating a can of soup for her dinner when Mrs. Hughes came calling through the screen door, "Another call, Elaine."

"Hello, Sister, is this the convent?"

"What? Chuck?" She recognized his voice when he started to laugh.

"I'll be back tomorrow, can you wait? Do you miss me?"

"You know I can't." Her heart was thumping.

"I'm going to be home tomorrow night, late. Should I stop?"

"You better," she said.

She was in bed, almost asleep, when Mrs. Hughes called out, "Another call, Elaine," knocking on the door.

The connection was so bad she thought it was her mother again. "Hello, hello, Elaine Walker? Chuck said I should phone you if I couldn't get hold of him. I'm Myra Sikes." She remembered the name, Chuck's friend's wife. "I'm sorry I have bothered you so late."

"No, no, I don't mind."

"Russ is supposed to be in San Francisco on May 27. I'm not going to make it, I don't think. I'm calling from Washington, D.C. I'm stuck here until tomorrow and I was only able to get a ticket on the train to Chicago. I don't know how I'm going to get out of Chicago. Transportation is terrible, no seats at all." Then her voice started fading in and out. "Tell Chuck, and he'll tell Russ when he arrives. Chuck is still there, isn't he?"

"Yes, yes, he's on bond tour but he's coming back tomorrow. I'll tell him." She was almost shouting. "Don't worry, Myra," she said, and they were disconnected.

All next day at school she couldn't pay attention. When the air-raid siren went off she got confused and thought it was lunchtime and said, "You're excused, class." They laughed and she laughed back, turning off the lights. She had confiscated from one of the boys a one-cell Navy flashlight that went on a life jacket, and she used the light now in the dark to read to them.

She was three-quarters of the way through *Huckleberry Finn* now. It was good the year was almost over. There weren't a whole lot of books that held their interest. Twain was really too wordy for reading out loud, but there were enough good parts to keep them listening.

She tried not to think about Chuck coming back. She kept busy when she got home, cleaning, for the first time in a month. There were dust puppies under her bed so big she thought they were shoes. She changed the sheets, though it wasn't Saturday. Walked downtown to get something to eat in case he was hungry. There was only canned Spam, but she was lucky and got a dozen eggs too. She went to four stores, but there was no sugar.

She didn't know what time he was coming. She polished all her shoes, then read the paper. Ironed enough dresses for the next five days. She took her bath at nine and put on her robe, then decided that might be too suggestive and put her dress back on again.

She was nodding off in her chair like Mrs. Hughes did reading the *Examiner*, her head slumping, chin resting on her chest. The neighbors traded newspapers back and forth. She could imagine how she looked. She checked for the time again at eleven. She was really going to sleep. She'd remembered to wind her watch, too; he would be proud of her.

She was awakened by a tap on the front-door window. She had left both doors unlocked. She wasn't sure if she was having a dream or not, but he was there in her bedroom and they were racing to take off their clothes, trying to help each other and getting in the way. She thought she'd got everything off but realized she still had her bra on. They were surrounded by the noise the bed was making, loud, but it stopped or she couldn't hear it after a while.

They lay on their backs, gasping. She was able to sit up first. He did the most work, but she wasn't quite sure yet what her part was. There was never any time to learn anything. But she felt completely unself-conscious. Unshy. She took her bra off and flipped it over her back onto the floor and curled up beside him, letting her breasts rest on his shoulder.

She remembered Myra's phone call. "You'll like them," he said. "Russ is the salt of the earth. Myra is smart like you." She couldn't really see him, just the outline of his face in the dark. When he'd come through the front door they hadn't touched at first. "I wasn't sure you were up," he'd whispered. It was 12:40. They were standing close. "Elaine, there's something I should tell you." But they had got off the subject when she touched his cheek with her fingertips. That's what started the frenzy.

She didn't want to sound coy, but she wanted to know. That he loved her? "What were you going to tell me, before? Tell me," she said.

"I'm not ashamed of the fact, but you should know. My mother was an Indian." He stopped.

"That's it?" she asked.

"Let me finish. She killed herself. She hung herself in a hotel room in Spokane. I don't know why she did it; no one ever said. My sister thought she had syphilis. I don't know why she thought that, she wouldn't tell me. I had a Wasserman test after I got in the Navy, when Molly wrote that. But I was clean."

"I'm sorry about your mother."

"I can hardly remember what she looked like," he said. "I try but I can't. I don't think of her as much as I used to before. But I have so much on my mind now, with giving that speech all the time." She was curling the hair on his chest around her finger, and she leaned forward and kissed his lips closed.

This time she was slowly being electrified in pink neon in the shape of a naked woman she had seen over a burlesque house, going off and on off and on. She shattered into pieces of light. She was falling asleep and waking up again. She asked him, really wanting to know, "Are you enjoying this as much as I am?" He tried not to make any sound as he laughed, pulled her up on top of him, and gave her face a big lick. She started moving. She felt awkward up there at first but then it started good better best bestest bestial beatific but there was so much noise from the springs it sounded like she was bringing the whole house down.

She wasn't sure where she was or if she was alive anymore, she had no memory, or why anyone should be shaking her shoulder. Her eyes wouldn't focus and she couldn't swing her legs over the side of the bed so her feet could be on the floor. She willed herself to feel the cold linoleum against her feet but it was impossible. Chuck was standing in his skivvy shirt, trying to find his trousers. Someone else was knocking on the door. She looked at the clock on the table. It was almost seven-thirty. She was going to be late for school. She had to answer the door, then dress. She looked over at Chuck, searching for his clothes. "Relax," she whispered, "I'll handle this." She found the dress she'd worn yesterday and slipped that over her head, went to the door, and opened it a crack.

"Are you coming to school today, Miss Walker? I'm ready to walk with you."

"I'm going to be a little late, Ruthie. Why don't you go ahead?"

"I can wait."

"No, no, you go and I'll be there as soon as I can."

She went back in the bedroom. Chuck had got back in bed. "How could we oversleep," she asked, "when you have all those watches?"

"Probably for the same reason you put your dress on inside out." She couldn't believe it, looking down, but he was right.

She made it to school fourteen minutes after the last bell. Mr. Allen had unlocked her door and was standing in front of the class with the world map down, discussing the latest strategy in the Pacific. He stopped when she came hurrying in. Smoothly, with aplomb, she said, "Why, thank you, Mr. Allen." Irma would be proud of her. "Class, please take out your arithmetic books and turn to page two hundred seventy-six. This will be our last fifth-grade math lesson."

She would stop in the middle of what she was doing sometimes and wonder where she was and why she was writing with chalk on the blackboard. But when the buzzer sounded she grabbed her coat and purse and was the first one out the door. She hurried over to Irma's room to pick up Ruthie.

Chuck was coming over tonight for dinner. She had to stop downtown for bread. By the time she got home he was sitting in Mrs. Hughes's living room, drinking tea and looking over her quilt squares. "Elaine's putting your name in her squares, but I have plenty of room to include it in mine, too," Mrs. Hughes was saying.

"I'd be honored," he said.

She made Spam and eggs with fried potatoes for dinner. Toast with the last of her mother's apricot jam. He was hungry and ate everything she put in front of him. She wished she had more. He teased her, "I didn't think you would be such a terrific cook. This Spam is out of this world." They both laughed at anything. Everything was good. Everything was funny.

"I'm off until Sunday," he said. "Then we're going to Portland. I'll be here when Russ comes." He seemed to brighten up then. He worried her, the way he talked about the bond drives now. "I'm going to tell them to go to hell," he said. "I'm not going to do it anymore. I'll go back to being the master-at-arms for the base. I did a good job for them. They still need me there; I'm supposed to spend as much time as I can helping out when I'm not on tour."

For dessert she put some margarine on warm toast, a few sprinkles of sugar and the last of her cinnamon. "Good, this is good," he kept saying. They turned on the radio and went into the bedroom. She thought to set the clock: he had to leave in enough time to go on duty at 2400.

Chuck had talked so much about Myra and Russ that she felt she'd known them for a long time, shaking hands with both of them and then hugging Myra. They went barhopping up in the city, to the Top of the Mark first, looking down on the lights, the bay. The place was full of servicemen. Jammed. Myra was making them all laugh, telling how she had got to California. "I stood up for hours before I realized I could sit on my suitcase in the aisle and just let everyone step over me. I wasn't the only one. You could barely make it to the end of the car to the toilet; there was no room. The conductor couldn't get through the car to take tickets. Somebody shared their bag of popcorn and Coke and I gave them half my cheese sandwich. Remember how elegant the dining cars used to be on trains? Forget it," she said.

Chuck was laughing, enjoying himself, but he was drinking one shot glass of whiskey after another, with a beer chaser. He'd dropped the last jigger of whiskey into his beer glass, Russ explaining the whiskey was heavier and stayed in the jigger when you drank it, and when Chuck raised his glass and yelled out, "Depth charge," people clapped and yelled back. He drained the whole glass without taking it from his mouth.

"In Chicago I got a bus to Denver, if I didn't mind standing, the driver said. I was getting used to it by then. But everybody moved over and we sat three to a seat most of the way. There was absolutely nothing out of Denver. I started talking to this other woman who got off and who was going to San Diego. She thought if we asked around we might get a ride in someone's car that was going our way, if we paid some of the gas.

"We got a ride with part of a crew of a B-25 who were going back to their base near Phoenix, nine of us in a '36 Chevy. We sat in the front with two of them, with the five biggest in the back. It was like riding inside a sardine can. There was no use griping about it; it was a ride. They took us to the bus station in Phoenix and we tried to get tickets, but people told us that the ticket window hadn't been open for the last twenty-four hours."

A serviceman clipped Chuck's chair as he squeezed by and Chuck yelled at him, "Watch yourself, buddy."

"Who you talking to, swabbie?"

"You, jarhead," and Chuck stood up.

Sikes tried to get in between them. The Marine was taking off his leather belt and wrapping it around his fist, the sharp shiny brass buckle hanging loose like a big razor blade. "Let's get out of here," Sikes said, pushing Chuck in front of him. Chuck was yelling back, "Seagoing bellhop."

"Come on, Chuck, it's over." Sikes was trying to soothe him.

"He made me sore," Chuck was arguing. "He did that on purpose."

They stopped at another place and Myra tried to get Chuck to eat something but he wouldn't. He fell asleep in the back of the car next to her, going back. "He was telling me he didn't like the duty he has now," Russ said.

"Who would?" Myra said. "Getting up there before a crowd and having to tell how you almost died, four or five times a day?"

They took her home first. Chuck didn't wake up. She didn't know what to say. Should it be, I'll take care of him, help me put him in my bed? Myra said, "We'll take him back to his barracks; he's got us a place on the base. Don't worry, Elaine, he won't be any the worse for wear tomorrow."

She couldn't sleep. She woke up Mrs. Hughes and used her phone to call the base. She got hold of Randy. "Is he okay?"

"He's in the sack. He has to go on tour tomorrow, but he'll be all right by then." She still couldn't sleep. She should have taken care of him, made sure he was ready for tomorrow.

She was up early and waiting with her coat and purse, sitting in her new chair, for Ruthie to knock. They walked to school. The second-to-last day: tomorrow they only went until noon. Ruthie was prattling on. She was going to go barefoot all summer. And she was going to help Avery with his new morning paper route delivering the *San Francisco Examiner*, pulling the wagon and folding the papers.

The class started coming in. They seemed to be wearing better clothes than usual, for the last full day of school. Some of them started putting presents on her desk as they passed on their way to their seats. She was surprised. Most weren't wrapped. She looked up, filling in the register. Thank you, thank you, she said each time. By the time the first bell rang there were piles of things. Three homemade pot holders, a pincushion, a fountain pen, a small bottle of perfume, hand cream, little bags of fudge and cookies. A five-and-ten charm bracelet, earrings, and a red scarf. She was touched. She would miss them over the summer. All of them.

Usually the class wrote a note to their new teacher and a farewell note to their old one. "Since we're going to be together next year," she said, "what if you wrote a good-bye letter to Mr. Allen and a hello letter to Miss Cameron, the new principal." Everyone set to work. There wasn't a holiday feeling: it was more subdued.

While they worked she handed back their president reports with long notes on how well they'd done. She probably overpraised most of them. But she also wrote what they should each study over the summer. *Work on your long division,* she wrote a lot. READ! she put on everyone's paper. Mary Maureen hadn't finished her report. *Save this. We'll complete it next year in the sixth grade,* she'd written across the top.

Sharon. She clipped a booklet on drawing to her report, and a sketch of her with her reading prize, like the ones she did at the USO. For Avery she wrote, *I expect even more of you next year. READ!*

At lunchtime in the teachers' room there was a festive air; it was like someone's birthday. There was a sheet cake and punch. Mr. Allen came in while most of them were eating their first piece of cake and proposed a toast, his coffee cup raised. "To the 1942–1943 school year at Edgemont Grammar School." She raised her glass of punch and felt a pang of sadness. It was over, school was over.

Russ's submarine left that afternoon from Mare Island. Myra hadn't spent one full day in California and was already on her way back to the East Coast. She'd phoned before she left. "I'll write to you if you write back," she'd promised.

She tried not to think of all the things that seemed to be happening at once. She wrote her mother a letter, telling her not to worry about Mona, things would work out for the best. She knew Chuck wouldn't phone that night, but she hated to leave the apartment, on the off-chance. She put the letter in an envelope and walked fast down to the corner where they'd put the new mailbox. She met Dora coming back from work. They walked back together and chatted about nothing. She wanted to bring up Mary Maureen, how she had just stopped doing anything in class, then thought, She has so much grief now; why add more? She'll know when she sees Mary Maureen's report card. She had given her all C's, and she didn't deserve even them.

She went to school earlier than usual to finish all the year-end things so she wouldn't have to go back, so she'd be ready for any madcap scheme she or Chuck could think up. He thought he could get a thirty-day leave. She still hadn't heard whether the superintendent had talked the trustees into hiring her for two months during the summer to develop an art program for the district. That had been his idea, after his wife, who had something to do with the USO, saw one of her drawings. That way she wouldn't be able to go back to Carson City; she'd have to work here. She'd go back for a visit, but not to stay.

They could go on picnics, go to the beach, see as much of California as possible. Among other things. Among a lot of other things. She had most of the texts counted and stacked on the back shelf by the time the students started coming in. She was ready; she had made some Kool-Aid and gotten all the leftover graham crackers out of the cloakroom to eat.

They cleaned out their desks, helped her wipe the blackboards with wet rags, pounded the erasers against the concrete ramp to get all the chalk dust out. They were exuberant. They could leave after she took roll and gave them their report cards and promotion certificates. Sharon started crying when she handed her hers. She didn't know what to say and put her arm around her shoulders. Leroy shook her hand. Arnold gave his loudest shriek.

A lot of them stayed around trying to help, getting in her way, finally going, yelling from the door, "See you in the sixth grade, Miss Walker," laughing like that was the best joke in the world.

When she saw the Navy uniform in the doorway she thought, Chuck? But it was Randy. "Can I talk to you?" he asked. He was wearing his SP rig, white leggings, armband, and a white belt and holster for his .45. "There's been some trouble at the base."

They were halfway to the base before he came out with it. "Chuck's in the brig. It was the XO who had him put there. I wouldn't have known, except the master sergeant down there phoned me. Said Chuck was going to stand a special court-martial for insubordination. Direct disobedience of an order. A long list of things, I guess. But what really's going to happen is he'll get sent to the fleet."

She could only listen. This shouldn't happen. It was almost summer.

"They do that, clean out the brig, send everyone over on the next draft to serve their time aboard ship. It's supposed to be better than a stateside brig," Randy was saying. "And they're going to bust him down. With a special court he won't be rated anymore; he'll be a seaman again. He'll have to start over."

All she could think was, I'm never going to see him again. "Can I write him?" she asked.

"Sure, as soon as he gets an address. Don't worry now, the worst is over. We thought he was going to get a general court, get sent to Portsmouth in New Hampshire for five years, but he didn't. He was lucky."

"I teach with a woman whose father is something in the government, high up; he could try and help."

"Elaine, I don't want to discourage you, but if the President came into that brig in his wheelchair with Falla, his wife, and all his kids plus his cabinet, it wouldn't mean a damn. Chuck has had the course; there's nothing anyone can do. He did the things he was accused of, that's what you have to understand."

She kept thinking there must be some way to stop this. They were on the base now. Chuck hadn't brought her here very often. Some of the teachers had been here on civilian tours, but he had never shown her around. They're all the same, he told her once.

Randy stopped the jeep near a new building and they got out. It seemed peaceful; the San Bruno wind wasn't blowing hard this afternoon, just enough to move the very tops of the trees. "This is a restricted area," he said. "The sergeant is doing me a favor. Chuck wanted to see you. You can say good-bye."

The guard at the gate started unlocking as soon as he recognized Randy. They walked through a big wire-mesh-covered cage. They were still outside the main building when Randy stopped in front of a wide double doorway covered with the same diamond-shaped wire mesh as the compound. A Marine guard on the other side of the wire said something to Randy, who nodded. The guard disappeared. Then he came back a second later, snapping to parade rest, and Randy did the same thing on their side, his arms behind him, elbows out, feet apart. The two men faced each other. She waited for something to happen.

She heard a noise then. Saw a sailor recruit, in blue denims, head shaved, shuffling toward the gate. Saw the chained manacles on his legs, chains going up around his waist to his arms, which were locked behind his back. It was when he smiled that she recognized him. "You didn't know me?" he said. "It must be the surroundings," he added, grinning. She tried to smile, say something, but she was frozen, couldn't think, couldn't move. Chuck had shuffled as far away as he could from the Marine. She moved sideways to be in front of him. His face was divided into diamond shapes by the wire mesh. You did this on purpose, you did this on purpose, she was thinking.

He whispered something to her. She thought he said, "I love you, Elaine."

She leaned forward and he whispered again, "Put your Elgin in your mouth. Not the band. Just the watch." She understood and slipped the band off her wrist. She got one side off, the one that always came off. In a normal tone he was saying, "You're on summer vacation now, I guess. That'll be nice." She hurried to work the other side off. The Marine guard was still looking straight ahead. She popped the watch into her mouth.

"I miss you most." He grinned again. "But I miss not knowing the time too. I need to know what hour it is."

"I handed out promotion certificates today," she said, speaking carefully, keeping the watch against her cheek. "We all made it up to the sixth grade. I'll be here, next year or however long it takes."

He seemed to think that over and was about to answer when the Marine guard snapped to attention saying, "Two minutes are up, prisoner."

Chuck forced his face closer into the mesh and she moved forward until she met his lips, not feeling the wire pressed into her forehead.

Avery

I wanted to die too when they said over the phone Mr. Mitchum was killed. I wanted to stab at my heart with the sharp knife. Stab. Stab. Kill it like a snake. I watched Mrs. Mitchum's face when they told her, and it didn't change. She didn't cry or anything, just put her hand over her mouth as she listened.

What if I hadn't stopped the letter by blowing up the mailbox, like I thought? What if Mr. Mitchum had found out that Michael had been caught and lost his leg, from the newspaper clippings? He had to have found out. Because why else would he have gone to North Africa, when he promised to stay in England?

Once you start the poison, it goes on and on by itself. If you don't die, someone else does. How can a person know where the end will be? The church God doesn't know; he wouldn't be where he is, if he knew. He'd be down here with us. He hides because he can't do any better than we do. You don't die when someone prints your name on the bullet; you just die because you're un-lucky enough to be in the way, or like Mr. Mitchum, in North Africa where they were shooting, instead of up in the city working in the shipyard. There are no German 88 artillery shells exploding up there. Did God put Abner's name on the two rifle bullets that went through him? Not likely. God should stay in the churches that buy his story and listen to the choirs sing and not try to pretend to come out here and know what's going on with the war and allowing all the soldiers and sailors to die. Mr. Mitchum should have never died.

I had been telling Ruthie for a long time I would take her to see the goldfish at the pond. When she cried or felt bad, I'd tell her about the fish, how they'd swim up to the surface to surprise you. It was hard on me to have to go back near where I used to live, but after Mr. Mitchum died I asked her if she wanted to go. It was the only place I ever saw that had wild goldfish, ones that lived on their own in a big lake. "Can we feed them?" she asked. I had forgotten the bread, and she went and got two slices. It was drizzling wet, just rain enough to keep the sidewalks dark. To get away, Ruthie pretended she was going to visit Miss Walker and we took off before Mary Maureen might see. I was wearing my leather aviator's hat and I put the goggles down, but the closer we got to the goldfish, the more worried I became. I didn't want to be in this part of town anymore.

It was a long walk and I kept asking Ruthie if she was tired but she wasn't. We got there at the right time, when no one was around the alley, and she followed me through the space between a cement wall and the fence, and we crawled on our hands and knees under the vines and shrubs until we reached the edge.

Why these goldfish were here I never understood, or the lake with a cement bottom, for that matter. It wasn't as deep as Sharon's pool, probably, but it was ten times bigger and had an island in the middle, with a statue the same size as Ruthie that looked like a mermaid. Water squirted out of a fish she was holding onto the surface of the lake. The place was so overgrown with the trees hanging down you couldn't see across the lake or what the statue really was. There was a boarded-up building that faced the road and had a name painted on a sign, 16 MILE HOUSE. Unk told me that was the exact number of miles from here to San Francisco. I never understood why anyone would care how far it was until Miss Walker told us the building used to be a stagecoach stop and they needed to know how much farther to the city. I used to come to the pond when I had nowhere else to go. Stay here until I was ready to go back. I was never scared at night, sleeping here. There was the moon or the stars, which never were the comfort the sun would have been, but I liked to think the fish were there too, and nothing had ever happened to them.

No one could see us, and when Ruthie started throwing the bread, the goldfish came right up to her fingers. "They don't look like the ones at the aquarium," she said.

"These are different," I said, kidding her, "they're made of gold." She just laughed. The water wasn't clear, so when the fish appeared for the bread it was like magic to see them all of a sudden at the surface to feed. The lily pads all had white flowers now and you couldn't see the water around the island, there were so many. The trees were so thick, tangled overhead, you couldn't feel the drizzle anymore.

I knew Ruthie would try and catch the fish. I did too. She used her hands first, then a rusty can. She took off her shoes and socks and waded in, but she didn't catch a goldfish. I had used a gunnysack once. Those goldfish lived a charmed life.

If a person could come back, return here, I wouldn't mind becoming one of these fat goldfish and swimming around in this pond for years and years. By the time Ruthie came out and started putting her socks back on, the sun had come out, and it was so bright by the time we got out into the alley I could barely see.

Ruthie started jumping up and down and pointing and I saw the rainbow too. It was the biggest one I'd ever seen. I put my goggles up to see better. It did make you want to run and find the end. I told Ruthie when I was younger I used to believe the pot-of-gold story and I used to go running. "We found the goldfish," she said.

I waited until Ruthie was listening again, and told her what I had been thinking about. "Ruthie, remember that time your father made the kite and it flew off on its own? It never came down; I could never find that kite. Maybe it was waiting for your father to fly it. Maybe that's what he's doing now, writing messages for that kite."

"He's not dead?" she asked.

"He's just not here where you can see him, but he's around. He can see the very same rainbow we can."

"He's in heaven, Grammy says. Mom doesn't say anything. Mary Maureen says he was blown into little pieces."

"You have to remember, Ruthie, even if you can't see the kite now, it was here, it was real. Just like your father, he was here and now you have to hope he's flying the kite."

"Like the birds," she said. "Those birds that came back alive in our hands, going to school in the morning."

I had to think back for a minute. "That's right, just like the sparrows."

We stopped at the garage on the way back and I bought Ruthie a Coke from the machine. I took my aviator hat off and Lloyd saw me. He came out and shook my hand. He had made a lot of changes in the place. Unk and I had a California license plate collection of over three hundred nailed to one outside wall of the garage, but there was metal sheeting over the outside now. The front was painted. The abalone shells that used to be lined up along the walks were gone. I didn't go into the office or house, when he invited me in for a cup of coffee, but I could see the new workbenches and the way each tool had a special place painted red on the wall with nails to hang it by.

The gas pumps were fixed and working. Unk had hated to wait on customers and put an out-of-order sign on the pumps, even when they were working. Lloyd kept talking. Business was good. Keeping all the old cars running on baling wire and spit was just up his alley, he said. The GORMAN'S GARAGE sign was still up on the roof.

Lloyd's son Warren came out too to say hello. Unk said he was a good worker but didn't have enough oil in his crankcase. He could bust truck tires, fixing flats, all day. He said he had had his physical and was waiting for his draft notice. I shook his hand and introduced Ruthie.

Unk had trusted Lloyd and the bank manager who handled the mortgage. Lloyd always gave a full day's work for his pay when sometimes there wasn't much money to split, and the bank manager could have taken the place a dozen times during the Depression, he used to say.

I did and I didn't want to see what the place was like now. I knew I would be reminded of Unk again, and what happened, and all those thoughts, but that wouldn't change things. Like Mr. Mitchum, Unk was dead.

I took my cap off once we got away from that end of town. I started walking slower, we were in no hurry now, Ruthie walking along, never stepping on the sidewalk cracks to break her mother's back, stopping once in a while to catch the beetles on the curb before they could get away down a hole.

Ruthie was happy. Her father was dead and she was smiling to herself. And she understood he wasn't coming back. "Do you ever think about your father?" I asked her.

"All the time," she said. "My mother told me, remember your father was a good man, and that's what I do." I wished I could be Ruthie for five minutes.

The sun was rubbing against where the sky and the earth came together on the horizon, heating up the two with the friction. The color wasn't the fiery red you sometimes see, but faded, like something red that runs in the wash. "What does that color remind you of?" I asked her. We had played this game before with different sunsets. "That's a pink cotton candy sky," she said.

I never trusted people who were too nice to me; they always had some reason. But I wanted to trust Miss Walker. Not just because she took me to the bond rally to see Chuck give his speech or helped me with my presidents report or got me out of the police station. I couldn't explain why, but I started reading more books instead of counting the boxcars at night. Ruthie and me went to the library every Saturday for more. I knew Miss Walker liked to see us come home with an armful of books. And she'd stop us and see what we checked out. "I remember this one," she'd say, or "I never read this at your age."

And the good part was, as long as I read, I never thought of the things that were waiting to worry me. They couldn't get past what was going on in the book. So I read until my eyes dropped out of my head, in my room, slowly turning the spool on the kite reel with my fingertips. I practiced not to let anyone know now when they made me want to shake or my eyes go crooked. I was able to control everything but my heart. That still hurt sometimes.

We each had to go up to the office and fill out forms for next year for the records. The secretary would type them in your folder. When she asked me my parent's or guardian's name I said Aunt May Fontana. And Mr. Allen was standing with some of the other teachers and he asked me if my aunt was an ant. "Does she crawl around on the ground and eat sugar, Avery?"

I didn't even know what he was trying to say. The teachers were enjoying the joke, and he kept saying, "Is your aunt an ant?" The secretary stopped typing, she was laughing so hard. When I understood, I was going to ask him if his club foot was named after the ace of clubs, but Miss Olds, Ruthie's teacher, told me to go back to my classroom.

She must have told Miss Walker, because she said I had to ignore some people that didn't know better, that thought something was funny but it wasn't. I told her what I was going to say back, and she got mad at me. "You'd be just like him, then, with no feelings. You have to just ignore people who don't or can't think." It was easy for her to say; she was the teacher.

But when she needed volunteers to stay after to stack the books, I always had my hand up. Sometimes I was the only one and she'd talk to me about what I wanted to be, and I always answered with what I thought she wanted to hear, like fireman or mechanic or sailor. I had already decided not to go in the Navy. If you had to work, you might as well do something steady, like a window washer. One used to come into Unk's garage who worked in the city, on big buildings. He'd start in on the bottom and by the time he reached the top he'd have to start over again. He'd been doing it for years. It seemed like the best job in the world. No one could bother you up there, and you always had work.

Miss Walker said I could do better. I ought to think of going to college, become a teacher and use my head. You never stop learning, she said. I was too surprised to answer. Dream on, I thought. No Gormans had never got out of high school that I knew of, much less gone to college. We left the oilcloth covers that students had put on the textbooks for next year too. You couldn't get oilcloth anymore. But we took off the ones made from brown grocery bags that everyone put on at the beginning of the year. They were all torn and marked up.

Ruthie always walked home with Miss Walker, so we all went together. I was going to miss this classroom. I had thoughts like that sometimes now. Chuck would come by once in a while and give us a ride home in his government car. He was becoming a regular fixture around here, I heard Grammy say. I didn't want to know what Mrs. Hughes was saying when his car was parked around the corner and all the lights were off in Miss Walker's apartment. They said thank you when he brought them vanilla extract and spices you couldn't get anymore. I was staying off people's roofs and letting the FBI do the spying for the country.

Chuck couldn't go by a fountain that he didn't want to stop for something. If there was a chance he might be back from a trip, we stayed near Miss Walker. Read on her front steps or did errands for her. He even got Mrs. Mitchum to take a ride with us when he picked her up at the streetcar stop. Then he wouldn't let her out on our street; instead we went to a place that made candy and we had some. "I forgot what it was like to ride in a car," she said.

We picked her up another time and we went to Redwood City to the movies. "I can't go to a movie," she said, "I have to work tomorrow. I'm not dressed up. I have to go home to dinner." Grammy knows, Ruthie told her. Grammy wouldn't come, but Mary Maureen did.

We went to the movies and then to Woolworth's after and had grilled cheese sandwiches for dinner. "I don't have my purse," she said. We all laughed until she stopped fretting and started laughing too.

I was just about getting used to what I had done when they sent Mr. Mitchum's footlocker home, with his name stenciled on the olive-drab top in white paint. Mrs. Mitchum put it in the garage after she went through it. She didn't want it in the house, she said.

Ruthie opened it for me and it was full of khaki uniforms and socks folded into balls. A pair of dress shoes. His overcoat. We sat on the floor and I took my time. There weren't any letters or his shaving things, just his Army clothes, until I got to the bottom. Against one side there was a booklet on the measurements for things made out of stainless steel. It had the Matson Lines stamp on the front, where he worked. He had taken this with him in the Army.

I leafed through it. Ruthie was talking to me. "Let's go," she said—no one liked to stay there for very long—when I saw the pink newspaper clipping, the one that had been in the *Call Bulletin* about Michael's capture. He had known. I hadn't stopped the letter. I hadn't stopped the letter because it hadn't been sent from the mailbox I blew up.

I slipped the clipping out of the book and into my shirt pocket. It burned my heart, burned through my skin, and I felt the pain and pressed both my hands over my pocket so it would hurt more. I knew it was my fault, I knew.

I must have groaned. I fell forward on my face. "Avery, what's wrong? Avery." I wanted to place the clipping around my heart and squeeze the life out. I didn't know I was hitting my forehead on the cement until Ruthie started screaming and putting her hands between my head and the floor to stop me. She was crying and screaming, and I said, "I've stopped. Ruthie, I've stopped."

At first it was just hard on all of us to stay in the garage long enough to accomplish anything, trying to figure out what was wrong with the Packard. The soldiers or police must have stolen some of his tools, because all the sockets and box wrenches were gone.

It wasn't only the battery; the generator needed new brushes too. I got it out and took it to Lloyd. I'll put it on your tab, he said, and we both laughed. He knew I didn't have any money. I had traded ten old batteries I found for the used one he gave me. He offered to come with me to put the generator back in, but I said I could handle it. Lloyd was a good man, like Unk always said he was.

The Packard ran fine. Mrs. Mitchum started driving that car and never stopped. It burned gas, of course, but it seemed to burn more oil. You had to check the dipstick more often than you did the gauge for the tank. Dora didn't look at it, either. She'd run that car until it didn't have any gas to get back to a station. We kept a can and funnel with us in case we had to hoof it. And the oil, it was used up faster than we could put it in.

Between Chuck and Mrs. Mitchum we went up and down El Camino so many times I knew each tree by heart. Mrs. Mitchum would come home from work and anyone that wanted to go had to be ready—Mrs. Hughes, Miss Walker, when Chuck wasn't around. Aunt May I talked into coming once, but she wasn't herself these days. Grammy wouldn't go. The one time Chuck came, Dora driving, we went up to the Golden Gate Bridge and tried to walk across. It was too windy; we all had to hold on to each other to make any progress. We got to the middle and were able to see all the ships going under. It was Miss Walker who wanted to keep going, and we did. I had Ruthie inside my Navy jacket with me, everyone was freezing, and we made it all the way across.

Last day of school, and all the kids were yelling and carrying on. They were going to do this and that during the summer, throwing their jackets and hats in the air and hooraying. I tried to join in but my heart wasn't in it. Before, I used to be the first to yell no more school. But I began thinking how I was going to miss coming here sometimes. And of course Miss Walker. When I was sitting at my desk I didn't think of what happened to Mr. Mitchum so much. I kept busy. I didn't wonder how it could have been different. If Michael hadn't been caught. If Mr. Mitchum hadn't died. They had buried him over in Tunisia and would bring him back after the war if Mrs. Mitchum wanted them to. That's the way it was. When you die, you're dead. It's the people left who feel bad.

Uncle Johnny. I didn't go, but a lot of people went to his funeral. He was well liked. Of all his brothers, he was the best one. And he had to die. I wasn't going to forget Unk. And I couldn't forget Mr. Mitchum. I just had to look at Mary Maureen; she looked and talked just like him. That whole business wouldn't let me alone. It was worse than the sea lion sometimes. There was not an hour passing that I didn't wonder why did things turn out this way.

Me and Ruthie delivered the *Examiner* before dawn every morning. I knew the route and we went fast. It was nice to be up in the almost dark morning. Neither of us woke up until we were halfway through. Ruthie didn't just watch; she did her share. I'd taken one of the biggest routes, and she delivered the side where we parked the wagon and I ran back and forth across the street.

On Sundays that paper was as heavy as a dictionary, at least four times the size of the everyday paper, and there was supposed to be a paper shortage too.

When we got back, Dora would be waiting with hot milk and toast. We'd have printer's ink all over our hands and faces, wet besides from the foggy dew. Ruthie would tell what we saw or found. We were the first ones out after the night, so there were always sailors still sleeping in parked cars or under the bushes at the library. Ruthie found pennies on Main Street, a woman's hat once, and a brand-new pair of cowboy boots that fit Mary Maureen.

Later, working in the garden, I would start to fall asleep, nodding off in the sunlight while irrigating. Once I lay right down and slept like a baby until I heard the gong of the streetcar and woke up. Ruthie was always sleepy too.

Dora took care of the money when we collected. Ruthie was the one that was best at that. When she rang the bell and said, "Collecting for the morning paper," they'd get the money. When I did, sometimes they paid and sometimes they didn't. Come back, they'd tell me. Dora said I got seventy-five percent and Ruthie twenty-five percent, and I put mine on the kitchen table for Aunt May. Ruthie saved hers to buy bonds. Mary Maureen had a job watching a woman's two kids that lived four blocks over, that Dora worked with. Miss Walker started doing something at the school district office in San Mateo, and took the bus down early in the morning right after we came back from the route. We always said hello and gave her an extra paper.

The people who loaned Aunt May the cash for Sammy said she would have to pay or sell the house and lots; they needed their money. It had been over two months and she hadn't paid on the interest yet. They started phoning and we just let it ring after we knew who it was. One time Dora and Ruthie were over when they phoned. Me and Aunt May pretended we didn't hear anything and talked in between rings like we didn't. Dora was too polite to mention the phone was ringing, and Ruthie was reading my comic books on the floor and didn't notice.

We sent a money order from the post office when I got paid from the paper and she got a government check. We're still behind, Aunt May kept saying, but the phone calls stopped.

On Monday it was still foggy after we delivered, and we were coming up the street, me pulling, Ruthie asleep in the big cardboard box we used to put the papers in—I had cut a hole in the side to reach in and get a paper, and looking back I could see Ruthie's fingers jiggling with the bumps the wagon made on the sidewalk—and when I looked ahead again I saw Miss Walker run across the street and start knocking on the Mitchums' door. "Dora, Dora," she was yelling.

"She's gone to work," I called out. "It's quarter to six."

"Where's Grammy?"

"She went with Mary Maureen."

"I need to use the car," she said. She just had her coat over her nightgown, and her feet were bare.

"I'll phone Dora and see," I said, "but I think the car's out of gas."

She got excited too. "There's no place open now. I have to get up to the city, to Hunters Point."

"I'll get the keys," Ruthie said. She was awake and climbing out of the box.

"You might want to put your shoes on, Miss Walker," I said. "It's wet this morning."

She looked down first and then ran back across the street. I called the plant and Dora said to go ahead and use the Packard. We warmed up the car, waiting for Miss Walker. The gas gauge was on empty and the oil didn't show on the dipstick when I checked. I couldn't keep up with everything anymore. I should have tried harder. I had never seen this to fail, when you needed something.

She came running then, dressed, and got in the passenger's side like me and Ruthie were going to drive the Packard, when neither of us could see above the dashboard. We hopped out and got in on the other side of her. She could drive, once she got used to the gearshift, but she didn't say anything about not having any gas, as if she could get us to the city without any. It was patchy fog now; you'd hit a cloud and wouldn't see anything and then you'd be in the clear dark again, able to see the streetlights and white lines. I told her I knew a place where she could get gas.

We got to the garage and I banged on the back until Lloyd answered. He had been drinking his first cup of coffee. I pumped the gas while he put some fifty-weight oil in. He said it was the thickest he had. Warren came out and put air in the low tire and wiped the inside of the windshield with the Bull Durham tobacco sack to keep it from fogging up. Warren told Miss Walker the easiest way to Hunters Point, when I asked.

Lloyd didn't mention paying for the gas, but he was waiting at the window. But Miss Walker didn't reach for her money. She looked like she wasn't listening or didn't understand, when he said, "Anything else, ma'am?" with his hand out, that the gas had to be paid for. Lloyd would have forgotten about the ration stamps. She held the steering wheel like the car was still moving. She hadn't even put on her lipstick; it was the first time I had ever seen her without any.

"I'll come back," I yelled to Lloyd as she gunned the Packard and we were on our way to the city. It got foggier as we went, but Miss Walker didn't slow down. We went faster. Ruthie was asleep again. When she said they were putting Chuck on a ship that was leaving this morning, I didn't understand exactly but didn't know what to ask. I hadn't seen Chuck for two or three weeks. She'd got a call from a friend who found out for her they were shipping him out.

I had to close my eyes, not because I was falling asleep but because Miss Walker was going even faster now. The Packard had a shimmy and the windows in the doors were rattling, the car was vibrating so much. There were only a few other cars on the road, and she always missed them once she saw the tail-lights, but it was getting closer each time. I didn't remind her about the 35-mile-an-hour national speed limit to save gas. I didn't think she'd hear.

When we got near the docks I could see the big ships under the yard lights, their gangplanks still down. There must have been fifty ships along the dock, miles of them, and we came to a gate and she had to park the car. There were other cars with families to say good-bye. The sailor at the gate said he wasn't supposed to let anyone through. "I'm going to walk the other way," he said, and he unlocked the gate and the crowd pushed through. "Tell them you jumped the fence," he yelled.

"Which ship?" I asked Miss Walker. We were all running, but I didn't know where.

"A ship," she said, "a ship."

"What kind?"

"LST, I think."

I stopped to ask a man who was moving crates with a forklift. "At the end," he said, pointing. We kept running, dodging the longshoremen trying to finish loading. There was black smoke coming out of the stacks of some of the ships, and horns going off as the tugboats came up, and we passed a gangplank that was being hauled away.

All the ships looked the same, some bigger and some smaller, but that was the only difference. We should have had ship identification in school too. I could tell an aircraft carrier from a tanker, but not much else.

There was more light, but not from the sky. They had turned on big spot-lights from all the ships in the convoy. We were getting closer to the end of the row of ships. You could feel the vibration under your feet from the ships' engines; whistles started going off; you knew something was getting ready to happen.

We got to the third to the last ship and we couldn't go any farther. Those two ships were on some kind of floating dock that wasn't part of the one we were standing on. There was water separating the two docks half a block long. There was no time to go back, even if we could have found a way to that dock.

We stood at the edge. We could see with the searchlights on. It was Ruthie who saw Chuck; he had his peacoat on and was standing with some other sailors on the dock, near where the ship was already loaded. It had a big opening in the bow where you could look in at the rows of amphibian tanks until they started to close up the front.

I didn't understand why Chuck was there, but when I saw the one Marine taking chains off him and another sailor, and the other Marine guard holding a shotgun, I didn't ask. But it was Chuck; he was standing at ease while an officer was talking to them. He was wearing a sailor's cap instead of a chief's.

Ruthie started yelling out, Chuck, Chuck. I didn't think he could hear. The Marine guards got everyone loose and went back to their truck and they drove away. I looked up at Miss Walker and she was just watching like she did when we saluted the flag, to see if we did everything right. The officer was still doing something with his clipboard but things began to happen then. He started walking toward the ship. And the sailors picked up their seabags, hefted them onto their shoulders, and followed him as he went up the gangplank. Ruthie was just waving now. When Chuck got on the ship he turned and waved and we all waved back and he was gone.

Chuck

*I*t was 1200 before he got away from the base, driving the big four-door sedan, to pick up everyone in San Bruno. They were all waiting out in front of Mrs. Hughes's. Ruthie sat in front with them, and Mary Maureen sat on her mother's lap in back. Mrs. Hughes had a cloth sun bonnet on. Avery was sitting on the edge of the seat to give Dora more room.

Ruthie and Elaine started singing "Take Me Out to the Ball Game." He was tired now. When he felt like that, he'd noticed, he needed to check his watches against each other. When no one was looking, he got a glimpse at the one on his ankle.

The sun was shining in the city and they were going to a ball game. Life couldn't get any better. Elaine. He reached over as she was singing, her eyes following his arm, and squeezed her shoulder. The back of his hand touched Ruthie's wet nose as he withdrew his arm.

They got to their seats just as the loudspeaker announced the Seals were coming up to bat the first time. The tickets were good, the seats right over the dugout. He'd bought programs and peanuts and rented cushions to sit on.

When the beer seller came around, he asked, "How many want a cold beer? Dora, naturally; Mrs. Hughes; not you, Mary Maureen, you're getting too tall and Avery is too short but Ruthie is just right; you all can have Cokes. And one for Elaine." He held up four fingers for the beers.

"None for me," Elaine said.

"You don't want a beer?"

"I don't want to drink one here, in public." She lowered her voice. "It might get back to the district."

"You're kidding." She shook her head. He held three fingers up.

He must have fallen asleep. Baseball was too slow to watch for long. He woke up in the fifth inning, woozy. He looked around. Everyone was watching the game. Avery had given Ruthie his cushion so she could see better.

Was it last time he was back from the bond drive or this time that Randy had mentioned Avery? "You know that kid that was in sick bay? The city cops had him. Hitting him with a telephone directory to get him to loosen up. One of them told me he blew up a mailbox. The kid just sat there like he didn't know what they were talking about. Then they'd whack him again in the face. Hard as a railroad spike. Never a whimper. Elaine had phoned me to go see. Two old guys couldn't identify him, so they had to let me take him."

"Avery, let's take a walk, give me a hand with the hot dogs. You stay, Ruthie, the Seals need you to root for them." They got in the end of the line at the concession stand. "You have some problems with the city cops?" he asked. Avery was good; his face showed he was trying hard to remember that particular instance out of the many in his busy life.

"It's me, Avery, don't go dumb on me."

"They thought I did something, is all."

"Avery, some people have to be more careful than others. You know what I'm saying?"

"Because of my family."

"Not only that; cops take the easy way and pick whoever is close when they want a crook to fit a crime. You have to be careful, more than careful; everybody does. It's the way things are. I could tell you stories that would make your hair stand on end." Shit, he thought, I'm giving a lecture.

"If you did something, Avery, and they didn't get you this time, they will the next time. It's the law of averages. That's the only important law we have when it comes to right and wrong. Don't give them any chance to even suspect you. You're supposed to be innocent until proven guilty, that's the law, but before you get to the law you've got to deal with the cops, and the odds go down if they happen to think you're guilty.

"Wait until you get in the Navy; it's even worse. They can court-martial you for what they think you're thinking, or even the way you look at them— silent contempt, they call it. But everyone knows when they're getting close to that line, so back off. Don't even let them think you did wrong. You look like I'm putting you to sleep."

"No you're not. I appreciate your telling me. I'll be more careful."

He smeared mustard on the hot dogs and handed them to Avery so he could spoon relish into the buns. The kid did blow up the mailbox, he thought, watching him, hair in his eyes, the careful way he handled each hot dog.

By the ninth inning the Seals were behind seven to one and everyone was yawning. "Who wants to stay for the second game?"

Mary Maureen shot up her hand.

"Maybe we should go back early," Dora said.

"That's a good idea," Elaine said. "I'm beat, and we can listen on the radio."

People had been leaving for a while, and Avery and Ruthie had been collecting their cushions. They were each sitting on a stack of at least ten now.

A batter fouled off a ball and it came back over the screen. He wasn't paying attention but put his hands up in time. It burned but he caught the ball. The people around them clapped and someone yelled, "Sign up the sailor." He gave the ball to Elaine.

"A perfect day," she said in the car, over the music on the radio. They were all asleep in the back. Ruthie had her mouth open and was snoring loud. Everyone had a red face from being out in the sun. His eyes were tired; he hadn't remembered his sunglasses.

He glanced over at Elaine at a traffic light. Her prominent nose was already peeling. He wanted to reach over and touch it, but kept his hands on the wheel. "I love you," he said. She looked over as if she didn't hear. He didn't want to repeat himself. It was as if the words would only escape that once from his lips.

"I love you too," she said.

He got out his new uniform that the base tailor had just sent over, and started packing for the trip. They were flying to Galveston that afternoon from Alameda. He'd get a chance to get some rest on the flight.

He took his time driving across the Bay Bridge to Oakland, but he was still the first there. Then the admiral came, his driver getting out to open the door. Richard had been living in one of the old staff officer mansions on Mare Island since he'd been activated for the bond drives. "He adds a little dignity to the group," Mills had said at the start, "and everyone knows what an admiral is, like a general. We needed some rank to make this sideshow look professional."

He helped Richard with his bag. "Chuck, it's good to see you." They shook hands. The admiral always treated him like a friend. They waited in an office for the others. He got them both a cup of coffee and they watched the plane being serviced for the flight to Texas.

They did five speeches the first day in Galveston. He concentrated on reading the speech off the cards instead of using his memory, and it worked. He never left the words and he stayed off the raft, but he was yawning all the time.

For a funny story at dinner, he told Ace about the raid. They were sitting at the banquet, the five of them at the head of the table. Mills overheard. "No more of that; you could get hurt. You're too valuable, Chuck. I'm going to chew Van Beek's ass out." Ace had been a high school geography teacher, the only one of them that had any college. He gave them advice on how to invest their money. Waiters were filling their glasses with champagne. The admiral was cutting Sarge's steak for him. Ronald had his brass and medals so shined up it made his dress uniform look like little lights were going off and on, flashing signals back and forth from the chandeliers in the ceiling. Everyone was getting along on this trip, so far.

Mills had found out somewhere about the ribbons he rated and got them from the PX and pinned them onto his uniform himself, before the speech. "Let the boobs know you're a warrior, Chuck." He didn't care anymore. Now Mills was standing up, tapping his spoon on the side of his water glass to get everyone's attention. There must have been a hundred men at the tables. "I want to propose the first toast," Mills said. "To our fine, fine young heroes, of course, who have proved themselves on the battlefields," and he raised his glass to them at the head of the table. "But also to the men in this other fight that is being waged in the shipyards, steel mills, airplane factories, and foundries of this great country."

"Hear, hear," one of the executives lifted himself to say.

"This terrible war has forced this country to become the great world power that was always its role by right," Mills went on. "We needed to develop the self-confidence to take our place in the family of nations. And American industry, the captains of industry, have put us there, in this year 1943, and for all time. Thanks to all of you," and he gestured around the room with his glass. Everyone started clapping when he sat down.

For the first time, they had each been given a five-hundred-dollar bond. It was more than he made in three months. And he got another watch. He had been in the room when Mills was talking to the chairman of the board of directors. "What's this shit?" Mills said, opening the Bibles with their names in gold on the covers.

"We thought the boys would like a little—"

"With all respect, sir, please don't think. Dig into your slush fund and go out and buy these men something they can use. They can't accept cash gratuities. Or here's a better idea; give me the money and I'll do the shopping."

This time the watch had chimes that sounded for each hour. He had once explained to Captain Mills his interest in watches. Since then his timepieces had all been different. One you had to wind with a key. Another had the rope and anchor in gold nuggets on a hunter case. He appreciated the effort Mills made.

After the speeches the women came in, all wearing long, lacy gowns, as if they were going to a ball. It had never happened this way before. Mills would tell them, Just ask the bellboy; it's all arranged. He'd never taken him up on the offer.

He was going to excuse himself. The lights were turned down, the hotel band was playing at one end of the banquet room, a woman was sitting on Ronald's lap. The admiral was sipping champagne out of a glass a redhead held to his lips. Sarge was dancing, stroking the woman's rear end with his one good hand as he wagged his tongue at them over her shoulder. He was the son of a dentist from the Midwest and a high school graduate, but he pretended he was raised in the gutter.

A woman wearing a pink dress put her hand on his shoulder and smiled down at him. "Sailor, can you show me a good time?" she asked.

"I can try," he said.

He got back to Tanforan at 1200 while everyone was at chow. He unlocked his footlocker, set out all the new watches on a blanket, and wiped each with a polishing cloth before putting them back in their boxes. He had a collection. Then he went out to the office to phone Elaine that he was back. When he got to his desk there was a pile of notes reporting phone calls, four from the sheriff's detective, Lou Schwartz. He called Schwartz, telling himself he wasn't going to take any shit from him. He was surprised when he heard the detective sounding almost friendly.

"Chief, I want to thank you for those reports from the state. They didn't lead to anything, but they eliminated that possibility."

"Since you're so good-humored today, I've always wanted to ask: did you find any fingerprints on the lighter?"

"None. I'm getting a definite feeling that it was left there on purpose."

"Not a sailor?"

"You could say that."

"How's the girl, better?"

"She's at home now, but the family doesn't want us to question her anymore. She can't help us, they say. Where are you?"

"I just got in; I'm at the base."

"I'll be over to pick you up. I have to talk to you anyhow, and I don't want to do it over the phone." It was the first time they'd talked to each other without ending up in an argument.

"What were you in civilian life?" Schwartz asked first thing, as he got in the car.

"I wasn't anything. I joined up when I was sixteen."

"What are your postwar plans, Chuck? If you had your druthers."

It didn't seem natural for Louie to be pleasant. "If I had my druthers, I'd be conductor of an orchestra." He had never told that to anyone before. He had never thought it before. "And what about you?"

"I'd be what I am, a cop. I'm a good one. I try to be fair. I've never issued a chickenshit ticket or given anyone too hard a time in my life."

"Except sailors."

Schwartz laughed. "You think I'm pissed off because my old lady ran off with a sailor?"

He didn't answer; he didn't want to argue.

"You're right. I am pissed off. I got two kids that my mother-in-law moved in to take care of. If my wife walked into the house tonight I'd take her back. Is there anything else you want to know?"

He shook his head.

"What I want to talk privately about is this. That raid you pulled over at the coast last week wasn't a good idea. In fact, it was a bad idea. You were set up to do the dirty work. The people that run this county, let me explain it this way: it's like they're in a big card game where they all know what's in the others' hands. One has a full house, another two pair, but no one's calling and everyone's more or less happy. Then the Navy comes in and it's like fifty-two-card-pick-up. There's more money than in the entire San Francisco Mint coming out of the base, and some of the players want a reshuffle." He stopped and looked over at him.

"I don't know any way but this roundabout way to tell you that most of the county officials, along with some from the city by the bay, are thieves. Gambling, black market, whores, alcohol, slots, and punchboards are permitted by you-know-who. Your raid was set up because somebody didn't get paid. So no more raids; it's upsetting everyone, and we're all trying hard to make the wartime adjustments.

"And by the way, I'm a thief too, but I happen to like police work. I take the free fight tickets and a white envelope every month. Don't look shocked. Graft isn't so bad. They say a stiff cock has no conscience; neither does President Jackson on a twenty-dollar bill. Don't think we're all crooks, because we're not; the split would be too small. Just pass the word along to your friends. Someone else is talking to your executive officer. He says he wants to get along with the civilians, but doesn't always know what your section is up to. So you have to try."

"You have the wrong sailor. I got the word today I'm finished as master-at-arms. They're supposed to have another chief soon to take my place. I'm TAD now."

"Too bad, I would have liked to work with someone who knew what *cuckold* meant. I'm a crossword puzzle nut; I take three papers a day just to work them."

"When I was a yeoman I wrote obtuse reports."

"You mean your intention was to obfuscate?"

"No, to prevaricate in a way those fornicators higher up couldn't discern."

"How feckless, Chief." They were both laughing, but Schwartz was laughing so hard tears were coming out of his eyes. He wiped them away with his thumb and forefinger. "Would you like to see the person who raped and almost killed that girl?" he asked. "You probably aren't aware the case has been closed, because the papers never mentioned the attack in the first place and won't mention it now to avoid offending the sensibilities of their readers."

He wasn't sure whether Lou was kidding or not, but he was driving as if he had a destination in mind, telling jokes as they left San Bruno and headed south. He guessed what the place was before Lou took him inside the refrigerated room to show him the body. "Here's the culprit. A tramp that was caught in the San Jose freightyards."

"Who shot him?"

"The report says the local PD. He tried to get away. They found articles of the girl's clothing in his bedroll. The family identified them."

He looked at the dead face, remembering the girl in the hospital, the burns. The man must have been insane. He said that out loud.

"It's hard to say. Sex crimes are hard to figure. You'd be surprised who commits them."

"Lou, no normal person would do that to a little kid, I don't care what you say."

"What's normal anymore? We picked up a soldier just back from the Pacific, another hero. He stabbed a cabbie and stole his taxi to drive back to Indianapolis. He had a necklace made up of gold teeth from the Nips for his wife. I asked him how did he get them out. He said he carried a pair of needle-nose pliers for that purpose. He told me they came out easy, unless the Jap was alive. That's normal?"

He had heard of the teeth bracelets; all the Japs were supposed to have gold teeth. He had seen the skulls with the skin boiled off that soldiers and Marines tried to sell to the sailors out on the ships. He felt weary, overwhelmed. What was there to say? None of the things he'd ever thought he understood about good and evil seemed to work anymore.

"Too bad we're not going to be working together, Chuck," Lou said when he dropped him off at the base. "You would have made a good accomplice."

She was insatiable; that was the only way he could describe what was happening between them. She was redefining the word *fuck* for him. It wasn't only that she would do anything, anywhere. She wanted to give her whole self to him, as if she could just hand it over, as if they were two parts of a zipper and she kept pulling them together farther and farther up. As if he ought to be handing over his own insides in exchange. Could he do that?

"Oh, do I love you," she said. "I do, I do." He was catching his breath. If his cock was like some flower determined to blossom, she was like the vase and was always waiting. "I love you," he said back.

"Was that so hard to say?" she asked. He was going to have to start buying rubbers by the gross, he thought. They'd been in the backseat of the car when she'd said, "I've got an appointment with a doctor to be fitted for a diaphragm." He wasn't sure he'd ever seen one. "Irma told me who to go to. A lot of doctors want a wedding ring or at least an engagement ring before they see you. I'm not suggesting anything; it was just a comment."

"You don't want to be a sailor's wife, Elaine. It's awful now and it's worse in peacetime. An enlisted man or his family, you're nothing."

"Didn't you tell me that they were thinking of making you an officer?"

"A commissioned warrant officer is the lowest, and officers have it just as bad as everyone else, but they don't get to moan and complain about it. The old admiral was telling me he saw his daughter all of three months from the time she was born till she was five years old. His wife drank, but he considered himself lucky that she loved him and waited. His kids, he says he doesn't even know them; he was gone most of the time the first fifteen years of their lives."

He and Elaine had talks like that all the time. He didn't want to lead her on, tell her he would marry her, and the rest. If he stayed in the Navy she'd be miserable. And he wasn't going to get out. There was no use fooling himself. He was a born thirty-year man.

But the way she loved him, it was overpowering, he thought; you could almost see it in the look on her face. He could feel the force with his fingertips when he touched her arm. It was as if she were capable of picking him up in a bear hug and squeezing her love into him. "Talk to me," he said.

"I want to try at Sutro's or in the bathtub, either one."

"I meant something else. What did you want to be, besides a fifth-grade teacher?"

"An artist. I wanted to be another Mary Cassatt. She was one of the first Impressionists."

"Keep going."

"She was a stupendous artist, and I wanted to be like her."

"Why aren't you?"

"Because it takes patience and years and years and, more than anything, pure luck, and when I realized that, I became a teacher. You can't be practical and realistic. That's the whole point, I guess. If you are, you stifle your vision. That doesn't mean you play the artist, that you'd rather play the role than paint. It means it has to be the focus of your whole life. What did you think that time I drew you naked?"

"That I was in the hands of a sex fiend."

"You are. You are."

And there were his questions: her family, the Catholic debate; he had no education, no job prospects. But she had answers she could run off on her fingers. My folks don't care about that. My father was a cowboy when he met my mother at school. I'll become a nun if you want me to be one, as long as you can live in my cell. You can go to school. Be a baker. Work in an office. You just have to start somewhere. There are jobs. Be my love slave.

"I'm already that," he said.

He'd gone into a bank and cashed all his bonds. Ace had worked it out that they were a bad investment. The savings account at simple interest was better. He'd never been a saver; he was always waiting with everyone else on the ship for the eagle to shit, ready to say with the rest, he only farted for me, but now he couldn't spend his pay; it was piling up on the books. He put it all in his account with his bond money, $4,382.46. He could buy a house in San Bruno, if there were any for sale. Hundreds of acres of land in Montana. Maybe a bakery. Or a thirty-day shipping-over drunk that he could talk about for years and years.

He liked to look at his bank book at odd times. It calmed him. Before he spoke. He'd be daydreaming about the money when he stood up to begin his speech. They were lying naked on her bed and he picked it up from the night table. Thumbed through it. She had her face close to his, looking at the rows of numbers too. He told her some of the things he had thought of.

"Let's not be hasty now. Figure out how many marshmallow sundaes you could buy me with that much money."

When they argued he felt like he could explode with rage at her, over nothing. She could scream and cry hot tears that would scald him. "You told Mrs. Hughes what?" he yelled at her, and she threw the alarm clock at him. But it was a prelude to something else, to an overwhelming feeling of warmth, well-being, like his bones were melting, that heightened the sex until it was so unbearably good that he never wanted to stop; it was too satisfying. "I can't stand it," he said once, no, he'd rather burst than end it.

It was good to see Sikes and Myra. They reminisced about before, when they were first at Tanforan, like nothing had occurred in their lives since then. "Remember the time we went to see the chief of police and the sheriff?" Russ said, and told the whole story again.

Elaine never said anything about what an ass he made out of himself, getting drunk and picking a fight. And when Myra wrote later, she only said how wonderful it was to see him again and how much she liked Elaine. But Sikes didn't let him off. "You better get over this bullshit," he told him next day. "Shape up or ship out. Stop feeling sorry for yourself. You're not the only one who suffered, and you won't be the last, either." He was going to interrupt, say wait until you get over there, but he didn't. "We're all responsible for our actions," Russ went on. "Especially you, because of your experience." He had to get a grip on himself; he knew that. He had to stop taking the easy way out.

"Let's get a tattoo," Elaine said one time. She was examining him as if she knew every inch of his skin.

"They hurt," he said. "And they're sore for a long time." She was looking at his feet. "As soon as I got them, I regretted it. I didn't want to be a billboard, but I wanted to be like everyone else. Some old-timer told me to use lemon to rub over them and they'd fade. They did, a little."

"What if I got *sweet* and *sour* on my chest?"

"You're not supposed to think such things, much less say them."

"Can a man be a prude?"

"I don't know, but I've had a strict Catholic upbringing and you've ruined me."

"I better have," she said, and bit him on the toe.

It wasn't only that she was all he could think of most of the time. When they were together, a kind of turmoil started. She was always asking or saying things that made him have to go over and over what he'd always done or accepted. Things that weren't important. "Why don't you just buy a clarinet, then, and you can play again?"

"It's not that easy." She didn't ask why, but he had to go on. "If I bought an instrument, I'd have to practice. It's not right not to. Brother Ralph used to say, he'd stand next to us to listen through a whole piece, 'Your bassoon is a machine. You have to make it human by pouring in your thoughts; then they'll come out as music.' I don't have any thoughts to spare anymore. It would always be a device. I can't allow myself to start over again." She gave him her look. "You don't want to understand. I don't want a goddamned clarinet," he was shouting.

"Do you think you said that loud enough for Mrs. Hughes to hear? She plays the concertina. Maybe she'll knock and ask you to play a duet."

He smothered her with kisses. "I love you even more when you're agitated," she said.

"If you're so smart, why don't you paint?"

"I'm afraid of failure, like everyone else, like you are. I'm starting to sketch again; give me time. Will you pose for me?"

She asked once, What do you plan to do with your life, then? I don't know, he'd answered. But for weeks after, he kept thinking over the question. Life, any life. What was a good answer? It bothered him.

They were at Stern Grove in a great circle of eucalyptus trees. He had been passing the place for weeks going to the city, and never known there were concerts there. Elaine had surprised him, taking him. They were sitting on the grass, listening to the San Francisco Symphony Orchestra play. He had never in his life seen a full symphony orchestra. Never. He'd listened to records, but now they were seeing the musicians too. "Irma told me about these concerts," she said. During the intermission he started telling her about what he'd been thinking.

"I don't lead my life so much as follow it. Life does the leading. I don't have that much to say; no one does. I'm in the Navy and I do what I'm told. The Navy is my life, and I follow after."

"That could be inertia," she said.

He was holding her wrist and he must have squeezed too hard, because she winced. "Excuse me," he said, trying not to get excited, to keep his voice low. She was always throwing him off with her answers, after he'd thought things out. "It's not inertia," he said. "It's not. That's how life is."

One time she asked about that night they were with Sikes and Myra. "Why did you start that with the biggest serviceman in the room? There were a lot of smaller men bumping your chair. Because you're a sailor and he was a Marine? I always thought it was the same branch of the service; there's a Secretary of the Navy, but there isn't one for the Marine Corps." She was straddling him, sitting on the small of his back as he lay on his stomach, while she massaged his shoulders. He opened his eyes not to see the raft, the man's face, and told her. "It was a Marine who gave up his place on the raft for me, after the shark bit me. A private. 'It's your turn,' he said. It was four hours on the raft and four off. I was keeping the time. It wasn't my turn. 'Up you go, swabbie,' he said, and he pulled me up. With the sharks swarming he jumped into the water. He died. And I didn't know his name. Buck Private, I called him." She was still rubbing his shoulders. "I don't know why I picked that fight. I don't hate Marines. I can't even hate the Japs. I don't hate anybody."

They were walking now, but five minutes ago he had come late to her place, leaping into her apartment, grappling with her, trying to get out of their clothes. It was amazing that she didn't start biting the buttons off his shirt to get it off him faster. She said, reaching back and unhooking her bra, "I'm having my period."

He was holding her sweater. "Maybe we should see if the creamery is open."

"It's eleven-thirty. 2330."

"Let's skip this."

"Because of my menses?"

"Just because. Let's take a walk around the heart."

They went, arm in arm. "Is this standard operating procedure?" she asked.

"Do you have to know everything?"

"Yes. Everything."

"Aren't you ever embarrassed about anything?"

She had to think it over. "I used to be, a lot more than I am now. I told you about the professor and buying Kotex in the gray wrapper. But that all seems like it happened a long time ago to someone else. When we went ice skating instead of swimming, it was because of my period. My mother told me that. And no PE. We'd whisper to the teacher, pssst, and we wouldn't have to dress down. Now you."

"Wait, what did you whisper to the teacher?"

" 'Moon time.' "

"I've heard men say it didn't matter to them, but now I guess it does to me. I've never thought about it before. When I was a seaman first, a prostitute told me that she got five days off every month and I asked what for and she laughed. In Montana the Indians at the school knew that too. I heard a girl tell another it was the sacred time. That's where I got it, I guess. At sea story time I heard a sailor say wading the bloody river was the only safe time, that you couldn't have kids then. We won't forget how in a couple of days, will we?"

"I don't think so," she said, "but I can think of a few other things we might try."

They were going into the El Camino Creamery next to the theater so often that as soon as the waitress saw them coming she started making Elaine her marshmallow sundae. They sat in the back booth on the same side. She could no more not ask questions than he could stop from answering them. "Why don't enlisted men like their officers, and why did you say those things about Damon and Daryl?"

"You want me to give you a long explanation, don't you?"

"The longest."

"So we can order another sundae. You're just like those kids in your class that want you to tell about living in the wilds of Carson City, Nevada, so they won't have to do their math." He reached behind her, feeling her rear end.

"What are you doing?"

"I'm just estimating how much weight you've gained."

"Unhand me."

"Do you think you're smothering me with your love?"

"What kind of a question is that?"

"It's exactly like your kind of question, designed to drive the questionee crazy with worrisome thought."

"What about enlisted men and officers? I really want to know; I never understand anything."

"Do you realize I'm over a quarter of a century old and have been in the Navy ten years?" She waited, spooning the ice cream into her mouth, the spoon always coming back for more, clean and shiny. He couldn't recall ever talking as much to anyone else. What happened when you told all your stories? Something else must occur in the meantime. You'd both see the same thing, but it would be open to interpretation.

"Sikes says that officers represent authority. That they are usually better educated, better trained, and therefore have more interesting things to do that require more responsibility. He's an officer, of course. But in the Navy I know, the chiefs are the ones that do the dirty work, the yelling and enforcing. And because most sailors don't deal with the officers on a daily basis, there's a kind of built-in awe, and sometimes antagonism when you do and find out they can be as stupid as anyone else.

"I've never got used to the officers on the bond drive. When the captain says, 'Call me Buck,' or the admiral says, 'Richard will do,' I'm still uncomfortable. Maybe because it could go back to *yes sir* and *no sir* in a minute. And I didn't mean anything when I said that about Damon and Daryl. I was just shooting my mouth off. I've been in too long now to analyze it clearly; the chucklehead officer, his wife, car, or pet, I'll salute them all. It's just a game I've learned to play. Officers are just as much a part of the Navy as the sailors, but not any more important.

"But the thing I started out to say—you're making me windy—is when we were in San Diego last time, the hotel had a swimming pool. It was a hot day and everyone was in that pool. Without their clothes on, everyone looked the same. A general didn't look any different from a private, undressed, or a politician that came to the rally or the businessmen who ran the shipyards. We were all the same until we went into the locker room. I don't remember what point I was going to make with that story. I can't even remember what I started out saying. I digress because you drive me wild with desire," he whispered.

She put her hand on his arm and said, louder than she should have, "I can never get enough of you, Chuck. It's going to take a lifetime." He was embarrassed, not just because someone could have heard, but because she meant what she said. All her emotions were that way; she did and said what she felt. It was as though he could see the veins and arteries working in her body. It was all too close to the surface. He wasn't used to that. This display. He wanted to slide under the table.

He wasn't sure that he'd set out to get drunk when he took Lou to the CPO club for lunch, or why, or at what point he decided not to stop himself. He didn't need to work up the courage, the nerve to ask to get out of the bond drive. He could say he needed a rest; the captain would give him a couple days off, rearrange the schedule. He was so important now, the captain said, that his reputation as a speaker and as someone who could sell bonds wholesale for the war effort was getting around. They were booked for the next two years.

Ace was gone. Another flyer, who'd crashed his crippled plane into a Jap tanker, had taken his place. Two weeks ago Sarge had taken down his trousers to show the audience what his legs looked like now. "You want to see what I gave for my country? I'll show you."

"What does he think this is, a freak show?" Mills yelled when he heard. He replaced Sarge with a blinded Marine PFC. "You understand what I'm doing,

Chuck. I'm trying to keep the same winning combination we started out with," Mills told him.

Ronald stopped talking about combat, killing Japs and cutting off their ears, except in his speeches. He cashed his bonds and sold his watches. "I took in four hundred dollars last month," he confided. "This is good duty. I can buy my mother a house. Two houses. We don't want to do anything to rock the boat, Chuck. We were made for this. We deserve this."

He'd had a run-in with Mills once already, when he let Sarge go. The admiral had spoken up first. "Could you reconsider, Captain? The man was an inspirational speaker."

"You're forgetting yourself, sir. You were living in a rented cottage in Monterey when we found you. You don't want to go back there, do you? We didn't have you activated to give advice."

"I agree with Richard," he'd said then. "Ace didn't want to stay, but Sarge does. Where does he go from here? They won't let him stay in the service. He'll get a medical discharge and pension; that's not enough to live on. He'd be lucky to get a cottage in Monterey."

"Are you listening to me, Chuck? Because I'm going to say this just one time. The staff sergeant is no longer part of our unit, period." Mills walked out of the room.

"This is good duty," Ronald said. "Don't forget that, Chuck."

"You bet," Richard said. "We're a team. One for all, all for one."

When he thought about standing behind the podium and beginning his speech now, bile rose in his throat and made him gag. Across the table, Lou was telling him something. "They're taking men with one eye now, Chuck. I'll probably be in charge of an aircraft carrier next week, with my brains." He hadn't been paying attention, but he laughed when Louie did. "They let you sailors live like kings. This bar is where the big bettors used to watch the races."

"Nothing is too good for the Navy during wartime; drink up."

"I haven't had a steak sandwich in a year, Chuck; this is an occasion. If you're not going to eat yours, pass it over here. I didn't realize how good you had it or I'd have come with the sheriff. It was a source of great merriment when you gave him PX privileges. He didn't realize what the sailors were going to mean to the business. When he got his first slice, he thought he'd died and gone to heaven. It was double what he got before. Live and let live is my motto."

"Lou, something's been bothering me. About that lighter . . ." Lou was waiting for him to go on, both his eyes turned as if they were listening too. "How positive are you that that hobo raped the girl? Why would he bother to leave anything, that Navy lighter? He got away; it wouldn't have made any difference to him who was blamed."

"That's a good question and I admire your perspicacity in this matter, but it's misplaced. It's not a question of who committed the crime anymore, but that there haven't been any more rape tortures. That's the point to remember. The Navy's happy and the civilians are satisfied. The case is closed. Do they have dessert around here, Chuck? Since you're paying, I might as well make a pig of myself. How about inviting me tomorrow, Chuck, and I'll bring my kids for dinner."

"I can't because we're flying to Ohio to some aircraft plant this afternoon. A couple of hours from now, in fact." He never drank this much in the daytime, but he wasn't feeling it. "When I come back, why don't you spend some of that money you have under your bed and take me to a civilian restaurant."

"Not so loud. If I don't spend it, I don't feel so bad. I tell myself that it's for my kids' education, but there's too much now; they'd have to go to Stanford for five or ten years to use it up. I never thought having money would be a burden. I'm too cheap to give it away. But that's the way it is; when there's an inordinate source of easy money available, you take some. Judas did, and Jesus would have if someone'd offered it to him first."

After Lou left he went over to the bar and had another drink. There were other chiefs there, and they started talking, buying each other rounds of the ten-cent drinks. He checked the time: he should be getting ready for the flight. They were leaving from Moffett. He started watching the clock over the bar as the hands moved from number to number. Mills was supposed to pick him up on his way. He worked over what he would say to Van Beek when he told him he wasn't going, he was finished with the bond drive. He'd go back to being master-at-arms of the base. He could do that for the duration.

He said good-bye to the two chiefs, put down a five for his share of the drinks, and went over to see the XO. He started telling Van Beek what was on his mind, that he wasn't going. Then Mills came in and he kept explaining. They let him speak, and it looked like he was convincing them, and he went on faster.

"I've paid for that experience now. I don't want to sell it. That's what I'm doing. When I joined up I could hardly wait, I was ready: fight, fuck, run a foot race, I wanted to see and do it all. I thought I was going to be the first one. But it wasn't like that.

"I realized that when I was on the raft. Ten years in the Navy. What I learned was what everyone else knew all along. I didn't have to go to Singapore to find that out; I could have stayed in Montana if I wanted. Experience is finding out what everyone else knows. And by standing up there giving those speeches, I'm allowing myself to sell that experience. And it's not all mine to give in the first place. In the end, it won't have any meaning for me or anyone. I worked too hard for it, staying alive on that raft."

Mills interrupted. "You have ten minutes to go, get your gear, and stand by for the ride to the plane. Or I'll give you an opportunity to gain some more experience. I hope you understand me."

"Let me add," the XO said, "that you won't even have a sleeve, much less any rank, when I'm finished with you."

"Don't you see, I worked hard to learn what I have; there's no shortcuts. I just can't tell people about what I saw and did for their money. They should have to learn from their own experience, not mine. I can't help them anymore. I'm all used up. Lookit, there's another thing too, I tell them, 'Take your money out of your mattresses, put it into government bonds, if you don't trust banks because of the Depression.' But someone came up after and explained to me, if inflation takes off after the war, wartime dollars won't be worth a fraction of what they are now. Bonds aren't a good investment for the workingman. I can't stand up there and say that anymore." He was losing his train of thought.

"Let's not give him ten minutes," Mills said. "Call the brig, tell them to send the officer of the day and two chasers to pick up an insubordinate sailor drunk on duty and disobeying a direct order."

He wasn't going to get angry and he wasn't going to get violent. He wasn't going to punch an officer in the nose. He had been in the Navy too long. It wasn't in him anymore. He kept trying to explain. When he saw the Marines he stopped.

"Lieutenant, take this drunken Indian to the brig to await court-martial," Van Beek said.

He wanted to say something succinct, sum up what he was explaining about experience. He was an Indian. He was a sailor. "Fuck you, Mills. Fuck you and the horse you rode in on."

No matter how stupid drunk you are, you always know. He knew what was going to happen. Maybe not all of it, but enough. He should never have thought they'd let him go back to being master-at-arms. They had sent Ace to some island in the Aleutians when he quit, instead of Texas, near his home. And he didn't need to lose his rank. What about Elaine?

It was when he thought of Elaine that he felt weak, as though he wouldn't be able to move again the next time a guard yelled double-time. He could have done this a different way. What if he lost her? He wouldn't be able to stand that. When she came to the brig and gave him the Elgin, it was more than he could bear, that look on her face.

They took it easy on him in the brig, no matter what Van Beek said. He started feeling better than he had for a long time. He was getting regular exercise, push-ups, sit-ups, and pull-ups. There must be some tradition in the brigs that if they punished you physically, your mental attitude would change.

He would overhear others talking that had been in awhile and were waiting to get out of the service with bad-conduct discharges. They didn't realize they could ruin their lives by something like that. Even now no one was supposed to hire them with bad paper. But maybe things had changed with the war, because they were laughing and kidding each other, I'm getting out, I'm getting out.

When he found out he was going to get sea duty, he had to accept that. He'd take his chances like the rest of the sailors. He could outlast the war. He didn't care when he saw that the ship was an LST flat-bottomed tub; it would be like sailing on a cast-iron frying pan. They were carrying amphibious tractors, amtracs, they were called, and a company of Marine drivers and gunners. Had he heard his name when he boarded? He'd waved but couldn't see anyone.

It all started again. Like the same dream, over and over, the sea had him again. He could look up now at the blue of the sky and down at the ocean and not feel the difference. He seemed to be above the surface of the Pacific. But for how long?

It usually took a week from San Francisco to Pearl, but they'd dropped out of the convoy when a boiler blew up and they were left to drift, trying to make repairs. Everyone realized that they were dead men if a Jap sub found them.

He wore his life jacket with two canteens of water all the time. He saw the grins, but they didn't realize how fast they could be in the drink. He added a flashlight and a signal mirror and fourteen packets of shark repellent. It was something new, you broke open the waterproof bag and shook the powder into the water. He stashed a one-pound bag of hardtack under his life jacket too. Let them laugh.

They finally got to Hawaii. He never got liberty when they reached Pearl— he was restricted—but he could write letters now, and he did. And Elaine wrote back. She was going to wait for him and she loved him. She wrote S.W.A.K. on the envelope flap under the lipstick print of her lips. He kept her letters in his shirt pocket and read and reread them when he could. She sent him cookies in a two-pound coffee can, and fudge. Mary Maureen and Ruthie sent him taffy they'd pulled themselves. Dora and Avery sent him homemade crackerjacks. Mrs. Hughes sent two blue handkerchiefs with his name embroidered on the side. They all wrote letters. It was more than he'd ever received in all the time he was in the Navy.

He was touched. He didn't have to pass the sweets around; nearly everyone was ashore. He ate a little of each, imagining them all in the Mitchums' kitchen. In October, Ruthie sent him a drawing of all thirty-two presidents, with their names underneath, rolled up in a cardboard tube. "Miss Walker is teaching me to draw," the note said. "I'm the best in the second grade." Mary Maureen sent a note in the same package. "If you have time, could you send me a hula-hula skirt? I want to become a dancer."

He wrote them all long letters. He wrote Elaine he was coming back soon, the war couldn't last much longer. "We're winning; you can tell the difference from stateside out here." He'd never seen so many ships and planes, or men in uniform. "The Japs are on the run."

He had been assigned to the deck crew, coming over, and the chief had given him the worst jobs. He'd been captain of the head, cleaning up the rows and rows of commodes the troops used. The weather hadn't been bad, but the LST was jammed with the heavy amtracs and the ship didn't float, it plowed, bouncing through the surface half-submerged. The Marines got sick. "Sweet, aft, clean up," he'd get called. He'd take his bucket and swab, the hot water strong with creosote, and pick it up. What was there to mind? They'd given him his watches back and he had Elaine's Elgin on a chain around his neck. He could follow orders. If anyone knew he'd been a chief before, no one mentioned it. He did what he was told and kept to himself.

While almost everyone else but the brig rats was ashore, the deck monkeys painted and chipped paint. Polished what brass there was that hadn't been painted black. "Sweepers, man your brooms," the squawk box said at 0700. He took a certain pleasure in doing the best he could, no matter what it was.

And he thought of Elaine. Things she said. The shape of her calves, the way her hands were attached to her long arms. Her face. The way she watched him when he talked. The way sweat beaded on her upper lip. Even her ears; he daydreamed about the way they turned red when she was angry.

He was hunkered down spreading paint on the bulkhead when he saw an officer's dress shoes by his other hand. He stood up. He wasn't sure at first because Sikes was wearing sunglasses and he'd lost weight, most off his belly. "Russ?"

"I see you're learning a new trade."

He wanted to clap him on the shoulder. "Damn, it's good to see you." He still looked as if he had slept in his khakis, but he was a full lieutenant now, wearing dolphins over his pocket.

"Elaine wrote Myra that you'd been transferred out here. I didn't learn the particulars until recently. I might be able to work it so you can come aboard the sub."

"I appreciate the offer, Russ, but this is fine." There was an awkwardness. Did Sikes look relieved?

"Well, we start another patrol tonight. You can't leave the ship, I understand. I better let you turn to. You know, Chuck, they have you down as a shit-disturber. Try and behave yourself."

"I'll do that." He'd almost said *yes sir*.

"I like the goddamn Navy," Russ was saying. "I might stay in if I can make lieutenant commander. I don't see what there is to bitch about. You keep yourself squared away, Chuck." They both saluted at the same time and then shook hands.

Early one morning he climbed the mast with a pair of binoculars. He could see the part of the USS *Arizona* that was out of the water. There was oil still coming up from the hull down on the bottom. My home, he thought.

They were in Pearl for five weeks, and he never left the ship. It didn't seem to matter. He had Elaine's letters, and he wrote back as often as he could. When he needed a haircut he had the acting barber shave it all off again. "I'm a brig rat and I might as well look like one," he told him.

He got two letters off the last night before they left port: a short one to his sister, telling Molly he was thinking of her, and one to Elaine. He missed her too much. He couldn't be too graphic when he wrote; the officer who censored the letters liked to recite the good parts at the officers' mess. He thought about the day they had the picnic up in the hills above town. "Remember when we climbed up to that eucalyptus grove?" he wrote. She'd made them sandwiches and he got beer and a big bag of potato chips. They hiked up to the stand of trees. It was a clear day and they kept stopping to look back and see more and more. They could see down the peninsula, the San Mateo Bridge going across the water, the San Bruno Mountains, the East Bay.

She was wearing brown wool slacks that got full of wild oat stickers from the tall grass all the way up. They saw a snake halfway. It moved almost on top of the grass. It was only a foot long and thin as a pencil, a green gray. "It's harmless," she said, "I'll give it a ride up," and she picked it up behind the head. The body coiled around her arm like a bracelet. Then she yelled, "I'll race you," and took off running.

They ran the last hundred feet to the trees. Her face was shiny with perspiration, and she let the snake go and lay back on the dried-out pinkish leaves and held out her arms. Later, when she was putting on her shirt, he saw the two green eucalyptus acorns stuck below her shoulder blade and picked them off and gave them to her, and then they ate their sandwiches. "I think of that picnic up on the hill pretty often," he wrote.

When they left Pearl they were moving in a convoy again. He read and reread the letters. Not just Elaine's. Lou had written too, and he was always funny. "I knew you were a criminal type, talking back to your superiors like that, telling them to go fornicate with pastry, or was it a horse? What's wrong with you? I happened to mention to the Sheriff your contretemps with authority, and on his own he made several phone calls. Randy got his transfer to a school in Baltimore, I hear."

They were supposed to be on their way to an invasion, that was the scuttlebutt. The Marine battalion that came on board believed it. They sat around the deck cleaning their weapons. Was he ever that young? They blindfolded each other to see who was fastest at assembling their M1s, Thompsons, and .45s, their skivvy shirts tied around their heads. They'd ask him to time them if he was working nearby.

The officers believed it too. They gave the troops lectures topside. This coming landing was part of the Pacific strategy to island-hop the atolls all the way to Japan. There would be a major bombardment from both the planes from the seventeen carriers and the battleships and cruisers in the two-hundred-ship task force, and then the troops would go in and mop up whoever had survived.

Ten days out they called him in, and he stood in front of the skipper's desk. "You're officially out of the brig, Sweet, and will be allowed liberty at the next port. But don't make the mistake of thinking we're not keeping our eye on you. The word is out on you."

"Yes, sir," he said, but wanted to snort. The irony of getting out, of being free out here on this ship in the middle of the ocean, and they were so serious. They assigned him to mess duty and he watched the Marines turn green when they smelled the food. The ship rode like a sash weight. He worked in the scullery, sweating in the hot steam in the small compartment, stacking up the metal trays to be washed.

On board ship there was a certain rhythm that you got into. Going to the galley at 0400, working, eating the chow that nobody wanted, sack time. He was getting used to the sea again. He'd never been on this small a ship before, three hundred feet, jammed with troops. The *Arizona* had been six hundred feet. The weather was summertime, the South Pacific in November; he slept on the deck, his head on his life preserver, his shoes knotted to his belt. He had sixty-one packets of shark repellent now in a bag around his neck.

He didn't allow himself to think of the future, what he was going to do after the war. He dreamed of Elaine, but it was always something they had done in the past. The day they went to the boardwalk in Santa Cruz. "You wanted to see something different," he kidded her. "Look at all those soldiers from Fort Ord and Camp Roberts." Could he stay in the Navy now? It was better to think of the raft, one of the funny things. It hadn't been funny then. Would he be laughing about being busted to apprentice seaman in twenty years?

There must have been sixty or seventy men on the rafts in the beginning. The first one to die of natural causes was a cook first class. He just died; no one could figure out why. No shark bites, and they still had plenty of water. They stripped him for his clothes and took his dog tags and were trying to roll him over the side of the raft, then they were going to paddle like crazy to get as far away as possible in case he drew the sharks, when some gunner's mate yelled from the other raft, "You can't do that. An officer is the only one that can authorize a burial at sea." It stopped them from deep-sixing the cook. There were no officers left. When he thought it over, he got mad. "You fucking sea lawyer, what do you know?" he yelled, and he tried to work the dead sailor over the side, pushing with his legs. "You're going on report," the gunner's mate said. "Report me, report me, you bastard," and he got the cook over the side. "Report me," he kept yelling, "and see what happens."

There was more scuttlebutt every day. It was the Gilbert Islands in the central Pacific they were headed for. These islands would be ringed with U.S. warships; they couldn't be reinforced, like Guadalcanal. This was going to be a cakewalk, one of the Marines who'd been there said.

The bombardment started from the battleships and the heavy cruisers, the big guns pounding the island, and then was joined by the planes from the carriers. It was hard to believe the number of shells and bombs the island absorbed without coming apart. It was like watching a Fourth of July celebration at night: the tracer and muzzle flashes, the boom-booms from the thousands of guns. There were secondary explosions from shore, ammunition dumps and fuel tanks that would light up the island suddenly. In the daylight the whole place disappeared in smoke, dust, and fire. No one could live through that, everyone kept saying.

The LST was standing off, waiting until the beach was secure, before their amtracs would go in. It was all so organized. It was a baseball game where the Japanese never got up to bat. They hadn't fired one shell back, that he saw.

He never thought the chaos would begin. He knew it could be there, waiting, but he didn't expect it this time. There were reefs, and the Higgins boats with their three-foot draft couldn't get over them, couldn't get close to one part of the beach. The men had to get out and wade in the water up to their shoulders. Small-arms fire started coming from the shore.

A destroyer hit a mine and rammed the LST amidships, cutting a twenty-foot gash in the side, flooding the engine compartment. The ship started listing and drifting toward shore. The Marines couldn't get the amtracs off. He started cutting the rafts loose and passing out shark repellent to the Marines milling around the deck.

A Marine colonel came on board, ordering the troops to get ready to disembark; Higgins boats were to be brought up. It was that chaos time again where the clock stopped and he felt that languid feeling of just coming awake. He moved easy, trying to help get the landing nets over the side. The small-arms fire from the shore started pinging against the steel plates of the ship.

As the men went down the net, some were hit and dropped into the sea and were crushed between the ship and the boat. Others got tangled in the net and hung there. He went down the net and got under them and lifted them up so they'd be grabbed from above, or took them back up himself on his shoulder.

He kept going back until another sailor who was helping was hit and fell on top of him, knocking him down into the Higgins boat. "Well, swabbie, you looking for some excitement?" a major said as the boat pulled away from the ship. "You mean this isn't the chow line?" he said. Some of the men laughed. The third-class manning the machine gun got hit and he took his place up on top and started firing, belt after belt, spraying the sand dunes that were getting closer and closer, bigger and bigger.

The coxswain somehow scraped the boat over part of the reef, and shells started splashing around them, some skipping past them over the water. The ramp was let down and everyone was running as fast as they could toward the beach. Some were hit in the boat and others were hit in the surf. Men were trying to crawl back to the boat or onto the beach. He got down and helped some back up the ramp. The coxswain was yelling he had to go back. He kept signaling one more, one more, dragging the wounded onto the boat until the ramp went up and he was left standing there in the water.

He made shore and ran over to the Marines that had been on the LST. They were all bunched up behind a seawall made of palm tree logs. He lay down near where a Marine had a radio strapped to his back. He wasn't tired or scared, just indifferent to the explosions, the smoke, the smell of blood and shit. There were dead all around them. "Get yourself a weapon, sailor," the major said.

"This is all I need," he said, yelling into his ear, and he showed him the shark-repellent packets. The major shook his head. He crawled over to where a sergeant lay holding his side and got the dressing off his belt and put it over the gash in his ribs. He took the first-aid kit off a dead corpsman and started using the morphine on the ones who were hit bad and were screaming. "Don't be so conspicuous," the major told him one time, "the Marines have landed," and another time, "See if you can get them to start coming for the wounded. It's bad for morale to have so many around."

Only the amtracs were getting over the reef and landing, and a lot of those were getting blown up. The Higgins boats were hanging up in the coral. Good targets. He found a wooden ladder, kicked out two rungs at one end so he could fit inside like a coolie inside the shafts of a rickshaw, and put the wounded on that and dragged them out toward the amtracs that were going back empty. He was running all the time but never felt tired, never out of breath. The first night the Japanese counterattacked, it went back and forth. The only thing constant was the dead. They were everywhere, in piles, half buried in the sand on the beach, some still afloat in the water. The island was a cemetery for both sides. It was to the death. Everyone was going to die before this was over.

On the second day he found an abandoned rubber boat and started ferrying the wounded back to the reef so they could be taken out to the hospital ship. He did it the third day. There was no end. The boat started taking on water.

He kept going back for more wounded until the boat swamped and an LSD was close by and he let the boat sink and grabbed a Jacob's ladder that someone let down. Somebody else handed him a mess kit of hot food and he was eating. That's all he remembered.

It was over when he woke up. The island was secure. But all the shooting and killing had done something permanent to the survivors. The troops came back to the LSD in shock, dirty faces tear-stained, staring with exhaustion and astonishment that they were still alive. The casualties were in the thousands, for a little island that didn't look any bigger than the neighborhood around the heart.

Someone was calling his name, Chief Sweet, shaking his hand. He didn't recognize the kid. "I was stationed with you at Tanforan."

"How are you? You're second-class already"

"Chief, it's good to see you, goddamn it. I learned a lot from you."

"I'm a seaman apprentice now," he explained. The kid got him a change of clothes. He had got a burn from somewhere, and a corpsman smeared salve on it and covered it with a loose bandage. He found out his ship had been taken out to sea and sunk; it was too badly damaged to repair.

He kept thinking, This is just one island. What are the others going to be like? There were hundreds more. He heard about a Marine who was going back stateside because his father was dying. He was to be flown back, he was going to depart in an hour, and everyone was writing letters that wouldn't be censored for him to take to mail in San Diego. He asked the kid if he could find him a piece of paper and an envelope.

Elaine's last letter had been in a box of oatmeal cookies. Every time he took a bite he could imagine her laughing as she made them, lifting them off the hot cookie pan with a spatula onto the cooling rack. Mona had a baby girl, was in Florida with her husband, who was ready to go overseas. It was newsy, full of what was going on with her family and in the neighborhood. "You won't recognize Ruthie now, she's shot up and is going to be tall." The cookies smelled different when he opened them up. There was a small package on top, wrapped in wax paper. He knew what it was before he opened them up. Eucalyptus acorns, two of them. "Remember me," on a little square of paper.

The last morning on the island, he'd had to drag his ladder farther and farther inland, where the fighting was, to get the wounded. He'd found a spring and was filling his canteen. All the palm trees were blasted down, just a few stumps left around. He had carried the acorns with him for good luck. He dug them out of his pocket and stuck his thumb in the damp soil and put them in.

He wrote Elaine. "Don't wait for me, Elaine. It wouldn't be fair to you. It would be a waste of time. I don't think I'm coming back, and I've never felt this, whatever happened before. After the last couple of days, I don't think anyone is. There's another island after this, and another after that. We are all going to die, both the Japanese and us. I've got to hurry. XXXXXXX Chuck.

"P.S. I planted the acorns you sent."

Ruthie

I phoned my mother or she phoned me at least once a week to pass the news
back and forth. "I had lunch with Mary Maureen yesterday." I told her. "I picked
her up at the store. She wanted to go to Woolworth's. She was really in a good
mood. We had strawberry sodas and hot dogs at the counter. I haven't been in
that store for years. We were having fun remembering back when we used to
go to the jewelry counter with our Saturday quarters and feel rich. How's
Grammy?"

"Fine as always. I think she's pretending these days that she has to work for
me for her room and board." My mother started laughing. "I don't know what
I'd do without her, now that I'm home."

"Did you get the invitation from Elaine for Linda's confirmation?"

"Should I buy a present for that?"

"Just something little. We could go up and see Elaine and Chuck."

"I'll have to think about that. I'll let you know by Thursday."

"So, what have you been up to?"

"We visited Aunt May. She was good today; she remembered us and talked
a blue streak."

"She comes and goes like that. What did she have to say?"

"We talked about flowers. She could have written a book. And I asked her
something I always wanted to know."

"What was that, Mom?"

"If she turned in Michael to the FBI. She said no, she didn't even know he
was in there until the night they came for him. The call couldn't have come
from Mrs. Hughes; she was on a party line and there was a woman who listened
to everything."

I was astonished. I didn't think my mother would ever talk about that time.
I had asked something about that once years ago, and the look on her face made
me never want to bring it up again. Maybe this was the time to try again.

"Mom, here's something I always wanted to know. Did Daddy know Michael was in the shed?"

"He didn't at first. I didn't either. Grammy knew; she took him food. But she had to tell us after a while; with rationing, you couldn't get extra without stamps. I went to speak to him, took some of my underclothes to wash by hand on the scrub board. He wouldn't even come down so I could see him, stayed up there in that loft and talked to me from there. He was upset; he didn't know why he'd run away, but he was never going back, and he wasn't going to allow them to take him alive. Grammy was trying to talk him into going back. The last time I went down there to the wash shed he was calmer and asked me if they'd believe him if he said he'd had amnesia. I just let him talk.

"Your father couldn't even go down there and speak to him, he was so ashamed. He told me to tell him to get the hell back where he belonged. I didn't tell Michael that. That's why your father joined the Army. Somebody from this family has to serve, he said. There was no talking him out of it. His mind was set."

Her voice was matter-of-fact. She talked about that time like it was last month. But so did Mary Maureen, for that matter, as if the last thirty-odd years hadn't made any difference in her life, like nothing significant had happened between 1943 and 1975. Time didn't function in her discussion.

"That reminds me, here's one for you, Mom. It was my turn at the clinic today and there were three girls from the continuation school waiting to have face tattoos removed. So we were examining them, another doctor and me, and the girls had a list of questions they were studying for a history exam, and they were asking everybody these questions. No one knew who Mussolini was, not even the other doctor. One of the nurses thought Tojo was a South American dictator."

"How could anyone forget that?"

"That's just it; each generation starts clean, every twenty years. They just live in their time and forget what's not necessary for the moment."

"Tojo, I'll tell Grammy. She'll get a kick out of that."

Sometimes, when I put down the phone, it begins for me. I start thinking about the past too, just like I was made up of switches that I could activate to make different times in my life appear. I could touch my thirty-eight-year-old nose and hear my mother say, "Don't make a pest of yourself, now," when I was thirteen and wanted to walk up to the Texaco where Avery was working. He worked at night after school and got his dinner from the drive-in and ate there at the station too.

I always had some excuse. A letter from Elaine in Sacramento to read. Something new I could play on my flute. Or I'd made cookies for us to eat. I would stand, one foot on either side of the oil rack, Avery listening to me chatter like I was the most important person in the world, while his friends went by, honking their horns.

He drove me north to Elaine and Chuck's for the summer when I was thirteen. Elaine had got me a job in a city swimming pool as a lifeguard, and Chuck had signed me up for the county youth symphony, which he'd started that year. It was Chuck's idea that Avery drive me and pick me up. Grammy said I could take the bus just as easy. "You work too hard, Avery," Chuck said when we got there. "Have some fun." Avery just smiled like he always did. We had a concert, the four of us, every night before he drove back to San Bruno.

Avery had started playing the trombone after Chuck came back from the war and married Elaine. They lived at Mrs. Hughes's while he went up to the conservatory in the city. Chuck got us all playing an instrument. My mother started taking piano lessons. Mrs. Hughes already played the concertina. Elaine had no ear but practiced on the xylophone. I had my flute. Grammy was the only one who wouldn't. Mary Maureen played the violin. In three years she was so good that the director of the conservatory arranged for her to have special lessons. She practiced and practiced, sometimes five or six hours a day. People would stop on the sidewalk to listen, thinking it was the radio. They were talking about recitals, playing with the symphony. Mary Maureen was better than anyone else Chuck knew of. Then she stopped and wouldn't play anymore. Avery played in the high school marching band.

I looked like my mother, slim, dark-haired, ordinary looking, but that was the summer I got breasts. At thirteen, in my swimming suit, I knew I was going to be beautiful. I presented myself in all the mirrors I passed. Boys were coming to the pool just to talk to me, not to swim. When Avery came to pick me up in August, I scooted over across the front seat right up next to him. He was surprised. I think he thought I wanted to get out his door. "It would be easier to drive if I had more room to shift," he said, and I moved back to my side.

Sammy came back when Avery and I were in Sacramento. It was only the third time he'd been home since he got out of the Navy. He was gone by the time we returned, but we heard about it for days after. Grammy said it was like listening to a dog and cat fight. They were making up for all the time he was away, I guess.

The next thing anyone knew, Aunt May's house was up for sale. The house had been in Sammy's name too, and he was going to sell his half. Aunt May was going into a home and so was Avery, Grammy hoped, though I didn't think that would happen because he was almost a senior in high school.

Then the sign came down and there was not another word about the house. Everything went on just like it was before. Avery worked at the Texaco for Mr.

Wright. Mary Maureen was picked to try out for the radio program "Whiz Kids." I was in junior high. Elaine had her second miscarriage.

She'd had the first when Chuck was still going to school and she was still teaching at Edgemont. I had her that year for fifth grade. "I'm not going to make the same mistake I did with your sister," she told me. She made me work three times as hard as everyone else. I thought she was so glamorous. That confident laugh when the class pleased her. She went to school a half hour early to be there to help everyone that didn't understand their homework. After school she stayed to teach drawing. Once a week we'd take our sketchbooks and hike somewhere high up, paint the old yellow San Bruno Mountains, the shape of the bay, eucalyptus trees shedding their bark in long peels like strips of leather. As soon as she found out she was pregnant she was over talking to my mother, showing her patterns for maternity clothes. She must have started wearing her smocks the week after she missed her period, my mother said. When the baby started to kick, she let me feel it. She had on the white linen smock with a bow at the neck that she starched, and we were talking in the kitchen, she was washing lettuce from Aunt May's garden at the sink and I was at the table sketching, when she looked down at the linoleum. I looked at the floor too and saw the spots and then more. She dropped to her knees, saying, "Oh no, oh no." There was blood all over and I ran for my mother.

Chuck was working as a dispatcher for the sheriff's department on weekends. Mrs. Hughes said it was so he and his friend could go eat free pie at the coffee shop. He met us at the hospital. They had stopped the hemorrhaging and my mother was holding Elaine's hand. A couple of weeks before, they had been laughing, giggling with each other in our kitchen: "You think you might be a little ahead of yourself, Elaine?" She had wanted to order a winter coat for a two-year-old that was on sale. You could get clothes now that the war had ended.

Nineteen forty-nine was the most peaceful year I can recall. Mary Maureen was chosen as exchange student by the Lions Club and went to Holland for a year. It was the first time she wasn't able to back out of whatever she was involved in. She was still getting good grades and they were already talking about sending her to Stanford on a full scholarship. But she had stopped the violin and had refused to go to the second interview for "Whiz Kids." "You can lead a horse to water but you can't make it drink," Grammy said.

"Then why does this particular horse keep acting like she wants water?" my mother said. After three weeks in Amsterdam, Mary Maureen wanted to come home; she hated the family she was staying with, the school, the city, and the country in general. But my mother wouldn't send her the money, and her return ticket was only good for the next June.

It was like turning the volume on the radio down to normal. There was no yelling, no slammed doors, no screaming, tears, and the rest. Taunts. "Your boy-friend is out there," she'd say. "Go see Avery, Ruthie." Avery had been working on our Packard. "The motor can be rebuilt, but something else will go. It's got over two hundred thousand miles on it now. It's just worn out," he was telling my mother. She went inside and I stayed to talk to Avery. Mary Maureen came out then. "You playing with my little sister, Avery?" He ignored her. He was putting the valve cover back on and I was handing him his tools. She was al-ways making comments like that.

When Mary Maureen was an exchange student I could talk Avery into doing more things. We went uptown to watch the TV at the appliance store. We'd get there just before "The Texaco Hour," stand near the window on the sidewalk. "You have to watch; you work for that company," I kidded him. The TV had a seven-inch screen but it had a fifteen-inch magnifying glass set in front, and we could all see. Sometimes there were a hundred people standing out in front of the store. It would get dark, and white moths would fly around the fluorescent sign over our heads.

In September of that year, when the new cars came out, my mother took Avery and me up to look at the Studebakers. The cars had a modern design; they looked like a P-38 airplane, with their chrome nose cone and the two fender lights mounted in front. She bought one, just like that, and we drove a maroon four-door sedan home. She gave the Packard to Avery. "You did what to Dennis's car?" Grammy yelled. It was a good thing Mary Maureen was in Europe.

When my mother's friend Maureen died in Tennessee, my mother decided to drive back. Elaine convinced her that it would be okay for me to miss school. I had to promise to do my schoolwork. "Ruthie will learn as much from the trip as she will in any classroom," she told my mother. I hugged her later because I thought she was making it up for me. She said it was true; my mother was a smart woman.

My mother took her two-week vacation from the electronics plant, and the three of us were packed and ready to go. Then at the last minute, Grammy wouldn't go. She and my mother had an argument over who they'd visit. "We only have two weeks," my mother kept repeating.

"I'm not going if we can't see everyone," Grammy said, and she wouldn't budge. It was the first time I could remember going to Tennessee. I was born there, of course, but had never gone back. Grammy had, right after the war, when they let Michael go and he went straight back to Tennessee to live. But she only stayed a month because she said she missed us too much.

We got there on the day of the funeral and went to the church. It was the first funeral I'd ever gone to. We sang in the church and everyone came up to say hello to my mother and me. There was a big dinner after, in the church.

Carl, Maureen's husband, gave my mother a brooch that Maureen had wanted her to have. It was the first time I'd ever been with so many colored people. I wondered if we would have stopped thinking so much about my father if we'd had a funeral like this, where everyone was talking about the good things they remembered about Maureen, and she was dead and at rest. My father was buried in Tunisia, but I still dreamed he'd come walking through the door. Then we went down to see Michael. I wouldn't have been able to pick him out in a crowd unless I really looked and saw the resemblance to Mary Maureen. I didn't remember my father that well. But Michael knew us; he whooped and hollered when we walked into his radio and TV repair shop. I don't think he was going to let me go. "Ruthie, little Ruthie." He tried to pick me up and hold me in his arms like I was still a little girl, but I was too heavy. He almost fell backward; his artificial leg must have given out.

We knew he was doing well because Grammy telephoned him and got letters. Customers kept coming into the store and he'd introduce us. A woman said to my mother, "You must be so proud, Mrs. Mitchum. Dennis died to free those people, and Michael gave his leg against the Japs."

My mother thanked her and looked away. When we were alone with him, Michael said, "I never started that rumor, Dora. I never told anyone how I lost my leg either, but I never said I was a hero." Neither my mother nor Michael ever said who did, but I knew who.

Michael had a TV and we watched that night in his apartment. He sold them, of course, so he had a seventeen-inch demonstration model bigger than any I'd ever seen. We talked and talked. My mother had given Michael a third of our father's GI insurance, and he wanted to pay her back. "It's yours; that's the way I meant it to be," she told him. "The girls get a third too; it's in an account in their name."

We went out to Michael's fiancée's home for dinner. She knew the truth, he said when we parked in front of the house. She was nice; her whole family was nice. They must have been cooking for days. Fried chicken, baked ham, homemade bread, three kinds of dessert. We never ate like this even at Thanksgiving. I had brought my flute along to practice, and I played for one of Lauren's younger sisters, who sang.

I watched TV that night until I got a headache. We visited my father's brother's family and my mother's sister and brother. Everyone moved slower back there, talked slower, laughed slower, even ate slower. It took a couple of hours to get through a big Sunday meal. In California it took ten minutes and you were on your way.

Tennessee is not California, I told my mother when we were driving back. She nodded. Lauren had made us a lunch that lasted all the way back on Route 66. We never had to stop at a restaurant once. We were only gone ten days, but I knew when we were back in California. It was that wonderful feeling you get when you start seeing things that are familiar: going up the coast, those big gum trees welcoming us, and the smell of the ocean.

Chuck had said something like that once, when he came back from the Navy after VJ Day in 1945. I could remember that time really well; I was almost nine by then. Chuck acted the same, kidding us all the time and laughing it up, but he was different from a lot of the veterans I saw. He never wore any part of his uniform, like some of them did, or the pin in their lapel they called a ruptured duck that meant they'd been in the service. He didn't say reefer for refrigerator or the rest of it. You'd never have known he was in the Navy. There were still some servicemen around, but not like before. Tanforan was a racetrack again, and what was left of the Navy base was across El Camino. But there weren't sailors everywhere like before. You could go for weeks without seeing one.

The peninsula was changing so fast you had to keep alert or something would be gone and you'd never know. They cut off some of the hills like you'd cut the top off a soft-boiled egg. Started building subdivisions on what was flat now, and hauled all the dirt down to fill in the bay so they could build more homes down there. "Everyone is making up for lost time during the war," Elaine told me once when she took me up where they were excavating and had discovered a mastodon. They were letting the town people go in and take pieces. I filled a peanut butter jar with chunks of bone.

The vacant lots were disappearing all over the neighborhood. Aunt May was always getting calls from people wanting to buy her back lots. The vegetable garden was much smaller now, and Avery just kept the weeds down mostly, and I watered. Our chickens were long gone. There were more people at the store you didn't know now, and they built the first supermarket, a Lucky, that was as big as a hangar. We'd wander down there just to watch the automated doughnut machine.

Chuck walked down to early mass at Saint Bruno's every Sunday morning like clockwork. Avery would be going to work at the Texaco and offer him a ride, but Chuck liked to walk. I went with him once or twice to see what it was like. It was too long a time to sit still. I didn't understand Latin, and everyone was old. But we brought a dozen warm doughnuts back and woke Elaine up to have some.

I knew about Avery's family; no one in the neighborhood could not know, with Grammy reminding anyone that would listen. But I never understood that everyone knew until Chuck's friend Mr. Schwartz who was in the sheriff's department saw Avery one time when he'd taken Chuck home.

"That's a Gorman," I heard him tell Chuck. "He live around here?"

"He's a good friend," Chuck told him. "A good friend of the family, too. I'd trust him with my life."

We were all sad when the Sweets moved to Sacramento so Chuck could teach music in one of the high schools. We all knew they were going, but I don't think anyone believed they really would, that they'd leave Mrs. Hughes's apartment, the neighborhood, the street, they were so much a part of everything that happened. We still all took walks around the heart. Sometimes we'd end up at the creamery. Even after the gas rationing stopped, we walked. Chuck always made sure Avery went with us. That he was invited to dinner over at their place Sundays, that he took something back with him for Aunt May, who we wouldn't see for days sometimes, because her legs hurt her all the time now, and she didn't like to go out. For weeks after they moved, I'd walk over to Mrs. Hughes's to tell Elaine something and be halfway up the stairs before I remembered someone else lived there now. Or I'd just wander around as if they might appear somehow on the street. Quit moping around, Mary Maureen would say.

When it came time to buy our school clothes and Elaine wasn't there, it wasn't fun anymore. The four of us used to drive up to the city, park, and march up and down Market Street, going to all the department stores. For my mother, I think it was always a chore; Mary Maureen told me one time she was going to get as many cashmere sweaters and plaid wool skirts as possible to make up for the way she was treated. But the fun started when the school clothes shopping was over and the trying on could start. We'd have lunch in one of the department store restaurants. Then we'd go into the Emporium or the City of Paris and Elaine and my mother would start trying on clothes. It took a few times before my mother got the knack of it, but she was good too. Mary Maureen and I would watch, both as excited as they were, to see them playing dress-up. My mother had never acted like this.

The more outlandish and expensive the clothes, the better. They'd giggle and cavort, coming out of the dressing room. "Buy it, Dora, it was made for you," Elaine would say to my mother as she posed in a dress that looked like a gold candy wrapper twisted around her body. Or "Just right for school," my mother would say, as Elaine pranced out in a black sequined sheath. They'd end up buying a pair of gloves or a scarf, though once my mother bought a sky-blue silk blouse.

Avery and Leroy doubled-dated for their junior prom. I watched Avery get into the Packard. He'd washed it and I'd helped him wax the hood. He had a gardenia corsage for his date, and a new crewcut. He waved to me when he drove off.

Mary Maureen's date came in his father's car. Rusty had red hair and was tall. He was the center on the basketball team. Mary Maureen looked nice. She had a blue formal Grammy had bought her at Macy's. He had orchids in a plastic box.

"Your turn will come," Mrs. Hughes told me, "and I'll make you a dress." I went back home and helped Grammy finish the dishes. Later I took Aunt May for a walk. I didn't know how old she was, but her legs were stiff, like matchsticks, and she moved like she was on stilts. "Brittle," she said. "They feel like they're going to snap off." Everyone knew her. She was a character. People waved at her, called out, "Aunt May, my geraniums are exceptional this year, help yourself."

"I was going to anyway," she whispered to me, and we'd laugh. She still had the most beautiful flower garden in the neighborhood. People would stop their cars in the middle of the street to look, when the iris blossomed, or later when the glads were reaching their colors up to the sky.

At the beginning of our walks I always asked, "Have you heard from Sammy?" and she'd add some part I didn't know before, until my mother found out and told me to stop. But I already knew the story about the house and how it was Avery's money that was used to buy out Sammy's half. My mother had helped when they all went to the bank. The Wright family at the Texaco where Avery worked had something to do with it too. "It's private," my mother had told me. So I always wondered. Aunt May would still drop hints, even after I stopped asking. "I'm not going to forget anything . . ." But she was also as nosy as I was. "Are you sweet on Avery, Ruthie?" she asked once. She liked to tease me if she could.

"We're just friends, Aunt May; he's like a big brother."

"I hear Michael is coming back."

"He's thinking about it. He'd like to open a store here."

"I never had anything against him," Aunt May said. "And stop mooning after Avery. You don't want to get mixed up with that family of his. His father is going to die in prison. Avery's a good boy, but when you marry someone you marry the whole family, not just the one person."

"I'm not going to marry anyone," I said. "I'm going to have a career. Like Margaret Truman." We both thought that was hilarious. She was a good enough singer, I guess. She was on TV all the time.

"You're your father's daughter, all right," she said.

My mother let me go up to Sacramento over Easter week to stay with Elaine and Chuck. Molly, his sister, who I'd never met before, came down to visit with her two kids. They could all play instruments; that whole family was talented that way. We played by the hour.

Chuck took out his watches for us to look at. Handed them around for us to hold afterward. There must have been forty or fifty of them. He was always going into pawnshops to look at watches. He wiped each one with a special cloth when he put them back. I'd seen them twice before. It was always a special occasion. The last one he showed us was his father's railroad watch.

When I came back, Mary Maureen was in a full love-swoon over Rusty. It wasn't just the phone calls, and them working out in the garage where they'd put an old mattress to practice tumbling. Grammy was right there to keep an eye from the kitchen window, ready to yell, "Keep that garage door open." When I started high school, he came to pick her up in the morning and dropped her off in the afternoon. They parked in front at night until Grammy would yell for Mary Maureen to come inside; it was time to go to bed. It was like she was playing the violin again; that's all she could do. Rusty was at our house more than he was at his.

High school was like you were dropped in the middle of an anthill and you were an ant yourself, lost in the crowd. I was confused at first. There was a lot of construction going on and it was hard to know what building to go to. I was tardy for my classes because I couldn't find the rooms, and I lost all my books when someone stole them out of my locker. Avery saw me one time wandering around trying to find my algebra class. He showed me where the room was, and was waiting outside when the bell rang. He bought me a Coke and a fried lemon pie at snack, and then took me to my next class. After the first week I decided I didn't like high school and as soon as I was old enough I was going to quit and get a job, I didn't care what anyone said.

Mary Maureen ignored me. I wasn't in any of her classes. I'd see her, just the top of her head, in Rusty's car, slumped down making out during lunchtime in the parking lot. I ignored her too. We didn't look like each other, but some of the teachers recognized the name. "Smartest kid we ever had in the math department." Or, "You're certainly not Mary Maureen." That didn't bother me. I was glad I wasn't.

We moved from the heart in 1955, the year I graduated from high school. The plant my mother had worked at since the war was bought by a larger electronics company in Burlingame, so we moved there to be closer to my mother's job. Elaine and Chuck came down for my graduation. They had come for Avery's and Mary Maureen's too, when they got out in 1951. Avery had enlisted in the Army the very next day, and Mary Maureen had gone up to Reno and got married to Rusty, three months pregnant.

Our ceremony was held on the football field, and afterward I crossed the grass and found everybody in a group on the sidelines. Elaine had her arm through Chuck's, standing next to my mother and Doug, her friend from work. Grammy, Michael and his wife, Lauren. Michael had been back almost two years now and liked to say he was in on the ground floor of the vacuum-tube revolution. He had one store and was going to open a second. He lived in the city. Mary Maureen had a home in Mountain View, where Rusty was a fireman and played basketball for a semipro team. "You made it, Ruthie," Elaine said, and she hugged me. They all knew I wanted to give my gown back and go to the graduation party, and they were giving me fast good-bye hugs and kisses again.

"Mary Maureen said to tell you congratulations," Grammy said. "She would have come, but one of us had to watch the boys." Grammy was living with Mary Maureen now to help. She had two kids and was pregnant again. I was anxious to go, but they were still lingering, so I started walking backward toward my friends, waving, watching them talking among themselves again, waving back to me, and I remember thinking, My family. That's my family.

I had decided to go to UC at Davis and was living in Sacramento with Elaine and Chuck. Elaine had had a stillborn child the year before and was moody, Chuck said, but so was he. If I made it a point to get Elaine laughing again, she and Chuck made an effort to stop me from being homesick. I missed the sound of the trains and the heart. I thought of my mother a lot. I missed everyone. I was too scared of failing at college not to study every minute I could, but I'd be sitting there reading, and little quick scenes of the past would appear on the page. The three of us kids sitting in the very first row of the El Camino Theater for the matinee, grabbing out of the same box of popcorn, our heads bent back like we were looking up at the moon. Delivering the morning papers with Avery, running down the sidewalk flipping the papers up on the porch in the early-morning dark. Mary Maureen and me getting one of the new cake mixes and eating all the batter raw out of the mixing bowl without ever pouring it into the pans. I'd remember and get a great big lump in my throat and want to call Mom, Mom, but it wasn't just her I missed, it was everyone, the house, the place.

I remembered Chuck phoning my mother and telling her Elaine was going to have a painting at the de Young, when I was still at home. We met them there, they'd driven down from Sacramento, and had lunch in the Japanese Tea Garden. They had just changed the name back from the Oriental Gardens. Grammy had come with us. "Well, let's see how good she is," she said. The exhibit was titled Young California Artists, and there were about twenty pictures in the small room. We were the only ones there, and we went to each one, looking for Elaine's. She wouldn't tell us which one was hers. Mary Maureen found it and we all looked. It was a landscape of the San Bruno hills with a grove of trees, and in the foreground there was a group of people eating around a table outside. I wondered if it was us, but I didn't want to ask Elaine.

When I lived with Chuck and Elaine they were so worried that I wouldn't have enough privacy that they stopped using the door to the backyard that was near my room. They had bought a big house with two bathrooms and three bedrooms. She used one for her studio. It was full of her paintings. "Pick one to hang in your room," she said. I chose the one that had been in the museum, which no one had bought. I could look up at it when I was lying on the bed and imagine things about the people.

Mary Maureen phoned me in Sacramento on Lincoln's birthday. I had been home for Christmas and New Year's break with my mother. "I just thought you'd like to know, Ruthie, that your mother is shacking up with that engineer from the plant," she said. "I caught them at it. I walked right in her bedroom and there they were, laying on the bed. 'What about Daddy?' I yelled. You can bet I told her what I thought of her, too. 'You're never going to see me or your grandkids again. Never.' That's what I said."

I didn't know what to answer at first. What to ask. "What did Grammy say?"

"Called her trash. That's what she is. Michael told me I should mind my own business. I told him he's not her son, goddamn it, and to butt out. You can tell Elaine she's got a slut for a friend."

I didn't tell Elaine anything at first. Chuck asked me how my mother was doing. She usually phoned on Sunday afternoon, but she hadn't yet. I told him what Mary Maureen had said. He was embarrassed or something. "Talk to Elaine when she comes back," he told me. She had a group she painted landscapes with on weekends.

When she heard, she asked me, "What do you think?"

I didn't know what I thought. "If she's happy, I guess it's okay. I want her to be happy is all."

"Phone and ask her," she said. "Go on, I'd like to know, too." They both went out in the backyard while I phoned.

"Mom, it's me, Ruthie," was as far as I got.

"I didn't know if you'd want to talk to me or not." I'd never heard her sound so abject before.

"Because you're a scarlet woman?" I asked, and we both started laughing at the same time.

"You know Doug," she said. "He's something like your father and then again he's not. I was lonely, I guess. You were all gone."

"How's Michael and Lauren?"

"They're fine; they had us over to dinner the other night and she made one of her famous meals. You know how Michael is; he told Doug, I'm not pushing you into anything, but I have you and Dora's wedding present all picked out. It all seemed kind of funny then. Mary Maureen made me feel miserable for a while. Does Elaine know?"

"She knows, and she wanted to know if you are happy."

"Tell her I am."

• • •

Chuck got letters from Avery sometimes, who'd reenlisted and was stationed in Italy, and he'd read aloud parts of them. "Can you believe this, Chuck?" he wrote. "I scored high enough in the language aptitude test I took that they are sending me to school to learn Russian. I can get along in Italian now, and I've never enjoyed myself more. The Italians are like the Chinese— family and food. And, of course, the women." I sneaked a look one time at what he didn't read. "In Germany the beer was cold and the women were warm. In Italy the wine is cool and the women are hot. What that means is I'm having a good time in Italia."

He wrote my mother too. He had taken a trip down the boot of Italy to Sicily and then across the Mediterranean by ferry to Tunisia. He sent her back photos of my father's grave. He had sent her a jade pendant and me a kimono when he'd been in Japan, and she wore it on special occasions. He'd sent Elaine china from Japan too, a setting for eight, that we were careful with and used every day.

At night Chuck and Elaine sat at either end of the dining room table reading or correcting papers, paying the bills or writing lesson plans. Chuck was teaching in a junior college now and always had something to do. Elaine opened a letter. "It's from the Second Marine Division again. They're going to be holding the fifteenth-year reunion for veterans of the Tarawa campaign. Did you hear me? It's in San Francisco."

"I'm not going," he said.

"No one said you were." When they argued it was subdued, gentle, like they each had a grip on a wishbone and were giving little tugs, waiting for the bone to split. "There's a handwritten note from someone who remembers you, encouraging you to come."

"I don't want to be reminded of all that. You know I don't." He put his book down.

"You went to see Russ Sikes at Mare Island when he got promoted to captain."

"That was different. You didn't go to that."

"I didn't because I don't like his new wife." He wouldn't argue anymore, just stopped talking. "You write them you're not coming, then. You're one of the guests of honor, not me." He got up and wound the grandfather clock, then went out to his music room in the back. We could still hear him playing his bassoon two hours later.

The four years in college went by so fast I never had time even to realize how well I was doing. I studied harder than I ever thought possible. I was a lab assistant twenty hours a week, and all summer I worked in my mother's department at the plant in Burlingame. Each quarter was harder than the last, but went by twice as fast. Then I was graduating again, and my family came up for the occasion. We got someone to take our picture as a group. I was in the middle, my arms around my mother's and Elaine's waists. Chuck. Mary Maureen. Rusty didn't come; they were having problems. My stepfather Doug with Mary Maureen's oldest boy, Dennis. Michael and Lauren didn't come because Mary Maureen would be there. Grammy didn't come because she was taking care of Mary Maureen's other three kids.

I didn't avoid Mary Maureen, but on the other hand I never went searching her out either. We saw each other on the holidays when I went home. Having four kids in eight years had left her overweight and shrill. "What does it take to turn a person into a shrew?" I asked Elaine once.

"It's a long process." She knew who I was talking about.

After the graduation ceremony we walked around the campus. "This place doesn't show me shit," Mary Maureen said. "I'm glad I didn't bother to go." She talked loud, salty, and in a kind of sisterly shorthand. That last comment meant her IQ was much higher than mine and she belonged to Mensa. Mary Maureen carried around a perpetual grievance. "You hear from Avery?" she asked Elaine.

"I think Chuck got a letter last month. And he sent me a present on my birthday."

"It was me he sent the last present to," Chuck said. "An antique clarinet with an ivory bell he found in some shop in Palermo."

"Still in the Army. Three hots and a cot," Mary Maureen said. "He wouldn't have done much better on the outside. I guess maybe he could have become a prom king sooner or later. He went often enough."

That was meant for me. I had asked Avery to my high school prom when he was back on leave, staying with Aunt May like before. He came over and checked with my mother. "If you want to," she told him, "it's all right with me."

"Ruthie," he said, "I'm too old now." But he went. Grammy didn't make a scene that time. She had when he'd sent me the kimono from Japan on R-and-R. She wasn't going to let me keep it; she said it was underwear and she was going to burn it. It took a lot of yelling to get it away from her. Avery wore a charcoal cashmere suit with a one-button roll he'd bought from a Hong Kong tailor, and I wore a dress Mrs. Hughes made me. I went over every night while she was working on it. It was emerald green taffeta with a white bodice. We double-dated and sat in the back of a '51 DeSoto. Avery was quiet, but he liked to dance.

I didn't know I was going to medical school. I wasn't officially in premed. I just happened to have taken so many of the prerequisites as a biology major that I qualified. It was Chuck who encouraged me to send for the applications and helped me fill them out. I applied to seven places, and I took the scholarship Stanford offered me.

When Mary Maureen found out, she yelled at me over the phone, "The only reason you got in there was Chuck knew someone."

"You're just jealous, Mary Maureen."

"Of you? Just ask him."

I didn't want to embarrass Chuck. I didn't know how to describe him, but he seemed almost fragile sometimes. It was hard to explain, but I didn't want to put him on the spot. I noticed sometimes he'd get nervous for no reason, and then he had a habit of looking at his watches, the one on his wrist, comparing that with his pocket watch. He'd put them away and then a couple of minutes later do it again, but faster this time. If Elaine was there she'd take his hand with the pocket watch and hold it in hers to stop him.

I asked Elaine. She said Chuck was friends with the county undersheriff, Mr. Schwartz, but she didn't know if he had any influence at Stanford. "You were accepted at those other places, Ruthie. Would you rather go to one of those? Don't torment yourself over nothing; do what you want." So I went back down to the peninsula and went to school in Palo Alto.

I had been asking Elaine from junior high on, How do you know when you're in love?

"You'll know," she always said. "You'll just know."

"I'll be smitten? Head over heels?"

"Something like that."

In high school I must have driven her crazy. "What's the difference between romantic love and commonsense love? Should you marry someone like a movie star or someone like a banker? What about arranged marriages, like in olden times?"

"Don't analyze everything so much. It'll happen."

In college I always had to work toward the concept, make love bend around some preconceived notion. When I thought I had a definition to fit with a person, I'd lose interest.

"What if I don't ever fall in love?"

"It would be awful," she said. Elaine was down staying with us in Burlingame; she was going to a fertility clinic for a series of tests.

"You're just saying that to make me feel good."

She laughed. "Change that to sad. Loving someone and marrying them, well, besides all the obvious benefits, you get to have two different perspectives on everything, his and yours, instead of just your own, and because you get to share experiences, it's like living it all twice. Ask your mother."

I got married the year I got out of medical school. It was the same summer Mary Maureen divorced Rusty, Doug had his first heart attack, and Elaine and Chuck had Linda, their first baby. And Avery was at Aunt May's for a week, on his way to Southeast Asia.

I was old enough, twenty-four, to decide for myself. I knew Alex loved me as much as I loved him. But it was like I had experienced the whole episode before, everything leading up to the wedding, and knew what was coming. I told that to Elaine on my wedding day. Mrs. Hughes had made my coronet and veil, and she'd just left after putting the finishing touches on the veil.

"It's normal to have second thoughts," she said.

"It's not second thoughts; it's like I've done this before, is all," I said.

"Ruthie, don't make me cry." She was wearing a dress that hid the weight she'd gained carrying Linda. Chuck had the baby out in front in the church.

"I'm just trying to understand what I'm feeling."

"Do you want me to go tell them you don't want to go through with it?"

"No, I'm just trying to explain it to myself," I said.

Michael gave me away. Later, at the receiving line, it was exactly like I'd remembered it. Elaine hugged me hard and I didn't think she was going to let me go. "Be yourself," she whispered. Michael and Lauren had brought Mrs. Hughes, and my mother had picked up Aunt May; we had the same arrangements for the holidays. I had explained this to Alex. "Why include them?" he asked. "It's not like they're members of your family." We always have, I told him.

I knew Avery was coming, but I wasn't sure I'd recognize him; it had been eight or nine years. He didn't look like a soldier in his blue blazer and gray slacks. Assured, suntanned, with that faint grin, he could have passed for anything. "This is Avery," I told Alex. "We grew up together, next door." They shook hands. "Good luck," Avery said, and he leaned forward to kiss me on the cheek. It wasn't the first time. He had kissed me like that when he brought me home from the junior prom and that time I had grabbed him and kissed him as hard as I could on the mouth. "Ruthie," he said, and he kissed me back the same way. This time I nodded and smiled and got ready to greet the next person. That seemed like it had happened to another person too.

Mary Maureen was reconciling with Rusty, and the two of them and their kids sat at a table with Aunt May and Avery during dinner. It was a traditional kind of wedding. I danced with Chuck, who was very good, after I had the first dance with Alex. With Michael. Doug. Avery danced with my mother and Elaine. I could hear them laughing. He danced with me. "I'm proud of you," he said. "You're going to be a plastic surgeon, your mother said." He didn't stutter now.

"What are you going to do?" I asked him.

"Stay in the Army." He added, "It's a good job."

"You don't miss California?" I asked.

"All the time. But your mother and the Sweets write me, so I hear about everyone. I keep up with things." Rusty came up to dance, already half drunk. "I'll see you," Avery said. Alex rescued me from Rusty after just a minute or two.

We went to England for our honeymoon. His parents gave us that as a gift, after my mother refused their help in paying for the wedding, plus three acres of land in the hills above Woodside. We started building our life, brick by brick, just like we built our house and stable and garden. I went back to school and Alex went back to managing the hospital his father owned.

My mother-in-law, Sue, took me in hand. She was the granddaughter and daughter of doctors, married to one, and the mother of two sons that were doctors. At first she treated me like someone who had just come out of a coma after a long period of time. She took me shopping, trying to develop my taste for clothes, and had my hair done so many ways that finally I found a style I was comfortable with. It was slow work. But Sue relished the impossible; she said that once, in a different context, of course.

I used to go visit my mother after these forays. Ask, "Do you notice anything different?"

"The new dress?"

I shook my head. "Me. Don't I seem different? Haven't I changed? Altered at least a little?"

"You're the same Ruthie. I don't see anything different."

And she was the same too, and I began to appreciate her more when I realized I was going to be like her. I was like my mother.

Sue and I both made fun of her project, but it was serious for both of us. Was I going to fit in? I knew I was. There was a certainty about me; it never gave me pause. I had what it takes, at least to be a good plastic surgeon. It must have been all the drawing I'd done. I was never close to being in Elaine's class. But I had a sense of the possibilities in reconstructive surgery that gave me an advantage. I could stroke some baby's chin to soothe her, planning how I would correct her cleft palate, and it was like making strokes with a pencil for me, rather than a scalpel.

With Alex, I wasn't so sure. Alex was always charming to my mother and treated Grammy with patience that no one else in the family had anymore, listening to her stories for hours, doing everything possible to be agreeable. I had told him a short version of our history. He'd sit at my mother's table for Thanksgiving, listening politely as Rusty and Mary Maureen argued or Aunt May said the world was going to come to an end if Richard Nixon was elected president. The time Rusty got drunk and threw up in the kitchen sink he told me, "They're all originals in your family."

Then, after a few years, he didn't go anymore, but I went to his family gatherings, which I came to enjoy. I never let Sue down. We had come to like each other. "You always seem like you're taking notes," she told me once at an opening of a Head Start school, "but I'm used to you now," and I hugged her back.

Alex came home tired, exhausted, he said, and he'd lie down on the couch and listen to classical music with his arm over his eyes. He had been in private practice with his father, a gynecologist, but left that to manage the hospital just before we were married. He explained he'd been bored as a doctor in private practice. "Put a paper gown on anyone and it's all the same." But he was bored at the hospital too. And he was bored with me.

"What did you expect out of marriage?" I asked him once. We were looking out over our meadow at the base of one of the old round hills above Junipero Serra, sitting out in the quiet of the late afternoon, watching the sun reflect off the surface of our swimming pool like it was on fire.

"This," he said, waving his hand at the property. "And I suppose to be like my parents, or at least a continuation of my conception of them. And to fill my professional, social, and familial obligations, that sort of thing. What did you expect?"

I didn't want to say what I thought, because I knew what he'd say. I had made myself stop thinking that this had all happened before, and that I was just a spectator. I didn't dwell on that very much anymore. Then I said it anyway: "To live happily ever after." I ruined it by adding, "Not literally, not in the sense of the fairy tale. Just to be together, grab the good times when they come by. Be constant."

"Like Elaine and Chuck?" he said. I had used them as an example once. He mocked them sometimes, and wouldn't go up to Sacramento with me, or stay around long if they came down on a visit. Mrs. Nice and Mr. Ordinary, he called them. Elaine had given me the painting I liked, the one I always thought was of all of us living around the heart. I had hung it in my office to avoid snide comments. "She paints like she's working for the WPA. She's really out of touch. Even more than Mr. Chuck the band man with two cymbals for a brain."

When I told my mother I was thinking about a divorce she seemed surprised. "I've been thinking about it a long time," I added. We were outside in her flower garden. The sweet williams were up and she was weeding around them.

"I never know what to say at times like this," she said. "To both you and Mary Maureen. You're going to have to find out for yourselves."

"About being alone, you mean?"

"No, I don't know what I mean. Hand me that trowel," she said.

After the divorce I moved, sold the house, and told myself I was going to throw everything away. I wanted to start over. I did it twice, but it never changed anything. I still couldn't part with the hubcap our dog used to eat out of. And I came across the medal Avery had given me. He'd just come back from Korea. He said he had something for me. He said it was to replace the one our father was awarded. I didn't know what he was talking about. When I went up to see the Sweets I showed it to Chuck. He said it was a purple heart; you got it if you were wounded or killed. This all happened when I was in high school. Elaine thought she remembered seeing Mary Maureen with something like that, thought she recalled telling her the string was going to break and she'd lose the medallion.

I had time to speculate. I was teaching three days a week now and working at the clinic the rest of the time. I opened the little box again. I had never asked Mary Maureen in the twenty years since Avery had given it to me. I phoned her, something I didn't often do anymore.

"I don't know what you're talking about," she said.

"Mom says she doesn't know what happened to Dad's medal either."

"Well, that's too bad. I don't know anything about it. You were too young to know how it was. None of this would have happened if Daddy hadn't died."

"Mary Maureen, you just remember what you want to."

She hung up on me.

Being wealthy gives you more time. I kept busy as a doctor after the divorce; I attended things, good works, galas for all kinds of causes. Sue was on committees and organizations that were endless, and I went when she phoned. But those spaces had to be filled with other people like yourself. I was looking over the ceramics at an art auction to benefit the City of Hope when a woman came over and said, "Don't I know you?"

"You look familiar," I said. This had never happened before because there was never anyone at these things I could have known before. "I'm from San Bruno originally," I said.

"You went to Edgemont?" I nodded. "You were younger. Your sister Mary Maureen was in my class. Miss Walker was our teacher during the war. She was the best teacher I ever had. I'm Sharon Lemke."

"I went to your birthday party." As I said it, I remembered that day. "With Avery Fontana." We talked on and on. Someone's name would lead to someone else's. She was the publisher of a newspaper in Ohio now and was back visiting her family. "Say hello to everyone for me," she said, "especially Miss Walker."

After Linda was born, Elaine and Chuck had the twins and then a fourth daughter. Sometimes now people took them for the grandparents. "I pretend that at times too, but no one else ever comes to pick them up," Chuck said when he came for me at the airport in Sacramento for the twins' twelfth birthday. Both he and Elaine had gray in their hair and looked their age, but there were times you could see them young again. When Elaine laughed. When Chuck did a double take, arguing with one of the girls.

The girls played in what Linda called the Sweet Quartet Plus One. Two violins, a viola, a cello, and Chuck on the bassoon. If happy meant you were satisfied with your lot, they were happy. I couldn't help but think, looking at them, that Mary Maureen was a grandmother two times over, and I was divorced, and hadn't wanted children.

They hadn't heard from Avery in five or six years. He had done four tours in Vietnam before it was over. He'd just stopped writing. He doesn't write my mother either, I told them. We were sitting around the table after dinner, talking about the past, the people in the old neighborhood. Aunt May was in a home now and most of the time didn't know any of us. My mother and Grammy still went to visit. Elaine and Chuck had come down when Doug died. Sammy came back and was working for Michael, I told them, but neither Elaine nor Chuck remembered him.

We went into the front room when the girls came in to do the dishes, sat in the semidarkness, and listened to a tape of the Quartet Plus One. Linda was going to be in high school next year. And I'd been asked to be on the committee for my class's twentieth reunion, and had been musing over high school ever since. Was that time so intense because you were on some kind of threshold where experience was accelerated, while you were still doing things for the first time? I was surprised when I discovered that for a lot of people those were the best years. For most of the committee, high school was not just a mutual experience; it was a mutual cultivation of the memory.

When I got home I phoned my mother to tell her about the Sweets. I waited till I was sure she'd be back from the rink. Now that she was retired, instead of going to the plant she went to the roller-skating rink most mornings for the two-hour senior floor time. "I always envied the way you and Mary Maureen used to glide up and down the sidewalk in front of the house. It looked so free and easy, swinging your arms like that, lifting your skates," she told me once. "So I tried it, and I was right."

"Mom," I asked, "are you ready for some ancient history questions? We were talking about old times, Elaine and Chuck and I, so it's in my mind." I didn't wait for her to answer. "Why did we leave Daddy over there instead of bringing him back after the war?"

She didn't hesitate. "It didn't seem to me then or now it was going to make any difference. He was dead; having his grave here or over there wasn't going to change that. It's funny you should ask about that. I've been thinking about it too the last few days. He died two days before the Germans gave up in North Africa. And he didn't have to go there in the first place." She paused, and I didn't think she would go on, but she did.

"I always thought he went where all the fighting was because Michael was caught; he felt he had to go then. I tried to keep him from knowing anything about that business, but he found out. I don't know how, but he did."

"Here's something else I remember. The war was almost over in Europe, we knew that at school, and if Daddy was alive, he'd be coming back now, but they were still fighting in the Pacific Islands. I remember walking home from school and the air-raid sirens went off and all the church bells started ringing. I caught up with Mary Maureen, and she had tears streaming down her face. 'Didn't you hear, didn't you hear?' she said. I ran home and Aunt May was out in the front yard and she was crying too. What was that all about, Mom?"

"It must have been when Roosevelt died."

"Was that bigger than when Kennedy died?"

"There was no comparison. Roosevelt had been in longer, of course, but it was like a member of your family had died. Kennedy was tragic, the way he died, but it was like you'd mourn for a favorite movie star. That night President Roosevelt died, we all sat around in the kitchen and cried. I think Mrs. Hughes and Aunt May were in the house at the same time, both crying. Grammy, the people down the street. The only one who was dry-eyed was Elaine. She voted for Thomas Dewey, she told me once, and her father was a big Republican. No one had ever heard of Harry Truman then. She was worried the war would go on longer with the President dead, and Chuck would never come home. She brought over a big dish of brownies; where she got that much sugar with rationing I'll never know. We all cried, drank Ovaltine, ate brownies, and talked about Franklin and Eleanor and what they did for us."

Avery and Mary Maureen's class had been the first freshman class in the new high school, and mine had been the fourth. All the classes had been small, two hundred, two hundred fifty kids; everyone knew one another. Every few years we had a joint class reunion, something informal at a park or a hall.

I had been my class president and I found it pleasant going back. The past didn't bother me. The present was all surprise, and after it became the past it didn't have the resonance to harm me. I could compete with my past. It was the future that kept me awake. Was I going to be doing the same thing over and over the rest of my life? The next five years, the next ten?

Mary Maureen was on the committee's mailing list, and when she got her notice of the next reunion, she was on the phone. I knew she would be. "Why do they keep sending me these goddamn things? This is the third this month. The reason you go is you've made it, you like to show off."

"Mary Maureen—"

"Don't Mary Maureen me. You think you're so smart. I never liked high school. I never liked school in general. Why would I want to go back?" She worked at Lucky's as a checker and lived in an apartment, now that the kids were grown.

What Mary Maureen didn't understand was the past isn't something static.

It changes with time and perspective. It's alive, fresh, growing, and waiting. But you have to be loyal to the past. Michael is an example, the family shame, the deserter. It's a joke now. His boys both went to Canada in 1971 when they drew low draft numbers; it's a family tradition. He's just opened his sixth store in the bay area at Tanforan Shopping Center. That place has gone from racetrack to assembly center for Japanese Americans being sent to the camps to naval base, then back to racetrack, and when that mysteriously burned down, to gigantic shopping mall. Michael is probably a millionaire. I don't think he's let the past use him like Mary Maureen keeps saying it has her.

Which is not to say that I don't have the same thoughts as Mary Maureen sometimes: there's no avoiding them. The whys and what-ifs. What if our father had lived? I remember how deft his hands were. He made a kite and took us over by the tracks to fly it away from the wires. He let me hold the line, and I can still feel the tugs and vibrations as the kite sawed back and forth in the wind. But when I see that image of the kite in the sky, my father's big hands around mine, I hear my ex-husband, after an argument, saying, "You're so easily pleased by the pedestrian. In love with the commonplace."

I don't know if it was Mary Maureen losing thirteen pounds or what, but she phoned me a few weeks later and said, "Let's go." I had mentioned once that the only people who go to reunions are thin and have all their hair. She bought a new outfit and had her hair lightened. My mother told me that when I phoned her.

There's always a little tension at first at these gatherings, trying to guess who people are before you can read their name tags. I was standing there alone, Mary Maureen had immediately seen someone she recognized and gone off, and I started to feel awkward. I'm not as calm as I pretend. Then Mary Maureen waved me over and introduced me to Leroy somebody and he remembered me. As I had walked up I heard Mary Maureen tell him, "Ruthie is a plastic surgeon." He taught math at a high school in Belmont. He hadn't lived on our street but across town.

"Remember, Mary Maureen?" he kept saying. "The canal? We built a raft together. Edgemont? Avery?"

"I remember Avery," I said.

"He wasn't in your class," Mary Maureen said. "Do you ever hear from him, Leroy?"

"Somebody wrote my mother and wanted to know if she knew anything about him. Some doctor up north, I think. She must have written ten pages. She knew the family, and I filled her in on the phone with some other things I remembered. She sent it back to some place. Washington. Either Tacoma or Spokane."

"That's all anyone knows?" I said.

"My mother lost the letter, so I don't know any more."

"He probably went haywire," Mary Maureen said. "Avery was always weird. Nothing would surprise me about him."

When Aunt May died in December of 1975, Sammy invited us all over after the funeral. I hadn't been back in a long time. I didn't recognize the street till I was halfway down. Our old house was gone. There was a twelve-unit two-story apartment building in its place. Mrs. Hughes's lot had more apartments. Aunt May's place was so small it looked like a doll house.

"They rezoned," Sammy said. "She'd never sell, and these lots are two hundred by two hundred. I got a blank check in the mail the other day from a realtor with a note, just fill in the numbers." He'd brought some vodka and scotch and we all had a drink. The place was cluttered with unopened mail and magazines but still pretty clean. "The last time we went to see May," Grammy said, "she said she was going to die in her own bed. She thought she was home. But she knew she'd outlived Mrs. Hughes."

Mary Maureen was explaining to Julie, her granddaughter, that we had lived next door. "They made El Camino Theater into a porno show," Sammy said. I shook my head. "Anybody want anything, take it. She'd like you to have a memento. And I'm just going to have to throw it away."

"I wouldn't mind some of the bulbs in the front yard," my mother said. "When we left here, I didn't take mine. They were all in flower."

"Help yourself," Sammy said.

Grammy got up and started for the kitchen. She had got old but hadn't changed that much. Still walked straight. Still did the laundry and ironing. I watched as she looked in a cupboard, taking down a dish and holding it to the light to read the back. Lauren had come too, and she went into the kitchen. I knew Michael wouldn't come: he'd never come back to the neighborhood as far as I knew.

"What are you going to do with this old Zenith radio?" Mary Maureen said.

"Take it," Sammy said without looking.

I wandered into Aunt May's room. I don't think I'd ever been in there before. Then into what must have been Sammy's room originally and then Avery's. Dresser, single bed. The empty closet must have had a hundred hangers, the wooden ones stenciled with the names of old laundries and clothing stores on San Mateo Avenue, El Camino Real. The bed had the old kind of springs, hundreds of wire coils. These were painted green. The mattress was half off, and I noticed something wedged between the headboard and the frame. I had to put my weight on the springs before I could work it out.

It was a handmade wooden box, and there was string on the wooden reel that was set inside. I got a rag and dusted it off. There were red veins in the grain of the wood. It was beautifully made, dovetailed joints, a few square nails in the bottom where it had been broken. I didn't understand what it was for, but it looked like a child's toy.

"Sammy," I asked, "was this yours when you were a kid?"

"Not that I remember. Take it," he said.

I didn't want it, particularly; I had too many things of my own from before, but I kept it in my hand, wandering around, and when I went outside, my mother looked up. She was on one knee, separating the bulbs she'd dug up. "The kite reel," she said. "It was your father's. I always wondered what happened to that. He and Michael used to make kites back in Tennessee every spring. It was something to watch. But when we came to California, they stopped; it seemed like there wasn't enough time for things like that here."

"I remember him making a kite and flying it over by the streetcar tracks once."

Grammy opened the front door. "Dora, are you going to say anything if I take a few things of Aunt May's to remember her by?"

"No, Grammy, I'm not." Both of them kept a straight face.

"I see you found Dennis's kite reel, Ruthie," she said matter-of-factly. "Your grandfather made that when Dennis was a boy. I don't think there were even any airplanes then. Everyone flew kites; the sky was free in those days and you could do what you wanted."

"If this was Daddy's, how did it get over here?" I asked.

"Dennis let that boy keep it before he went in the Army. That's what he said to me when I asked."

"Why would he do that, Grammy?" my mother said.

"Probably the same reason you gave him Dennis's Packard, because you wanted to," she said. I had to think a minute to remember everything, but then I started laughing with them.

My mother was on her hands and knees again, digging in the soft ground with a trowel she'd found. Her hair was almost all gray now and she wore glasses so thick that when you looked directly at her they distorted her face. She had always looked distracted, like her mind was somewhere else. Driving over, I'd taken the old way, around the heart. I don't know what made Mary Maureen ask her all of a sudden, "How could you hide Michael in the wash shed like that?"

Before she had a chance to answer, Grammy said, "He wanted us to."

"Well, it was nothing but a big embarrassment for the rest of us."

My mother, sitting in front with me, had turned her head and was watching the conversation between them in the back as if she were seeing those events over again.

"Why didn't he go in like everyone else? Daddy went, didn't he?"

"He didn't want to go either, but they would have called him up too. We were losing the war," Grammy said.

"I had to live here after they caught Michael. I had to go to school, and everyone looked at me."

"He lost his leg," Grammy said. "And he worked up in that sawmill in Oregon until the war was over. He did his part, just like your father did, who fell for his country." Grammy took off her glasses and wiped her eyes with her fingers and Mary Maureen stopped then.

I watched Mary Maureen in the rearview mirror. She had a satisfied look on her face, as if she had just touched a secret talisman. It was the same little smile she had when she talked about me eating caterpillars or wetting the bed when I was small.

After I found a bag for my mother to put the bulbs in, I helped Mary Maureen put the radio in the trunk of the car and we all went back inside. The phone rang and Sammy picked it up, handing me a stack of unopened letters he was going through, pointing with his chin toward them for me to continue. "Sure, I can see your side," he said into the phone, "but can you see mine?"

It was all junk mail and I threw it away. I picked up an old shoe box full of receipts next. They were stubs from Army allotment checks from the fifties to the seventies. My mother looked over my shoulder and I handed them to her. I picked up some more recent mail and started dropping the useless ones into the big cardboard box Sammy had put in the middle of the floor.

I was scanning the front of the envelopes, opening any that looked promising. MSgt. Avery Fontana RA42478735. Information that might help us evaluate his condition would be appreciated. There was a doctor's name and address. The letter had been sent over a year and a half ago. I opened my mouth to say something, but I stopped. I couldn't speak a word. I slipped the envelope in my purse. My hands had got dirty and I went to the kitchen sink to wash them.

Sammy put down the phone. "If I can't get five hundred thousand for the house and lots, there's something wrong with me. The market on the peninsula is going crazy."

"Sammy," my mother said, "I haven't looked at the bank papers for a long time, but this house isn't yours to sell. I've been thinking about that time after the war a lot lately, and I remember the day I drove your mother to the bank."

"I'm her son, Dora, let's not forget that."

"The people who bought the Texaco station and the garage from Avery were there, Sammy, and the bank manager took that money to pay off the mortgage to this house, so you could get your share. And Avery's name was put on the new deed. Just Avery's. It was the way your mother wanted it."

"I'm the executor of the will, Dora; there are a lot of expenses too. That convalescent hospital didn't come cheap." He went on, but my mother didn't say anything more.

Grammy came out of the kitchen carrying two little glasses with red and green flowers that cheese had come in years ago. "We better go, Dora," she said. "I have to work, you know, to earn my keep." I started laughing at that, I couldn't help it, and hugging Grammy. "You're going to make me drop my glasses, young lady."

"You don't have to worry, Dora," Sammy said at the door. "I'll do what's right."

"I know you will, Sammy," my mother said, going out with her bag of gladiolus bulbs.

When Leroy had mentioned Avery at the reunion, I'd let it go. I hadn't tried to find out anything. I just let it go. But this time I was on the phone as soon as I got home. I made an appointment with the doctor in Seattle for Tuesday morning. It was as easy as that. After I put down the phone I thought, This may be a mistake.

When I knew Grammy would be taking her nap, I phoned my mother. "Should I travel a thousand miles to find out something that's probably going to make me feel awful?"

"I'll come with you," she said. I was so surprised I didn't know what to say. I got two tickets instead of one.

I phoned Sacramento next. Elaine answered and I told her what I'd found out about Avery. "What are you going to do, Ruthie?" she asked me. "I'm going up, and my mother's coming. We'll tell you how he is as soon as we get back."

"At least we know where he is now," she said.

The grounds of the state psychiatric facility looked like a park. There were benches under tall trees, and several picnic tables. But a uniformed guard was at the entrance to the administration building, and when we said we had an appointment with Dr. Rossi he checked our names against his list before he unlocked the door. I was having second thoughts about coming and wondering if I had locked the rental car we'd driven in from the airport.

Dr. Rossi was younger than I was. He seemed genuinely pleased at our coming. "It's supposed to be sunny weather the next couple of days," he said. "I've never seen such rain, and I'm from the Upper Peninsula of Michigan. I've only been here four months, and I'm already complaining." Given enough time, he'd tell us this was his first job and that the woman and child in the photo on his desk were his wife and daughter. He'd go on to say he went into psychiatry because it was interesting and he wanted to help people. Without the mustache and family, he was me, twelve years ago.

"Let's get started," he said. "I'm afraid I have a time conflict I wasn't aware of when I talked to you on the phone." He began reading out of a file folder. "After serving twenty-three years in the Army, separated from the service at Fort Lewis with an honorable discharge, Mr. Fontana took a room in a Seattle hotel, and two days later began shooting at a nearby store window with a .22 rifle from the window of his third-story room. Fortunately, no one was injured; it was a Sunday, and not many people were on the street at that hour of the morning. He was intoxicated and incoherent when arrested. He said he hadn't meant to hurt anyone.

"After a hearing at which Mr. Fontana exhibited diminished capacity, re-fusing to respond to questions, he was sent here for observation, being a possible danger to himself and others, and he's been here the past twenty months. I know what you're thinking. But he insists it wasn't a flashback from his military service."

"Can we see him?" my mother asked. "We'd like to talk to him."

"Yes, in a little while. I'm afraid that I scheduled your appointment at the same time as a staff meeting. I forgot this is the first Tuesday in the month. As soon as I get back, I'll have him sent for. In the meantime, I'd like you to read this. It's something he wrote. I don't know what to make of it." He handed us some typed pages from the folder and left the office.

My mother read first, passing me each page as she finished. The first page was titled *The World Is Flat* and began:

When I was young and small in stature (I am larger now) I wore a very small sized shoe, which immediately upon buying I began to destroy by striking the toes against curbs and green-topped yellow fire hydrants. I used to mutilate and then de-stroy my shoes, for I, young as I was, preferred not to wear them. I wanted to walk in the wet grass in vacant lots and leave no trail. Hide without being seen.

During the time I am going to tell you about and even before then I knew someone I liked very much; he was my friend. We would sit on the curb, always picking one where lots of cars drove by, and each of us would take turns naming the makes of the passing automobiles. We never debated the other's decision, even though I will admit now that I often took wild guesses. And we would journey from one favorite place to another and bury the dead birds we found. Most of the time we found them looking as if they were asleep, but they never moved. Some of the birds were broken and blood came out of their beaks; others were smashed flat by cars. We would scrape them off the street, in between oncoming cars, and wrap them in paper. Then we would carry them down to the tracks—very close to the tracks was the burial ground. When a train came we would have to leave the bird because of the noise. But no, I should in all honesty—and it's very easy to be honest with myself now, safely away from the dishonest condition—say this: I was also frightened of trains; that is why we ran, not because of the steam from the engine, which might burn you, or the noise. My friend ran with me, holding my hand. He wasn't frightened, and I didn't tremble when he was with me. We dug the graves deep enough, we thought, so that cats would not be able to get to the birds. Usually I helped in this task, but once we found a bird that was very beautiful, it had red and yellow on its wings. I knew that it was dead and that if we didn't bury it the red ants and the cats would get it, but the colors on the wings looked alive, and I couldn't push the dirt in on it and bury it: after that, he did all the filling of the graves. After the burial we made a cross from the Popsicle sticks we saved, splitting one halfway down and then fitting the other into the crack. Sitting there looking at a new addition to our burial ground with all its Popsicle crosses protruding above it and thinking of all the birds and the four mice that we buried there, wondering if they would go to heaven too, tears would come to my eyes and his too, until the next train came, and then we would run.

Fourteen days before the day I am going to tell you about, I was walking through the city alone, looking at windows and sometimes at the objects behind them and once in a while at people whose bodies were not like mine because pieces were missing. I bought a balloon for two pictures of Abraham Lincoln and blew it up and walked on to a flower stand to smell the pink gladioluses wrapped in newspaper. I released the balloon, fully expecting it to rise into the air as high as the white pole with a gold ball on top and the flag wrapped securely around it. A truck ran over the balloon. I didn't even hear it pop. The flag wrapped around the pole looked like it was painted there. It certainly was not like the one we had in our classroom in the brick building I went to every morning with a brown paper bag, water-combed hair, and the words of my now-dead grandmother in my head that patches do not make any difference as long as your clothes are clean. I was so clean the other clean children were dirty.

The flag was in the corner of the room. One student picked by the teacher would lead us every morning in saluting the flag with our arms outstretched, hundreds of fingers pointing at the corner where the flag was stuck in the wall. Sometimes I would point my fingers at a picture of George Washington, but most of the time in the general direction of the corner. Something happened; we changed, and in the morning we were never again to point at the flag with our fingers, or anywhere else, for that matter, for our hands were to be placed over our hearts. I could feel my heart beating most of the time; it beat rhythmically and I enjoyed this much more than pointing my fingers, but sometimes I could not feel my heart beating, and I would search frantically for it, unbuttoning my shirt and probing my chest, because even at that time I realized that without a heart I would be dead. The teacher caught me when I was searching and slapped my face. Then I had to stand in front of the class facing her desk every morning, which was embarrassing, for I did not know my left hand from my right; with my back turned from the class I could not determine which hand the majority were using that morning. When I guessed wrong she would hit the offending hand with a ruler, but both hands were bruised in this way and this led to more confusion.

I put a tack on the chair in which she sat, most of the time very heavily. The tack, really a roofing nail with a very wide head, was dipped in mercurochrome—they had told me where I used to live that mercurochrome was poison. She knew the tack was there before she sat down, much to my disappointment, and due to information given by my friend, who sat behind me in the first row, second seat—I was obviously in the first seat in front of the teacher's desk—she made me extend my hands, fingers pointing to the corner where the flag was, while she hit them with the steel-edged yardstick. For three months afterwards the black blood stayed under four fingers on my right hand. Also during that time of pain but not tears or screams I called her a son of a bitch, which I now realize was not appropriate, and they put me in another classroom with another teacher who gave me free milk and graham crackers during milk period and let me watercolor all day in the back of the room. I became very proficient at drawing pictures of Betsy Ross, who I hated—if it hadn't been for her, my fingers would not have hurt on cold mornings—trying to sew three-pointed stars on a black flag with a long, swordlike needle and sticking herself, the blood running down her legs, covering her feet and my futile attempt at drawing them.

Every day after that whenever I saw my former friend I thought of how I would get even with him. He tried to explain that I would have had worse punishment if I'd killed the teacher with the poisoned nail, but I wouldn't hear his reasons; I just held out my hands. Before I could do anything, they took him away, his whole family with the rest of the Japanese. Some kids came to school the next day with I AM A CHINK written on paper pinned to their sweaters, so they wouldn't get beat up. I wanted a sign that said DIE KILL.

I went to the racetrack where they put them but the problem was there were too many Japs at the assembly center. I couldn't find him from the outside of the fence. I couldn't go inside because there were guards at the gate. I went back again, circling the place on my hands and knees, trying to find the best way. Then again.

During that same time, someone's father on the street next to mine had his head chopped off by the enemy in the Philippines. When I passed the house, I could hear the family wailing inside. Screaming. When the President sent the family a flag, the mother cut it up in little pieces and let the wind blow them down the sidewalk. I read that they were going to move the Japs from the racetrack. I had to do something. It was an eye for an eye now.

When I got to the place I took my time until I reached the grass and took off my shoes. I walked barefooted until I got close enough to hear them talking. The faces of the men near the fence looked just like the Jap soldiers on the posters. I had to get closer. And closer. I kept my head down carrying the bag of explosives.

I'd had to walk every alley in the town to find it all. Five spools of 16mm film that burns like a ten-foot flash, then makes enough smoke for a cloud, which I found in the garbage behind the camera shop. Thirty-nine Chinese firecrackers I'd saved, and a big wad of cotton soaked in lighter fluid that was connected to the clothesline fuse. By the time I got to the fence, the Japs were gone, so I decided to just burn down one of the buildings instead, where they were hiding.

It took time to get through the barbed wire fence. I never saw so many strands and rolls of wire. I crawled across the hard-packed dirt on my belly and under the first building, which, like all the others, was up on stilts. I always had matches. I set the bomb just behind the stairs. I got my book of matches out and closed the cover like it said, to avoid accidents, and lit the fuse, watching the wonderful way the flame went down the cotton rope. Then I started crawling backwards, out from under. I looked up then and saw the little girl watching me through the space between the stairs. I knew I couldn't stop the explosives because the fuse was almost burnt down. She had her face over the brown paper bag and was trying to catch the smoke.

I moved as fast as I could out from under the building, then grabbed her by one leg and dragged her away. Her crying, people coming. Then the explosion. The smoke. I couldn't see and ran for the fence too fast and got tangled in the wire that cut into my neck and caught my shirt and I was left dangling in my bare feet. A man who looked just like the pictures of the Japanese soldiers—the same glasses, the teeth— came to where I was caught in the wire. He lifted the barbed wire away from my neck and stopped the bleeding with his handkerchief. I was shaking so hard I could barely speak. "A man on the next street was killed by the Japs," I told him. "They cut off his head, and he lived near my street." With his other hand he rubbed my shoulder. "It's okay, buddy," he said. "It's going to be all right."

Thousands of days later on a hill with no trees or grass where we dumped our empty ration cans, a small girl in a dirty white dress was sitting, plucking feathers out of the breast of a bird. Her cheeks were covered with red sores. The bird was black. I emptied the magazine of my rifle until all I could see was two dirty knees and a dirty white dress, and then I picked up the bird and buried it.

Neither of us had a chance to say anything about what Avery had written because Dr. Rossi came back in as I was finishing the last page. "What do you think?" he asked. Before either of us could reply he went on, "We encourage them to write: diaries, stories, journals, anything to get them to open up. I've tried to talk to Avery about this story." He stopped and looked at his notes. "He says he didn't shoot the little girl. She was real, but he says he took the bird away and gave her some C rations in exchange. He says he thought it would make a better story, the way he wrote it. He said, and I quote, 'Endings are too hard.' I believe him. I don't think he's capable of that kind of violence against a child, or anyone, for that matter."

"Then why is he here?" I asked him.

"There's a lot I don't understand, and I don't think Avery does either. It's like the shop window, the place he was shooting up with the .22. It's a hobby shop, I pass the place on the way here every morning; the windows are full of big model airplanes, gliders, all kinds of kites. He says he was just shooting at nothing, that he was drunk. I don't know about that. Chiefly, he's here because he wants to be here. We received a letter from a woman who knew him and his family before and after his father killed his uncle. Before that he lived with a grandmother, who died, and with the uncle. Then he went to live with an aunt, and if I understand the chronology, he met your family in the fall of 1942. That's all we know about him, because he refuses to talk about any details of his life before he entered the military."

"Can we see him?" my mother asked again.

We waited for another ten minutes in a bigger room with wire mesh on the windows and a peephole in each door. A thick glass partition ran across the room with a table on either side of it. The walls were painted beige. "Why do you think he called it 'The World Is Flat'?" she asked me.

"I don't know. I don't understand what it's about, either."

I must have been thinking hard about what Avery had written because I didn't see him come in at first. All of a sudden my mother started talking. He was sitting on the other side of the glass, smiling at us. My mother was still talking when he pointed to the phone and picked his up and put it to his ear. She picked up hers, laughing at herself. He smiled at us again. It was as if four different people I was thinking about came into focus. It was the same eleven-year-old who pulled me in his wagon, the same eighteen-year-old who worked at the Texaco. The twenty-year-old who took me to the prom. I picked up my phone.

"It's sure nice to see you, Mrs. Mitchum," he was saying. "I would have known you anywhere. It's been eleven or twelve years." My mother started talking about the old neighborhood. He didn't seem surprised that Aunt May was dead.

Dr. Rossi came back and picked up a phone. "Avery, you've got some good friends here who came all the way up here to Seattle to see you. What about that?"

"It was kind of them," he said.

"How would you like to go on a picnic with Mrs. Mitchum and her daughter, out under the trees? It's a beautiful day. The sun's out, and you know in Seattle that's an occasion."

Avery hesitated. "Do they want to go outside?"

We both nodded. Avery got up and went out the door on his side.

Dr. Rossi turned to us. "I shouldn't have done that without asking you," he said. "But I couldn't pass up the opportunity. I never thought I'd see him so animated, talking like this to anyone. And go outside, he won't leave the building. He works in the cafeteria or stays in his room, reads, watches TV, listens to the radio. Exercises. Takes his medication. It's hard to help someone like that. It was his idea to see you here in this room instead of face to face. We don't normally use this now. He told me he likes it here, wants to stay. Has no desire to ever get out. Is perfectly happy. That's what I don't understand."

I hadn't said a word to Avery yet, and he seemed to be ignoring me, or maybe he didn't recognize me. We followed the doctor out to a hallway full of vending machines. We all started putting coins in for the packaged food and soft drinks.

"I never thought anyone would come up here to see him," Dr. Rossi said. "I really appreciate this. We get very little support from our patients' families, much less friends. I was given his case two months ago and just let it ride, like everyone else."

We sat in the sun at a picnic table, Dr. Rossi chatting away. Avery came across the lawn toward us. He wore sunglasses and he walked hesitantly, as if he wasn't sure of his footing. He didn't look his age, much younger. It could have been because he wore his hair short, as if he were still in the military. His Levi's had been ironed, creased. He wore a starched white shirt and polished shoes. He sat down across from my mother.

"Do you remember me, Avery?" I asked.

"Ruthie," he said. "Of course I remember you." But he kept looking at my mother. He opened the plastic wrapping of a sandwich and offered it to her. She took half and he took the other. "It's good," he said after taking a big bite.

"Will it bother you to answer some questions, Avery?" Dr. Rossi asked.

"I haven't anything to hide," he said, and he started laughing, but way too loud.

"Why did you decide to leave the Army, Avery? Forty-one's pretty young to retire."

He was slowly eating all the food that no one else wanted. "I was in the Rangers from the time I enlisted. Then in '72 they put me in a support unit. There was a night training exercise and I was a little overenthusiastic. I butt-stroked some recruit with my M16 when he came up on me in the dark. He wrote home about it to his mother and she phoned her congressman. They were going to bust me, so I got out."

"Wasn't that sudden?"

"Not really; the whole rigmarole lasted a year. The recruit testified for me that it was an accident, but it still didn't make a difference. 'We can't permit random violence by an individual in the U.S. Army,' the colonel said." It was the only time so far he'd spoken like the old Avery. His voice rose, and he moved one arm in a gesture.

"Avery, do you remember buying the .22 rifle?"

"I always wanted one when I was a boy. I might have got confused there. I wasn't sure about anything. I expected to stay in the Army. I was in all that time, and the next day I was out. It caught me by surprise. The drinking surprised me too. I usually don't drink, it's poison in my family. I remember thinking, This is unusual. But I didn't stop." My mother had pushed the rest of the food closer, so he could reach it. He was musing out loud. Dr. Rossi let him go on.

"I used to think when I left the Army I'd head for Alaska or Idaho, somewhere out in the country. It wouldn't be expensive and I could live on my pension. I never gave it a lot of thought. I had plenty of time ahead of me to decide. But when I got out, I just let go. I could feel it happening, but I couldn't stop. I never meant to hurt anyone. Ever. I've seen enough of that." He took a big bite out of an apple.

My mother started telling him about Aunt May's house and Sammy's plans, and how Chuck had phoned someone who called the superior court that dealt with probate, and a judge wrote Sammy. "He's changed his tune a little now," she said. Avery just looked at her like he wasn't hearing very well. He reacted with a kind of nervous impatience while she spoke, as if he wanted to talk now.

I asked, "Avery, why haven't you written to Chuck or Elaine? It's been years."

"I got out of the habit. I was moving around a lot. I thought of all of you, but I never wrote. I kept thinking I'd start again, but I didn't." He was picking up the small pieces of corn chips, one by one. My mother stood up suddenly. She was holding her purse in front of her with both hands.

"You remember Dennis, Avery."

Still smiling, he said, "Yes ma'am. Mr. Mitchum."

"You remember what happened?"

"Yes ma'am. He was killed in North Africa." He'd stopped eating the corn chips.

"And Michael?"

He nodded now.

"Dennis joined the Army to take his place. Then the FBI found out Michael was hiding in the wash shed and came for him. You remember all that?"

Avery was sitting rigid, as if his body was turning to stone.

"Mother, this hasn't anything to do with him."

"Yes it does, doesn't it, Avery? I've been going over this in my mind for years now. The FBI agent said they'd got a call that afternoon at two. That was sewing circle day. I didn't recall that until recently. Mrs. Hughes was on her porch; I could see her through the screen door. Aunt May was in working on the quilting frame with Grammy, Elaine, and the girls. You phoned, didn't you, Avery?" My mother asked it like she wanted to know the time.

"Mrs. Mitchum," Dr. Rossi said.

"Didn't you?" my mother repeated. He didn't move. She had taken a step toward Avery, and she leaned closer. "I'd like to slap your face, Avery. He treated you like a son." She stood there a minute watching him before she turned and started walking away from us toward the parking lot, calling back to me, "I'll wait for you in the car." It had happened so suddenly, I couldn't react.

Avery jumped up and yanked off his sunglasses. "Do you know how many times I've picked up that phone in my life?" he called out. "Do you know what it's like? I didn't know he would get killed. I didn't know Michael would run and get his leg cut off. I phoned." His voice was hoarse, painful to hear, like a broken roar. "I phoned."

My mother stopped and looked back. "I'm not going to hate you, Avery, now that I've seen you here. But I'm never going to forgive you for sending that newspaper clipping to Dennis. That's why he went to Tunisia. When he found out about Michael. That's why he died."

"I joined the Army," Avery shouted after her as she moved away again. "I did everything they told me to. I was a good soldier, ma'am. He would have been proud of me. I tried to be the best man I knew how. I I I . . ." He couldn't go on.

We were staying overnight in Seattle, and had an early-morning flight back to San Francisco. We had dinner, then window-shopped in the mall near the hotel. She didn't talk about what had happened at the hospital. I wanted her to start first. I had been going over and over that time, and now I was ready to speak. I was waiting to get back to the room to say something, do something, anything. I couldn't leave it like that.

When we got back there was a phone call. Dr. Rossi wanted to speak to my mother. She wouldn't come to the phone. "Mother, talk to him." She went in the bathroom and shut the door. "I'm sorry," I said, "she doesn't want to speak to you. We're leaving on the eight-o'clock flight. We wouldn't have time to come out anyway." It looked like my mother wasn't going to talk to either of us about this. I kept thinking about Avery's story. It wasn't really about killing a child. Like he said, that was just an ending. Was it about betraying a friend? Was that why he was looking for an ending now, for himself?

I slept a dreamless sleep. When I woke in the morning, my mother was already dressed. "I'm going back to the hospital," I said. "You can come with me, or I'll take you out to the airport first, but I'm going back."

In the car she talked about her garden, how she was going to plant a fragrance bed with lavender and star jasmine and daphne. I waited with her at the airport lounge until she had to board. I wanted to say something, but all I could do was peck her on the cheek. I still couldn't bring up Avery.

I phoned first. Then I drove back to the hospital. "We're not his relatives," was all I could think to say to Dr. Rossi.

"He wants to say good-bye, I believe. I've arranged for him to meet us outside again."

"Not outside. This is not fun for me. I'm not here to enjoy myself and have a nice visit. I don't like to see my mother upset like that. I'd like to talk to him alone."

"Avery mentioned that you are an M.D. You should have told me."

"Would that have made any difference? What professional courtesy would you have extended me, Doctor, that you wouldn't have given anyone else, my mother, say?"

Why was I this angry? I didn't even know at whom. The doctor? Avery? Why had I come back? I was shaking. But I couldn't just leave him here like this. He didn't deserve to spend his whole life in an institution. Twenty-three years in the Army was enough for anyone.

Avery was already inside the small conference room. He didn't smile this time when he saw me. I sat down across from him at the table. "I'm glad you came back, Ruthie," he said. Then he stopped. We just looked at each other.

I started speaking. "There's something I don't understand, Avery. I've been thinking about that time too, when I broke my arm. We were trying to get a letter out of the mailbox, but I couldn't reach the envelope. Who mailed that letter?" He just sat there. "What was inside? Is that how the clipping got to my father? In that letter?"

"I phoned the number to turn in deserters. Your mother was right. I did that."

"But who sent the clipping? You know, Avery. It was you who burned up the mailbox, when we couldn't get the letter out. Who sent the clipping?"

"What difference does it make now? It can't change anything."

"You mean it can't bring my father back?" He just looked straight ahead. I said the next thing that came into my head. "Do you remember Abner, Avery?" He moved his chair. "I still have the hubcap we put his dog food in."

"I was afraid of that dog. He would bite you and hang on and never let go. I was afraid even after the three of us buried him."

It came to me then who sent the clipping. "Avery, it was Mary Maureen. You burned the mailbox after Mary Maureen sent the clipping, to try and stop her. But she must have walked down to the post office to mail the letter."

"I phoned and told where Michael was. It was my fault. That's what killed your father."

"But you couldn't know that would happen. Just like Mary Maureen couldn't know. My father died from a bullet from a German sniper's rifle, not from your call or that clipping. It's just self-pity to dwell on that. It's self-indulgent. You're just hiding here, Avery. You're going to be the one to die for nothing if you stay here. You didn't make my father die."

"That's just it, Ruthie, everyone always dies. They die. My grandmother. Uncle Johnny. Your father. My friends in the unit." He closed his eyes and laced his hands over the top of his head like we used to do during the air raids. I didn't know what to say now. Where to go from here. I thought of just getting up and walking out. Walking out of the house and around the heart.

"Do you know, Avery, when I think of before, I remember that time we were walking to school, you, me, and Mary Maureen. There was thick white frost on all the roofs and the lawns. And you saw the sparrows on the ground underneath that magnolia tree. They were just lying there like they were dead. It was so cold my toes and fingers were hurting. We started picking up the birds. Do you remember that?" He took his hands down and opened his eyes and looked at me. "You do."

"That's what I know when I think of the past. When I want to recall the heart. The birds coming alive. Feeling them move in the palms of my hands. When you picked up the birds, I had to too; I couldn't leave them there for the ants. They flew away just like that, leaped into the air and were gone. Every one. It was like pieces of myself had taken flight." He was nodding and opened his mouth to say something, hesitated, then stopped. "You were the one who guessed they'd come alive again."

He was waiting for me to go on. And I was going to tell him about Elaine and Chuck and their daughters. Mary Maureen. Anyone. Anything, to convince him there was something besides this place and himself. But he was the one who had to decide. I wasn't going to do it for him.

"Did I get a chance to say that I'm on the high school reunion committee? You were on the missing list for years in our records." What was there to forgive an eleven-year-old boy? But it was easier for me than for my mother, who'd had a different thirty years to think about that time.

"There's a class reunion coming up next April. On a Saturday, I think. You could come, Avery."

He was listening, staring at me as if he could read my lips too, and nodding as I spoke. "You'll try, Avery?"

"I'll have to think it over," he said.